THAT WAY MURDER LIES

THAT WAY MURDER LIES

Ann Granger

headline

First published in 2004
by HEADLINE BOOK PUBLISHING

10 9 8 7 6 5 4 3 2

Cataloguing in Publication Data is available
from the British Library

ISBN 0 7472 7473 8 (Hardback)
ISBN 0 7553 0847 6 (Trade paperback)

Typeset in Plantin by Avon DataSet Ltd,
Bidford-on-Avon, Warwickshire

Printed and bound in Great Britain by
Clays Ltd, St Ives plc

HEADLINE BOOK PUBLISHING
A division of Hodder Headline
338 Euston Road
London NW1 3BH

www.headline.co.uk
www.hodderheadline.com

To all those readers over the years who have followed
Mitchell and Markby

Chapter One

The three envelopes lay on the mat inside the front door. The postman, having sent them flying through the letter box with the insouciance of one who had no idea what would follow from his action, could be heard driving off, scattering gravel chips as he went. Betsy, the old black Labrador, was pushing the new arrivals around with her nose and sniffing at them suspiciously. As Alison walked slowly down the hall towards her, the dog looked up at her with questioning, anxious brown eyes and whined, giving an uncertain wag of her tail at the same time.

She knows, thought Alison. She senses something is wrong and it has to do with the post, although she can't know what it is. You can fool people but you can never fool a dog.

She dropped her hand to touch the old dog's head. 'It's all right, Betsy.'

Betsy wagged her tail more energetically, half reassured, and thrust her head against Alison's knee as she stooped over the envelopes. One was a long brown official type. Any problem that presented could be dealt with by Jeremy. The second looked as if it came from a credit card company. Any problem that held would be another ordinary, everyday one. The third was smaller, white and square, with a printed address to Mrs Alison Jenner. Alison's heart lurched and seemed to drop like a stone down into her stomach. Momentary dizziness overwhelmed her, her knees gave way, and she sank down to sit on the floor by Betsy, ankles crossed as if she were about to engage in a spot of yogic meditation. For a

1

moment she just sat there, her eyes fixed on the envelope, until the dog pushed her wet nose into Alison's ear, following it with a tentative lick.

It brought her out of her haze but the biting pain of dismay was still there. The envelope was still there, too. *It's another one*, she thought. *Please, no!* But it was another one, another one, another one . . .

For a second or two, the dismay turned to anger against the writer. 'How dare you do this to me?' she raged aloud in the silence of the empty hallway. Betsy cocked her head and her furry brow crinkled in concern. 'You have no right to do this!' Alison shouted, the words echoing around her.

The uselessness of her rage flooded over her. Nausea rose in her, filling her mouth with sour, acid bile which burned her throat and tasted foul. She forced it back and picked up all the envelopes. Scrambling to her feet and followed by the dog, she took them back to the dining room. Shouting out like that was worse than useless, it was dangerous. Mrs Whittle might hear her.

The room was cool and quite dark. The sun didn't reach this side of the house until the afternoon. The polished oak refectory table had been cleared of the breakfast things. They didn't eat much in the way of breakfast these days, she and Jeremy, just toast and a pot of coffee. The table was one of Jeremy's antiques, acquired long ago, before Alison had even met him. Its dark surface with ancient scratches and dents had probably witnessed more than one crisis. It was quite frightening, Alison thought, how inanimate objects could survive so much and human beings just crumble. She tossed the two oblong envelopes on to the table and turned the small square one in her fingers. At least Jeremy wasn't at home. He'd taken the car and gone into Bamford on some errand. He didn't know about the letters and he must never know. He'd want to do something and whatever he did, it would make it worse. She tore the envelope open and took out the single folded printed sheet it contained. The hate-filled words had a horrible familiarity by now. They seldom varied by more than a phrase or two. Though few in number, the pain and terror they caused were immeasurable.

YOU KILLED HER. YOU KILLED FREDA KEMP. YOU THINK YOU GOT AWAY WITH IT BUT I KNOW. SOON EVERYONE WILL KNOW. YOU WILL GET WHAT'S COMING TO YOU. BLOOD WILL HAVE JUSTICE.

'Why are you doing this to me?' Alison whispered now. 'Do you hate me? If you do, why? What have I done to you? Who are you? Do I know you? Are you someone I think of as a friend, see regularly and share a joke with, sit down to dinner with? Or are you a stranger?'

Far, far better that the poisonous thing came from a stranger. The betrayal by a friend, the thought that someone she trusted could do this to her, would be so much worse that Alison felt she understood now why Judas' betrayal was especially dreadful. He had been the friend who had sat at table. Alison could imagine the particular pain his treachery must have caused. Was the writer of the letter just such a smiling acquaintance?

Another question buzzed about her brain. 'How do you know about this?' she asked the unknown writer. 'Nobody hereabouts knows. It all happened twenty-five years ago, miles away from here. Did someone tell you? Who was it and how did they know? Or did you read a report in a yellowing newspaper used to line a drawer? I was a twenty-three-year-old! I am, I was then, innocent. And now you are trying to make me pay for something *I didn't do!*'

She would destroy the letter as she'd destroyed the others. But another one would come and, next time, Jeremy might get to the post first. He wouldn't open it, of course, not if it was addressed to her personally. But he would probably ask her who it was from and she'd have to lie to him. She didn't want to lie to him. So far, to avoid the necessity, she had invented ingenious ways of getting to the post before he did. Because the deliveries seemed to come later and later these days, she spent half the mornings listening for the crunch of the postvan's tyres, the driver's cheerful whistling and the rattle of the letter box. Sometimes, on fine mornings, she used the pretext of taking Betsy for a walk to intercept him. She dragged the unwilling old dog up and down the lane until the little red van appeared and she could waylay it. But she couldn't do that every day without the postman becoming suspicious. He was young and she knew he already found her behaviour odd. She could read it in his bemused expression. He had probably told all his mates at the depot that the woman at Overvale House was potty. But better tales should spread of her eccentricity than that he should realize she really dreaded the arrival of the post because of something in it. He was young enough to be curious. That might lead to the existence of the letters becoming known. But for how long would this go on? Would the writer eventually tire of his cat-and-mouse game? What would he do then? Just stop writing or make his information public as he threatened?

The nausea returned. Alison dropped the letter on the table where its pristine whiteness showed up startlingly against the blackened oak. She dashed to the downstairs cloakroom where she threw up into the lavatory bowl, retching violently until her diaphragm muscles ached. She burned with heat and sweat trickled over her entire body. To remedy it, she splashed cold water on to her face and mopped it dry. She peered into the little mirror and decided that, though still blotchy, she looked fairly normal, enough for Jeremy, anyway.

Jeremy! She had left the letter on the table and her husband would be home soon. Alison ran back to the dining room.

She was too late. With her head stuck down the loo, she hadn't heard his return. Jeremy was standing by the table holding the small white sheet. He held it up as she entered.

'How bloody long has this been going on?'

It was Thursday, Maundy Thursday to be exact. After lunch, Meredith Mitchell would clear her Foreign Office desk and take off for the Easter break, not returning until Tuesday. The knowledge made her light-hearted. The weather had been good all week and, with luck, would stay good over the short holiday. There would be time to relax with Alan, time to discuss the house they were buying and all that needed doing to fix it up. The pressure of work would be gone and they both needed the break. At the other end of the room, Polly, with whom she shared a spacious office, was packing away already. Meredith stretched out her hand to her in-tray where a ray of sunlight from the tall window fell across a single slim file. Get this one out of the way and she, too, could be off, free.

The ray of sunlight was abruptly cut off. Someone was standing in front of her desk. She looked up.

'Toby!' she exclaimed. 'Where on earth did you spring from?'

'Beijing,' said Toby Smythe. 'I've just finished a tour of duty there. Now I'm home for a spot of leave before they find me a new posting. At least,' his expression grew troubled, 'I hope they do find me a new posting. I've been telling them that this morning. I don't want to be stuck at a London desk for ages, like you.'

That wasn't very polite but it was true. She had been stuck at this desk for quite a while now. Ever since her return, a few years ago, from what had then been the Federal Republic of Yugoslavia, in fact. She had been consul there. But now she was just a desk in this room. The Yugoslavia she'd known had fallen apart and it seemed to her that her career had stalled about the same time in an empathetic parallel. Despite repeated requests, no long-term new overseas post had been offered her, only slots of a few weeks at a time, filling in for someone sick or to lend an extra pair of hands in an emergency. At first she had minded, minded very much, knowing that there was a reason for her being grounded like this that she would never know. Somewhere she had crossed someone, or gained a reputation perhaps for a maverick style which made senior heads uneasy. But now things had changed. She no longer felt the need to 'flee the country' as Alan Markby always described her desire to work abroad. Alan had never wanted her to go. She smiled to herself and then up at Toby.

'I don't mind being in London,' she said. 'I'm getting married in the summer.'

Toby started back in theatrical manner, both hands upraised, palms outwards. 'You're not getting married to that copper you've been hanging out with for years?'

'His name is Alan,' Meredith said crossly. 'As you very well know! Nor have I been "hanging out" with him.'

At the other end of the room, Polly was laughing at them. Meredith felt her brief anger evaporate. It was no use getting ruffled over anything Toby said or did. Toby was just Toby and this was the beginning of the Easter break, for goodness' sake.

'There's no hope for me, then?' he was asking. He gave a melodramatic sigh. Polly giggled.

'There never was any hope for you,' Meredith told him. 'But I am pleased to see you.'

'I couldn't come here and not look you up.' Toby put his hands on the desk and leaned over it towards her. 'I was wondering, if you're not dashing straight back to the arms of Mr Plod, if I could take you out to lunch?'

'Not if you're going to call him Mr Plod!'

'Sorry. Come on, come and have lunch. I promise I won't call him anything even slightly disrespectful. We can catch up on the news, talk over old times and—' Toby hesitated briefly. 'I'm rather glad you're still together, you and Markby, because I've got a bit of a problem. That is, I haven't, but a friend of mine has. Markby might be able to give some advice.'

She shook her head. 'If your friend has a problem which might involve the law, perhaps he ought to consult a solicitor? Alan isn't an agony aunt. If it's really a police matter, then the procedure's simple. Your friend should go to the nearest police station and ask to speak to someone. Alan can't interfere outside his own area, anyway. If it were a serious criminal investigation which took him outside his own boundaries he would make arrangements with whichever other police force was involved. But he isn't going to do that for your chum's little problem! You know that, Toby.'

'Ah,' said Toby cunningly. 'But all this is taking place in Markby's neck of the woods. That's why he's the ideal chap.'

Meredith sighed. Toby wasn't Alan's favourite person at the best of times. She felt instinctively that an appeal to help Toby would fall on deaf ears. But Toby was standing there looking at her so hopefully, and he was an old friend. One stuck by old friends. She studied him. Tidiness had always eluded him. His suit was so crumpled it looked as if he'd spent the flight home in it. But Toby wasn't the sort of person who travelled in a suit. It had probably been crushed in his suitcase. The top button of his shirt was undone and the knot of his tie nestled some two inches below it. Suddenly Meredith realized that she was truly very pleased to see him.

'Of course I'll come to lunch with you,' she said.

Toby, perhaps mentally still in Beijing, took her to a restaurant in Chinatown. It was busy, packed out, the waiters rushing to and fro. The activity and buzz of conversation meant it was easy to talk in confidence.

'Seriously,' said Toby when they'd ordered. 'Congratulations and all that on your forthcoming nuptials. But what changed your mind? I know he's been keen on getting married but I got the impression you weren't.'

'I didn't change my mind. I was just a bit slow making it up.'

Very slow. The idea of marriage, settling down, had previously sent her into a spin. But oddly enough, once it was all decided upon, her misgivings had vanished.

'The big event is to be in the summer, you say?' Toby was saying. 'I'd like to dance at your wedding, of course, but with luck they'll have found me a new posting by then. No, sorry, that doesn't sound right. You know what I mean. If I'm anywhere in Europe I could get back home for it, if I'm invited.'

'You're invited. We've picked a summer date because the house won't be ready until then. We're buying the vicarage in Bamford. The Church authorities have long wanted to sell it and Alan's always yearned to own it, its garden especially. But it's in an awful state. It needs a new kitchen, new bathroom, rewiring and redecorating top to bottom. There will be other things, too, once we start work. There always are.'

'What will they do with the vicar?'

'James is being moved into a brick box on a new estate. The Church imagines he'll be among his parishioners there. Some hopes. James says he doesn't mind. His housekeeper has retired. She's incredibly ancient, no one knows how old. Mrs Harman's age is like a state secret. But she's hung up her pinny at last and James is having to "do" for himself. He'll manage much better in a new house with a fitted kitchen and a postage-stamp-sized garden, so everyone's happy. Only, I refuse to camp out in a house that's completely topsy-turvy with workmen tramping up and down the stairs. I'm still living in my terraced cottage in Bamford and Alan's still got his house. Both houses are on the market. If one of us sells, that one will move in with the other one. If we both sell, well, I suppose we shall have to camp out among the paint pots.'

'I've still got my flat in Camden,' Toby said, as their food was plonked down in front of them by a harassed waiter who sped away. 'It's apparently worth an obscene amount of money now. I can hardly believe it.'

Meredith manoeuvred her chopsticks round a prawn and dipped it into the sweet and sour sauce.

Toby took a bite of crispy duck. 'Everyone's got their problems, which brings me to mine, to my friend's.'

'Look, Toby,' Meredith said firmly. 'If it's really your problem, stop pretending it's a friend's. It's daft and I won't let you tell me anything unless you are absolutely frank. That's the first thing. The second is that I don't promise to ask Alan about it. All I can do is give you my own opinion, for what it's worth.'

'Fair enough,' agreed Toby. 'It isn't my problem, honestly. The person whose problem it is, well, he's a relative – Jeremy Jenner. He's a cousin of my father's. When I was a kid I used to call him

Uncle Jeremy. Now I just call him Jeremy. He made a pile working for the multinationals and retired to a country estate near Bamford to live on his ill-gotten gains.'

'Are they ill-gotten?'

He shook his head. 'No, absolutely legit. Unless you happen to be one of the anti-globalization bunch. Then you'd probably think him a public enemy. But Jeremy is as straight as a die. He's married to a really nice woman called Alison. She's a bit younger than he is. She's in her forties. He's sixty-something. He doesn't look it.'

'I see. What's his problem, then? He's seems pretty well fixed.'

'It isn't really his, it's Alison's.'

Meredith groaned. 'Another degree removed!'

'I rang him up,' went on Toby. 'As soon as I got back to England. I wanted to touch base and, to be honest, I wanted to wangle an invitation down there for the weekend, this Easter weekend, as it happens. He has invited me. But I also had to listen for twenty minutes while he bent my ear about Alison's problem.'

'Is it going to take you that long to tell me about it?' demanded Meredith.

'No, hang on. I'll make it brief. The old chap was obviously distressed, I could tell, and pretty angry as well. It seems poor Alison has been getting poison pen letters, and he'd only just found out.'

'He should take them to the local police,' said Meredith promptly.

'They've only got the one example because she burned the others. He had taken it to the local copshop that very morning and he wasn't at all happy at their reaction. That was why he was so upset when I spoke to him. He said they were uncivil, incompetent and short.'

'Short?' asked Meredith, wondering if she'd heard him right amid all the surrounding din. 'Short meaning brusque? Or short meaning lacking height?'

'Short as in not tall. Jeremy reckons they must have lowered the height requirement for coppers. According to him, the ones at Bamford were practically midgets. Unimpressive, he called them.'

'I don't think I'm going to let your cousin Jeremy anywhere near Alan!' said Meredith. 'If he said that to Alan, Alan would hit the roof.'

'I admit,' said Toby, 'old Jeremy can be rather outspoken. I think it's all those years as a captain of industry. He's used to giving orders and seeing minions scurry to obey his every command. He probably harangued the cops until they politely told him to naff off.'

'I am *not* letting him near Alan!' said Meredith firmly.

'Wait! He wouldn't be like that with Markby because Markby is the right sort.'

'Right sort?' A prawn fell from Meredith's chopsticks back into the sauce. 'What on earth is the right sort?'

'He's high-ranking, a superintendent, isn't he? Jeremy is used to dealing with the top men. Markby went to public school, he's polite to ladies and wears polished shoes. He's even, as I recall, quite tall. Tall enough to satisfy Jeremy's idea of a copper. They'd get on like a house on fire.'

'I doubt it! Your cousin Jeremy sounds a real snob.'

'He isn't, not really, just conditioned by all those years in the boardroom. He's a bit stuffy, that's all. Alison, bless her, hasn't a snobbish bone in her body. She's a sweetie. You'd like her.'

'I might like her. I don't think I'd like your cousin Jeremy. Incidentally, I'm probably tall enough for his idea of a police recruit!'

'Don't take against him,' pleaded Toby. 'He's really a decent guy, but right now he's in a terrible state over this letter business. He needs help. Believe me, he isn't the sort who seeks help unless the situation is desperate. He adores Alison. He must be ready to kill whoever is writing the letters. He's got a slight heart condition. It can't be good for him.'

Meredith gazed at Toby's face, puckered in worry lines. He scratched his mop of light brown hair and gazed back at her.

Well, thought Meredith, what are friends for? Toby seems genuinely to care about this awful cousin. The least I can do is try and help.

'Did the police,' she began, 'say if anyone else in the district had received a similar letter? Because, as far as I know anything about it, the writer is often someone with a grudge against the community. He or she sits down and pens these wretched things to any and all. It'll probably turn out to be someone no one suspects.'

He shook his head. 'No, only Alison's been getting letters. Or rather, no others have been reported to the police. We and the police think it's probably only her because they aren't the usual run of poison pen stuff. There's no foul language or accusations of unnatural sex, any of the stuff twisted minds usually come up with. The letters refer to a specific event in Alison's past, something that really happened. That's why she's so upset and Jeremy, too. Just think, this weirdo has got hold of some very personal and, up until now, private information about her. No wonder she's sensitive about it.'

'That is more worrying,' said Meredith soberly. She wondered if Toby was going to tell her what the specific event was, or if she was going to have to ask outright. The problem with family secrets was that people were reluctant to disclose them even when forced to seek help. Jeremy, Alison and Toby would have to learn that they needed to open up. She tried the roundabout approach. 'He, the writer, isn't asking for money, is he?'

'No, not yet, anyway. It's just an accusation, repeated over and over again, and a threat to make it all public.'

'Where is the letter now?'

'The local cops have it. They're trying to see if they can get a sweaty fingerprint off it or something. Alison's going crazy at the idea of all those coppers reading it. It's not something she wants anyone to know about. Jeremy knows, because she told him when they married. I know because he told me all about it on the phone. But no one else around there does, unless the writer carries out his threat to tell everyone. If it *is* a man, which we don't know. I fancy it's a woman myself. It seems like a woman's thing.'

'Poison is a woman's weapon, whether it's in a bottle or written on paper, you mean? Plenty of men have written letters of that sort.'

'All right. We'll call the writer "he" for the purpose of discussion. Look, Alison's panicking. She says they'd have to sell the house and leave, if the facts in the letter got out. They're a funny lot in the country. They take an unhealthy interest in one another's affairs and rumours run like wildfire.'

'Not more than in the city,' Meredith defended rural life.

'Don't you believe it. The green-welly brigade are sticklers for form, and can be merciless if they think you don't fit in. There's so little going on in the country that your social life is everything. Being cut from everyone's guest list really matters. In town you can make new friends, there's a bigger pool, if you like. In the country you're down to your neighbours. If the contents of the letter get out, they'll freeze out Alison and old Jeremy too. In the city there's far too much going on for anyone to worry what his neighbour is doing, or care.'

'Conan Doyle,' Meredith objected, not willing to give in to this argument, 'wrote that it was the other way round, or at least he has Holmes say so in one of the stories. Holmes tells Watson that nobody knows what goes on in the country because people are so isolated.'

Toby considered this point. 'Either way, all that rural peace and quiet isn't good for you. It makes people strange and who knows what they get up to?'

'You're saying, one of them found out Alison's secret and is writing to let her know? But how did he find it out? Because if we know how, we might well know who.' Meredith frowned. 'Why torment Alison with threats? If, as you say, the knowledge would result in social exclusion, why not just tell everyone, if the writer's aim is to do her harm? Instead, he just writes about it. What's his purpose?'

'That's a question none of us can answer. Alison wouldn't hurt a fly. She hasn't got any enemies.'

'She's got at least one,' Meredith pointed out, 'unless the letters are just a sick joke. Did she keep the envelope? If the writer licked it, there might be a DNA trace.'

'You see? You know all about that kind of thing. I knew you were the one to ask.' Toby's manner was that of a man who had successfully passed on a burden to another's shoulders.

I'm a sucker, thought Meredith. Why did I let him drop this in my lap? 'One more thing,' she said. 'And it's important. Before I'm convinced this matters enough to bother Alan with it, I need to know exactly what this episode in Alison's past is, because that's the cause of the trouble. I'm the soul of discretion. I won't blab it around. But what you're asking me to do is ask Alan to get on to whoever is handling this at the local station and make waves. Alan's got plenty on his plate without that. I need to know it really matters. Sorry, but Jeremy and Alison losing all their friends isn't enough. They must be fair-weather friends, by the way.'

Toby nodded. 'Yes, I realize you have to know. I warned Jeremy about that.'

'You told Jeremy you'd speak to me? Honestly, Toby—'

He cut short her spluttered indignation by plunging into his story, knowing full well, she told herself wryly, that her curiosity would outweigh her anger.

'Twenty-five years ago, Alison stood trial. She was found not guilty. That is, she wasn't guilty and the jury agreed.'

'So, why is it a problem now? Why should she worry if the neighbours know? I think country people are a lot more tolerant that you believe they are.' Meredith paused. Toby was avoiding her gaze. 'Toby? What did she stand trial for?'

'Murder,' said Toby simply.

Chapter Two

'I've been looking forward to this Easter break,' said Alan Markby. He scowled at an overweight youth who had just lurched past their table. The beer in the boy's glass had slopped dangerously near them. 'Now you tell me the wretched Smythe is staying in the neighbourhood.'

'Hey!' said Meredith. 'I don't let him call you nicknames, so I don't think you should call him "the wretched Smythe". He's really very nice, good-hearted. You just need to get used to his sense of humour.'

'Do I, indeed? I'll try and remember that. As far as I'm concerned he's a walking disaster area. He exerts a malign influence on all around him and especially, I might add, on you when you move into his forcefield. He's a Jonah. Look what happened when he leased you his flat, only for him to turn up unannounced because he'd been chucked out of some country, *persona non grata*. You had to go and stay with Ursula Gretton in a caravan on an archaeological site, up to your knees in mud and, incidentally, dead bodies! Then he broke his leg and you had to—'

Meredith threw up her hands. 'Alan, stop, please! He didn't break his leg on purpose. Nor was he thrown out of that country for something he'd really done. It was a tit-for-tat thing. We'd expelled one of theirs and so they expelled one of ours. It happened to be Toby. I'm sorry you don't like him, but he's an old friend—'

'It isn't that I don't like him!' Markby interrupted her. 'I agree, he's a likeable chap. He's just accident-prone. What's he like at his job?'

'Very good, as it happens. He's conscientious. He tries hard to help people. He's trying now to help his cousin. Toby wouldn't turn his back on anyone in need. In that way, I think he's like you.'

'Hah!' said Markby, momentarily silenced by this devious thrust.

It was Thursday evening and they'd driven out into the country for a meal at a riverside pub. From their seat by a window they could watch the sun go down, scattering red-gold flashes over the rippling water.

'Like,' Meredith had said earlier, 'that glitter stuff you buy to decorate home-made Christmas cards.' She hoped Alan wasn't going to be difficult about Toby. But she had expected a certain lack of enthusiasm and prepared for it. At any rate, she wasn't going to be put off. 'Have you,' she asked now, 'ever met this Jeremy Jenner?'

'No, not that I recall. I've heard the name. I know of the property, Overvale House. I used to know the people who lived there years ago. It's a nice place. In today's market, it's certainly an expensive one. You and I couldn't afford it. Jenner must be pretty well-heeled.' Markby picked up his glass and drained the last of his wine. 'Would you like coffee?'

'Yes, please.' At least, she thought, he seemed prepared to talk about it.

'I'll have to go over to the bar and order it. Won't be long.'

In his absence Meredith sat back, pushed her thick brown hair from her face and looked around her. This pub was very old. That wasn't unusual in the Cotswolds which was dotted with such places. Other buildings, she thought, are demolished or altered or change their usage, but the village pub goes on for ever although subject to change in other ways. The villages themselves had changed. Wealthy high-flyers lived in cottages built for country labourers to which they added extra bathrooms and home offices. The descendants of the original cottagers were banished to housing estates. The new inhabitants of the town centres wanted a quaint pub – but a quaint pub with all the trimmings. The result was that to remain viable, the pubs had nearly all turned themselves into quasi-restaurants. It varied, of course. Some kept only a minimal bill of fare. Others, like this one, had virtually given up being places where people went just to drink and socialize. The old timers wouldn't recognize it. Although, to be fair, many of these inns had been on the old coaching roads and had supplied food and lodging for the weary and bruised travellers who stumbled through their doors. In providing food, they were returning to a traditional use.

She spoke her thoughts aloud to Alan on his return.

He smiled at her. 'This place is believed to have been a stopover for medieval pilgrims making their way into the West Country to Glastonbury.'

'As old as that?'

A young barman brought the coffee and when he'd left them Markby said in a conversational way, 'So Mrs Alison Jenner has been receiving unpleasant correspondence?'

'Yes, she has. And you will look into it yourself? I know it's already in the hands of the local police, but Toby is counting on your help with his problem.'

This didn't go down well. Alan struggled to repress whatever remark had leapt to his lips, threw up his hands, brought them down with a slap on the table and hissed, 'It isn't his problem, is it? It's the lady's. Can you persuade your very good friend Smythe that I am a regular copper and not Philip Marlowe? If Mrs Jenner does wish to speak to me about her problem, I am willing to listen. But the request must come from *her*. Honestly, you wonder why Smythe annoys me? Of course he annoys me. I don't doubt he has all the excellent qualities you give him. But you know the old saying, the way to hell is paved with good intentions?'

'I think that's unfair,' she said obstinately.

Markby studied her. Whenever she was sticking to a point of dispute (and Meredith did stick to points. It was one of the things which made verbal jousting with her such a satisfying mental challenge) she had a trick of tilting her chin and jutting out her lower lip. He found this trait both endearing and comical. It always made him want to kiss her. But he couldn't kiss her here in the middle of the restaurant. There were free souls who did that sort of thing but he wasn't one of them.

'Well,' he said cautiously, because he knew he was going to cede the point but he didn't want to make it obvious. 'If Mrs Jenner does approach me and I do agree to look into it, it's because I don't want to spend my entire Easter break fending off reproachful looks and remarks from you. Don't look so injured! I know you well enough to know you never give up. Incidentally, you and Toby haven't got any wild ideas about doing a little amateur investigating yourselves, I hope!'

'That's not what Toby wants,' said Meredith, avoiding the direct answer.

'It's not what I want! It's a police matter. I don't mind discussing it with the Jenners but I just hope Toby and his cousin don't think I'm going to sort it all out in ten minutes. *With a bound, Jack was free*! That sort of stuff. Winkling out the writers of poison pen letters can be a lengthy process. We waste time going after every suspicious character in the neighbourhood and it turns out to be a dear old lady who lives alone with a pug dog and goes to church every Sunday.'

'I said something of the sort to Toby. I'm sure they don't think it's going to be easy.' Meredith took a deep breath and plunged on. 'We've been invited to lunch at Overvale House tomorrow. I haven't accepted, of course I haven't! I wanted to ask you first, naturally.'

'Oh, thanks very much!'

'I said I'd ring first thing in the morning and let them know.'

Alan grimaced, pushed an unruly hank of fair hair from his forehead and sighed. 'That doesn't give me any time to look into

18

the background. I don't like going into things blind. I know you've told me what Toby has told you but I'd like to look up this old murder case just to see what Alison Jenner's unwished-for pen pal has got hold of. But yes, tell them we'll go to lunch, by all means. I can understand the state they're in.' After a pause he added, 'It does sound to me like the first move in a plan to blackmail the Jenners.'

'Toby says no demand for money has been made and Alison insists on that. She's received five of the letters, four of which she burned. All contained the same threat to reveal her secret to everyone.'

At this Markby muttered crossly, 'Why must they always do that, destroy the letters? They come in to their local police station, at long last, to tell us they're being targeted by hate mail, and we ask, how many letters? Then they get shifty and don't want to say but eventually admit there have been several, all torn up, thrown away or burned. Burning is the favourite. How are we to do anything without any evidence?'

He drummed his fingertips on the table. There was a faraway look in his eyes. Despite himself, he was interested. 'If the threat in the letters to make the old scandal public is real, the intention being to harm Alison's social standing, why not just go ahead and tell someone about it? Why mess about writing letters? Just a word in the right ear would do it. Toby's correct in one thing. Rumours do run round small communities like wildfire.'

'It's what Alison fears, Toby says. She thinks that after making her sweat for a while, the writer will do just what he threatens. To me that speaks of a real hatred. But Toby says Alison is a quiet, friendly, harmless woman.' Meredith had noticed the faraway look and knew it meant Alan would grumble – but he'd do it.

'A nice woman who was once on a murder charge? You and I are already viewing this in two different ways. You speak of hatred. I'm thinking along the lines of extortion. When a man's got as much money as Jenner, it has to be considered as a motive. He, the writer, hasn't asked for money yet, but he will. He's softening them up. When they're in a complete panic and pretty well in his grip, then he'll suggest a one-off payment and they'll leap at it to get him off their backs, poor souls. But it won't be a one-off, that's the thing. They'll get another demand and so it'll go on. I'm inclined to stick to my blackmail theory.'

'What you're suggesting doesn't sound like an old lady living with a pug dog and getting her kicks from sending anonymous letters to her neighbours,' Meredith argued. 'It's a big jump from trying to frighten someone to demanding money.'

'It is, but sometimes a person starts out with one aim and then thinks up an improvement on his original plan.'

'Perhaps,' Meredith said soberly, 'the Jenners would almost prefer blackmail as a motive. That someone wants your money is easier to bear than the fact that someone hates you and is delighting in tormenting you.' She drew a deep breath. 'They can't think how the wretched writer got on to them in the first place, or on to Alison, at any rate.'

'That might not be such a mystery. Her trial will be a matter of record. Anyone might have come across a reference to it or an account of it.'

'But he wouldn't know it referred to Alison, would he? Because her name was Harris in those days, Toby says. But for the last ten years it's been Jenner. Why connect Alison Jenner with Alison Harris? Even if there was a photo with the account of the trial in some magazine or similar – supposing that's how the writer found out about it all – in twenty-five years people change. Alison must be forty-eight now. She was twenty-three at the time of the trial.'

Markby had been listening to her objections. He nodded as she fell silent. 'Fair enough. Look, Inspector Winter over at Bamford is a conscientious type and I'm sure he's taken all the necessary action with regard to these letters. But he might be more than pleased to pass the investigation on to someone at Regional Headquarters, partly because if it does turn out to be blackmail, then investigating that is going to take time and manpower Winter doesn't have. Also because the Jenners are the sort of people the tabloid press would be interested in. Wealthy man, younger wife, scandal in wife's past. Incidentally, was Jenner married before? He must have been over fifty when he married Alison.'

Meredith rubbed her nose. 'Don't know. I'll ask Toby.'

'And then,' said Markby. 'There's Jenner himself. He could well have made enemies during his long and successful career. You don't get to the top in business without a streak of ruthlessness. Perhaps someone is trying to get at him through his wife?'

'He does sound,' Meredith admitted, 'pretty grim. Toby says he's all right really, he's just used to being in charge.'

'And doesn't like being put in a position where he doesn't know what to do? I can understand that.' Markby nodded. 'OK, we'll go to lunch with them and hear what they've got to say. I'll phone Winter in the morning and tell him what I intend. I can't go behind his back. I'll also get him to give me a quick rundown on any forensic evidence the one surviving letter may have thrown up. The problem for me is, if we take it on at Regional HQ, who do I put in charge of it? I'm going to miss Dave Pearce but he's at the other end of the country now and unlikely to return to us. There's his replacement, Jessica Campbell, of course.'

'Do I know her?' Meredith asked frowning.

'I don't think so. She's recently arrived to replace Pearce. With luck, she'll be a great addition to the team. She seems keen. I'm sure she'd like to get her teeth into this. But she'll have to be careful. These cases are always awkward, apt to spring surprises.'

'I bet,' said Meredith with a sudden impish grin, 'old Jeremy Jenner won't fancy the day-to-day responsibility for this being given to a woman.'

Markby's returning smile was tigerish. 'Old Jeremy, as you call him, is going to have to accept that if I run this investigation, then I call the shots!'

'Stand still!' ordered Jess Campbell. 'You're shifting about.'

'Then hurry up! The light's fading.'

The camera clicked and at the same time the flash exploded. 'There you are!' said Jess.

'At last!' The young man climbed down from the stile and watched her pack away the camera in her canvas bag and then sling the bag over her shoulder. 'Send me a copy?' he asked.

'Of course I will. I'll send one to Mum and Dad as well.'

The setting sun touched their heads and made their hair glow with the same deep red fire. They'd always been alike. No one took them for anything other than what they were. 'What's it like, being a twin?' people had asked them since infancy.

Jess had often replied, 'I don't know what it's like not being a twin, so I can't tell you.'

But sometimes being a twin was quite a painful business. They fell into step now, walking down the rough track towards the spot where they'd parked Jess's car.

'I'm glad you were able to come and spend a couple of days,' she said. 'Before you go away again.'

The words 'go away' hung in the quiet evening air. In the bushes to their right, something rustled and then, almost at their feet, a small rabbit bounced up and fled before them, leaping over hillocks, its white tail disappearing at last into a ditch.

'There were no rabbits in England before the Norman Conquest,' said Simon. 'Did you know that?'

'It sounds like one of those facts people bring out when there's a lull in a dinner-party conversation,' she said. 'Did the rabbits stow away on William the Conqueror's ships?'

'They were brought over to be bred for the table. The Norman knights fancied a bit of rabbit stew. They were a rich man's meat. There were severe penalties for stealing them.' Simon grinned. 'I'm full of useless information like that.'

'You never know,' his sister said. 'You never know when it might come in handy.'

'Not when you're sitting in a sweltering tent, swatting flies and trying your best to inoculate howling babies,' he said. The silence fell again.

'I'm not going to say I wish you weren't going,' Jess said at last. 'Because I know what a necessary job you do and how difficult it is to do it. I see harrowing sights as a police officer. You, dealing with refugees, you see every sight multiplied by hundreds.'

'Of course it's distressing,' he agreed. 'I hope I never cease to find it distressing. But I don't have time to worry about how I feel, when I'm there. I've too much to do and emergencies take place every few minutes so that you're constantly having to make decisions or improvise. I've never wished myself somewhere else or not doing it. I feel guilty when I grab a couple of weeks' leave. But it gives me a chance to talk to people here, explain to them what we're up against.'

'I saw you on that television breakfast show. You made a good job of that.'

He grinned wryly. 'Thanks. I think I'm more afraid of the TV cameras than I am that a bunch of machete-wielding so-called soldiers will come bursting out of the undergrowth, demanding we give them our drugs.'

She shivered. 'That's one of the many things I'm afraid will happen to you.'

'Look,' he said. 'If I really spent my time thinking about that, I wouldn't be able to work. You must feel the same way.' He grinned. 'Especially when you're stuck in a police car on a Saturday night, watching yobs smash windows and beat one another up!'

'That's not what I do. Not now, anyway. I did my turn at that when I joined up.'

'I know! You're after the big boys now, the real criminals. Mum and Dad are really proud of you, Jess.'

'Are they? I don't want them to be proud, just satisfied would do. But I know Dad wishes I did something "less dangerous" and Mum just doesn't understand why I want to be in the police force at all. Dad doesn't mind the police as a career; he just wishes I sat in a back room somewhere rattling the keys of a computer.' Jess sighed. 'Mind you, some days that's just all I do.'

'Believe me,' he insisted. 'They are proud of you.' After a moment he added, 'And so, at times, am I.'

'Only at times?' She gave him a look of mock dismay.

'Wouldn't want you to get swollen-headed!' He reached out and ruffled her cropped red hair.

'Some chance of that!' she said ruefully. 'In the police force.'

Simon frowned. 'Ah, I detect a note of dissatisfaction. You don't think you're going to like this new job of yours?'

'I like my job. I think I'm going to like the rest of the team, providing they don't keep telling me how my predecessor did things. You know how it is when a woman turns up to replace a popular male colleague. The chap I'm replacing, Dave Pearce, is being quoted to me at every turn. He seems to have been the best-liked officer in the history of the police and he was, in addition, a local man. He couldn't go wrong!'

'Whoa!' exclaimed Simon.

'I know I sound grumpy but it's only because I'm nervous. Not that I'll let any of them see it.'

'They probably know it,' said Simon. 'What about your boss, Superintendent, whatsit? Maltby?'

'Markby? I haven't seen much of him. But he's another one everyone seems to credit with superhuman powers, even more than Pearce. I get Markby quoted at me, too. I've only met him briefly when he welcomed me. He seemed all right, not quite the usual sort of copper.'

'Oh? How? Not broken-nosed from playing rugger and with a suspicious squint in his eye?'

'I don't know if he played rugby. He hasn't got a broken nose. He's quite a good-looking chap, tall, fair hair, remarkable blue eyes. No squint.'

'Blimey,' said Simon. 'You haven't fallen for this guy, have you? That'll stir things up.'

'It certainly would, if I had, because he's about to get married. But I haven't. It's just that when I met him, it rather threw me. I expected to be given the usual welcome talk combined with a lecture about clearing up the crime rate and turning in my reports on time. But it was more like being granted an interview with the headmaster of a rather good school. I gather, by the way, that he did go to a rather good school. But although he was very nice, I wouldn't like to cross him. I got the impression that behind the expressed hopes that I'll be happy here and that I've got some-where to live, he was summing me up pretty accurately. I reckon he's as tough as boiled boots, but he doesn't let it show.' Jess paused. 'In fact, he rather scared me.'

'You'll be all right, Jess,' Simon said. He touched her arm. 'And so shall I.'

Above them the sky darkened for an instant as a flock of swarming starlings passed over them, heading for nearby trees. Jess, looking at her brother, saw that he had turned his face upwards to watch the birds.

'Sometimes, though,' he said quietly, 'I do feel I've been in too many places where wheeling birds mean dead bodies on the ground beneath.'

Jess bit her lip. They reached with car without further conversa-tion and bumped away down the track. At the turning into the surfaced road, they saw a pub on the other side. It looked welcoming with a row of coloured lights draped along the façade beneath its slate-tiled roof.

'A drink?' Simon suggested. 'I know you coppers don't drink on duty but you're not on duty now.'

'No, but I am at the wheel of a car!'

'Oh, come on, one drink. Or sit there supping tomato juice and watch me, if you prefer.'

She grinned and turned into the car park, but as they were about to get out of the car, she suddenly exclaimed, 'No, not here!'

'What not here?'

'We can't, or I'd prefer not to drink here. Look, see the BMW? That's Markby's car.'

'Are you sure?' Simon peered through the windscreen.

'I recognize the number plate. One thing we coppers are trained to do is remember number plates. If it's all the same to you, I'd rather not drink my tomato juice under the eye of the super-intendent.'

'Perhaps he's in there with this woman he's going to marry? Aren't you curious to see her?'

'No,' Jess said. 'I'm not. And I didn't think you were such an old busybody! We'll stop at the next decent pub, I promise.'

'I didn't know,' her brother complained, 'that being a copper made life so difficult.'

There's a lot you don't know about being a copper, Jess thought, but didn't say aloud.

Chapter Three

Meredith wasn't prepared for her first sight of Overvale House. They drove up hill and down dale through wooded countryside before suddenly emerging at the top of a steep rise to find an open panorama spread out below them in a flat-bottomed valley. Here and there the landscape was dotted with the virulent yellow patches of rape fields. The rape seeds had escaped and established themselves by the roadside, where they nodded lemon flower heads at passing cars. In a sheltered low-lying spot an orchard of cherry or plum trees was a riot of pink blossom. But they turned aside from all this, following Toby's pencilled road map, on to a badly surfaced lane which was little more than a track. This took them away from the bright open vista back into the shadows of overhanging trees.

They rattled and shook their progress over potholes until, suddenly, they burst out into the open again and an equally arresting sight. Overvale House was before them, on rising land on the other side of the valley, a square white Georgian building among steep green fields and dark patches of woodland. In one field horses grazed peacefully and on the valley floor an irregular oval patch glittered in the sunlight, sending out flashes of bright light. Meredith gasped. Alan drew into the side of the track and they both got out, crossing the road to stand on the narrow verge, overlooking the scene.

'That's the lake,' said Alan, pointing down at the oval of dancing lights. 'It's not very large, as you can see, and it's artificial. It was created early in the nineteenth century as a boating lake, to amuse guests, I suppose.'

'You know the house and grounds, of course. I'm longing to see them.' The wind whipped up her hair as she spoke and she put up a hand to smooth it down.

'Ask the Jenners. I'm sure they'd be delighted to show you the property.' There was a dry note in his voice.

She glanced at him. 'I'm sorry, Alan. I shouldn't have landed you with this.'

He shook his head and grinned at her. 'Don't, please, apologize. It isn't like you and makes me nervous. Anyway, it's not necessary. If this turns out to be blackmail, then it would probably end up on my desk. In a sense, I'm quite pleased to be in on the action early. As I was saying to you last night, we usually get called in far too late.'

She was gazing at the view again. 'It's such a lovely house, the whole setting, everything. It's – it's like coming on an enchanted palace in a fairy tale.'

Markby asked gently, 'Is it a good or an evil enchantment?' Then, when she turned a surprised face towards him, he smiled and added teasingly, 'It's not like Bamford vicarage.'

'No, we couldn't afford this – or afford to keep it up if we had it. Nor would it be suitable for us. Wildly over the top. But his cousin's made a lot of money, Toby says. If I were a millionaire, which I gather is Jenner is, I'd buy this. Wouldn't you? Anyway, when we've finished with the vicarage, it will be pretty good too. Though not, I admit, in this league!'

They returned to the car and Markby drove on. They were going downhill now, down into the valley bottom and back into trees. They lost sight of the house. Then they began to climb again. The trees thinned out. They passed a cottage of reddish stone and then came to high gates which had been opened, presumably to let them in. Markby drove through the tall stone gateposts. They were committed to whatever lay ahead.

The drive had been laid out perhaps two hundred years earlier with the clear intent that visitors arriving in carriages should be impressed. At first only part of the house façade was glimpsed through the straight lines of chestnut trees standing as sentries to either side of the drive. But at the last moment the view was cleared and they had unimpeded sight of a graceful, perfectly proportioned mansion, not overlarge, its long, narrow windows reflecting the spring sunshine.

'I feel,' Meredith said to Alan, pointing at the porch with its white pillars, 'that the door should open and the Bennet sisters come out.'

The semi-circle before the house was gravelled. Markby drew up in a swirl of small stones. As he did, the front door of the house opened and two figures appeared, but both, as it happened, male. The younger of the two, easily recognizable, ran forward and greeted them as they emerged from the car.

'This really is good of you!' Toby pumped Alan's hand. 'We're just so grateful, the whole family.'

'Alan's only come to listen!' Meredith said quickly as she could see the beginnings of exasperation already on Markby's face.

'That's what we want, someone to listen!' declared Toby.

'I'm sure,' Alan said stiffly, 'that Inspector Winter at Bamford listened. Nice to see you again,' he added politely.

'Oh, that chap, Winter,' Toby dismissed doughty Inspector Winter. 'Good chap but swallowed the rule book. Let me introduce my cousin, Jeremy.'

Jenner had arrived during this brief exchange. He was, Meredith was amused to note, rather as she'd imagined he would be. A tall man, he'd kept a trim figure probably by visits to an expensive private health club. His thick grey hair was neatly trimmed and beneath bushy eyebrows deep-set eyes treated them to a sharp scrutiny. His deep voice, however, was affable and his manner smooth.

'I can only repeat what Toby has said. We are extremely grateful to you. This is a wretched business. I want to see it cleared up, as

29

you'll understand. I agree, Inspector Winter is a solid sort of chap but I don't know that he quite appreciates the ramifications which could follow from this.'

Alan's right! Meredith thought. Jenner, too, fears this is a prelude to a blackmail demand.

They were ushered into a spacious hall where they were greeted first by an elderly black Labrador and then by a pretty woman of middle height. Her thick fair hair was streaked with the first signs of grey but they blended well with the rest, and as she grew older she wouldn't probably change much in appearance. She gave them a ready, if slightly nervous, smile.

'My wife, Alison,' Jenner said and, as he said it, something, an echo in his tone, a softening in his glance combined with a sudden and brief warm glow in his otherwise hawkish gaze, told Meredith all she needed to know about this relationship. She guessed Jenner loved his wife deeply. She was perhaps more than a partner; she was the centre of his existence. If so, he would be determined nothing would harm her, both because of his love and because, in harming her, the unknown letter-writer had shaken that cherished domestic stability which must mean so much to Jeremy himself.

On the threshold of marriage herself, there was something both endearing and slightly frightening about this dependency. Agatha Christie, she thought, in one of her Mary Westmacott novels, wrote of the burden of being loved. You were a shrewd woman, Agatha! And then Meredith remembered that in that particular novel the burden of love had led to murder.

They moved into an airy drawing room and there a fourth person turned to acknowledge their arrival.

Meredith had not expected anyone else. Toby hadn't referred to another person. But when she saw the girl standing by the Adam-style fireplace she guessed that this, originally, was the reason that Toby had phoned his cousin to wangle an invitation to stay.

Alison was attractive and as a younger woman had probably been distractingly pretty, but this girl was beautiful in the classic mould. Meredith supposed her about twenty. She had a flawless skin, straight nose and rounded chin with full, slightly pouting lips. Her long, thick, ash-blond hair was braided at each temple in two narrow plaits which were drawn back and joined at the rear of her head. The rest of her hair hung straight as a waterfall from a central parting. The effect was to suggest the female subject of some painting of the Italian Renaissance. This impression was furthered by the scoop-necked loose blouse of some floating material with smocking at the bust and upper arms which she wore with her jeans. The mixture struck Meredith as successful even if oddly matched. There was something of the same effect in the girl herself. She seemed both to be at home in this comfortable room and yet wary of the newcomers. Her clear, steady gaze held either defiance or arrogance and Meredith wasn't sure which.

'Hi,' she said in low throaty voice, 'I'm Fiona.'

'My daughter,' Jenner said with some pride.

Yet it was a pride, Meredith thought, without that fierceness of emotion she had sensed in his previous introduction of 'my wife'. It should be obvious this was Jenner's daughter. She had something of her father's way of assessing newcomers directly without troubling to disguise the fact. Beautiful, wealthy, confident, indulged. Trouble in top-of-the-range trainers, thought Meredith.

It answered another question, however. Yes, he had been married before. Toby, during their conversation in the Chinese restaurant, had said that Alison and Jeremy had been married only ten years. So, Meredith asked herself. Where is wife number one and did the marriage end in death or divorce?

They were offered drinks in a comfortable drawing room and then led out to eat lunch in a large Edwardian conservatory. The house must have a formal dining room so Meredith guessed this informality was not without its purpose. It made people more relaxed and chatty. At the end of the meal they retired to the drawing room again and coffee was brought there by a middle-aged cook-housekeeper of ultra-respectable appearance.

'People do still live like this!' she managed to whisper to Alan.

'Oh, yes, they do . . .' he murmured and she glanced at him. His attitude was deceptively relaxed. She could see that he was assessing the surroundings and the people in the room every bit as keenly as Jenner had assessed them on their arrival.

'Right,' said Jenner briskly when they'd finished their coffee. He set down his own cup on a small polished table and pushed the delicate porcelain away from him. 'To business.'

This was the chairman of the board speaking but he was being honest. They were here, after all, for a specific reason, not just to enjoy what had been an excellent lunch. Meredith was interested to see that Fiona had settled back in her chair with a slightly bored expression. So she was to remain and hear everything and, from her attitude, had heard it all before. Whatever Jeremy and Alison had to say, it would spring no surprises on her, yet Toby had claimed that 'nobody knew' of Alison's past history. At least four out of the six people in this room did. How many people, thought Meredith uneasily, do actually know about this?

'You know the details, Alan? Toby's told you?' Jeremy was impatient to cut to what he saw as the important part of the discussion: what the police were going to do about it.

'Well, no, not exactly,' Markby said, refusing to be rushed. 'I know about the threatening letter. I've not had time to do much other than exchange a few words with Inspector Winter on the phone. I understand that examination of the letter you gave him has not revealed anything very helpful. The writer is literate and motivated by considerable ill will.'

Alison winced and looked down at her hands folded in her lap.

Fiona said in her husky drawl, 'Can't they tell things from the print and all that?'

Alan smiled at her. 'Alas, not since the demise of the type-written letter. I take it that's what you mean. The old typewriters grew worn with use and were often quite distinctive in what they produced. And, of course, if it was a question of cuttings from newspapers glued on to a sheet, then the newsprint of individual papers could be distinguished. But we live in the computer age and this writer has access to a computer and an ink-jet printer. The paper is a standard sort such as you buy in one of those stores which supply office necessities. The envelope is of the self-sealing type, probably from the same kind of store. The postage stamp is also of the self-sticking variety. No saliva to go on like the older standard do-it-yourself stamps. The Post Office has a lot to answer for. Besides no trace of DNA material, there are no distinguishing marks of any kind, no fingerprints, nothing.'

'There's one of those office supply places on the outskirts of Bamford,' Jenner said.

'Quite. They're everywhere these days. He could have bought it there or anywhere in the country. Even if it turns out to be the sort supplied to a particular chain, such stores sell thousands of packs a week, often in big boxes of two and half thousand sheets. I've got a box of the stuff at home myself.'

'He was very careful, though, wasn't he?' Meredith said thoughtfully. 'To leave no trace at all like that? He thought about it all before he did it. He bought the self-sealing envelopes and the self-sticking stamps. He bought general purpose paper of the bulk sale type. He's methodical, isn't he? A planner.'

Alison, who had been watching her as she spoke, shuddered at the last words.

Alan was nodding. 'Yes, he's careful. He isn't going to help us.'

'You think it is a man, then?' Jenner demanded, his bushy eyebrows meeting in a frown.

'I wouldn't like to say. We'll say "he" for convenience's sake.'

Fiona was twisting a finger in her long blond hair. She said unexpectedly, 'What does he want?'

Yes, she was her father's daughter, all right, Meredith thought. Behind the sharp gaze lay a sharp brain. She guessed that more than spite lay behind this campaign against her stepmother. Did she also suspect blackmail?

'Until he tells us, we don't know,' said Markby. 'It may be his sole aim is to embarrass and distress you. He may want money for his silence. He may still be mulling over his options.'

'I don't know,' Alison said very quietly, 'why anyone should hate me so much. And how does he know about it?'

'Well, I'm afraid,' Markby said to her gently, 'that any criminal process is a matter of record. There are a dozen ways in which someone may come across the details.'

'But not link them to Ally here!' Toby said forcefully. 'It all happened donkey's years ago! She had a different surname then.'

Markby shifted in his chair and turned to Alison Jenner. 'I'm afraid, owing to lack of time, I haven't been able to look up the details of your trial. Without them—'

Jenner and his wife exchanged glances. Alison straightened her posture in the chair and said firmly, 'I can tell anything you want to know now.'

'Are you sure, darling?' Jenner asked her. He reached out and touched her arm.

'Absolutely sure, Jeremy. Not talking about it all these years, pushing it away as if it never happened, that's what's led to this situation, isn't it? If everyone knew, no one could threaten me now.'

'We can talk about it in private, if you wish,' Markby said.

She shook her head. 'No, the family members here have been told. When Jeremy found out about the letters, Alan, we discussed it. I said Fiona and Toby must be told because it seemed likely now it would all come out about the trial. I didn't want either or them to learn about it from newspapers. When we told Toby, he said at once he'd ask Meredith to speak to you. I know that wasn't correct procedure. It's probably put you on the spot and you're privately cursing us. I don't blame you. But we are desperate. One clutches at straws. Meredith should hear all the details because she's the one Toby asked to approach you. You, of course, have to know. I was accused of the murder of my great-aunt, Freda Kemp.'

She paused and heaved a sigh. 'It's hard to know where to begin. You need some background facts if it's to make sense. My parents were in the Diplomatic Service, as you were, Meredith. They lived in various parts of the globe and I was sent home to school. My guardian for practical purposes in this country was Aunt Freda. She was a single woman who ran a successful business finding nannies and domestic staff for people. By the time of the – the events which led to the trial, I was twenty-three. My parents had retired to St Lucia to spend the rest of their lives in the sun. Aunt Freda was long retired herself but she was still my remaining family link in this country. I used to go and see her when I could, though it wasn't easy. She lived in Cornwall, rather off the beaten track, near Rock on the Camel estuary.'

'I know it,' Markby nodded. 'A beautiful spot.'

'Yes,' Alison agreed. 'I always loved it there. Aunt Freda had had a holiday cottage there for years when she lived and ran her firm in London. When she retired, she chose to make the cottage her permanent home. It had a large garden and she loved that particularly.'

'That,' Alan said, 'I can certainly understand!' He smiled.

Alison didn't return the smile. 'Moving to the cottage was, if you like to use the expression, her undoing.' She paused and they waited. As they did a shadow passed the window which gave on to the front of the house.

Both Markby and Meredith turned their heads and Meredith had a fleeting impression of a tall ungainly shape.

'Harry Stebbings,' said Jenner briefly. 'The gardener.'

They sat and listened as Stebbings' footsteps crunched away heavily across the gravel.

'He maintains the grounds alone?' Markby asked.

'He's got the help of his son in holiday times. A gormless youth by the name of Darren whom his parents hope will benefit from attending the local college of further education. I doubt it. I gather he's studying photography!' Jenner snorted.

Fiona giggled. 'He wants to be a snapper of the stars, that's what he told me, in those words. You know, part of the paparazzi pack.'

'He'll find that a cut-throat world,' Markby observed.

'Oh, he hasn't got a clue,' Fiona said carelessly. 'He's got one of those little digital cameras and he thinks he's going to do it all with that. He's never heard of any of the famous photographers and he's got no artistic or dramatic sense. He thinks as long as you have the figures dead centre in the middle of the picture, that's it.'

'I'd be happy,' Meredith observed, 'if I could get the subject in the middle of the snap. When I take a photo, the subject always comes out on the bottom right-hand side.'

Markby gave her a brief conspiratorial grin before he turned back to Alison who continued her story.

'I wish I could have visited Aunt Freda more often. She was getting frail. She was, after all, my mother's aunt and my great-aunt. She was eighty when – when the tragedy happened. Perhaps I should say the additional tragedy, because it was already the saddest thing to have watched her decline. Living on her own down there, after such a busy life, she just went downhill. It was certainly a mistake, after a lifetime in a city, to cut herself off in such a peaceful but pretty well deserted place, at least it is out of season. Spending holiday breaks there had been fine. She hadn't counted on the way permanent residence would result in making each day exactly like the one before and the one to come, the lack of stimulation which comes from meeting people, visiting museums and exhibitions, being part of the general buzz. I used to phone her and chat. I knew she was lonely. But she was obstinate, too. She wouldn't admit she'd made a mistake. Also I fancy the thought of moving house again, having done it once when she left London, appeared daunting to her. I did suggest it and offered to help, but she would have none of it. She had company of a sort during the day because a local woman, Mrs Travis, used to go in and clean for her and get her lunchtime meal. Not that Mrs Travis was a great companion. She was a dour sort of woman. I don't think she liked any-one much, that's the impression she gave. She certainly didn't like me!'

'Any particular reason?' Markby asked.

'At the time I supposed it was just her disposition. Her husband had bolted and left her with a young son, a sullen kid about ten years old. He seemed to live in wellington boots and have a nature just like his mother. He tagged along with her during school holidays and sat drawing pictures on scrap paper but wouldn't show them to me. I think his mother had warned him I wasn't to be trusted. I wasn't surprised she hadn't warmed to me. I wasn't the sort of person she'd ever had much to do with. I was working in London on a good salary in the advertising world, an independent young woman pretty sure of herself. No man had dumped me. I didn't have a kid to worry about. I had choice of employment. You might not think it looking at me now but in those days, I really did have all my marbles!' She gave a deprecating laugh.

Jenner frowned and said reproachfully, 'Don't put yourself down!'

'You know what I mean,' she said. 'Everything was going for me. I'd drive down from London when I had a free weekend, city chick with wheels, and there would be Mrs Travis standing in the doorway wearing an apron and hand-knitted jumper and radiating disapproval. I was inclined to find it rather funny. My mistake. She did look after Aunt Freda very well, I have to admit. I think that probably, in her own way, Mrs Travis thought she was protecting her employer.'

'From you?' Markby asked.

'Yes, even from me. She was the sort of person who thought badly of everyone. No generosity of soul herself and unable to see good in anyone else, except in Aunt Freda. And Aunt Freda's kindness was probably seen by Mrs Travis as a weakness, making her vulnerable to conniving fast hussies from London. She

37

couldn't bar the door to me, though she'd have liked to, but all that scowling was to let me know she was "on" to me.

'One Sunday, it was in August and a lovely day, I was getting ready to drive back to London. I had to leave in the morning. Mrs Travis didn't come in on a Sunday so she wasn't around. I was a little concerned about Aunt Freda because since my last visit she seemed to have gone downhill even faster. Her hair was untidy, which wasn't like her. She rambled a bit and got a little muddled from time to time. Twice she called me by my mother's name, Lilian. I knew Mrs Travis would be going in the next morning and I had to be back at my desk on Monday bright and early, so I had to leave. I decided to ring my aunt's doctor as soon as I got a chance and report my concerns. The last I saw of my aunt was standing by her gate, waving goodbye to me.' Alison paused and bit her lip. 'I think I shall always see her like that.'

There was another awkward silence. The old Labrador which had been lying at Alison's feet looked up anxiously at her mistress.

'Drop of brandy!' said her husband firmly. He got up and fetched it. 'Here you are, darling, knock it back! Anyone else want one?' He held up the bottle.

They all shook their heads, even Toby after a momentary hesitation.

The brandy seemed to do the trick. Alison began again briskly. 'The police turned up on my doorstep at seven the following morning, I was up and about getting ready for my usual working day. It was just one policeman, a young constable, very sympathetic. He was sorry he had bad news for me. Miss Kemp had been found dead in her garden. It appeared to be an accident but he had no details. Early as it was, I rang my aunt's doctor in Cornwall. He hadn't heard about it. He was not the doctor called in by the police to certify death. He promised to ring me back as soon as he knew something. He kept his promise. He rang me at lunchtime to say my aunt had been found by her housekeeper at around nine that morning. She was in the garden and had apparently fallen into the fishpond and drowned. It was only a small pond and if you put your whole arm straight down in it, the water would have come up to about your elbow. But my aunt had fallen forwards with her face in the water and it had been enough. She'd lain there overnight. The accident probably happened mid-afternoon on Sunday. There would have to be a post-mortem, the doctor said. But he wouldn't be the one performing it. That was for the local pathologist. I could tell the doctor was upset, not only because he'd lost a patient in those circumstances, but because he was being cut out of the loop.

'I was more than upset. I took the rest of the day off. In fact I took the week off because I was executor of my aunt's estate and I needed to go and see her solicitor. He was a London man. I already knew what was in the will. She had left everything to me except for five hundred pounds to Mrs Travis. The cottage was mine, everything. I had the keys already. I went down there so that I could see the local vicar about the funeral, that sort of thing. I was there when the police came on the Thursday. The post-mortem had discovered a wound on my aunt's head but there were no stones round the pond on which she could have hit her head by accident. Worse, there was no sign of pond water in her lungs. She'd been dead when she went in the water. Mrs Travis had been busy spreading poison. She told them how I had an expensive London lifestyle. She said I was always coming to see my aunt and I had hopes of inheriting. I had been there that very weekend. My aunt was wealthy. I had borrowed money from her.'

'Was that true?' Markby asked her.

'As it happened, yes. I had a good income but London is expensive. I wanted to put down a deposit on a flat. I told Aunt Freda about it and she said straight away that she didn't want me borrowing money from strangers, as she put it. She advanced me the deposit. It was always understood I'd pay it back, but there was nothing in writing. "When you can," she'd said to me. "But it's yours, anyway." She was referring to her will. We left it at that.'

'It was a family arrangement!' broke in her husband loudly. 'It's normal. One lends money to youngsters. They always need something.'

Fiona put a hand to her long hair and smoothed it. She then turned her attention to her polished nails. For a second a faint frisson ran through the air.

'Well, to cut a long story short,' said Alison, 'the police decided it was murder. The investigating officer was a Chief Inspector Barnes-Wakefield and I'll never forget him! Everything about him was narrow, his head and body, his hands. His hair was straight and oiled with some preparation or other and brushed back from his forehead. He looked as if he'd been squashed flat between two hard surfaces, like a pressed flower or, in his case, a pressed weed. I soon found out his mind was as narrow as the rest of him. I knew, as soon as I met him, that he had me in his sights. The way he saw it, I was the most likely suspect. I stood to gain.'

'It's a question all detectives ask,' Markby said quietly. '*Cui bono*? I don't mean they ask it in Latin, but it's the first line of inquiry. Who stands to profit by the crime?'

'Of course,' said Alison simply. 'I understand that. I stood to profit. But you don't stop at asking just that one question, do you? Mind you, Barnes-Wakefield had what he called a case. I'd been there that day. I'd known no one would call by until the following morning when I'd be safely back in London. If you add that to the fact that I'd borrowed money . . .'

'All circumstantial evidence, surely,' Meredith objected.

'Who else was in the frame?' Alison retorted bluntly. 'Besides, I was the outsider, the one who came down from London. My aunt had lived in London too, but she'd owned the cottage for years and locals knew and respected her. Mrs Travis was hard at work blackening my character and building up every little incident into something it wasn't, determined to see I got my come-uppance. She and Barnes-Wakefield were soulmates, if you ask me.'

'There is another point,' Jenner interrupted again. 'A number of people hire holiday cottages in the West Country. It's necessary that they feel safe in lonely properties. The local police needed to solve the crime quickly and, if possible, show it to be the result of something like a family dispute, an in-house crime, if you like. No hint of a lone prowler, nothing like that.'

'Hum,' said Markby. 'Nevertheless, I'm surprised they went to trial on such evidence. However, twenty-five years ago, things were done differently, I know.'

'One thing about being known in the city and having money,' Alison said. 'I could hire a good lawyer. He's still around. Now he's Sir Montague Ling. Then he was plain Monty Ling but going places.'

'Montague Ling!' Markby exclaimed. 'I bet he knocked all their circumstantial evidence into a cocked hat!'

'Yes, he did. But even so, I mightn't have squeaked through had not, quite unexpectedly, a pair of witnesses turned up. They were a young couple on a cycling holiday. They read about the trial in the papers and in one paper there was a picture of the cottage. They remembered it. They'd cycled past it at one o'clock that Sunday afternoon and stopped to ask the elderly woman in the garden if they were on the right road. She said they were and they remembered her clearly, could identify her photo. Well, at one o'clock I was nearly a hundred miles away, buying petrol, with a timed and dated receipt to prove it. The garage didn't have a security camera at the till. It was before they became standard equipment. But they were shown a photograph of me and the young man at the till recognized me. He said yes, I'd definitely been in on that Sunday.' Alison blushed faintly. 'He remembered me because I was what he called a looker. So that was that. I was cleared or, as Mrs Travis probably told everyone, got away with it.'

'Don't say that!' Jenner told her. 'You were rightly cleared. The case should never have gone to court, as Markby indicated.'

'Tell me,' Markby asked Alison, 'what do you think happened to your aunt?'

She met his gaze frankly. 'I've spent a long time puzzling over that and I have got a theory, though I can't prove it. It was such a lovely day and Aunt Freda loved the garden. She would stay out in it until teatime, I'm sure, just popping into the house for the odd thing. The cyclists saw her there. There were no rocks around the pool, but much further away there was a rockery. I think my aunt, who was frail and unsteady on her feet, stumbled and fell near the rockery. She hit her head, probably knocked herself out. She came round sufficiently to get to her feet. But she was disorientated. She wanted to go back to the cottage but she went in the other direction, towards the pond. There she collapsed and died, falling face forwards into the water.'

'The local police didn't search round the garden to see if there was anywhere like that where she could have struck her head?' Meredith asked.

'Apparently not.'

'You bet they didn't,' said Fiona unexpectedly. 'They wanted to stitch Alison up.' She stared defiantly at Markby. 'Clearing up the crime rate, that's what it's about, isn't it? Closing the file?'

'Darling . . .' murmured her father, looking slightly shocked.

If he was shocked, thought Meredith, it was because his daughter had been rude to a guest. He had suggested much the same thing earlier himself, albeit in a rather more circumspect manner.

Markby met Fiona's challenging stare with an easy smile. 'I couldn't say. I don't have the details of the investigations the police carried out.'

Fiona flushed and retorted, 'Nor do I. That's what you mean, isn't it? Well, I don't. But one hears about these things. You heard what Alison said about this guy, Barnes-Wakefield. He had a mean disposition and he wanted to pin it on Alison.'

Jenner stepped into the situation smoothly. 'So that's the story, Markby. As you say, the writer of the letter could have learned the facts anywhere.'

'Yes, especially if the case was an early success for Sir Montague Ling. Whenever he has another triumph the papers usually refer to his earlier exploits.'

'But,' said Toby obstinately, 'whoever read it still would have no reason to link it to Alison.'

'That's something we're going to have to look into, isn't it? Well,' Markby said, 'we'll do our best to trace the writer quickly. But, as I hope you'll have understood, it could take time. If you get another letter bring it to me at once together with the envelope.' He smiled at Alison. 'In the meantime, *nil desperandum*, eh?'

'Thank you,' she said.

'I wonder,' Markby said to Jeremy Jenner, 'if, before we go, we might take a look at your gardens? Meredith would like to see the boating lake.'

'Yes, of course!' Jenner said, getting to his feet.

Everyone else stood up and the atmosphere was suddenly lighter. There was a sense of palpable relief as if a disagreeable chore had been done and minds could be turned to more pleasant matters.

'If you're going down to the lake,' said Fiona. 'Count me out. I don't like that bird. It's vicious. I'm going to see the horses.'

Meredith saw Toby hesitate. He clearly wanted to go with Fiona. But he must have decided quickly that, as she and Alan were here at his instigation, he could hardly abandon them. He watched Fiona walk quickly away, his expression wistful.

A complication, thought Meredith.

'We'll have to shut in Betsy,' Alison said. 'He goes for her.'

These ominous references were not explained.

'I remember these gardens,' Markby said to Jeremy Jenner as they walked down a well-raked path, 'from when the Grays lived here.'

The route led them steeply downhill between banks of shrubs. Gardening on this slope must present problems. Birds fluttered up at their passage but it was very quiet, a place of peace.

'We've made a few changes,' Jenner replied. 'Alison's a keen gardener. She's got a lot of ideas.'

They were passing by an arrangement of rustic chairs and a table as he spoke.

'Those are nice,' Meredith observed.

'Yes, well made.' Jenner nodded approvingly. 'A couple of fellows run a small business turning them out, down on the Watersmeet industrial estate. The firm's called "Rusticity".' Jenner snorted. 'Sort of name that appeals to people, I suppose.'

'We're taking over a run-down garden at the vicarage,' Meredith said. 'When we get it cleared up, something like those chairs would be nice.'

'Ted and Steve,' Alison said, overhearing. 'Those are their names. Their prices are quite reasonable and they'll make anything you like to order.'

They had reached the bottom of the slope where it flattened into a shallow valley floor. Here a stream trickled its way through and fed the lake ahead of them. Not only was it bigger than Meredith had expected, but its whole appearance was surprising. She had imagined from Alan's casual description, and the distant view she had had of it, that close to hand the lake would present quite a formal appearance. But this was a more irregularly shaped patch of water than appeared from across the valley, ringed with trees, willow and birch, and clumps of large ornamental shrubs. Rushes grew in banks at the water's edge and further out she could see the large flat dark green pads of waterlily plants. All of this had been carefully laid out by the Victorian gardener who had created it to look natural and romantic. There was even a small island in the centre of the lake. To reach this, or just to amuse oneself out on the water, there was a rowing boat moored to a wooden jetty. The boat rocked gently as the breeze rippled the water and whispered in the rushes. It was an idyllic spot.

Between the visitors and the lake, however, was an obstacle, not a large one, admittedly, but a determined one.

A Canada goose stood by the water's edge facing them. It spread out its wings and hissed warningly.

'Allow me to introduce Spike,' said Jenner. 'He started by being something of a pet and has now turned into a first-rate nuisance.'

'What happened to the rest of his flock?' Meredith asked.

'He was injured,' Alison told her. 'We found him with a damaged wing. We're not sure how it happened. The others had flown on and he was waddling up and down by the edge of the water looking very sorry for himself. So we took him to the wildlife sanctuary down the road and they patched him up. But when they released him, he made his way back here. He'd decided he liked it here. Our mistake was to make a bit of a fuss of him. Now he thinks he owns the lake and the approaches to it. He accepts Jeremy and me in a grudging sort of way, but he's tricky with strangers. We have tried taking him away and releasing him in suitable spots but he always turns up back here again. Stop that, Spike, go on, shoo!'

Alison clapped her hands. Spike responded by flapping his wings but shuffled a short distance away from where he kept a baleful watch on them.

'That bird,' said Toby, 'is the avian equivalent of crazy.'

'Poor Toby.' Alison smiled at him as she addressed Meredith and Alan. 'He tried to take the boat out on the lake with Fiona. Spike attacked them and they both had to run for it. It was such a pity. They'd wanted to row over to the island.'

'Bloody bird! If I had my way I'd take my gun and scatter his feathers. I suppose you want me to catch him again, take him well away and release him,' said a harsh voice behind them. 'Lot of good that does.'

They all jumped and turned to face the speaker. None of them had heard his approach across the grass and Markby and Meredith were certainly unprepared for the actual sight of him. The man was tall and angular and gave the impression of great strength without muscular bulk. His greying hair was long and tangled and his beard also long and untrimmed. His nose jutted between deep-set eyes which glittered in his sunburned face. He wore an old baggy waxed jacket and strong workboots. The sleeves of the jacket had ridden up, or else his arms were unusually long. His bony wrists and huge knotted hands hung from them like the dangling arms of marionette at rest. He raised one now, rather as though it had been activated by an unseen puppet-master, and pointed at Spike who appeared, Meredith thought, understandably disconcerted. The goose managed only a token flap of its wings and backed further away. From this safe distance, it gave a derisive honk.

'I know we've had no luck removing him, Harry,' said Alison. 'But it's the only way. I'll ring the RSPCA in the morning and see if they have any ideas.'

'I still think you ought to let me shoot him,' offered the man.

'No, Harry! Certainly not! We'll think of something.'

Spike's would-be Nemesis snorted and, turning, shambled off, his long arms swinging by his sides.

'That's Stebbings,' said Jenner. 'He's got a quaint way with him but he's a good chap.'

His listeners made no reply to this, and they all began to walk back to the house, leaving Spike in triumphant possession. Alan, Toby and Jeremy had forged ahead and Alison slowed her step so that she and Meredith fell back out of earshot of the three men.

'Some things I can't say in front of Jeremy,' she said a low urgent voice. 'But I'm so worried about the effect this business is having on him. I know he gives the appearance of being in control, but he's had years of practice at that. He's really very, very angry. It will come out, won't it? It will all get in the papers now?'

They had reached the arrangement of rustic table and chairs. Alison made a gesture towards them and she and Meredith sat down. The other members of the party were now out of sight.

'It's always so difficult,' Alison said, 'to explain family matters.' Her hands smoothed her skirt nervously. She was looking down and her fair hair fell forwards, obscuring her face. 'Being accused of killing my aunt was horrible. Worse than anything I can describe.'

'I can imagine it,' Meredith said sympathetically.

Alison looked up sharply. 'No, you can't. I'm sorry. I don't mean to be rude. But quite simply, you can't. You haven't been in that situation and I hope you never are. I wouldn't wish it on my worst enemy. The trial was a nightmare. Afterwards, living with what had happened, was almost unbearable. Dirt sticks. The papers had painted me as a fortune-hunting, hard-hearted, scheming woman. It's true my aunt had given me money on several occasions. But she didn't mind. She liked to help me. She would have been hurt if I'd turned her offers down. Barnes-Wakefield couldn't understand that. Over and over again, he kept asking me about the money Aunt Freda had given me over the years and about her will. Had I known she'd made me her sole heiress? Yes, I had to tell him, I did know. So, he kept asking, what did I feel about that? What kind of reply could I give him?'

'You're quite right,' Meredith told her. 'I have no idea what I would have replied in your situation.'

'But I carried on. I still had my job. People there were kind and supportive. But I'd still catch one or two or them watching me when they thought I was busy. There would be a question in their eyes, a sort of prurient curiosity. They got a sort of kick out of working with someone who'd been accused of murder. Eventually, in the natural process of staff turnover, they left. I stayed. I thought it was forgotten. Then I met Jeremy. Our firm handled an advertising campaign for him. When he proposed to me, I told him all about the trial. Fifteen years had gone by and I really, stupidly, believed I had, at last, left it behind me. Or so I thought. But I had to tell Jeremy. It was only fair. He was splendid about it. From then until just the other day when he found I'd received another letter, we didn't speak of it again, not once in ten years of marriage. Now it's as if we can't speak of anything else. Jeremy wants it all cleared up quickly, so that we can get back to normal. But will we ever be able to do that? Get back to normal?'

'Yes!' said Meredith. 'You will. It doesn't seem like it now but you must hold on to the belief that it will all be sorted out eventually.'

Alison gave her a wry smile. 'Thanks. I can see why Toby wanted to bring you and Alan in on it. Jeremy's talking of hiring a private detective but I don't want that. What could a private investigator do anyway, that the police can't?'

'In this case, not much, I imagine,' Meredith said. 'You're right to discourage Jeremy.'

Alison gave a little laugh. 'Discouraging Jeremy is a bit like trying to stop a bolting horse! I just want all this cleared up before he starts bringing in goodness knows who. The stress isn't good for him. He looks calm but he's fizzing away underneath it all. If it's not settled soon, I really do fear for his heart.' She hesitated. 'Another reason I don't want a private detective involved, someone reporting to Jeremy, is that, if the gumshoe did find out who was responsible and told Jeremy, then I really fear Jeremy might take the law into his own hands.'

Chapter Four

'So what do you think?' Alan asked Meredith as they drove away from the house between the long lines of chestnut trees towards the main gates.

'I think Alison is very frightened and Jeremy very angry. She's frightened because she's been targeted by hate mail and she's scared of what her husband might do if he finds out the writer's identity. He's talking about hiring a private detective.'

'Is he?' Alan said thoughtfully, 'I may have to have a word with him about that. He's entitled to do it but we wouldn't welcome it. Hello, what's this?'

A figure was waiting for them just inside the main gates. Fiona Jenner had stepped forwards from the dappled shade of the last tree, and held up her hand to signal them to stop. A breeze had sprung up and caught her long fair hair and the gauzy smocked top, causing both to flutter. Meredith felt a spurt of unease, as if they had been presented with a form which, if not quite unearthly, was at least an unknown quantity. Markby stopped the car.

Fiona came to his window and stooped. 'I want to talk to you,' she said in her direct way.

Markby's only reply was to stretch his arm over the back of his seat and disengage the rear door latch. Fiona slid elegantly inside and pulled the door shut. Both Alan and Meredith had twisted in their front seats to be able to face her. There was a silence.

Fiona used it to stare at them with that casual arrogance of youth. She was leaning back in the corner of the car, her head resting against the inner lining. Her windswept long hair lay in tangled skeins across her shoulders. Her cheeks were flushed pink, either from the wind or because she was in the grip of some emotion. It wasn't, thought Meredith, because Fiona was in any way embarrassed at having flagged them down.

Fiona asked suddenly, 'Do you think you'll find him?'

The question was addressed to Markby and he answered it. 'I should think so. It may take a little time but we usually get these jokers.'

Her smooth forehead puckered briefly and she began to twist one strand of long blond hair round her index finger. 'Do you think he wants money?' The twisting finger was stilled.

'Yes,' he said. 'He probably does. Your father is a wealthy man.'

A look compounded of scorn and something very like quiet satisfaction crossed her face. 'Then he's got it wrong. Daddy won't pay. He's not that sort. My father is boardroom man, writ large. If you want anything from Daddy you have to put it in writing, three copies, and justify the expenditure. He's furious.'

'So are you, I fancy.'

She sniffed. 'I couldn't give a toss. But, you know, it's making life bloody difficult at home. Alison's twitchy. Daddy's brooding darkly. Toby keeps on saying it will be all right. How does he know?'

'Look, it's an upsetting business—' Markby began.

She interrupted, shaking her head. 'You don't understand. You don't know my father. What upsets him is that he can't control this "in-house", as he'd describe it. He's had to turn to the police, outsiders. When Toby said he knew you personally, Daddy jumped at the idea you should come today. You're a policeman but not the usual sort. You've got Toby to vouch for you, do you see? It's like you're part of the company. One of us, as Daddy would put it. Daddy liked everything to run smoothly in any company he was in charge of. I bet working for him was hell. He likes everything to run smoothly in family life, too. No problems and no bloody backchat. Just get on and do it. That's Daddy's attitude.'

There was bitterness in her voice. There had been rows in the past, Meredith thought. What about? Perhaps about the school she'd been sent to? That was a common cause of dissent. Or the friends she'd associated with? A career she'd chosen but which wasn't to his taste?

Markby said quietly, 'I'm not part of the company. I'm a police officer, just like Inspector Winter at Bamford. Senior in rank to him, perhaps, but just the same. Your father and Toby Smythe will both have to accept that.'

Seeking to defuse some of the tension which now crackled inside the car's confines, Meredith said, 'Your father is very worried and that makes him touchy, perhaps. People do get a bit brusque when they're upset.'

Fiona dismissed this with another sniff. 'You mean he's worried about Alison, I suppose? Alison will cope with it. Daddy likes to think Alison is a frail little woman who needs protecting but, believe me, Alison is as tough as old boots!'

She had opened the door almost before she'd finished speaking and jumped out. The door slammed. She gave them a farewell wave and set off back towards the house.

'Well,' Markby observed, as he let in the clutch and they rolled forwards again. 'What do you make of that?'

'She doesn't like Alison,' Meredith said promptly. 'She didn't come out and say so but it was pretty clear. She knows better than to let her father see it, or Toby. But it seems to me this business of the poison pen letters is going to shake a few more family secrets out of the closet.'

'And what do you make of the girl herself?'

Meredith considered her answer carefully. 'She's very attractive but stroppy. Perhaps she's just a chip off the old block. She wouldn't like anyone to say she's like her father but I fancy she is. This poison pen business has upset things in the family circle.' Meredith frowned. 'I hope Toby hasn't really fallen for her.'

'Why?' There was a touch of asperity in Markby's voice. 'He's well able to handle his own love life.' Steering the BMW between potholes, he added peevishly, 'I don't know if this lane is a private stretch of road. If so, I wish Jenner would use some of his money to have it resurfaced.'

'Perhaps,' said Meredith, 'he wants to discourage casual visitors or people just driving by.'

He glanced at her. 'That's a very shrewd observation.'

'Thank you, but, like Alison, I am still in possession of most of my marbles!' she retorted. 'And as regards Toby, he can fall in love with anyone he likes, but Fiona will chew him up and spit him out. Besides, she's a cousin of sorts.'

'Only distantly.'

'She's very young. Toby's in his late thirties.'

'Sounds young to me! You're in your late thirties and you don't think you're old, surely? I'm in my mid forties and determined to cling to what little of my youth I have left!' Markby chuckled. 'But we all believe ourselves to be young,' he added. 'The outside changes but the inside doesn't, isn't that it?'

'This is metaphysical meander I don't want to follow. What I meant about the difference in age between Toby and Fiona is that it might not be obvious now, but it will become obvious later.'

'I don't think it matters a jot. Look at Jeremy and Alison. He's got to be at least twenty years older than his wife. Lots of couples cope with a wide age-difference and the marriages work just fine.'

'All right. If you want to know, my real worry about Toby falling for Fiona is that Fiona might turn out to be the writer with the poison pen!'

'Aha! Despite all that back there?' Markby jerked his head backwards to indicate the scene they'd left behind them.

'Partly because of all that back there. I think she stopped us for a private quiz session not so much because she's fed up with the family being upset, but because she's worried, now you've turned up. She didn't bank on you. Toby sprang quite a surprise when he said he had a contact in the police force, a senior copper who was local and engaged to marry an old friend of his, me. Her father leapt at it, she says. You can bet she didn't.'

He hunched his shoulders. 'It's a possibility. But if she has been writing the letters, would she let us see that Alison isn't her favourite person? Wouldn't that be rather stupid?'

'Or she's smart enough to be upfront and honest about it because that would put you off the scent.'

'You have a suspicious mind,' he said with a chuckle. 'You should have been a copper.'

They were passing the cottage they had noticed on their way to Overvale House. Meredith took a closer look at it. It was surrounded by a well-tended garden. Beds were dug over ready for spring planting. There was a row of what looked like gooseberry or blackcurrant bushes in new leaf. A woman was pegging clothes to a line. She stopped what she was doing to stare inquisitively at the car and its occupants. Just then, a familiar figure rounded the rear corner of the building. Meredith had fleeting sight of Stebbings, the gardener, before Markby had swept them past and beyond the cottage.

'That was Stebbings,' she said. 'That must be where he lives. Do you think Jeremy owns that cottage, too?'

'Very likely. There are probably estate workers' cottages like that scattered all over the place. If so, I expect it'll be tied to Stebbings' job.'

'Difficult,' Meredith mused. 'To have your home linked with your job like that. Anything could happen. Stebbings could lose his job or retire or just die. Where would that leave Mrs Stebbings? Homeless? It's not very satisfactory.'

'On the other hand,' Markby pointed out, 'I doubt he pays any rent. Incidentally, he struck me as an odd fish. He looks like the Ancient Mariner.'

'Long grey beard, glittering eye and all, I agree.' Meredith laughed.

Markby picked up the previous thread of conversation. 'What are your grounds for suspecting Fiona? Other than dislike?'

'I didn't say *I* disliked *her*!' Meredith protested. 'I didn't warm to her, I admit. To be brutally honest, I thought she had all the hallmarks of a spoilt brat. But perhaps that isn't all her fault. It's fairly clear there have been some tremendous family rows in the past. I'd like to know about her mother. Is she still alive? Married to someone else? Did she leave Jenner or did he dump her? Did they part by mutual agreement? How old was Fiona at the time and how did she feel about the divorce? Is that why she doesn't like Alison?'

'And then there is the money,' said Markby thoughtfully.

'You're picking up on that remark of Jeremy's about youngsters always wanting something and it being natural to lend them money. Despite that crack she made about having to put in any request in triplicate, I imagine the money's been given outright to Fiona pretty well when she's wanted it. All that trendy gear costs a packet. I wonder if she works at all? Any kind of job, even a voluntary one, something charitable.'

'I can't imagine Fiona in a soup kitchen or handing out clean clothing to down and outs,' he told her. 'Like you, I'm thinking not so much about the present time as the future. I wonder how the two women, Alison and Fiona, stand to benefit from Jeremy Jenner's will.'

'Hold on, let's see what we've got.' Meredith ticked the points off on her fingers. 'Let's suppose Jeremy has been giving Fiona money. Perhaps he's starting to ask where it all goes? Perhaps she needs money for something she can't admit to. She might have a drug habit.'

'She might but we've no reason to suppose she does.' There was enough of the stuff out there on the streets, Markby knew. He also knew the dealers targeted the children of the wealthy. Doing a line of coke before going to a party was routine these days for many youngsters and many not so young. But a serious habit? 'She hasn't the look,' he objected. 'There are no signs of it.'

'OK.' Meredith accepted his argument in that way which meant she was only putting her own to one side temporarily. 'How about this? Jeremy absolutely dotes on his wife. He's almost certainly left her very well provided for under his will. He has a heart condition. This poison pen business is putting a strain on that. He could pop off and then the blackmailer could put the squeeze on Alison directly.' She paused. 'Or it needn't be primarily about money. The writer hasn't mentioned money yet. Perhaps he just wants to discredit Alison, wants to make her suffer. It's a revenge thing.'

'Revenge for what?'

'For marrying Jeremy?'

'You're back to Fiona again.'

'All right, I am. I have her down as prime suspect. She could be motivated by both revenge and blackmail. In her case they'd fit neatly together.' Meredith's tone challenged him to find fault in that line of reasoning.

'How did she come to know the facts of the murder trial? According to the Jenners they didn't tell either the girl or Toby until this poison pen business blew up.'

Markby was playing devil's advocate. Once Meredith got her teeth into a theory, he knew, she could build it quickly into an ingenious case. That was where the amateur always had the advantage over the professional who was tied to mundane things like facts and evidence. But she was clear-headed and shrewd and even if her theories lacked facts, they seldom lacked cohesion.

'It's a matter of record, you said so yourself,' she retorted impatiently. 'You keep knocking down my ideas. Let's hear yours!'

'Do I suspect her? It's too early to say. I'm not ready to point at anyone nor can I rule anyone out. That, by the way, includes your chum, Toby.'

'What!' Aghast, she stared at him. 'But that's ridiculous! What possible motive could he have? He asked me to ask you to investigate!'

'Sure he did. It wouldn't be the first instance of double bluff. Just as you said only minutes ago you thought Fiona stopped us by the gates in a similar game. As for motive, let's say he's in love with Fiona, as you obviously fear he is. Men have done strange things for love.'

There was an ominous silence in the car and then Meredith said stiffly, 'It's still ridiculous. I know Toby. Why on earth would he do a thing like that? Besides, he's been out of the country. Alison would've remembered if the letters had been postmarked Beijing!'

'I didn't say he *wrote* them. He still might be involved. He and Fiona together may have cooked up some plan.'

'He's fond of Alison and Jeremy! Honestly, Alan, it's a crazy idea!'

They had reached the outskirts of Bamford and Markby, perhaps sensing it was time to change the subject, pointed through the windscreen. 'There's the Watersmeet trading estate.'

Meredith looked past him to a collection of low brick buildings. 'A romantic name for a pretty prosaic development.'

'It used to be a farm, Watersmeet Farm,' he explained. 'Then the land was sold for development. I think it was one of Dudley Newman's projects.' Newman was a local builder and entrepreneur.

'Just up his street,' said Meredith morosely. 'Dudley's never as happy as when covering open countryside with bricks.'

'He's even moved his own builder's yard there now. Why don't we turn in here?' Markby suggested. 'We could find this place, Rusticity, and look at the garden furniture.'

Markby parked the car in an area marked Visitors Only. As they got out, he pointed across the lot to one of the warehouses. 'There's one of those office supply places. That's where I bought my box of paper. Just imagine how many individuals and how many businesses that supplies with paper in Bamford alone.'

Rusticity lay at the far end of the trading estate and proved to be a low building bearing the name and, in smaller print beneath, the words: S. Poole and E. Pritchard, Props. A small yard alongside the building was filled with lengths of wood and completed items of furniture. Prospective customers had to pick their way between the contents with care. There were plenty of splinters ready to embed themselves in the flesh of the unwary. A battered white van was parked by the entrance, the name of the firm painted on its side.

Meredith and Alan inspected the random collection of tables and seats. The hallmark of the design appeared to be the use of 'natural' – looking wood, complete with bark, knotholes and minor damage.

'It's well made,' said Markby, testing a rustic bench.

'Nothing goes out of here that isn't properly made,' said a voice behind them. 'We're craftsmen. We're proud of our work.'

The speaker moved into view. He was youngish man in his thirties with thinning hair and very fair eyebrows. A stub of pencil protruded above one ear.

'You run the business?' Markby asked.

'I run it with a partner. I'm Steve Poole.' He held out a work-callused hand and Markby shook it. 'Do you want to see the workshop?' Poole offered, nodding towards the building behind them.

'Yes, we do. We've just seen some of your furniture in the gardens at Overvale House.'

The fair eyebrows twitched. 'We made that set to order for Mr Jenner. We make anything you like to order.' He turned and led them into the workshop.

Inside it was cool and the air was filled with the smell of timber and the sound of hammering. The floor was covered with a thin layer of sawdust, chippings, and, despite a notice requesting No Smoking, squashed cigarette butts. In a corner another man was busy making what appeared to be a bird table.

'That's Ted,' said Poole. 'He's the other half of the business.'

Ted stopped his work and looked up. Like his business partner, he wore dusty work clothes and he was about the same age as Poole. But in appearance he provided a startling and even comic contrast. Poole was lanky and pale, of sober appearance. A regular Eeyore, Meredith had judged him. Ted, on the other hand, had a round impish face with a snub nose and curly fair hair. He had a countryman's complexion of red cheeks and tanned skin. If Poole suggested gloomy spirits, Ted suggested the life and soul of the party. Such people could prove a mixed blessing.

'Hello,' he hailed them affably. 'What can we do for you, eh?' He grinned widely at them, revealing a gap in his front teeth. Somehow this increased his likeness to one of those corbel heads in medieval churches which, from high up in the roof, pull their stone faces into all manner of grimaces at the hapless worshippers below.

They asked if they could inspect his work and he stood back to allow them a good view of it, his hands on his hips.

'Not so much a bird table,' said Markby in admiration, 'more a desirable residence!'

The feeding table itself was a flat surface. At each corner of it stood little pillars supporting a roof in Chinese style with tip-tilted ends and covered with flat wooden tiles. An ornamental frieze ran along the top.

'It's designed to be practical. You can hang things from the roof,' Ted pointed out to him. 'Like bits of fat, nets of peanuts, the stuff the birds eat. But it's not a house. They can't go nesting there. That's not what it's for!'

'Well, no,' Markby sounded slightly abashed. 'I realize that. I wasn't being facetious. I meant only that it's a splendid piece of work. I've a bird table in my backyard but it's a primitive thing compared with this.'

Ted stretched out his hand and passed it over the nearest gable in a gesture which was almost like affection. 'I do a good job. I take pride in it, see? I can make you a nesting box, if you want one. But you don't want to put a nesting box over a feeding table, mate. You see that sometimes. It's a waste of time. A nesting bird needs a bit of peace and quiet, not a lot of sparrows and starlings scrabbling for seed right under it as it sits on the eggs.'

'Do you have a catalogue?' Meredith asked him.

Ted looked at Steve, who scratched his sparsely covered skull and shook his head. 'They haven't come yet from the printer's. If you want, you can leave your address and I'll send you one.'

'Yes, we'd like that.'

Steve removed the pencil stub from above his ear and asked, 'You got a bit of paper? If not, no matter. I got plenty in the office.'

The office was presumably the area shielded from the work floor by makeshift partitions. But Meredith had a notebook in her bag. She tore out a clean sheet and with Steve's pencil wrote out her name and address.

Steve read it through carefully, folded it and stuffed it in his pocket. The pencil stub was returned to its home above his ear.

'Thank you for showing us round,' Markby told them.

'Come again!' said Ted.

Ted and Steve stood side by side and watched them leave.

'Do you know what, Ted?' said Steve when they'd left. 'I know that feller.'

'That right?' said Ted, taking up his hammer and beginning to whistle through the gap in his front teeth.

'He's a copper.' Steve's face twisted into disapproval. 'I don't like them. It's never a good idea to have them hanging round.'

Hammer aloft to strike a nail, Ted paused, then turned towards his partner. 'Why? You haven't got anything to worry about, have you? What sort of copper? How do you know?'

'Seen him before, years ago. He used to be in charge over at Bamford police station. A chief inspector he was back then. Then I heard he'd got promoted and he left, went over to that big HQ building they've got over beyond Cheriton. He'll be something important by now, I reckon.' Steve sniffed. 'They're always canny, are coppers. They don't let on who they are when you meet them off duty. They know people don't cotton to them. He let that woman write out her name but he didn't give his. Mitchell, she's called.' Steve slapped his pocket in which the paper with Meredith's address resided. 'But he's called Markby. What do you reckon he was doing up at Overvale House?'

Ted shrugged and struck the nail with an unerring aim. He picked up another and placed it carefully. The hammer was raised again.

'But then,' said Steve with concentrated distaste, 'I don't suppose old Jenner deals with the small fry. If he's got a problem, he'll call in the top brass and top brass will come running for someone like Mr Jenner!'

Clunk! The hammer missed the nail and hit the wood. Ted swore. 'If you'd stop rabbiting on about Jenner and some copper, I'd be able to concentrate and not go hitting my thumb!' He put the bruised digit to his mouth.

'All right, all right,' said Steve placatingly. 'There's no law against being curious and no law against not liking coppers. I'll get out of your way, then.'

'You can clear the table, Mrs Whittle,' said Alison on Saturday morning. 'I don't think Fiona will be down for any breakfast.'

'I don't understand,' grumbled her husband, 'how young people can lie in bed so long of a morning! You'd think they'd want to be up and about. They're supposed to have energy, for goodness' sake!'

'Fiona is up and about,' Toby said, sneaking the last piece of toast from the tray Mrs Whittle had just picked up. 'Saw her earlier,' he added indistinctly.

Jenner glanced at his wristwatch. 'Earlier? Good Lord. It's only half past nine now. If she got up, why didn't she come down and join us?'

'She went out,' said Toby.

'Out?' Jenner and his wife both stared at the speaker in surprise. 'Out where?' Fiona's father demanded.

Toby shook his head. 'No idea. That is, I think she's gone out for an early morning run. She had running pants and a red sweatshirt on and she was jogging away from the house. It was about eight, a little after? I saw her from the bathroom window.' Toby swallowed his toast and looked wistful. 'If she'd said she was going for a run, I'd have turned out a little earlier and joined her.'

'You saw her at eight? She's been gone a long time for a run. What's she doing, running right round the estate? Well, I suppose I should be glad she's keen to keep fit,' Jenner muttered. He stood up and picked up his newspaper. As he did, some commotion could be heard outside in the hall.

Mrs Whittle returned, flustered. 'Here's Stebbings,' she said. 'I made him take his boots off and he's making no end of fuss. But I wasn't having him walk over my clean floor in dirty boots! He says he's got to see you, sir, right away! It won't wait!'

She had scarcely finished speaking before the gaunt hirsute figure of Stebbings appeared. He wasn't wearing his waxed jacket, only his shirt and a thick knit pullover with holes in the elbows, and his trouser legs were soaked with water up to his knees. His wet socks had left dark footprints on the parquet. He ignored everyone except his employer.

'You'd best come, sir. There's been an – accident.' He had paused fractionally before the last word and glanced briefly at the other two.

Jenner pushed back his chair and asked sharply, 'What sort of accident? Where?'

'It's not far.' Stebbings' expression grew mulish. 'I'll tell you about it as we go, sir.'

'You can tell us now, Harry, don't be silly!' said Alison unexpectedly.

'I don't want to be the one to bring you bad news, ma'am,' returned Stebbings.

'Out with it, Harry!' ordered Jenner.

Stebbings shrugged his shoulders. 'It's the young lady, sir. Miss Fiona.'

They all crowded towards him, expressing dismay and shock and asking questions at the same time.

Mrs Whittle, who had lingered in the hall, was heard to demand, 'What are you on about, Harry Stebbings?'

But Stebbings wasn't going to divulge any more. He simply turned and strode out. They followed, pausing impatiently while Stebbings resumed his boots at the kitchen door. Jeremy Jenner was growing angrier by the second.

'Speak up, man! What's happened? Where is my daughter?'

Stebbings didn't reply but strode on and they hurried after him.

They were making directly across the lawns and appeared to be heading downhill towards the lake. After three glorious spring days of sunshine, the wind had moved round and brought with it echoes of the departed winter. The sky was clouded over and beneath it the lake was a dull grey disc absorbing the light and reflecting none of it. As they neared it there was a flap of wings and the goose rose from the water's surface and flew, honking agitatedly, across the landscape towards the horses' paddock. Above it, it turned back towards the lake and landed on the small island in the middle.

'It's got Spike upset,' Alison exclaimed. 'Is Fiona hurt, Harry? Why won't you *say*?'

'For goodness' sake,' Jenner snapped. 'What's happened to my daughter? Have you gone deaf, Stebbings?'

But Toby had spotted something ahead of them and broken into a run straight past the gardener towards the lake. Stebbings watched him, muttering into his beard. Jenner and his wife also began to run forward. The Labrador, Betsy, who'd followed, lumbered behind Alison. All arrived at the lake to see Toby on his knees beside Stebbings' waxed jacket which lay on the ground near the jetty, covering something.

Jenner stopped, put out his arm and seized his wife's elbow. 'No, Ally, you stay here. Please. Hold the dog.' The words were barked out as an order.

Alison, her face frightened, obeyed, grabbing Betsy's collar. Jenner walked towards the jacket and the huddled thing beneath it. Stebbings had halted and watched him. Jenner walked very straight, his whole manner that of a man who knows that an unpleasant task lies before him but is determined to handle it correctly.

Toby had turned back the jacket. They could all see long blond hair spread on the ground and a sodden red sweatshirt. Toby looked up at the approaching Jenner, his face ashen. 'Fi – Fiona . . .' Toby stammered. 'She's—'

Stebbings' harsh voice broke in. 'She was floating in the water, sir. I waded in and pulled her out. I covered her over because that blasted bird started pecking at her. I phoned my boy on my mobile and told him to bring a sack over to catch the brute. He should be here by now,' added Stebbings discontentedly, glowering into the distance.

'You called your boy!' Jenner had dropped on to his knees by his daughter. He dragged away the rest of the jacket. Fiona was lying on her stomach. Her head was turned to one side away from them and her open eyes stared blindly at the grass tussocks. 'Why didn't you call an ambulance?' he went on furiously, before adding in a desperate voice, 'Toby, do you know first aid? Resuscitation techniques?'

'It's too late for that, sir,' said Stebbings in a flat voice. 'She's a goner. Face down in the water, she was.' Unexpectedly he reached out and touched his employer's shoulder in a gesture of sympathy. 'I had a go, sir, at bringing her to her senses, getting the water out of her. It wasn't any good. So I came up to the house to tell you.'

'But you didn't tell us, did you?' Toby snapped at him. 'You said there had been an accident. We thought she might be hurt, sprained an ankle or something! We didn't expect this!'

'Dad?'

They had all been unaware of the presence of another person. A youth had approached them and stood nervously a few feet away. 'I brought the sack.' He held up a rough hessian sack.

'Right,' said his father curtly. 'Took you long enough. Just get in the boat and row over to the island and see if you can catch that bird.'

Darren edged towards the jetty, his frightened eyes fixed on the body of Fiona.

'Is she all right?' he asked.

Jenner looked up at him, his face distorted with despair. 'All right? No, of course she isn't bloody all right! She's dead!'

Darren scrambled into the boat with a terrified look at Jenner. His father cast it off and the youngster began to row towards the island where Spike patrolled the shore.

'How could it happen?' Toby asked bewildered. 'Did she fall out of the boat or off the jetty? She could swim.'

Stebbings cleared his throat and made an awkward gesture with his long arms, flapping them to either side a little like the goose its wings.

'There's something else, sir.'

'What?' Jenner's voice cracked as he looked up at the man. 'What else?'

'I turned her head that way so as you wouldn't see it straight off. But if you just turn her to face the other way, you'll see there's something on the other side, an injury like.'

Both Toby and his cousin stared down at the body of Fiona, their attitudes frozen in horror. Jenner started to put out his hand and then withdrew it. It was Toby who said gently, 'I'll do it, Jerry.' He cupped his hands around Fiona's head and turned her to face them.

Her hair fell back and revealed broken skin and a faint indentation at her left temple.

'She hit her head,' said Stebbings. 'Or something like that.'

They had forgotten Alison who had been sitting and listening. At Stebbings' words, she let out a sharp cry. They looked towards her and saw that she had buried her face in her hands and was rocking herself backwards and forwards. The dog was nuzzling at her, trying to get her attention, but Alison was lost in dreadful anguish.

Jenner got to his feet and hurried across to her. 'Take it easy, darling. Perhaps you'd better go back go the house—' She seemed not to have heard him. He prised her fingers gently from her face and said anxiously, 'Alison?'

She looked up, wild-eyed. 'It's happened again, hasn't it? Fiona's dead and she's died just the way Aunt Freda died!'

By the time Alan Markby arrived on the scene it was quite crowded. The family were not to be seen but the police were there, including Jessica Campbell, easily identifiable by her short-cropped dark red hair. In addition he saw Stebbings and a youngster who must be his son, Darren the would-be photographer of celebrities. The boy was holding a large hessian sack which bulged with unknown content.

Markby had left his car under the chestnut trees and walked to the lake. Jess Campbell saw him coming and came to meet him.

'This is a funny business, sir.'

Markby, his hands thrust into his pockets and the wind whipping up his fair hair, muttered, 'Yes.' Then he took his hands from his pockets and said more politely, 'It may be even stranger than it already looks. I'd meant to ask you to take over investigating a campaign of poison pen letters aimed at Alison Jenner. Now there's a sudden death in the family and I have an inbuilt dislike of coincidences. Who found her?'

Jess nodded towards the Stebbingses, father and son. 'The gardener. I'm afraid he moved the body but it's understandable. She was in the water, face down, so he says. He thought there might be just a chance of saving her if she'd just gone in, so he pulled her out. He tried to resuscitate her but had no luck, so he covered her with his jacket and went to tell the family.'

Markby nodded. In theory a dead body ought not to be moved before the police arrived but the average member of the public would naturally try to save a life if there was the slightest chance it was possible. It was a pity Fiona wasn't exactly where she'd been when discovered. They'd have to rely on Stebbings for details. It would be better if there were a second person to back up Stebbings' account.

This led Markby to ask, 'Was that boy with him?'

'His son? No, not when the body was found. There was a large bird here, a Canada goose. Apparently it lives around the lake. It began pecking at the body, that's why he covered her up. Stebbings has a mobile phone and called his own house to ask his son to come with a sack to catch the bird. He didn't call an ambulance because, he says, he saw she was dead. Nor did he call the family because, again he says, he felt he ought to go up and tell them in person. He's a funny sort of bloke. So that's what he did and they all came running down here. The goose was still causing trouble. It's taken them until now to get hold of it. It flew out to that island.' Jess pointed. 'The lad rowed out there and tried to grab it whereupon it flew back to this side. So he had to row back and both of them tried to catch it while waiting for the police. They managed it about five minutes before the first police car turned up. It's in that sack. It was creating a heck of a fuss when they put it in, apparently, but once inside, it quietened down.'

Markby's heart sank. Was there anything about this scene of an unexplained death which hadn't been thoroughly disturbed before the arrival of the first police officers? 'You mean, not only has the boat been moved, too, but they've been running up and down the shoreline after the goose?'

She understood his meaning. 'I'm afraid so. Great bootprints everywhere. The boy skidded about and fell over twice, he says. There are great gouged areas of earth to prove it. Before that Stebbings himself and then the Jenners and a chap called Smythe had all trampled the entire immediate area.' She paused. 'I understand you know the family, sir?'

'It's a very recent acquaintance. I lunched here yesterday with them because they wanted to talk to me about the poison pen letters. That was my first and only meeting with Jenner and his wife. Has a pathologist attended?'

'Dr Fuller's on his way. A local doctor's been already and certified her dead. He was here when I got here. He'd been called to attend Mrs Jenner.'

They had been moving as she spoke, nearing the body. Beside it they stopped.

'She's received a blow on the left temple,' Jess went on. 'Dr Fuller might be able to tell us, just by looking at it, whether it could have been fatal or not. She might have drowned, of course. It's possible she climbed down into that little boat and fell out. She could then have struck her head. I'll arrange for a diver to go into the lake.'

Jess stared thoughtfully at the rippling surface. 'Stebbings waded in and brought the body out. It can't be very deep near the edge. I don't know about further out but it's deep enough to need the boat if you want to get to the island. That was still tied up, Stebbings swears, when he found her. The boy untied it to row over and try to catch the bird. She wouldn't have gone for a swim in all her clothes and there's no reason to suspect suicide.'

Markby contemplated the body. 'We all came down here yesterday to look at the lake. The dead girl, Fiona Jenner, wouldn't come with us because of that Canada goose. It had attacked her before. It patrolled the area and was very territorial. In view of that, it's strange that she should die here. She avoided the spot.'

'Dr Fuller's here, sir,' said a nearby officer.

The pathologist was making his way towards them, bag in hand. He was a short, rotund man and had donned a one-piece protective suit which made him look like a child's toy. The impression was enhanced by the cheery smile which he seemed to have at all times in all circumstances.

'Good morning, good morning!' he greeted them. 'And what have we here?'

They stood back and let him get on with his preliminary examination. 'That's a nasty blow,' he said, 'but I doubt it would have killed her. I'll do the post-mortem as soon as possible. Have you been in touch with the coroner's office?'

'I'll do it right away, sir,' said Jess.

'Then, provided the coroner gives clearance, I'll do it this afternoon.' Fuller got to his feet. 'We have a rather important family gathering this weekend. I'd like to get business out of the way.'

It was, of course, Easter Saturday. Markby found that, in present circumstances, he'd forgotten that. But it was a holiday period. Not only Fuller but others had family visits and social outings arranged. That applied to the team who would have to be assembled to investigate this unexpected death. No one was going to be very happy about that. With a start of guilt he remembered that he and Meredith were supposed to be lunching at his sister's house today. Paul, his brother-in-law, was a trained chef and a cookery journalist. Lunch with them was always to be savoured and preceded by Paul's devoting the entire morning to creating delicacies in the kitchen. Cooks could be temperamental and Paul was no exception. If they got to his sister's house at all today, it would be late. Lunch would probably be ruined.

Families, thought Markby, were nice to have but the relationships involved had pitfalls of their own. Yesterday he and Meredith had been discussing the Jenners. Now, look at Fuller over there. The pathologist was well known to be a family man. He had three highly talented musical daughters, all of whom Markby found terrifying. Markby himself was tone deaf, or as near tone deaf as made little difference, and conversation with any of the Fuller girls was agony. Knowing of his musical incompetence, they treated him politely but with a kindly tolerance, as one who suffered an irredeemable handicap.

'Have you been up to the house?' Markby asked Jess.

'Not yet, sir. Mr Jenner was still here when I got here. He'd got the local doctor with him. Jenner identified the body and the local doctor confirmed she was dead before he dashed back to the house. Mrs Jenner's apparently broken down and a guest here, a Mr Smythe, had escorted her back to the house, so I didn't see either of them. It was Mr Smythe, I gather, who called a doctor to Mrs Jenner.'

Markby was silent for a moment. Then he said, 'As I sat at their table on Friday, I'd better go up and make my condolences. I'll leave it to you to organize their statements.'

At the house a red-eyed housekeeper showed him into a study where he found Jeremy Jenner and Toby. Jenner looked grey and every one of his sixty-eight years. Markby had seen the effect of a great shock and sudden bereavement before. It was always pitiable but in this man, whom he formerly seen so confident and in control, it was devastating. Jenner appeared as a figure from Greek tragedy. The man even seemed to have lost height, as he rose to greet Markby. There was no sign of Alison.

Now that an outsider had arrived, Jenner managed to summon up at least an appearance of his normal manner. It must have taken almost superhuman effort. He shook the visitor's hand and received his condolences with a composure which must have cost him a great deal to maintain.

'How is your wife?' Markby asked him.

'My wife?' For a moment Jenner looked fierce as if the question were impertinent. Then he shook his head and went on, 'She's upset, of course. Very upset. We had to call our family doctor and he's given her a sedative.'

That meant Jess Campbell wouldn't be able to take a statement from her today – or possibly even tomorrow. Markby was beginning to feel this whole investigation was going to be jinxed. Unfairly, he knew, he was tempted to attribute this to the presence of Toby Smythe on the scene. Wherever Toby went, disaster seemed to follow. But he mustn't think this way, let personal prejudice colour his view.

'You've met Inspector Campbell, I understand,' he said.

'The young woman? Yes. This isn't going to be left to her, is it? It's not an accident. It can't be. It's the lunatic who's been writing those damn letters! He's responsible.'

Toby was sitting on a window seat, leaning forward, hands loosely clasped. From that vantage point he would be able to see the gardens and although not the lake itself, he would have been able to observe some of the movement of police vehicles. He looked up and said in a low voice, 'Fiona wouldn't have gone down to the lake alone. She was scared of Spike, the goose.'

'Even to meet someone?' Markby asked.

'No! Why should she want to meet anyone at that unholy hour of the morning, anyway?'

'Toby saw my daughter leave the house just after eight,' Jenner said. 'He assumed she was going for an early-morning run. She might have met an intruder in the grounds, of course. It could have been the letter-writer. He might have been hanging round the place, spying on us. He's clearly demented.'

'Insanity is quite often claimed as a defence but seldom found to be genuine,' Markby observed.

'Nevertheless,' Jenner replied obstinately, 'it must occur to you that possibly my wife has been stalked for some time and the letters are an integral part of a vicious and obsessive campaign by this – this person.' Jenner fell silent, unable to add further words. He merely gestured hopelessly.

'You understand a post-mortem examination will be carried out on your daughter?' Markby asked him gently.

Jenner winced. 'I hate the idea. But it has to be. I know that.' He and Toby exchanged glances. 'Fiona had also been struck on the head. That's what has upset my wife more than anything. It – it's as though her death is a carbon copy of Freda Kemp's. Can that be a coincidence?' Jenner gave a short, mirthless bark of laughter. 'I don't think so. I tell you, Markby. There's a maniac out there and he's hell bent on persecuting us.'

Markby studied him for a moment. 'No other member of the household left the house before breakfast? Only your daughter?'

'No! For goodness' sake, do we need alibis? I didn't leave the house. I'm sure my wife didn't.'

'I didn't,' said Toby. 'I saw Fiona from the bathroom window. I opened it to let out the steam. If I'd known she was going running I'd have got up earlier and gone with her. I wish I had.' His face twisted in misery. 'She might be alive now. She *would* be alive now!'

'I shall, of course, be overseeing any investigation,' Markby told them. 'But Inspector Campbell will be in charge of things on the ground. She'll be along to talk to you shortly. Tell her everything you've told me and any other detail you may remember. You can have every confidence in her. She has shown herself very able officer in her previous division. She is new here but I'm sure she'll handle it well.'

As he spoke these words, Markby felt a twinge of an emotion he couldn't at once identify. He told himself it wasn't doubt. Campbell had come to them with an excellent reputation in her job. But perhaps the momentary twinge had been one of envy? Campbell was young. She was at the beginning of her career. He was nearing the end of his. His past successes had resulted in promotion to a rank putting him behind a desk for most of his time. He'd much rather be out there where the action was. Yes, dammit, he did envy Campbell!

'I don't like it!' Jenner snapped. 'She's too young. I want someone with experience. And a newcomer, you say?'

Markby smiled. 'That could be a good thing. Newcomers are usually keen. Don't worry. I'll keep an eye on things.'

'I should damn well hope so!' Jenner's face had flushed an angry red. He recollected himself and said stiffly, 'I apologize. I'm not myself. Of course you'll see everything necessary is done.'

Markby left them and drove slowly back to Bamford. Thus he wasn't at the lakeside when one of the constables called out to Jess Campbell that there was a tyre mark some distance from the water's edge.

'Here, ma'am.' The man pointed. 'It's not too good.'

It was almost obliterated. Either Darren or his father, careering round the lake in pursuit of Spike, must have lumbered straight across it.

'Accidentally or on purpose,' Jess said aloud.

'Inspector?' The constable looked puzzled.

'I'll send the photographer over here and get forensics to make a cast of it,' Jess said. 'Well spotted.'

Markby pressed his finger on the doorbell and heard it buzz inside the house. It was an electronic gadget. You pressed the button; it sent a signal to the buzzer inside and a tiny spot glowed on the button to show you it had done it. The trouble was that half the time it hadn't done it. It meant he strained his ear every time to make sure he caught the buzz.

This time he heard it and the quick approach of Meredith's footstep. She pulled the door open, relief on her face.

'I was beginning to wonder where you were. It's almost two. Laura's been on the phone to me. Paul is getting jittery and wanting to know when he can put in the soufflé. She thought you might be here or I might know where you were but I couldn't help her. She said she'd rung your place but there was no reply and you hadn't left the answerphone on. That was an hour ago. I thought about trying your mobile but I had this horrible feeling you might have been called in on something and that lunch was scrapped.'

'I'm sorry I'm late,' he told her as he followed her inside. 'I'll phone Laura and apologize to her and to Paul but I don't think I fancy lunch.' His voice and manner had registered with her now.

She asked quietly, 'What's happened?'

He smiled at her ruefully. 'I always seem to be the harbinger of bad news. In this case, it involves the Jenners. I'm afraid your prime suspect for the role of poison pen wielder is dead.'

'Fiona?'

He saw her hazel eyes widen in shock and the colour drain from her face. Instinctively he put out his hand to grasp her.

'It's all right,' she said at once. But she gripped his hand, even so, for reassurance. 'That's terrible. Poor kid. Poor Toby . . . Jeremy, Alison, everyone . . . What happened? Was it an accident?'

'To know that exactly we'll have to await the post-mortem results.' He explained about the blow Fiona appeared to have received to the head and that she'd been found in the lake. 'Very like Freda Kemp.'

He watched this register with her. She turned her face away so that her expression was partly concealed from him. He felt her hand, still in his, twitch.

'I feel awful,' she said quietly. 'I'm so sorry for all the things I said about her, for accusing her of being the letter-writer. You'd say I was theorizing without facts, wouldn't you? Of course I was. It was stupid.'

'Don't feel badly about it,' he told her gently. 'No one expected this. We none of us had enough facts. We still don't.' Markby released her hand and stared thoughtfully past her towards the window, but it was doubtful he took in the limited view of the back yard. 'Poison pen campaigns don't usually end in . . .'

Meredith was watching his face and rubbing her forearms as if she were cold. 'In what? You think this is murder, don't you?' she said soberly.

'Yes,' Markby replied, turning his gaze from the window towards her. 'I think it very probably is.'

Chapter Five

Jess got to the morgue at four o'clock, having been informed that the coroner's office had given Dr Fuller the go-ahead to carry out the autopsy. This was a police matter but the corpse was still technically the coroner's body. The idea of being shut up in the cavernous dissection room with its background noises of running water, its air smelling of antiseptic, was never to be welcomed. But the morning's clouds had vanished, the sun returned to sparkle teasingly outside the dusty windows, and this just wasn't the place to be, and at Easter to boot. Still, it couldn't be helped. She was accompanied by Sergeant Steve Prescott, an amiable giant whose features bore the honourable scars of collisions on the rugby field. He stood by the stainless steel dissection table with its sinister central drainage channel; his hands folded one over the other as if he were at a church service or, alternatively, a Mafia bodyguard awaiting orders. There was also a long-faced photographer fiddling with his camera but as a conversationalist he rated zero. After a brief exchange of greetings on their arrival, that had been that.

The body was covered by a sheet. The silence seemed less respectful than unnatural and Jess felt impelled to break it.

'Pity it's happened over Easter.' A daft remark, she thought. Death doesn't look at the calendar before it picks its victim and police work wasn't held up because the rest of the country took a holiday.

Prescott seemed to consider the remark from all angles before replying, a little unexpectedly, 'Always seems wrong when it's a young person. Makes you think.'

So even the impassive Prescott had been filled with intimations of mortality.

Perhaps Prescott felt he needed to explain his remark. 'I mean, there she is.' He nodded towards the sheeted corpse. 'She'd be fit and healthy if she wasn't dead, bags of money in the family – and as cold as a cod on a fishmonger's slab.'

There was no arguing with that diagnosis.

There was a slam of a distant door and Dr Fuller bounced in, his pink face still wreathed in smiles, which, Jess thought crossly, hardly suited the occasion. Still, the pathologist was one of those fortunate beings who genuinely enjoyed their work. His green plastic apron reached from his neck to his ankles. Add in his bushy grey eyebrows and he appeared not so much a child's toy now as a jolly green-clad garden gnome.

'Here we are again!' Dr Fuller hailed them. He didn't actually rub his hands, but Jess had the feeling he would have liked to. 'To work, then! With luck this shouldn't take long. Just a moment, let me switch on the machine.' Fuller set his little tape recorder whirring and, as he worked, he would make a running commentary. 'Before I begin, I've got a little surprise for you, I think,' he said happily like the kindly paterfamilias he no doubt was.

Beside her, Jess was aware that Prescott's battered features had taken on a suspicious slant. His acquaintance with Dr Fuller was of long standing.

Deftly Dr Fuller turned back the sheet and the body lay revealed. 'Now then, what do you make of that?'

They leaned forward and studied the area indicated by the pathologist. The photographer moved in for a close-up. Fuller was right. It was a surprise.

'Stabbed?' Markby exclaimed. He stared at the inspector. She looked a bit pale, but they usually did on returning from morgue duty. Even so, her excitement could be heard in her voice.

'Yes, sir. A single thrust which went right through her clothing, between her ribs and straight into her heart. We didn't realize it at first because she'd been floating in water and the blood had washed away. Also she was wearing a red sweatshirt and it's a very small puncture mark. Dr Fuller thinks it probably didn't bleed much. They found the wound at the morgue when they stripped the body.'

'What you're saying,' Markby said tersely, 'doesn't sound like a wound made by a knife.'

'Dr Fuller thinks not. He thinks some possibly home-made, thin weapon with the end sharpened. In diameter it would be rounded. Rather like a thick needle, he guesses.'

Markby drummed his fingers on his desk. 'Is that diver still down at the lake?'

'I've got a message to the underwater team, sir. They've failed to find any underwater rocks on which she might have struck her head as she went in and they were about to pack up. Now they're looking for anything which might have been a weapon, but that means going further out in the lake. It will take time.'

Markby still looked discontented. It wasn't, Jess thought, either at the slowness of the underwater search or at her handling of the case. It might be because of the added cost involved in keeping the diving team on. Increasingly they worked with the word 'budget' hanging invisibly over their heads, but she didn't think it was that, either. It was something else.

'Does he think death would have been instantaneous?' The superintendent's voice was abrupt and his bright blue eyes bored into hers.

'Dr Fuller thinks she probably lived for up to a minute but no longer. There's no lake water in the lungs, so she was dead by the time she went in there. As for the head wound, he thinks that was inflicted after death, almost certainly deliberately.'

'And then her killer put her in lake, knowing full well we'd find the real cause of death. He wasn't trying to cover that up. He was just making a point. He wanted to recall the death of Freda

Kemp. Pah!' He slapped his hands on the desk top and scowled ferociously but not, she was pleased to see, at her.

'Freda Kemp?' Jess asked cautiously, lest the scowl be turned in her direction, after all.

His expression faded to one of mild surprise and then became apologetic. 'You haven't had an opportunity to examine the details of the poison pen campaign Mrs Jenner's been subjected to. But it may turn out to be very much part and parcel of this business. Let's hope that tyre tread turns up something.'

'It's a very poor impression, sir, forensics are doing their best.' She paused. 'I haven't told the family yet. There's a bit of a problem interviewing Mrs Jenner. Her doctor gave her a sedative and she's out for the count. She probably won't be too clear-headed tomorrow. I won't be able to see her until Monday morning.'

Markby nodded. 'It will give you a chance to read up the file on her trial.'

'Her trial, sir?' Had she heard that correctly?

'Yes, yes, her trial for murder. Twenty-five years ago. She was acquitted.'

'Merry hell!' said Jess, hastily amending this to, 'I'll do that, sir.'

'No, you were right the first time,' he corrected her gloomily. 'Merry hell describes matters pretty exactly.'

Dorcas Stebbings was seated at her kitchen table. It was late and had grown dark. She could barely see across the room. Lost in her thoughts she had been unaware how gloomy it had got and it wasn't until the rattle of the old 4×4 roused her that she stood up and went to switch on the light.

The action seemed to set off another train of thought and she remained by the wall with her hand still upraised to the light switch, staring at the room. All these objects were things she touched every day, the scrubbed pine table laid now for their evening meal, the chairs, the kitchen stove, the Welsh dresser with its array of old decorative plates, most of which had been her mother's. Each piece of furniture had its place, so unchanging that if by some disaster she'd been struck blind at this very moment, she'd still have been able to navigate her way round without collision. Yet this very familiarity now seemed a fragile thing. It was almost as if she looked at a mirage, about to disappear and be lost for ever.

She heard the stamp of her husband's feet and a shuffling in the back porch which indicated he was taking off his boots. She moved away from the wall, tidying her hair and straightening her apron in automatic movements, and went to the cooker where she took the lid off a saucepan and peered into it. The sight which met her wasn't encouraging. The potatoes had boiled dry and begun to stick to the bottom of the pan. She gave it a vigorous shake and dislodged them. Another minute or two and they would have burned.

The back door opened. Stebbings ducked his head and entered.

'You're late,' she observed from the stove.

'Of course I'm late! You heard what happened? I found her. The police kept asking me the same damn-fool questions over and over again. If that wasn't enough, I had to drive right across the county, didn't I? To get rid of that damn bird, Mr Jenner's orders. I felt like wringing its neck.'

'You didn't?' she asked, looking up with a frightened face. 'Mrs Jenner wouldn't like that.'

'Mrs Jenner wouldn't know, would she? But I didn't, though I swear if it comes back again I will. I took it to another of those wildlife parks. They reckoned they can keep it until the next time a flock of Canada geese comes over. They've got a big pen where they put the injured birds and it's in there. They get the flocks in from time to time. They didn't think it would be long.' Stebbings sat at the table and asked, 'What's for my tea, then?'

'I made a meat pie, but I expect it's dried out now. My potatoes have nearly boiled away.'

'I should've phoned you, I suppose,' said her husband. 'But it clear slipped my mind with all that's happened today. One bloody thing after another and no idea what's going to happen next! I don't want another day like it.'

'It doesn't matter.' His failure to let her know he'd be late wasn't the reason for the spoilt meal. She hadn't been able to keep her mind off the awful news. With her hands encased in padded oven mitts she stooped to take the pie from the oven and carried it over to the table where she set it on a wooden stand.

'So what's up with you, then?' Stebbings asked, watching her.

'Should there be anything wrong with me?' she retorted.

'Face as long as a fiddle. Just because the pie is burnt, is it?'

'I'm upset, aren't I? Just like you!' She sank down on the nearest chair and divested her hands of the mitts. 'I'm afraid, too, Harry.' The confession gained her no sympathy.

'What have you got to be frightened about?' he demanded.

'How can you ask? All this business, the poor young lady . . . Liz Whittle came down and told me what the police were doing. She's terrible distressed. I'd seen all the police cars going up there earlier, of course. I knew it had to be something bad.'

'It's got nothing to do with us,' he growled. 'I've done my part, pulling her out of the lake and going up to the house to tell them about it. Just forget about it now, can't you? It's what I want to do.'

'It could affect us, though, couldn't it?' she persisted and began to tinker with the knife and fork set before her, moving them away from the plate, bringing them closer. 'Mr Jenner might take against living here now his daughter's died here like that, so horribly. If he sells up, what'll happen to us?'

'I'll work for the next owner, won't I? It was old Mr Gray who took me on first and he dropped dead not eighteen month after, but Mr Jenner, when he bought the place, he wanted me to stay.'

'Another new owner still might not want you. You don't know who'd buy. It might be some company that would turn the place into something like a, like a retirement home or a business centre.

They might contract the upkeep of the grounds out to one of these firms that goes round doing that sort of thing.'

Her husband's fist came crashing down on the table top, making all the cutlery jump. The salt cellar fell over and the grains spilled on the table. His wife gave a little cry and hastened to scrape up a pinch of salt and throw it over her left shoulder.

'What are you doing that for? That's bloody superstition, that is!'

'It's bad luck, Harry, to spill the salt. And bad luck is what's coming to us. It's here already with the young lady drowning and if Mr Jenner decides to up and leave—'

'For crying out loud, woman! Why worry about something like that before it happens? Why should he want to leave the place?' Stebbings howled in exasperation.

'His wife might want to.'

'It's always the same with you women,' he grumbled. 'If one argument doesn't work, you find another. The girl was Mr Jenner's daughter, not his wife's.'

'Mrs Jenner will still be terribly upset, she must be! Anyway, she's been not too happy these last few weeks, even before this awful thing happened. Perhaps she's tired of living out here and got a fancy to go and live in town? I dare say it's a bit quiet for her here. This death, well, it could decide her.'

He stared at her fiercely. 'Who told you that? That Mrs Jenner's been moping?'

'Liz Whittle. She says Mrs Jenner's been acting odd, well, different. She's been on edge like her nerves were bad.'

Stebbings twisted his huge knotted hands together and scowled. 'There could be any reason for that. You don't want to go gossiping with Liz Whittle.' He straightened up and dismissed the matter. 'I want my tea. Where's Darren?'

'He's up in the attic in his work room. I'll go and call him.'

'I'll go,' Stebbings said, getting up. 'Just you get those spuds on the table.'

★　★　★

He climbed the narrow stairs. At the landing he stopped and looked up. The recessed hatch in the ceiling was closed but a ladder propped against the wooden frame showed how someone might get up into the roof space.

'Darren!' Stebbings called up. 'Your mum's got your tea on the table. Come on down here!'

There was a sound of movement above his head. Footsteps caused wooden boards to creak.

'I'm coming!' a voice called.

Stebbings made to turn away but then stopped, chewed his lower lip in thought and climbed a couple of rungs to reach up his long arms and raise the hatch. He shifted it to one side and hauled himself up into the attic.

It had been converted into extra living space. His son was sitting there in front of a flickering computer screen. On the table beside it, an ink-jet printer whirred and delivered up coloured prints in a steady progression. On the far side of the room, a table was laden with dusty jars of chemicals and basins. But if Darren had once made a foray into traditional photographic development, he'd apparently abandoned it in favour of technology. At this father's appearance Darren started guiltily and flung a nervous look over his shoulder. Stebbings looked round him with disgust.

'It's about time you stopped messing with this lot!' Stebbings pointed at the computer and then at the printer. 'Look at the money you've spent on that. And that fancy camera. Gadgets, that's what they all are, just fashionable toys. A waste of good cash. You youngsters, you've got more money than sense.'

'It's going to be my career!' his son said defiantly. 'I earned the money to pay for all this myself. It's an investment.'

'Don't talk nonsense. How are you going to earn any kind of a living doing this? You'll need to get a proper job.'

'I can make this pay,' Darren said obstinately.

'I'll believe that when I see it!' was the paternal retort.

'Well, just you wait then, and you will see it!' Darren told him. 'There's good money to be had. Magazines and newspapers, they'll pay for a good pic!'

'Pic? What the hell's a pic? Don't tell me, I know. Listen to me, boy, where do you think you're going to get these snaps that the press are going to pay you so much for?'

'You have to find out where celebrities are. Then you wait, catch them unawares.'

'I never heard anything so daft in all my life. I think there's something wrong with your brain!' Stebbings suddenly reached out and grabbed one of the glossy prints as it emerged from the machine.

'Hey, leave that!' Darren darted forward to rescue it but his father put out a long arm and pushed him back roughly. Darren stumbled and grabbed at the computer bench to steady himself. 'Leave that, Dad, please,' he pleaded. 'It's not dried off and you'll get fingerprints all over it.'

'Just want to see your work!' Stebbings said. 'Since it seems it's going to earn you a fortune!' He studied the print and then picked up the others, studying them one by one, his expression growing darker. Finally he held up one of the sheets. 'Where did you get this? And the others like it?'

At the quiet menace in his father's voice, Darren blanched, but managed to reply with a show of confidence. 'I took them.'

'I know you bloody took them!' his father shouted. 'When?'

'Friday, Friday evening,' Darren muttered, avoiding his father's eye.

'Did she know?'

'No, Dad, honestly. I – I was practising, you know, pretending I was snapping a celebrity. She wasn't a celebrity but she was the nearest I could get to it. I watched her and I reckon I managed some good pics. Of course she didn't know. The whole point was that she didn't see me. She was only interested in the horses and I was over behind the trees. Don't damage them, Dad, please! Don't go putting your fingerprints all over them or creasing them up! I'll have to print them again. That photo-quality glossy paper is expensive!'

'I always thought you didn't have much sense,' his father said, breathing heavily. 'But now I know you're plain stupid!' In a sudden movement he tore the photograph in two.

'No!' Darren flung himself at his father and tried to wrest the remaining photographs from him but in vain. He was thrust back again and this time tripped and sprawled on the floor.

'Where's the film?' Stebbings demanded. 'Come on, hand it over!'

Darren scrambled to his feet and whimpered, 'There's no film, it's a digital camera! It's some of my best work, Dad! Don't destroy it!'

'And who are you going to show it to, eh? If anyone sees these you know where you'll end up? In a prison cell, that's where! What were you going to do with them, anyway?'

'Nothing, just keep them. Dad, what are *you* going to do with them?' Darren's voice trembled. He was near to tears.

'Do? Burn them. And you think yourself lucky that I'm doing it! Are there any more?'

Darren whispered, 'No.'

Stebbings pointed at the camera. 'There's none in that thing?'

Fatally, Darren hesitated.

'What's it got, then, if it's got no film?'

'It's got a memory card,' Darren muttered.

'Then let's be having it!'

Darren slipped out the little card and handed it to his father, who stared at it mistrustfully. 'You'd better be telling me the truth about this damn thing.' Stebbings was struck by a thought. 'Your mum seen these?'

Darren shook his head.

'Then we don't tell her, right? We don't tell anyone!'

Easter Sunday morning. The bells were ringing out from Bamford's churches. The sky was still overcast although there were signs the sun might break through later. But it was still cool and people who, only days earlier, had worn light spring clothes hurried to church in winter wool jackets. Jess Campbell, in the cramped little flat she was renting, was in the middle of a long and difficult telephone conversation with her mother.

'Yes, Mum, I know I said I'd come down on Easter Day while Simon's home and have lunch with you, but I can't. I'm on duty. There's been a serious incident.'

'But I wanted us all to be together!' Her mother's voice was plaintive. 'It's special, and not only because it's Easter. Simon's hardly ever in the country these days.'

'I can't help it.' Jess drew a deep breath. 'It's not like I haven't seen Simon. He was here Thursday and all Friday morning. I'm really sorry, Mum, but I just can't come.'

'What kind of incident?' Mrs Campbell was asking, her voice suspicious. 'What's so serious you've got to be working over a holiday?'

'It's a – a sudden death. It might be linked to something else. Look, Mum, police work is like that. Things happen. We have to deal with them. They just don't always happen at convenient times.'

'I know it's important, your work,' her mother said. 'But you never seem to have any free time. We hardly see you. I keep wishing that you'd get a job nearer home.'

'This is a good move for me, Mum. I've got real responsibility here and if I can make a go of it, don't blot my copybook, well, that's got to be good, hasn't it?'

'Yes, dear, of course it is,' said her mother in that way which meant she hadn't a clue what Jess was talking about.

When she put down the receiver Jess was surprised at the strength of the regret she felt.

She went to the window and threw it open. The flat was in a small block which had been built on the site of a former grain merchant's store. It overlooked a dull road of crumbling Victorian houses, most of which seemed to be in multiple occupation, if the number of dustbins cluttering the tiny neglected forecourts was anything to go by. At least the flat, although dimensionally designed to accommodate munchkins, offered privacy of a sort, far better than sharing a house. But it wasn't home any more than any rented accommodation could feel like home, not a true home. There was always the knowledge that it was somebody else's really.

Jess had always rented, for convenience's sake. But she knew she ought to buy. Getting on the property ladder, that was what it was called. Now she'd come to Bamford she'd thought more seriously about it than ever before, even to the extent of looking in estate agents' windows. But it wouldn't be easy. Any decent place carried a hefty price tag. She didn't really want another flat. She fancied a small house or cottage. Not too much garden, though, because she had no time for that. Not stuck out in the countryside, either, but near enough to shops to be able to scurry out for a pint of milk or a takeaway meal when necessary, because cooking was another thing she didn't have time for.

She moved back into the flat and gazed round her with increasing dissatisfaction. It had the look of a place which had been furnished with a view to renting it out. Every stick of furniture was cheap and some of it second-hand. The coffee table was marked with rings from the drinks glasses of previous tenants. There was an unsightly stain on the cord carpet which suggested someone had had an accident with a curry. Perhaps this thought of food prompted her to go out to the kitchen, a mere cupboard of a place in which it was just possible to turn round. She opened the fridge. It contained some butter, a pack of cheese and half a bottle of white wine which she'd opened the previous evening. When you sat alone before the television of an evening, drinking wine and watching made-for-TV films which had obviously rolled off the conveyor belt of some production company, put together from assembled parts like so many kit cars, then you knew your private life wasn't a life. It was an existence! The two days of companionship afforded her by her brother's visit had only served to underline the loneliness. Jess slammed the fridge door shut. She'd have to stop off somewhere and pick up some groceries, bacon and eggs. She couldn't go on living on takeaways. Her rubbish bin was crammed with little foil cartons. Her diet was probably nutritionally unsound. She was becoming deskilled in kitchen tasks to an extent which would shock her mother.

That brought back the memory of the recent phone conversation. Of course she wanted to be there with them. She could imagine her family, what they might be doing. They'd all been to church, her mother had said. The meal was cooking. Jess could almost smell it in imagination, each of the savoury aromas wafting from the kitchen. It would probably be roast beef. Or it might be chicken. No, Simon was there so her mother would have bought a nice piece of beef. The best china would have been brought out for the occasion. Of course Jess wanted to be sitting there with them to eat it. But she couldn't and that was that. She was twenty-nine and far too old to be suffering homesickness! Snap out of it, she told herself sternly.

To dismiss the images, she first ate two of the chocolate crème eggs her brother had left for her in advance of the festival, then got in the car and drove over to Regional HQ. That had a deserted air about it; far fewer people than usual could be seen around the place, just the duty team looking glum because they had to work and everyone else was enjoying the Easter holiday. The office they'd given Jess had previously belonged to Inspector Pearce whom she'd never met but of whom she'd heard so much. Pearce had cleared out his belongings but had missed one, a snapshot of a pretty girl holding a puppy. That must be either his girlfriend or his wife, she'd thought when she'd found it in the drawer. She had put it in an envelope, meaning to send it on to him, but hadn't yet done so. The only other thing he'd left behind was a depressed-looking dusty cactus with a spider living in the heart of it. Jess had shaken out the spider and was doing her best to revive the plant but didn't hold out much hope for it. It had the look of a cactus with a death wish. Jess collected a cup of coffee from the dispenser to wash away the cloying sweetness of the eggs, and settled down to work.

The annoying thing in all investigations was the time-consuming composing of reports and despite several other things she wanted to be doing, she had to complete her report on Saturday's events. To ensure accuracy she opened up the notebook in which she kept a virtually minute-by-minute account of her actions on Saturday, her thoughts and her reasoning. She frowned now over her note on the discovery of the partly obliterated tyre mark. Sergeant Ginny Holding, who had been given the job of checking it against all the vehicles owned by the Jenner family and anyone resident at the house at the time or visiting, was out there somewhere even now about this task. Her remit included the dead woman's car, a blue Volkswagen Golf. The visitors' cars, of course, included Markby's own. He'd understand that his tyres would have to be checked against the imprint, along with all the rest. Any other vehicle used on the estate would be checked as well. She hoped to have Holding's report by Monday afternoon.

Jess paused at this point to read through what she'd written. She needed urgently to talk to the Jenners again. That was, she needed to talk to Jeremy again and to Alison for the first time. Her last job the previous evening had been to drive to Overvale House and inform Jeremy Jenner his daughter had died from a stab wound. Jenner had at first been shocked in a buttoned-up sort of way, but Jess's tentative request to see Mrs Jenner before Monday caused an eruption.

'You know the doctor gave her a sedative. She'll still be woozy tomorrow and as soon as she's thinking clearly I'll have to break the news of Fiona having been stabbed. She'll need time to get over the shock. I'm also still trying to get in touch with my ex-wife, Fiona's mother. That's going to be a damn difficult business. What the dickens am I going to say to her? How can I explain it? You'll have to come on Monday.'

Smythe had been more visibly shaken at the news, repeating over and over again that he wished he'd joined Fiona on her early-morning run. He had been the last member of the household to see the dead girl. Smythe, thought Jess, was an interesting young man. She'd sensed that behind the casual appearance, disorganized manner and the grief, there was a sharp brain. Smythe wasn't a fool. He was an FCO high-flyer. There was a possibility, which she'd have to investigate, of a romantic connection between him and the dead girl. The time he gave, ten minutes past eight, was important. It was a reasonable time for someone to go out jogging. It wasn't a particularly reasonable time for that person to meet an intruder in the grounds. Burglars were all at home and in bed by then, thought Jess wryly. Or perhaps not? Perhaps Fiona had encountered someone using that early hour, when he could expect to be undisturbed, to case the property? Jess scribbled a note to herself about this. She must check and find out whether other large houses in the area had been burgled recently or disturbed intruders in their grounds.

Fiona. She had to learn more about Fiona. But before Fiona, there was Alison, the recipient of the poison pen mail.

'I'm losing the advantage,' muttered Jess. 'If this is murder, this is vital time and I'm sitting here writing out a report and kicking my heels waiting to interview the stepmother who was once on a murder charge and has now been getting abusive letters. Ginny's wasting time chasing after a tyre tread that will probably turn out to be weeks old.' Her frustration was well founded. After seventy-two hours the trail went cold. Every police officer knew that.

There was, however, some new reading matter which had appeared on her desk in the form of two files. The top file, the slimmest, contained the brief details of the letter received by Alison with the negative forensic report. The second file was thicker. She picked it up curiously. The sheets it contained appeared to have been faxed from elsewhere. It dealt with an old trial, a murder trial. The accused: Alison Harris. The hairs prickled on Jess's neck. She forgot her regret at not being with her family and having to work the holiday weekend, even the frustrations of the delays, and opened it. There was a note pinned to it and, to her surprise, she saw it was from the superintendent and addressed to her, brief and to the point.

'Alison Harris is Alison Jenner. This is the material which the poison pen writer has got hold of and has used as material for his/her letters. So far no one has made any suggestion how he/she linked Harris with Jenner.'

Jess stared at the note thoughtfully. She was struck by Markby's scrupulous use of he/she. No jumping to conclusions there!

Jess began to read the file.

An hour and a half later, having read the file twice and taken a break to fetch some more truly horrible coffee from a dispensing machine in the corridor, Jess switched on the computer and began to put her thoughts up on screen.

'Certainly the circumstances of Fiona's Jenner's death recall those of Freda Kemp in 1978 and suggest the writer of the poison pen letters may have had a hand in Fiona's death. I am worried by one aspect of Alison Harris's defence. On the face of it, no one can argue with a timed, dated till receipt and a positive ID by the till cashier. But the young man only saw her that one time, very briefly. It could have been someone like her. Could she have had an accomplice? Another young woman, much the same age and wearing identical clothes, same haircut etc. Alison could have met the accomplice before leaving Cornwall and exchanged cars. She could then have driven back to Freda Kemp's cottage and killed her aunt shortly after the one o'clock time given by the cyclists as the last known sighting of Miss Kemp alive. At the same time, the accomplice could have stopped at the petrol station, chatted to the cashier to make sure he remembered her, and obtained the till receipt. It would have needed careful timing but, working together, two people could have pulled it off. Incidentally, if this is what happened, then the arrival of the cyclists at Ms Kemp's cottage at one o'clock, rather than support Alison's alibi, might well have ruined it. The killer must have arrived at the cottage very shortly afterwards and missed being seen by the cyclists possibly only by minutes. I admit there is no evidence of this. The question which arises from my theory is, where is the accomplice now? Why did she agree to be a party to murder? For money? Alison stood to inherit a small fortune from her aunt. As for where the accomplice is now, perhaps she is out there, writing poison pen letters, having spent the money she was paid twenty-five years ago and hoping to replenish her bank account with blackmail. Against this: the poison pen writer has made no demand for money. However, we've seen only one letter and have only Alison Jenner's word for the content of the others.'

Jess read through all she'd written and printed it out. When she'd done that, she folded the sheets carefully and put them in her bag. These were her thoughts, her ideas. She'd take them home and mull over them. This was her first case here in a new job. She was going to get it right.

On her way out of the room she paused by the cactus. It still had that depressed look. It wasn't a cactus with a future. It belonged to the past. She picked it up in its pot and dropped the whole lot into the waste-paper basket.

Then she went home and ate the rest of the chocolate eggs.

Chapter Six

Jess Campbell's view of Overvale House on Monday morning was obscured by a fine haze of rain. It was the sort which appears light but can soak you through in a few minutes, as she found out when she left her car. The gardeners would be glad of it, no doubt. By the time she was admitted to the house her hair felt unpleasantly damp and a quick glance in the hall mirror as she passed by revealed that her face glistened with moisture. She pulled out a handkerchief and rubbed it over her features hastily before going into the room to which Mrs Whittle had directed her.

The housekeeper had welcomed her in a hushed voice as if it were illness, not death, which had visited the house. Grief, of course, might be termed an illness. It had symptoms. It laid the sufferer low. It took time to recover from it. It left scars. But for grief there was no medicine, no quick fix. Moreover, grief had a palpable presence. Jess felt it in the hallway. It didn't need the muffled tones of Mrs Whittle or her reddened eyelids to show it was there. For this reason, she'd told the woman she'd announce herself. It was always bad enough facing a bereaved family without a lugubrious herald going before.

Jess tapped at the door, called out her name and opened it. As she stepped inside her face tingled from the warmth of a log fire crackling in the hearth. Despite the fact that this was a household in mourning, in here the atmosphere seemed at first sight quite uplifting. It was the sort of room which bid you welcome. The contrast between this and her cheerless rented flat could not have been more marked. The furniture was good, but old and comfortable. There was a baby grand piano in one corner and Jess wondered who played. The old dog, Betsy, who had been stretched out before the heat of the flames, struggled to her feet and padded over to inspect the newcomer. Jess dropped her hand to fondle the animal's ears. Betsy responded by wagging her tail. Pass, friend.

'Pity about the weather,' said Jeremy Jenner, following behind the dog. Either he had no gardening interests or this was a version of the standard British conversation opener. 'Is Mrs Whittle there?' He sounded slightly critical.

'I said I'd announce myself.' Jess wondered whether Jenner felt she was guilty of some social faux pas. Heck, she was a police officer, not some toothy county neighbour.

But Jenner had walked past her out into the hall and his upraised voice could be heard calling, 'Mrs Whittle! We'd like some coffee if you can manage that.'

If I were Mrs Whittle, thought Jess, I'd be tempted to pour it over his head. But Jenner, in leaving, had left the floor to the other person present, someone who, when Jess had entered, had been hidden by his bulky frame.

'I'm Alison,' said the woman. Her tone was subdued and Jess had to strain her ears to hear. 'Jeremy's wife and Fiona's step-mother. I'm sorry I wasn't able to speak to you on Saturday or yesterday. I've been a bit of mess. I'm better today.' She gave Jess a hesitant smile.

So here at long last was Alison Jenner, previously Alison Harris, accused but cleared of murder. Jess saw one of those women of very English type with a fair skin and light brown hair, not exactly pretty but pleasant in appearance and looking much younger than her forty-eight years. She wore woollen slacks and a black silk polo neck sweater. The colour denoted bereavement, Jess supposed. It drained the residual colour from the wearer's pale complexion. But in the circumstances, she could be expected to be pale. The fire in the hearth, perhaps not entirely necessary today even though it was raining, had probably been lit because Alison had felt cold. Shock did that. However, apart from the pallor and a touch of understandable nervousness, Jess thought she seemed composed.

Alison spoke again. 'It's not a very nice day, as my husband said. Do sit by the fire.'

Her voice was louder now and firmer; she felt herself on surer ground in performing the social niceties. She would be a good hostess, thought Jess. No matter how difficult the guest or tedious the occasion, Alison would preside over it with charm and grace. Somewhat to her surprise, Jess found herself filled with resentful admiration. She knew that she lacked the sort of skills Alison could call up automatically. But then, when had she the time or occasion to practise them? She had other abilities. She could stand by and watch an autopsy without throwing up. She could question witnesses and listen to tales of appalling brutality and degradation. She could deal with hardened criminals in the confines of the dingiest interview room. But she couldn't have hosted a formal dinner party to save her life. But I don't want to, she told herself. I didn't choose that sort of life. I chose to be a police officer.

'Thank you,' she replied politely, taking the designated armchair.

Jenner had returned and retook his seat. He cleared his throat. Jess had the impression of a meeting being called to order. 'We want to help, of course we do. But my wife and I have discussed this sad event at length and we really can offer no explanation other than the one I thought of when my daughter's body was found. Some maniac did this, the same one who has been writing odious letters to Alison. Find him and you'll find my daughter's killer.' Jenner ended his speech on a flat, formal note and stared at Jess, challenging her to dispute his conclusions.

'You know . . .' Alison began in her quiet voice but then seemed to realize how difficult it was for Jess to hear her. She began again and said more loudly, 'You know what the letters referred to? About my aunt's death? Alan Markby told you?'

'I've seen the file,' Jess admitted.

For a moment Alison Jenner looked as if she was going to be physically sick. The woman was under tremendous stress. Jess felt an instinctive burst of sympathy for her and, at the same time, a twinge of guilt because in her memo to Markby, she'd suggested Alison might have been guilty of Freda Kemp's murder after all. But nice, kindly-faced women with all the social graces had killed before. This one, however, had been cleared of the murder. Jess was more than conscious that she had to be careful how she questioned Alison.

As if he read her mind, Jenner said sharply, 'There has been an attempt, a clear attempt, to drag up the sorry details of the death of my wife's aunt. To arrange my daughter's body in the same way—' He broke off. 'It's disgusting,' he said after a moment. 'It's sick. He is sick, whoever this is.'

Jess said, 'I'm sorry,' and meant it. She turned to Alison and asked, 'Mr Jenner has told you the result of the post-mortem?'

'I know my stepdaughter was stabbed.'

Alison's voice was calm and there was even something close to relief in it.

To Jenner, Jess asked, 'Can you tell me about your daughter? Did she live here with you?'

He had placed his hand over his eyes as his wife spoke. Now he took his hand away from his face. 'Good Lord, no. No, she has – had a flat in London. Not much of a place, just a pied-à-terre. It's what they call a studio flat these days, just one big room really with the usual offices and a balcony.'

It sounded expensive to Jess, even though Jenner dismissed it. 'Whereabouts in London?' she asked.

'In Docklands.'

Jess made a note of that. 'Did she work there?'

He shook his head. 'No, but she had a fancy for a new place and for living there. It's very much an area for young people.'

Wealthy young people. But Fiona had had a wealthy papa. 'May I ask,' Jess put the question cautiously. 'if Fiona bought it with her own money?'

'Yes,' he said shortly.

'What line of work was she in?' Well-paid work, it would seem.

'She worked in television for a while, nothing glamorous, just office work. I think she hoped it might lead to her being spotted and offered something in front of camera but it didn't work out like that and she chucked the job in. These last few weeks she hasn't – hadn't – been working.'

'But if she had a mortgage,' Jess asked, 'wasn't that rash?'

'She didn't have a mortgage. She bought the flat outright. She was left a considerable amount by her grandfather and at eighteen gained control of it. She wanted to invest it and thought property the best option. She consulted me. I made enquiries about the flat and it did seem a good investment. I told her to go ahead.'

Jess was momentarily bereft of speech and hoped her jaw hadn't dropped. Rich people, she thought wryly, saw ordinary life and its daily necessities through a different pair of spectacles to the rest of us mortals. But a flat in Docklands, just like that. No skulking before estate agents' windows, hoping one of the cheaper properties would turn out on viewing to be better than it looked. A hope usually vain since she'd already discovered that estate agents were skilled at finding a photogenic angle from which to snap the dreariest property. She'd learned an important fact, however, from Fiona's very different experience. Fiona hadn't lacked money and the price tag hadn't been an obstacle.

'I'd like to take a look at this flat,' Jess said. 'Do you have the keys?'

Jenner stared at her very hard and breathed heavily down his nostrils like a suspicious horse. 'Is that necessary?'

'It's routine,' Jess told him.

'It still seems an unnecessary intrusion. What do you hope to find there?'

'That I can't say. Possibly nothing at all. We have to take a look.' Jess met his outraged glare and held it. She had the satisfaction of making him look away first.

Alison reached out and touched his arm. 'They're trying to do their job, Jerry.'

Jenner got to his feet and began to turn restlessly up and down the room. Eventually he fetched up by Jess's chair and said sulkily, 'The keys will be in her room, probably in her bag, upstairs.'

'That's another thing,' Jess said. 'Could I see her room?'

Alison jumped to her feet before her husband could protest at this further intrusion, and said quickly, 'I'll show you the way.'

Jess's spirits rose. She had been wondering how to detach Alison from Jenner but now an opportunity was being given her. She wondered whether Alison realized that Jess would need to speak to her privately and had offered to escort her upstairs to create the necessary situation.

Jess decided to waste no time. As she climbed the staircase behind Alison, she asked, 'Did you see Fiona leave the house on Saturday morning?'

Alison shook her head but didn't turn it. 'No. Toby saw her. He was the only one.'

'You didn't go outside yourself?'

Now Alison stopped at the head of the stairs and turned to give her a surprisingly knowing look. 'I didn't, neither did Jeremy. We can vouch for one another. Before breakfast we were pretty well under one another's eye all the time. You want to know about alibis, don't you? Mrs Whittle saw me, too. I went down to the kitchen and asked if she'd scramble some eggs for Toby. My husband and I only eat toast. I didn't have time to go down to the lake.' She gave Alison a sad smile. 'You see, Inspector, I've been through all this before. I know what you want to ask and why. Oh, and I didn't kill Fiona.'

'I hadn't suggested you did, Mrs Jenner.' Jess felt she was being wrong-footed here and didn't like it. As a police officer, she ought to be past being shocked. But somehow Alison's direct denial and the almost serene way in which it had been spoken were deeply shocking. But this serenity might be a result of the tranquillizers Alison had been taking since Saturday afternoon. Alison had been deeply affected by the event. She had required medical assistance.

Alison gave her a wise smile. Perhaps Jess's face had betrayed her. 'But that's what some people might think.'

Jess said bluntly, 'You were relieved when I referred to the fact that Fiona had been stabbed, not bludgeoned to death or drowned.'

'Yes,' Alison admitted calmly. 'What happened to her was unforgivable. Jeremy will never come to terms with it. For me it was horrible not only because Fiona had died, but because someone tried to make it look like the death of my aunt. Ashamed as I am now for feeling it, it was a relief to hear Fiona hadn't died that way. Oh, yes, I am selfish enough to be glad poor Fiona didn't die in the same way as Aunt Freda.' Alison gave Jess another of those knowing looks. 'Perhaps you haven't had the experience, Inspector, but I've found that when one hears of a death, so often one of the emotions one feels is guilt because one feels one ought to have been able to prevent it. When I believed Fiona had died as Aunt Freda did, I thought it must be my fault because it must be connected with me. The stabbing is something new, something outside my experience. It allowed me to think perhaps this hasn't happened because of something involving me, years ago.'

'Your husband thinks there's a connection.'

Alison's face clouded. 'Yes, Jeremy still thinks the writer of those wretched letters did it. The blow to the head, the placing of the body in the lake, all that window-dressing, can any of that be coincidence?' Her eyes searched Jess's face.

'We don't know,' Jess replied cautiously. 'At this stage it would be a mistake to assume we know anything.'

Alison considered this and nodded. 'I wouldn't expect you to say anything else. Do you know what's so wonderful about Jeremy? Even though he's sure the letter-writer did this, he doesn't blame *me.* I love my husband, Inspector Campbell, he's a special man. He's honourable and fair.'

She turned away before Jess could reply and walked down the corridor. Like the walls of the staircase, it was lined with small dark oil paintings of trees and meadows, with the occasional child picking flowers or wooden-looking domestic animal. The sort of views young Victorian ladies turned out by the dozen, Jess thought, and wondered if they had been handed down through Jenner's family or bought at a country house auction.

Fiona's room was at the back of the house. It was painted entirely throughout in white and the curtains and duvet cover were lilac. On the windowsill was a vase of fresh flowers and beyond them, through the panes, could be seen a narrow path leading across a lawn to an area surrounded by an ornamental wall. Jess guessed that behind that was the family's swimming pool. In a house this size it would be strange if they didn't have one.

She turned her attention back to the bed. It had been made up, the duvet smooth, the pillows plumped up, Fiona's expensive-looking nightgown neatly folded. Not just the bed had suffered the attentions of a careful hand. Everything had been tidied away. She sighed. She'd slipped up. Pride went before a fall, and she had been so determined that Markby should see how efficient she was that she had made a basic mistake. She should have asked to see this room on Saturday, immediately the body was discovered. If there had been anything of interest here, by now it might well have been removed. Families, she knew, were keen to protect their good name, and no one wanted to do that more than a father to protect the reputation of his daughter. Not even a book with a raunchy cover would be left. The only reading matter in this room was on the bedside table. It was a copy of *Country Life*. Do me a favour! thought Jess in exasperation. You might at least have found a copy of *Cosmopolitan* or *Marie-Claire*.

Alison had gone to the far side of the room and opened a cupboard. She turned towards Jess holding out a bag made of multicoloured leather patchwork. It was the pear-shaped sort with a wide band, designed to be worn fitting snugly against the spine, an upmarket backpack. It did not pass Jess by that Alison had known immediately where to go for it. They had been through this room, probably both Jenners together.

'This is the bag Fiona brought with her.' Alison put it down on the bed. 'I expect you want to look round. I'll leave you to it. I dare say the coffee's arrived by now downstairs. You'll join us when you've finished?'

'Mrs Jenner!' Jess called out as the woman reached the door. Alison turned towards her, eyebrows raised. 'May I ask, did you get along well with your stepdaughter?'

Alison came back inside the room a few steps. 'Yes. That is, I didn't get along badly with her. The truth is, I never really felt I knew her. She was brought up by her mother, largely in France, except for the time she spent at boarding school in this country. Chantal – Fiona's mother and Jeremy's first wife – is French. Fiona occasionally spent a school holiday with us. But it's only this last year or so that she'd taken to coming down to Overvale for a few days at a time. It's not because I didn't invite her. I thought it was important that Jeremy should have close contact with her. She's – she was – his flesh and blood, after all.' Alison paused. 'How difficult it is,' she mused, 'to remember to use the past tense. It seems so wrong that a young person should die like that. I can hardly take it in, even though I saw her myself, lying there by the lake.'

'Mr Jenner has no other children?'

'No.' Alison folded her arms as if she were cold and the room was a little chilly. 'Jeremy's taken this very hard, as I told you. He keeps up a brave front but he's devastated.'

Without waiting to find out if Jess wanted to ask her anything more, Alison turned and left.

A quick search through drawers and cupboards revealed nothing and confirmed her first impression of the room. Every item of clothing was carefully folded or hung up. Twenty-year-olds are not normally so tidy. At twenty-nine, Jess herself wasn't. She thought about her own bedroom back at the Bamford flat with its clothes tossed over the back of a chair and jumble of make-up items on the dressing table. This dressing table was dusted and neat. Not a bottle of nail polish out of place.

As for the contents of the leather bag, they were also disappointing. There was a bunch of keys. Good, Jess tossed them up in the air and caught them. But apart from two crumpled Kleenex tissues, a purse with a little loose change in it, a credit card holder with an impressive selection of plastic and a lipstick, there was nothing which gave any clue to the dead girl's interests or contacts. No notebook or diary. No personal organizer. No contraceptives either in pill or barrier form. Had Fiona had a sex life?

Jess rummaged through the pockets of a jacket in the wardrobe and found Fiona's car keys and a crumpled scrap of paper bearing the legend 'buy milk'. Somehow this creased snippet of domestic ephemera was the most poignant thing of all. Yet it told her nothing.

Jess stared round the room with dissatisfaction. The only thing apart from her clothes that could be said to be personal to Fiona was her electric toothbrush plugged into a socket. There wasn't even the stuffed toy mascot beloved of many young people. The wicker waste-paper basket by the dressing table was empty and freshly lined with a plastic sack. There was no ensuite bathroom but instead an individual washbasin. That sparkled with cleanliness. Even the piece of soap lying on it was new. It was like a hotel room. Was that just because Mrs Whittle had cleaned it so thoroughly and the Jenners had removed anything they deemed embarrassing? Or had Fiona not wished to leave any clues to her personality? Jess recalled Alison's words. 'I never really felt I knew her.'

'I'm not going to get to know her either,' Jess muttered. 'Unless someone opens up.'

She went back downstairs. An enticing aroma of good hot coffee seeped from the drawing room and when she opened the door she saw the tray with the coffee things on a low table. Alison and her husband were seated close together on the sofa and appeared to have been having some kind of disagreement. Not of the acrimonious kind, thought Jess, just the difference-of-opinion sort argued out with affectionate obstinacy. As soon as she saw Jess, however, Alison picked up the coffee pot and poured out a fresh cup.

'Thank you,' said Jess, accepting it. 'I have the keys, Mr Jenner, and I'll give you a receipt for them. Now I need your daughter's London address.'

Jenner picked up a small piece of paper from the coffee table and handed it to her. 'I've written it out ready for you.'

As Jess's fingers closed on it, Jenner added, 'You have to understand. I've lost my daughter. I know her death has to be investigated. But I feel as though everything about her is being violated. The autopsy, her room searched, her personal effects, now her flat . . .' His voice trailed away.

'We'll leave everything neat, sir. Can I ask, did Mrs Whittle tidy the room upstairs?' She didn't ask them directly if they had been through the room, but waited to see their reaction.

Alison put her fingers to her mouth in a gesture of dismay. 'Yes, I didn't think to stop her. Of course, everything should have been left as it was . . . But Fiona was a tidy person. I don't suppose Mrs Whittle did very much.'

The gesture looked convincing. That meant Alison might be a good actress or it might be genuine regret. In any case, it might be unfair to blame her. She had been sleeping most of the weekend and any search through Fiona's effects might have been instigated by Jenner himself. If so, he wasn't the sort of man to admit he'd done anything improper.

'All the same, I'd like a word with Mrs Whittle.' Jess put her cup down. 'That was lovely coffee. Will I find her in the kitchen? No, don't get up. I can find my way.'

'Intrusion,' muttered Jeremy Jenner. 'Wandering all over the damn house. None of us is going to have a bit of privacy left!'

★ ★ ★

Mrs Whittle was sitting in the kitchen drinking a cup of coffee of her own and reading the *Daily Mail*.

'Sorry to bother you,' Jess said, taking the seat across the table from her. 'I just wanted to ask, when you tidied Fiona Jenner's room, did you throw anything away?'

Mrs Whittle stared at her in bewilderment. 'No, miss, why should I?'

'I saw there was a waste-paper basket in there and it was empty.'

Understanding dawned on the housekeeper's face. 'Oh, I emptied that but it wasn't anything much, some tissues with lipstick on them I think. Oh, and a pair of tights that she'd put her toe through.' Mrs Whittle flushed guiltily. 'I kept the tights. I mended them. It was only a little hole but young people nowadays, they don't mend anything, do they? They throw anything like that away and buy new. They were good tights and I couldn't bring myself to put them in the bin. When I sewed up the hole you could hardly see it but I knew she wouldn't wear darned tights so, well, I just kept them.'

'I'm not worried about the tights,' Jess assured her. 'If I could take you back to Saturday morning, the morning Miss Jenner died.'

Mrs Whittle looked distressed and said, 'Poor young woman. She was such a lovely girl, just like one of those fashion models. To think of her lying dead like that.'

'Yes. Did you see Fiona leave the house on Saturday morning?'

'Now,' said Mrs Whittle, suddenly confidential. 'As a matter of fact, I did and I didn't. I'd taken a tray of breakfast things into the dining room and she ran past the window. I suppose you'd say I didn't exactly see her *leave*. But she was outside the house. She was running, jogging, like they do to keep fit.'

'Can you describe her?' Jess asked. 'What was she wearing?'

'It was Miss Fiona, I recognized her. I saw her clearly. She had on a red top. It had long sleeves and a little hood at the back. She'd got her hair tied back with a red band round it and as she ran the ponytail of hair bobbed up and down just like a real pony's tail. It amused me at the time.' Mrs Whittle paused to sniff, take out a handkerchief and rub the end of her nose with it.

'What time was this?' The picture the woman had drawn of Fiona Jenner running past the window was a good one and yet there was something wrong with it.

'It would have been around, oh, a quarter past eight? I couldn't swear to the time, not to the minute. But about that.' Mrs Whittle nodded as if agreeing with herself.

The feeling of something wrong still niggled at Jess. Before her inner vision swam another picture. In it, Fiona lay dead on the edge of the lake, her long blond hair spread out. That was what was different! Where was the red scrunchy which had secured the ponytail?

'The red band, as you called it,' Jess said. 'Was it a small thing?'

'On her hair? It was an elasticized red satin ring, quite a pretty thing. I'd seen her wear it before. She'd pull her hair into a ponytail and twist this ring thing round it two or three times until it was tight.'

'Right,' Jess said briskly. 'Thank you, Mrs Whittle. Oh, I was hoping to talk to Mr Smythe but he doesn't seem to be about. Has he gone back to London?'

'No,' said Mrs Whittle decidedly. 'But he won't be in for lunch. He's gone out to have lunch with a friend.'

'Why on earth did you choose the Feathers?' whispered Meredith across the table.

'It looked all right from the outside,' Toby defended himself, gazing round him.

The Feathers was an old pub and had the necessary quaint features to make it picturesque but they were spoiled by ancient tobacco-stained anaglypta wallpaper, a lot of dark wood and an array of faded photographs which provided the decoration. It wasn't a popular hostelry but it had a core of doggedly loyal patrons, themselves of a dauntingly uncommunicative nature. The entry of Meredith and Toby had been met with surly stares.

'I should have warned you,' she said. 'My fault.'

'We'll go somewhere else,' he said. 'Drink up.'

'Too late. Dolores is coming over. We can't slip out now.'

'Who is—'

'Miss Mitchell, isn't it?' A voice cut across Toby's question. He looked up and his expression became startled. A woman of Amazonian build wearing a tight purple sweater over an impressive bust, black leggings and stiletto heels had arrived at the table, clearly ready to take their order. She had long bottle-blond hair and a great deal of make-up. She also had a glint in her eye and a no-nonsense manner which would have done credit to the matron of a nineteenth-century workhouse.

'Hello, Dolores,' said Meredith. 'How are you? This is Mrs Forbes, the licensee, Toby.'

'Nothing wrong with me,' said Mrs Forbes briskly as if Meredith's enquiry had suggested the possibility of weakness. 'Mr Markby well? Not with you today?' She raised her plucked eyebrows and gave Toby a look intended to quell. It did. Toby gulped and picked up his glass, burying his nose in it.

'Alan's working,' Meredith explained. 'This is a friend, just down for a couple of days.'

'Oh, yes?' Clearly Mrs Forbes didn't believe in innocent friendships. 'That'll be the murder, I dare say, over at Overvale House?'

'What?' Meredith made the necessary mental leap. 'Yes.' She couldn't deny it but it was a nuisance to have Mrs Forbes take an interest in the reason for Alan's absence. She wasn't prepared for it to throw up a nugget of curious information.

'She came in here one night,' said Mrs Forbes unexpectedly.

'She?'

'The dead girl. Mr Jenner's daughter, was it? We had a visiting darts team here at the time and you never saw so many blokes with their eyes out on stalks. The darts were going all over the place. We've got lasagne today.'

'Was she on her own?' Meredith disregarded the offer of lasagne.

Mrs Forbes frowned and tapped a menu card against her teeth. 'It was that crowded in here, with the darts match, that I couldn't say. I suppose she must have been with someone. A girl like that doesn't go into pubs on her own. Funny thing, I can't remember anyone with her exactly, at least, not anyone I didn't know. Of course with the visiting darts team and their girlfriends, the bar was full of strangers. She might have come with them. If you don't want the lasagne, I've got a Thai green curry. That's new on the menu.'

Dolores' manner indicated that she'd spent enough time on chit-chat and they should make up their minds, sharpish. They settled for lasagne.

'I don't suppose,' ventured Toby, 'that you've got a wine list?'

The landlady gave him a fierce stare. 'No, we're a pub, not a restaurant. We've got wine, red or white. Which do you want?'

They ordered the red.

'What a ghastly battleaxe,' whispered Toby in awe when Mrs Forbes had marched away to deliver their order to the kitchen. 'Is she the cook?'

'I don't think so. She's got a partner, a little chap who never speaks and is hardly ever let out of the kitchen, so I guess he does it. You do realize, she thinks that you and I are engaging in illicit shenanigans behind Alan's back?'

'Then she'll have to think it, won't she?' Toby frowned. 'What on earth was Fiona doing in here? It's not her sort of place at all.'

'Toby,' Meredith hesitated. 'Were you very keen on her?'

'I liked her a lot,' he said. 'I suppose you mean, was I in love? I don't know.'

'Then you weren't,' she said firmly. 'I have to say, I'm a bit relieved. I thought you might be heart-broken, although you don't look it. I don't mean that unkindly.'

'I know what you mean,' Toby said with unaccustomed sharpness. 'People think I'm superficial. Generally it's people who don't know me very well. You do know me pretty well and even you think it.'

'No . . .' she protested. 'I didn't mean it to sound . . .'

He leaned forward. 'It's a protective disguise. I developed it when I was a kid. At boys' schools it doesn't do to be sensitive. We all worked hard at seeming tough and cool. What you see now is my adult version of it, I suppose. I'm really upset about Fiona. I did like her a lot, even if I didn't – I wasn't what people would call *in love* with her. I think she liked me in the same way. We were both oddities, if you like. That's why we got on so well. We always were good mates, even as kids, although I saw little of her after the age of about ten when Jeremy and Chantal divorced. Fiona was abroad with her mother. You know how it is when you spend most of your time abroad? You lose touch with daily life in your own country.'

Meredith nodded. 'Yes, I felt that very much when I first came back to England permanently after so many years abroad. Odd periods of leave at home aren't enough. You find you're operating from a whole different mindset. You feel like a foreigner in your own country. It's weird. I suppose you mean Fiona felt like a foreigner here in England.'

'That's it. She did and so do I. Most of my school friends are married now with kids. I haven't got much in the way of relatives, none that I can drop in on easily, anyway. People I've met in the service and got on well with are scattered round the globe. Fiona was in much the same boat. Her mother's French. After she and Jeremy split, Chantal, Fiona's mum, took her back to France. But it wasn't a settled life, even then. Chantal took up with some bloke who took her and Fiona to live in Belgium. Then that relationship broke up and Chantal brought Fiona back to France, but to a different part. Finally, when Fiona was fourteen, Chantal and Jeremy decided through their lawyers that Fiona should go to boarding school in England and Jeremy foot the bill. So she was sent off to some scholastic institution for young ladies which she hated. She didn't fit in there. In the holidays she either went back to France or to stay with Jeremy who'd married Alison by then. I think Chantal had a whole string of boyfriends and some of them wanted Fiona there and some didn't. Whether Fiona went to France depended on whom Chantal was shacked up with at the time. Also,' Toby pulled a face. 'Fiona was growing up and she was real stunner, you saw that. I think Chantal didn't want competition under her own roof. You haven't met Chantal but ·Jeremy's trying to contact her about this and we are expecting her to turn up here as soon as she gets the sad news. She's – not easy.'

'That's sad,' Meredith said. 'But I suppose it's a common enough story.'

Unexpectedly Toby said, 'I know Fiona gave the impression of being a tough brat but you can see why. Like me, she'd learned young to put up a defence. She wasn't really that bad but people hadn't treated her all that well. There was enough money, you see, for both her father and her mother to salve their consciences with expensive school fees and presents.'

'And all she wanted was love?' asked Meredith a little drily.

'I don't say both Jeremy and Chantal didn't love her. I know Jeremy did, I don't doubt it for a minute, but I don't think he was any good at showing it. I suppose Chantal did. But they both managed to persuade themselves they were doing everything that they needed to do and Fiona was well taken care of.' Toby paused. 'Love's s funny thing,' he added. 'Sort of, you know, adjustable. Like a conscience.'

'Hello, there, Miss Mitchell,' said a male voice.

They looked up and saw Ted Pritchard standing by them. He wore a washed-out T-shirt with a faded advertisement for a popular lager on it, probably a promotional gift from a brewery. His curly hair was sprinkled with wood dust like a bad case of dandruff.

'Popped in for my lunch,' he explained his presence. 'We take it in turns to go out for a bite to eat, Steve and me.' He bent an eye on Toby. 'The other gentleman not with you today, then?'

'I don't believe this,' said Toby.

'No, Ted, he's working. We're both making the most of the Easter holiday break.'

'Nice for some, eh?' said Ted amiably and wandered away to the bar.

'Don't tell me,' said Toby with deep feeling, 'that they don't spend all their time in the country poking their noses into other people's business. Who is that guy?'

'He makes garden furniture. Alan and I want him to make some for us, for the vicarage garden when we get round to fixing it up.'

'I've never understood the obsession some people have with gardening,' said Toby morosely.

'About Fiona. Did Jeremy give her a lot of money?' Meredith asked him after a moment's silence.

Toby shrugged. 'When she was younger, I think he did. But then, you see, when she was eighteen she came into her own money, from her grandfather. So she was independent.'

This surprised Meredith. It also knocked a plank out of the motive she'd been building for Fiona to be the poison pen letter-writer. It wouldn't do, she decided, to suggest to Toby that Fiona might have had a hand in the letters. At least not yet.

A hand appeared between them holding an opened wine bottle. 'The red!' announced Dolores and vanished.

'We're not to get a chance to sample it, then,' muttered Toby and took hold of the bottle. He released it at once with a yelp. 'Where the hell has she been storing it? It's warm!'

Meredith touched it. It was certainly alarmingly warm. 'By a radiator or the oven?' she suggested. 'Under those electric lights always on in the bar? There are some bottles up there like this one.'

'Right!' said Toby grimly, gripping the offending bottle by the neck. 'I'm not paying for this. I'm resigned to paying over the odds for a bottle of plonk but not for a bottle of hot plonk!' He strode towards the bar.

Meredith watched with interest as an animated conversation took place at the bar. Dolores flung back her blond locks and placed her hands on her hips. Toby's gestures grew ever more Mediterranean. Ted, leaning on the bar with cigarette smoke swirling around his head and consuming an apparently all-liquid lunch, was watching with interest. At the instant Meredith was about to jump up and intervene before it came to violence, Dolores grabbed the bottle and, looking even more like the figurehead on a galleon, surged out of the bar and through the kitchen door.

Toby returned looking flushed, baffled and disconcerted.

'Well?' Meredith asked him.

'I said I it was warm,' Toby informed her. 'And she said it was room temperature which it ought to be. I said only if the room was a sauna. I told her I wanted another one. She said they were all the same. I said I wasn't going to pay for a bottle of warm wine and was prepared to argue my case before the magistrates. She offered to put it in the fridge for a bit.'

By this time Meredith had buried her face in her hands and was helpless with laughter.

'It will be undrinkable!' growled Toby at her shaking shoulders. 'But arguing with that woman is like arguing with a tank!'

Meredith wiped her eyes. 'That's Dolores, for you.'

A small depressed-looking man emerged furtively from the kitchens bearing two plates on which stood brown glazed terrines. He placed these before them. 'The lasagne,' he whispered. 'I'll bring your wine in a minute. I've popped it in the freezer for a couple of minutes.'

'Look forward to it,' murmured Toby. He picked up a fork and plunged it into the lasagne. 'I wonder what's in here.'

'It looks all right. I'll have to tell Alan about Fiona being seen here. You're right. It's not her sort of place and I can't believe she came here for a night out. Do you reckon she was meeting someone? Did she know anyone local?'

Toby shrugged. 'Search me. She didn't say.' He tasted the lasagne cautiously. 'Edible,' he said. 'Something, I suppose.' He put down his fork again. 'Meredith, I've got a sort of confession.

Fiona and I weren't in love in the way I suppose you and Alan must be, but we were good friends, and I was getting round to asking her if she'd marry me.'

Meredith was startled into silence. Eventually she asked simply, 'Why?'

'Why are you and Alan getting married? No, don't answer that. Ignore it. Forget I asked. I know why you two are getting married. Anyone seeing the pair of you together would know why. In my case, I just thought I'd like to be married. Fiona seemed to me a person I'd like to be married to. It wasn't a spur-of-the-moment decision. I'd been thinking it over for a few weeks.'

'You're not going to tell me you were considering a marriage of convenience?'

He had the grace to blush. 'You could call it that. You see, over the last couple of years I've discovered I've turned into the embassy bachelor. It's not a role I'm that keen to play. Fiona, well, she was living in that flat of hers in Docklands and coming down here occasionally for a few days with Jeremy and Alison. It seemed to me she didn't have much of a life, not really. People always thought, because she was so good-looking, she must be out every night painting the town red. But the way she talked, it wasn't like that. I knew she wasn't working now, so she didn't have colleagues she could have a drink with, nothing like that. But as a diplomatic wife, she'd have had a ready-made role to play, a social life, chance to travel. She had no proper roots in England. We got on OK. It might have worked.'

His manner had grown steadily more defensive as he spoke. 'All right, I admit it, now I'm telling you about it, sitting here, it sounds pretty stupid. But when I just thought about it by myself, it didn't. You'll say that no man in his right mind would consider asking a girl he'd never even kissed to marry him.'

'I'm not saying that, Toby. I'm just wondering whether she'd ever, you know, given you any encouragement. Did you get the impression she'd quite like to be married to you?'

Toby looked uncomfortable. 'To be honest, no. She was always very friendly. I think she liked talking to me. Although, now I think about it, I did most of the talking. She didn't tell me much about herself. I didn't ask personal questions because I thought I knew her and because something in her manner didn't encourage it. One does think one knows relatives. I suppose I was making assumptions. Right or wrong, I'd made up my mind to put the idea to her.'

'But you hadn't actually asked her?'

'No. I was hoping to work my way round to it this weekend.'

Impulsively Meredith put out her hand and covered his which rested on the table top. 'Oh, poor Toby. What can I say?'

'Harr-um!' A throat was noisily cleared above their heads. 'Sorry to disturb you, I'm sure,' said Dolores Forbes. A bottle was set down between them with a thump. 'Your chilled wine!'

Jess Campbell got back to regional HQ at midday and was rummaging in a drawer of her desk when she became aware someone had entered her office and was standing by the door.

'Just a sec!' she called. 'Be with you in a jiff.'

'No hurry,' said a pleasant male voice.

Jess jumped and spun round. 'Oh, sorry, sir. Didn't see it was you.'

'I came to see how you got on at Overvale,' Alan Markby said.

'I turned up a few things, one of them a bit of a surprise. I was just about to write out a report,' Jess added quickly.

He nodded. 'About this time of day, in these circumstances, if it had been Dave Pearce still in this office, I'd be offering to stand him a pint in the pub on the corner.'

'Oh,' said Jess. At the mention of her predecessor's name she'd felt herself bristle but the follow-up was totally unexpected. 'I don't know about a pint,' she ventured. 'I might manage half a cider.'

Unexpectedly he gave a broad smile. 'Meredith, my fiancée, is a cider-drinker. Come on, then. You can tell me what you found out this morning in rather more comfortable surroundings than these.'

★ ★ ★

The pub Jess found herself in was quite unlike the one in which Toby and Meredith were sharing an indifferent bottle of wine. The Feathers, with all its faults, was genuinely old. This was a fairly new building furnished in a way to suggest 'character'. Bookcases along the walls were filled with a motley selection of second-hand volumes. Whatever the overhead beams were made of, it wasn't wood. There was a fire burning in the hearth but it was gas-powered.

'Sorry about the kitsch.' Markby had noted her critical study of their surroundings. 'They do a good ham baguette if you're hungry. That's what I'm having.'

'Oh, right, sir.'

Somehow Jess felt that Markby being friendly in a relaxed way was more alarming than Markby being professionally courteous. What was this supposed to achieve? That she, Jess, would blurt out her innermost secrets? I haven't got any! she thought crossly. Yes, you do, replied that inner voice which delights in disconcerting us. Everyone does.

He had returned holding the cider in one hand and a pint in the other. 'The baguettes are coming,' he informed her. 'Cheers!'

She raised her glass cautiously. 'Cheers, sir.'

'What did you make of the Kemp case?' He put down his glass. At least he wasn't going to beat about the bush.

Jess felt he expected her to be equally to the point. She began, trying not to let a nervous tremor invade her voice. 'It does seem too much of a coincidence that Fiona Jenner should be found dead in a way which suggests the death of Freda Kemp. At the very least, the murderer knew about the Kemp case. That, in turn, suggests the killer might be the poison pen sender. That's what Jeremy Jenner thinks and he might be right. Or, we might all be thinking along lines suggested by the killer to throw us off the scent. The killer might not be the writer, but he or she knows about the letters and wants to point us in the direction of the letter-writer.

'As for the Kemp case.' Here Jess faltered but controlled the moment's weakness and went on firmly, 'The original investigation seems to have been botched. Either there wasn't enough evidence and the case shouldn't have come to court, or there was evidence, but it wasn't properly checked. The inspiration for the letters may lie in the mistakes which were made then.'

Markby said quietly, 'We are not investigating the Kemp murder. That's for others to do if the case is ever reopened. Alison Harris, as she then was, was found Not Guilty. I should tell you that Alison doesn't think Freda Kemp *was* murdered.' He repeated Alison's explanation of her aunt's death.

'It would make sense, I suppose.' Jess was unable to keep the doubt from her voice. 'I wasn't intending to question Alison Jenner about the earlier case. I just thought we ought to keep it in mind.'

'I quite agree. The senior investigating officer in the case was a chap called Barnes-Wakefield. He'll be retired now but I thought I might get in touch with him and hear what he's got to say. The roots of the murder of Fiona Jenner may indeed lie in the distant past. I can be getting on with that while you're concentrating on what's happening at this end of things. I'll be tactful. I won't suggest he botched things.' Markby smiled.

'No, sir. I wouldn't say it to him directly, either.'

'I'm not suggesting you would. But it's best I get in touch with him. He might be happier chatting to a serving officer of the rank of superintendent—'

'— And male,' said Jess, before she could stop herself.

'Quite so.' Markby raised his glass to her.

Jess laughed ruefully. It was true the old fellow, as Barnes-Wakefield must now be, probably wouldn't be so forthcoming with a young female inspector of the type virtually unknown when he'd been an active police officer.

'I'll dig him out,' said Markby affably. 'These old fellows usually jump at a chance to reminisce.'

The baguettes arrived and there was a pause while both of them ate.

'So,' the superintendent asked after a while. 'How about this morning?'

'I spoke to Jenner and his wife. Smythe wasn't there. He'd gone off to lunch with a friend.'

Markby nodded. 'He's lunching somewhere with Meredith. I dare say I'll get the breakdown on that later. If anything of interest came up, I'll pass it on.'

Jess took her time replying to this. To have the superintendent's fiancée a close friend of one of the suspects didn't help. No wonder he'd invited her to this pub with its off-duty atmosphere. He had a good reason to want to know what she was thinking. If things got awkward, he'd want to extricate his fiancée, Meredith, was it? Yes, he'd want to get her out of an embarrassing situation.

'One thing to come out of the interview was that Fiona Jenner was financially independent,' she explained.

Markby nodded thoughtfully. 'That would certainly prove significant. I wonder if she'd made a will? Being so young, she might not have done.'

'If she hasn't,' Jess observed, 'then Jenner would have a claim on the estate and so would her mother, who is French. Her first name is Chantal but I don't know her present surname. I don't know where she is, here or in France. I don't think Jenner is sure of her whereabouts, either. He told me he was still trying to get in touch with her.'

'I had Fiona down as possibly the letter-writer,' Markby said thoughtfully. 'So did Meredith. That now looks highly unlikely.'

'What did you think of her, sir? The dead girl? You met her and I didn't.'

'I only met her once. Self-assured and pretty hard-boiled was the impression I got. It might have been a false impression. Why don't you talk to Meredith? She might have more insight. She's pretty good at judging people's characters. It's that consular training. That's what she used to be, a British consul, dealing with all sorts of odd bods with British passports and unlikely yarns of mishaps abroad.'

116

'I'd like to talk to her,' Jess said.

'Fine, I'll tell her. She ought to go back to work tomorrow but perhaps she could take a morning off. I'll ask. What else did you find out this morning?'

'The housekeeper saw Fiona at about a quarter past eight, jogging past the window. That supports Smythe's story that he saw her leaving the house at about ten past eight. One detail: she says Fiona's hair was tied back with a red satin scrunchy.' Helpfully Jess began to explain what this hair adornment was. 'It's an elastic—'

'I know what they are,' he said. 'My niece has one. I don't have any children but my sister has four and they keep me up to speed.'

'Oh, right, sir. Well, there wasn't any sign of it by the lake. She might have lost it jogging.' Jess paused. 'Quite possibly she wasn't killed at the lake. There's that tyre track. She could have been attacked somewhere on the estate and the body driven to the lake. In that case, she could have lost the hair band at the time of the attack.'

'And if we find the red scrunchy, we'll know where the attack took place?' Markby considered this. 'It's a fair assumption.'

'I looked at her room but it had been cleaned up.' Jess drew a deep breath. 'I should have looked on Saturday evening before they got to it. It's now as clean as a whistle. At least I've got the keys to Fiona's flat in London. I thought I might go there tomorrow and take a look round.'

'In that case I'll tell Meredith to expect you on Wednesday morning.' When Jess had admitted her failure to search Fiona's room on Saturday, he'd merely nodded. That didn't mean he wasn't aware of the mistake. But he appreciated she hadn't pleaded tiredness after a long day culminating in attendance at the post-mortem and a difficult visit to tell Jenner his daughter had been stabbed. Own up to your mistakes and Markby would be reasonable. Attempt to conceal them and he'd be down on you like a ton of bricks! That was the unspoken message.

Jess thanked him and added, 'The diving team didn't find anything in the lake which might have been the weapon and we've had no luck so far with the impression of the tyre tread. It's a popular pattern. There is a vehicle on the estate which has some like it. It belongs to the gardener, Stebbings, an old 4 ×4. But his tyres are reasonably new and would've made a better imprint. I'll phone through to the Met this afternoon and clear it with them,' she concluded, 'if it's OK for me to go to London tomorrow.'

'Fair enough. But make sure someone's following up the original investigation into the letters themselves. It's even more urgent that we find the writer. Because,' Markby added, 'if the writer *didn't* have anything to do with Fiona Jenner's death, then he or she is now one very frightened person.'

When Toby got back to Overvale House, he saw a florist's van before the porch. The front door was open and Mrs Whittle was taking delivering of a large spray of purple iris and mauve tulips. The florist got back in her van and rattled away.

Toby went indoors.

'Look at these,' said Mrs Whittle to him. 'Lovely, aren't they?'

Toby turned the attached card so that he could read it. 'Who are Michael and Caroline Fossett?'

'They live about a mile away, sir. Their land adjoins ours. They farm and Mr Jenner, he leases out some of his land to them for the grazing. It's nice of them to show their sympathy. I'll just go and put them in some water. Mrs Jenner is lying down. There was a woman police officer here and I think it upset her. Best not to disturb her,' Mrs Whittle added and bustled away.

The door to Toby's left clicked and opened. 'Oh, Toby, there you are,' Jeremy Jenner said. 'Come on in.'

Toby followed him into the study. There was a distinct whiff of whisky in the air.

'Want one?' Jenner held up the decanter.

'I've been drinking at lunch, better not.' Toby paused. 'Some flowers came for you both, from some people called Fossett. Mrs Whittle's taken them to put in a vase.'

'Oh?' Jenner didn't appear very interested. He slumped in a chair and stared up at his cousin. 'We had that woman inspector here again this morning. It upset Alison.'

'Sorry to hear it. What was she after?'

'Snooping around, asking personal questions. It's a damn awful business.' Jenner hesitated. 'Look, Toby old son, you wouldn't do a favour for a chap, would you?

Chapter Seven

Jess Campbell's first sight of Fiona Jenner's flat on Tuesday morning was, as she afterwards admitted to Markby, an eye-opener. She had set off for London early in the morning by train, not trusting herself to drive in the nation's capital with its unfamiliar patterns of one-way systems. She had found her way to Docklands via the light railway and after wandering round a maze of buildings which still gleamed with comparative newness in the returned spring sunshine, and almost deserted streets, she found herself before a converted waterside warehouse. She gazed up at the deep red brick building towering above her. Its large windows, affording a spectacular view of the Thames basin, sparkled in the clear light. She consulted the scrap of paper Jenner had given her. Yes, this was it!

And there again, it wasn't, at least not as Jess had imagined it would be. To begin with, the flat was situated on the ground floor and had an independent entrance, more in the style of a maison-ette. The door was reached by crossing a minute patio containing a tub with a bay tree in it. Jess reached out and fingered one of the shiny dark green leaves. Was this just for decoration or had Fiona been interested in cooking? Jess had an idea these plants were expensive to buy. To leave it unattended out here showed a certain trust in the neighbours.

She put the key in the lock. It turned easily and the door swung open. She stepped inside.

Two things struck her in quick succession. First, a

confirmation of the discovery she'd already made, that Jeremy Jenner's description of his daughter's purchase had been hopelessly inadequate, not to say misleading. One room, perhaps, but one room of majestic proportions, large and so high that a spiral staircase had been installed up to a mezzanine bedroom platform, supported by an iron girder. It reached halfway across the whole space. This must be what Jeremy had meant when he spoke of a balcony. Light streamed in through high windows in the far wall. Everything gleamed: the stainless steel kitchen area, the minimalist décor and furnishings, a white leather sofa, a glass-topped coffee table. There was an off-white dining set with uncomfortable-looking chairs with high narrow backs made up of a sort of framed trellis-work. In one corner was the inevitable computer work station. The walls had been left in their red brick and there was one big unframed canvas on the far wall. Jess wasn't into art. It was just a lot of black splodges and zigzags on a white background to her eye, but it was clearly an original and probably by some well-known modern artist. The only other piece of decoration was a long mobile of silvery shapes hanging from high ceiling. It turned slowly in the draught from the opened front door with a faint metallic tinkle like distant bells. The whole place looked like something from the Ideal Home Exhibition, pristine, untouched and out of most people's league. It also, in its cleanliness, neatness and all that white, reminded Jess of a hospital ward.

Her trained eye took in all these things in one quick sweep of her surroundings. The second thing she became aware of, almost at once, was that she wasn't alone in here. There was someone up in the mezzanine bedroom. She closed the front door softly and stood listening. There it was: a hiss of expelled breath as someone exerted some effort, the creak of a footstep on the wooden floor and then a male voice uttering a quiet but heartfelt imprecation followed by a rhetorical question.

'*What the hell am I doing here?*'

'Just what I was thinking, sir!' Jess called up.

There was a thud from above as something was dropped. Footsteps clattered on the spiral staircase as the other began a hasty descent which stopped abruptly, midway.

'Inspector . . .'The dismay was almost laughable but Jess wasn't laughing.

'Mr Smythe. Do you mind telling me just what you are doing here?'

'Jeremy asked me to come, as a favour,' Toby said dejectedly from Fiona's white leather sofa. 'I didn't want to do it but the poor guy's in such a state. How could I refuse? He's my cousin.' He was slumped forward with his forearms resting on his thighs. He put up his hands and rubbed them over his head so that his dark hair became more tousled than ever.

'Family obligation doesn't excuse what looks remarkably like an attempt to remove evidence,' Jess told him and wished the words hadn't come out sounding so damn prissy. She was sitting opposite him on a tubular chair and between them the silver mobile twisted in an air current, shimmering and rustling. She was angry because his presence suggested the Jenners intended to carry out the same clean-up operation on Fiona's flat as they'd done on her bedroom at Overvale. At the same time, she felt herself curiously out of countenance. Embarrassment was what Smythe was feeling, unless he was a better actor than she gave him credit for being. And so he should be embarrassed! Her awkwardness came from the fact that she sat here like an old-fashioned mother superior and he sat there like a kid who'd been found smoking behind the toilets. He should be wriggling with guilt, but she shouldn't feel like this. It was unprofessional.

'I haven't removed a damn thing. I haven't found a damn thing.' He was defiant now. (*I wasn't smoking it, Sister, honest. I just picked it up to throw it in the rubbish bin.*) He smoothed his untidy hair with both hands in an attempt to restore it to order, and glared at her. 'I'd only been here about ten minutes when you turned up.'

'How did you get in here?' Jess asked briskly.

'I had a key. Jeremy knew that.'

'*You* had a key. Why?' Damn Jeremy Jenner! Why hadn't he told Jess that his cousin held a key to Fiona's flat?

'Through an oversight, really. When Fiona bought the place and it was still empty, she kipped over at my place in Camden. I was home on a spot of leave at the time. She had the bed and I had the sofa, in case you're wondering. She'd bought some stuff which she stored in my flat and left me a key for this place because I'd agreed to bring it over here. At that time I still had a car in London. I sold it when I left for Beijing and bought another when I got out there. I did well on the deal. Diplomatic perk.' He gave a wan smile which faded quickly in the face of Jess's stony expression.

'I'm not interested in your car,' she said sharply. 'So, you were given the key by Miss Jenner, so that you could deliver some property of hers.'

'Yes,' he said defiantly. 'She was going away for the weekend, not to see Jeremy, somewhere else, I don't know where.'

Toby looked round him and waved a hand vaguely in the direction of the kitchen area. 'It only was pots and pans and stuff like that. I came over here and dumped it all. My leave was up and I flew out back to Beijing a few days later. While I was away, she moved in here. The key – the key to this place which she gave me – was left in my flat in a drawer. I mentioned it when I arrived at Overvale. We were all sitting at dinner the first evening and I said I had the key and had meant to bring it down with me for Fiona but had forgotten it. Fiona said to put it in an envelope and post it to her. Jeremy remembered.'

Remembering that cleaned and tidied bedroom at Overvale, Jess's conviction that something was being deliberately erased from the record increased. Now was the time to find out what it was.

'And what did Jenner want you to search for?'

Toby hunched his shoulders. 'I don't know. Look, honestly, I *don't* know. I asked him and he turned vague. He just said I should take a look round and see if there was anything potentially embarrassing. He didn't mean anything directly to do with her *death*. It was anything to do with her *life* which would give a story to the press. We don't know why she died or who killed her. Jeremy's afraid the redtop papers might get hold of all this. Fiona was a single girl and he didn't want anything found here which might, I use his words, besmirch her reputation.'

'Mr Smythe!' Jess burst out. 'Given the job you do, you can't be so naïve! Fiona Jenner was murdered and anything here might give a clue to her killer! Even if there is something her father doesn't want to come to light, he has to face the fact that now it must! So must you! As for her posthumous reputation, I'm sorry, but in these circumstances the victim has no rights in that.'

' "I come to bury Caesar, not to praise him," quoted Toby gloomily. "The evil that men do lives after them, the good is oft interred with their bones." '

'Mr Smythe! This is a very serious matter.'

'I am being serious!' Toby snapped back irritably. 'Why does no one ever believe that I take things seriously? But old Shakespeare got it right, didn't he? He was a wise old bird. Now Fiona's dead anyone can say anything about her and any grubby journalist write up every little human failing for the titillation of his prurient readers. This whole thing is a nightmare. I sympathize with old Jeremy. However, believe me or not, I didn't intend to remove anything. I work for the government. I know things have to be done by the book. If I'd found anything embarrassing I'd have gone back and told Jeremy about it so he'd be ready for it when the police found it. Forewarned is forearmed, and all the rest of it. I know, believe it or not, about evidence.'

'Do you also know about fingerprints?' Jess retorted silkily. 'Yours, I presume, are now all over the place here?'

'What?' he gazed at her. 'Oh, yes, I suppose they are.'

'No "suppose" about it. Now, let's say, for the sake of argument, you wanted to confuse the police. You might come and leave some fingerprints here today to disguise any you might have made on previous visits.'

Toby ran his fingers through his hair, dishevelling it again. 'I've hardly ever been in here! I came once when it was brand new and empty, to see it, and once when I brought over the kitchen pots I told you about. I've been in Beijing, for crying out loud! I'd never even seen it fully furnished like it is now.' He gazed round him critically. 'I suppose this *is* fully furnished. It's not my style. It looks like a reception area in a posh block of offices. Look, all I meant to do was have a good look round and if there was anything iffy I'd have gone back and told Jeremy about it but I wouldn't, I repeat, *I would not* have removed it. You probably don't believe that but it's true. I'm between the devil and the deep blue sea over this. I didn't want to upset the police but I didn't want to argue with Jeremy in the state he's in.'

Jess stood up. 'You'd better show me what you've done and put things back as you found them.'

'I'd just begun,' Toby explained as they climbed the spiral stairs. 'I started up here and meant to work my way down. But up here was bad enough. I felt like some kind of grubby pervert, looking through her stuff. It's all perfectly ordinary. Lord knows what Jeremy thinks I might find. I'm beginning to wonder if grief has sent him a bit funny.'

On the mezzanine were twin beds, both neatly made up in matching bed linen. On one of them a well-worn teddy bear was propped surveying them with its one remaining glass eye. Jess frowned. 'You're sure Jenner didn't tell you what he thought you'd find?'

'He didn't tell me anything. I wish he had. It was bloody impossible, looking for something when I didn't know what it was. I looked in the drawers there.' He pointed. 'And I'd just opened the wardrobe when you called up. I nearly had a heart attack.'

'I didn't expect to find you, come to that,' Jess said drily.

'No, I suppose not. It's full of clothes and shoes and things. Nothing interesting.' He gestured towards the wardrobe.

Jess put her hand through the door and riffled through the rack of clothes. There were plenty of them all right, packed in tightly, something for every occasion. Fiona must have been shopping mad. Two or three business suits hung together. Did people who worked in television wear that sort of thing? Jess uttered a soundless whistle between her pursed lips. It was curious. Hardly any furniture in the place, yet masses of garments of all sorts, and shoes. Aware that Toby was watching her, Jess stooped and picked up a pair of low-heeled tangerine slip-ons. They looked new. She turned them over and saw on the instep the stamped impression giving the size, 5½. She replaced them and picked up a pair of ankle boots next to them. She turned them over. Size 6½.

Toby's sharp gaze had registered the puzzlement on her face. 'What's up?'

Jess retrieved the first pair of shoes and held both out to him so that he could read the sizes. 'What do you make of that?'

'Bought them on sale?' suggested Toby. 'Thought she could squeeze her size six and a half tootsies into a pair of size five and a halfs?'

'Unlikely. She might have varied by half a size between different designs of shoe, but I wouldn't have thought a whole size. What size did she take, did you know?'

'Search me.'

'If I've any reason to think you've removed any item, believe me, someone will.' Jess returned both pairs of shoes and picked up a third pair, then a fourth and fifth. 'They're all either one or the other of those two sizes.'

'So?' Toby folded his arms and leaned against the wardrobe, looking mutinous. 'What does that tell your trained brain?'

'First, it tells me you're sulking, which you're far too old to do. Second, it suggests to me that—'

From below came the sound of a key in the front-door lock and then the slam of the door. Footsteps crossed the wooden floor below and someone turned on the tap at the kitchen unit. They could hear water splashing into a kettle. They exchanged startled looks and, as one, moved to peer over the mezzanine rail.

A young woman in a trim charcoal grey pants suit was moving about in the kitchen area, getting out a mug and milk from the fridge. A briefcase lay on the kitchen counter.

'Making herself at home,' whispered Toby.

'That's what I was about to say,' Jess whispered back. 'Two different sizes of shoe suggests two different people—'

They had been heard. The girl below dropped a spoon into the sink with a clatter and whirled round, looking up. 'What – who the . . .?'

Jess scrabbled hastily for her ID and held it up over the balcony though it was unlikely the girl could make it out from down there. 'Police. Inspector Campbell.'

Still holding out the ID she hastened down the spiral stairs, Toby on her heels.

The girl was tall and slim and her dark hair was trimmed into a twenties-style bob. Freckles spattered her nose and high Slavic cheekbones. She snatched Jess's ID from her and glowered at it before returning it. She didn't, thank goodness, ask to see Toby's.

'It doesn't explain what the hell you're doing here. Why were you up in the bedroom? It's not a ruddy drugs bust, is it? Because, if it is, you're out of luck. Neither Fiona nor I do drugs.'

'May I ask who you are?' Jess retorted. She ignored the bit about the drugs bust. To have immediately leapt to this conclusion suggested this girl had been through that particular procedure somewhere before, but was sure there were no banned substances on these premises at the moment.

'I'm Tara Seale. I live here with Fi, with Fiona.'

'Oh,' said Jess. 'I'm sorry if I seem to have barged in. I didn't realize Miss Jenner shared the flat.'

'Well, you know it now,' was the ungracious reply. 'And you still haven't told me what you're doing here.'

Jess eyed her. There was surly defiance and suspicion but no grief, as yet, anyway. Tara didn't know what had happened. There was no way she could know, of course, unless someone from Overvale had contacted her. The death had made the local press in a couple of lines but, as yet, Jess didn't think it had reached the national papers.

'I'm afraid I have some bad news for you,' she said.

Tara Seale's gaze sharpened. She snapped, 'What sort of bad news?'

Belatedly, Jess remembered Toby Smythe behind her. She turned to him and said, 'I don't need you any more.'

'Right,' mumbled Toby and left.

Tara watched him go with something akin to contempt. 'Who's that? Don't tell me he's a copper. He didn't show any ID, you didn't introduce him as a colleague and he doesn't look like a policeman.'

I suppose, thought Jess crossly, I look like a policewoman! Well, so what if I do? That's what I am.

'He's Fiona's cousin, Toby Smythe.'

Tara's eyebrows twitched. 'I've heard about him. Fi told me.' She almost smiled.

Jess's antennae twitched. 'Told you what?'

'Oh, that he was showing signs of being smitten. She liked him very much, don't get me wrong. But she'd realized she was going to have to tell him about us.'

'You're Fiona Jenner's partner.' Jess said it as a statement, not a question. She remembered the pair of neatly made-up beds on the mezzanine and all those clothes and shoes crammed in the one wardrobe.

'Yes!' Tara replied impatiently. 'What's this bad news? Has something happened to Fi?'

'I'm really sorry,' Jess said gently. 'She's dead.'

As a police officer she'd been given all kinds of advice on breaking bad news, especially news of a death. But in the end there wasn't any other way of putting it, other than a bald statement.

She saw Tara's eyes widen in shock. The young woman swayed and Jess stepped forward hastily but Tara put out a hand to ward her off.

'I'm not going to faint! What do you mean, dead? Rubbish. She's going to be twenty-one next month. I'm organizing the party. There's nothing wrong with her. She couldn't just die!'

Denial, a common first reaction to the news.

'I'm afraid not. She died on Saturday.'

'This is crap,' said Tara, but with less conviction. Abruptly she sat down on the white leather sofa where Toby had sat earlier. Her complexion had drained of colour, leaving the freckles startlingly obvious. She was seated beneath the white painting with the black squiggles and, in her charcoal grey, she formed a grey, black and white unity with her surroundings.

'I'll get you a cup of tea,' Jess offered. 'You were just going to make one, weren't you?'

'Coffee,' muttered Tara. 'I don't drink tea.'

Jess went to the kitchen area and made a mug of coffee. Bringing it back, she glanced at the briefcase on the breakfast bar. Tara was sitting as she'd left her, staring at the floor with a pinched angry face. After denial would come fury, and Jess was going to have to bear the brunt of it.

'Here,' she handed the other woman the mug.

Tara took it without thanks. After taking a sip, she put it down on the floor by her feet. When she looked up her eyes sparkled fiercely. 'Was it an accident?'

'No. I'm sorry to have to tell you this is a murder investigation.'

'Somebody *killed* Fi?' Incredulity mixed with outrage. 'Who'd do that? When did this happen and where? Is it possible you've got this wrong? It's a wrong identification, it wasn't Fi—'

Jess shook her head, interrupting the flow of protestations. 'Her father identified the body. She died in the grounds of her family's house, while out jogging it seems, at around eight thirty on Saturday morning.'

'You mean someone got into the grounds? Was she raped?' Tara's ferocity increased.

'No. There was, as far as we know at the moment, no sexual motive.'

Tara asked in a low hoarse voice, 'How did she die?'

'She was stabbed. Yes, in the grounds somewhere, but we're not sure where. We believe her body was moved and placed in an ornamental lake where it was found.'

Tara sat for a few minutes absorbing this. Her expression was still fixed in angry disbelief but she seemed to be in control of her emotions. Jess nodded towards the briefcase on the breakfast bar. 'You've been to work today? You're home early or do you always come home for lunch?'

'I'm a financial journalist. I meant to work at home today. I went into the office to collect some documents, that's all. I need the article for tomorrow. I thought, as Fi was away . . . I thought, it would be a good opportunity to work undisturbed.'

'Fiona didn't work?'

'No. Not at the moment. She was talking about getting another job. She'd tried television but it hadn't worked out. She was interested in journalism, because of me. She was talking about doing a degree course. I told her, she'd do better trying to get back into television and learn the ropes there. I warned her, it's a tough world.' Tara shook her head as if to clear her brain of a mist. 'Fiona wasn't tough . . .' she mumbled. 'She took things to heart. I can't believe this. It doesn't seem real.' A tear trickled down her cheek and was angrily brushed away.

'How long have you been together?' Jess asked sympathetically.

'Five months living here. We've known each other longer.' Tara leaned back against the sofa's pneumatic leather upholstery. By her feet the cooling mug of coffee sent up a spiral of steam. 'I should have realized when I called her mobile on Saturday night and she didn't reply, not even to the message I left. I should have guessed something was wrong.' Tara narrowed her eyes, shining brightly with unshed tears, and asked suspiciously, 'He didn't do it, did he?'

'Who?' Jess asked, startled.

'That guy, Toby. Fiona thought he was getting round to pop the question. We had a bit of a laugh about it but we knew it was a serious situation. She was going to have to tell him and her family about us. Her father's a bit stuffy and her stepmother one of those clingy women who feel they've always got to be hanging on some guy's arm. She'd always meant to tell them, of course. But she was waiting to pick her moment. Toby complicated things by getting lovesick. She hadn't allowed for that. Perhaps she did tell him, Toby, and he flipped, you know, offended male ego. Some men are like that about lesbians. They see us as some kind of an insult to their virility.'

Jess digested this information. She'd had no idea Toby had had plans involving his cousin. 'We'll investigate all avenues,' she said.

'Investigate all avenues?' Tara jerked upright. Her foot struck the coffee mug and sent it spinning across the wooden floor, the contents spilling out in a dark puddle. 'Is that police-speak? You've got to do a bloody sight better than that! You've got to find him! You've got to find that bastard!' Without warning, she burst into a flood of wild tears and, with her arms wrapped round her body, began to rock to and fro, sobbing.

Jess left the flat and set out to walk back the way she'd come. It had taken a while to stem Tara Seale's grief and even longer to persuade her to let Jess go through Fiona's private papers and belongings. But once Jess had started, Tara became helpful. Her outburst of grief seemed to have cleared the air. In the end, however, nothing of significance had been found.

At a waterside wine bar, Jess noticed quite a few people sitting on an open area outside it, enjoying the spring sun. Several were eating. It was still lunchtime, she thought, and wondered whether to join them. Then she saw a figure sitting alone, hunched over a coffee. Oh dear, first she'd had to console one of Fiona's lovers, now she was going to have to console the other one.

She walked up to the table and asked, 'May I join you?'

Toby glanced up. 'Go ahead.'

Jess pulled out the chair and sat down. She waited.

'You must think,' Toby said, not looking at her, 'that I'm a complete fool.'

'No. I don't think you're a fool at all. I think you were daft to let Jeremy persuade you come here and go through the flat. But that's not the same thing. You know yourself it was daft.'

'I feel a fool,' said Toby fiercely, looking up now and straight at her. His face was flushed. 'I should have known, shouldn't? That she was a lesbian? But she didn't say. She didn't look it. She didn't act like it.'

'Mr Smythe,' Jess said, 'don't you think you might be in danger of assigning people to stereotypes here? What did Fiona have to do to qualify, in your mind, as looking or acting like a lesbian? Wear dungarees and big boots? Shave her head and go in for body-piercing?'

'All right, all right!' Toby said irritably. 'Point taken. I'm not that stupid. It's just that I thought I knew Fiona quite well and it's come as a surprise, a shock.' He eyed her. 'You're not one, too, are you?'

'Me? No, actually, I'm not. Not that it's any of your business or has any relevance here. Why? Do I qualify because I joined the police force?' Jess heard the sharp note in her own voice.

'You're not going to let me forget this, are you?' Toby said with an unexpected grin. Then the grin faded. 'Now I know what Jeremy wanted me to find out, why he sent me up here. The silly old devil, why didn't he warn me?'

'You think he knew?'

Toby considered the question before replying. 'I'm pretty sure she hadn't told him. I think he'd have told me or Alison would have done. It'd have been general knowledge in family circles, wouldn't it? I'm also sure he didn't know she was sharing the flat with anyone of either sex. I think, though, that he must have had his suspicions because Jeremy isn't a slouch at summing up people. Probably she'd never brought a boyfriend to meet him, never spoken of a boyfriend. She was a stunner, wasn't she? There ought to have been a horde of blokes trying to date her. It did cross my mind that it was curious she hadn't got someone in tow. But I didn't ask myself why. I just assumed she didn't want to talk about her love life. Why should she? Jeremy was smarter than I was. He must have asked himself what was going on. So he sent me to find out and I, prize idiot, obediently came along here and, well, I did find out, didn't I? And now I'm going to have to go back and tell him.'

'He'll be upset?' Jess asked.

'Of course he'll be upset. He's a traditional sort of bloke. But he's not the kind who'd have thrown her out of the house. He'd have accepted it if that was her choice. She should have told him.'

'According to Tara Seale she was going to.' Jess hesitated. 'She was going to tell both her father and you. Fiona had the idea, and told Tara, that you might be going to ask her to marry you.'

'Oh, right,' said Toby crossly. 'Everyone knows everything about everybody except me. I just blunder along in a world of my own.'

'I'm curious,' said Jess. 'Something must have given you the idea she'd accept you.'

Toby looked awkward. 'It wasn't a great romance, obviously, in view of what we now know! But even before I knew, I couldn't have kidded myself there was any real deep feeling between us, other than friendship. But it was a good friendship. We really enjoyed one another's company. I'm on my own. I thought that, living on her own, because I thought she *did* live on her own, she didn't have much of a life.'

Tell me about it, thought Jess ruefully. 'And she'd rather be married to you?'

'It makes me sound conceited, doesn't it?' he said. 'Not to say desperate. I can't explain it to you. I explained it to Meredith and she understood. Working in embassy circles, your social life is known to everyone. Everyone goes to the same parties. Everyone passes round the latest gossip. If you get romantically interested in someone, everyone knows and it pours cold water on any relationship. Perhaps I was lonely, and although I don't think I was, or am, desperate, I felt I ought to make some positive decision about finding a partner. Possibly I was conceited to think Fiona would marry me. After all, I'd never even kissed her. If I'd tried, she wouldn't have let me, I now know. She'd have explained about her preferences. I could have accepted that, but she didn't say a thing! If that Tara person is right and Fiona did guess I was going to suggest we get married, then she could have put me off, couldn't she?'

His manner changed. 'Hey!' he said sharply. 'Did you ask that woman, Tara, to account for her movements on Saturday? Perhaps she was jealous? Perhaps she thought Fiona had decided that lesbianism wasn't for her? Perhaps Tara followed her down to Overvale, waylaid her when she was out jogging and they had a row about me. Tara whatsit lost her temper, and stabbed her with – with something she'd got with her.'

'Funny you should suggest that,' said Jess. 'Tara thinks perhaps you were the jealous one and you did something like that.'

'Me?' howled Toby so loudly that people at a nearby table turned their heads in alarm. '*Me?*' repeated Toby in a stage whisper. 'Of course I didn't!'

'How do you account for Fiona being found in the lake?' Jess asked. 'I mean, if you think Tara went down there and killed Fiona in a fit of jealous rage, why did she put her in the lake?'

'Cover up. Make it look like a drowning, an accident.'

'Tara Seale is an intelligent woman and if she stabbed Fiona, she'd know that a post-mortem would discover it. Putting the body in the lake mimicked the way in which Freda Kemp died. That's just coincidence, you think?'

He paused again to consider his reply. 'It might be. Coincidences happen. On the other hand . . .' Toby hesitated again. 'Fiona might have told her about Alison's trial. Tara might have remembered and she decided to make it look like a copycat thing.'

'You think Fiona would have told Tara Seale about such a sensitive family matter?'

'They were partners,' said Toby simply, 'as we now know. Partners tell one another things about their families. Besides . . .' He paused yet again and looked embarrassed. 'To tell you the truth, Inspector, Fiona had a quirky sense of humour. She could be quite cruel.'

A waiter appeared at the table and Toby added, 'Look, let me buy you lunch. I'm really sorry about messing about in the flat without telling you I was going there.'

'I'll join you at lunch but I can't accept your kind offer. You're a—' Jess glanced briefly at the waiter. 'You'll understand why.' She picked up the menu card and scanned it. 'I'll have the Caesar salad.'

'Rabbit food,' muttered Toby. 'I'll have the hamburger.' When the waiter had departed, Toby asked, 'I'm a what? You were going to say I'm a suspect?'

'I was going to say you're a witness. The funny thing about witnesses in this case is how little they have to tell me. Apart from your family's peculiar sense of *omertà*, there was nothing in the flat and even Tara Seale hadn't much to tell me.'

Except, thought Jess, one thing of interest.

'Tell me,' she said to Toby. 'This last weekend, did you ever see Fiona use a mobile phone? Or notice one in her possession?'

Toby shook his head. 'Don't think so. I certainly didn't see her using one. I don't remember her carrying one or a phone sticking out of a pocket. Why?'

'Tara Seale tried to call her on her mobile phone. I didn't find one in your cousin's bedroom at Overvale House or in her bag. There certainly wasn't one on the—in her clothing.'

'She might have dropped it, then,' Toby said immediately. 'Either while she was jogging or, more likely, when she was attacked.' His face grew grim. 'She may have tried to call for help and the killer took it off her! In that case, he's got it!'

Toby leaned forward excitedly at the very moment the waiter placed Jess's salad on the table, and sent the plate skimming to the ground in a shower of green, yellow and gold.

When apologies had been exchanged all round, the salad replaced and Toby's hamburger had arrived, Toby's appetite appeared to have disappeared. He prodded the hamburger listlessly and asked, 'Are you going to tell Alan Markby I was in the flat?'

'Of course I am.'

'He already thinks I'm accident-prone. This will confirm it. Still, he has to know. I'd tell him myself if you didn't. I am sorry about it and I am sorry I knocked your salad off the table.' Toby paused and scowled thoughtfully into space. 'Perhaps I've got a clumsy gene.'

Jess struggled to suppress her laughter. 'I think you're inclined to overdramatize.'

'Meredith will tell me off, too. Have you met Meredith?'

'Mr Markby's fiancée? No, but I'm hoping to have a talk with her soon about your cousin. I want her impression of Fiona. It's difficult for me to feel I know her. That's because I didn't know her, I realize that. But the more I know about the victim, the better it is and, as I've already told you, no one seems very keen to tell me anything.'

'I'm not going to ask you why you became a police officer because you must be sick of people asking you that. But doesn't it ever get you down?' Toby asked curiously. 'You always see people at their worst. You know, the one thing I've always admired in Markby is that after all the years he's been doing the job he hasn't become cynical.'

'Well,' Jess said, 'I hope I don't become cynical.'

'How did your family react when you told them you were going to join the boys in blue?' Toby asked suddenly.

'My mother was bewildered. My father was worried. My brother laughed his head off.' Jess smiled at the memory.

'Is he an older brother or a younger one?'

'He's older by three minutes. Don't ask what it's like to be a twin, either, will you, please?'

'He's not a policeman, too, is he? I mean your brother. Or your father, come to that? Yours isn't a police family?'

'No, I'm the first one. Simon, my brother, works for a medical charity. He's overseas most of the time.'

Toby looked interested. 'Where is he based now?'

'In the Congo. But he's been home on leave just recently. You know, Mr Smythe, I'm the one who's supposed to ask the questions.'

'That means you're not going to answer any more,' Toby replied. 'You can ask me about myself if you want. But you probably don't want to. I wish I could tell you more about Fiona but right now I feel I knew as little about her as you do.'

'There is one thing you might be able to confirm,' Jess said. 'Can you cast your mind back to when you saw Fiona jogging away from the house on Saturday morning? Describe to me again exactly what you saw.'

Toby expelled breath in a long soundless whistle. 'I was in the bathroom and it had got steamed up, so I opened the window. There was Fiona, with her back to me, running away at a gentle jog-trot. I just saw her briefly because it was pretty chilly standing at the open window wearing nothing but a towel.'

'But you've no doubt it was Fiona? What was she wearing?'

'It was Fiona, no doubts about that at all. It couldn't have been Alison, could it? Because she's shorter and her hair's different.'

'Ah,' said Jess. 'Her hair. How did Fiona's hair look that morning?'

'I don't know what you're getting at,' Toby said in some exasperation. 'You're like old Jeremy. You don't tell people what you're thinking and yet you expect them to come up with the right answers!'

'I'm trying not to lead a witness,' Jess defended herself.

'Well, she had long blond hair. In the morning sun it looked very pale. She'd got it tied up in a ponytail.'

'You've got no doubt about that?' Jess stopped and turned to face him. 'Could you see the ribbon or whatever it was fastened the ponytail?'

'No. Not at that distance. Why, is it important?' Toby broke off and thumped one clenched fist into the palm of his other hand

and Jess prudently grabbed her plate. 'Of course it is,' he said enthusiastically. 'When we saw her down by the lake, her hair was loose.'

'Mrs Whittle saw her leave the house, too. She says Fiona's hair was tied back with a red satin scrunchy.'

'I remember that thing,' Toby said. 'Not on that morning but on other occasions. She used it to fix her hair back when she went riding. Now it's missing?'

'Now it's missing,' agreed Jess.

They rode the light railway back to Waterloo where they parted. 'I'll just go for a bit of a wander round,' Toby said. 'Clear my head. I'll probably walk up Concert Hall Approach and round the Festival Hall, over the Hungerford Bridge and pick up the Tube on the other side of the river.' He looked at her hopefully.

'I have to go straight back,' said Jess, not taking the bait. 'I'll pick up the Bakerloo line Tube here.'

Toby stood silently before her for a moment, his hair ruffled and his face set in despondent lines. 'When you tell Markby about this,' he said. 'He'll probably have a bloody good laugh.'

Toby was upset now but when he'd calmed down, he might want to continue his own investigations. Jess decided to put down a marker.

'Don't deceive yourself, Mr Smythe. When he hears all this, I expect the superintendent to be a very angry man. Laughter, I think, is going to be very far from his mind!'

Chapter Eight

'So, where's Alan?' James Holland asked. 'Making sure we can all sleep peacefully in our beds?'

'He's working, if that's what you mean. Would you believe it, he's been working all over Easter?' Meredith shook her head.

The vicar cleared his throat and said mildly, 'So have I.'

'Sorry, James. Yes, of course it's one of your extra-busy periods. But Alan and I were hoping for some time together. That Alan's working isn't by choice, of course, and, what makes it worse, I feel it's my fault.'

'Ah,' said the vicar, scratching his bushy black beard and fixing a quizzical eye on her.

'Originally, I asked him to talk to a friend of a friend, as a favour, but it sort of escalated. Serve me right.'

'Mighty oaks from little acorns grow. Would you like another cup of coffee?' When they both had mugs of coffee, James went on, 'It's a great pleasure to see you but I thought that on Tuesday after Easter the civil service managed to drag itself back to work?'

'I should be back at work. But I rang in and arranged to take the rest of the week off. It didn't make me popular but I explained that the police wanted to interview me at some point, I didn't know when.'

'They do?'

'Yes, Inspector Jessica Campbell is apparently keen to talk to me. I thought she might choose today but she's gone out of town.

Besides that, this friend I mentioned needs moral support. I felt I should be around.'

The vicar sipped his coffee and fell silent.

'James,' Meredith asked. 'What are you planning to do with all this?' She indicated their general surroundings.

They were sitting in the normally roomy kitchen of the vicarage, but today they were hemmed in on all sides by packing cases and stacks of newspaper. Every worktop and ledge was piled high with assorted pots, pans and crockery.

'I thought,' he said, 'I ought to start packing up my stuff so that I can move out and you two can move in with your paint pots. The new vicarage is ready for me.'

'Are you taking all this? Where will you put it? The new place is half the size of this one and its kitchen won't hold a tenth of this stuff.' She gazed round in disbelief. 'Where did you get it all?'

'I inherited it,' said James, looking slightly abashed. 'My predecessor died in harness here in this house. His personal effects were removed but no one cleared out his domestic possessions. I inherited the housekeeper, Mrs Harman, from him, too. She liked cooking with the pots she knew and so we left it at that. Just carried on. If you see anything you like, please feel free. Take your pick.' James picked up a blackened frying pan the base of which had become unaccountably rounded so that it wouldn't stand flat on any surface. He gazed at it thoughtfully.

'Thanks, and all that. But I don't think so.' Meredith lifted a teapot with a chipped spout. She took off the lid and peered inside. 'This hasn't been used in ages. It's got an old bus ticket in it.' She set it down. 'James, honestly, have you thought of just putting the lot in a jumble sale?'

'I might, eventually. Tell me, this police business that necessitated Alan working over Easter, it wouldn't be the death of Jeremy Jenner's daughter?'

'Yes. I feel really bad about it all. I mean, I feel very sorry for the Jenners and, of course, for the girl herself. But well, it's difficult to explain. In fact, I can't explain, it's confidential. It's a terrible thing to happen. At the moment no one has any idea why, that's what's so awful. Alan isn't actually at his desk. He's gone to see the Jenners. He asked me if I wanted to go with him but I said no. I wasn't copping out, exactly. OK, I was, to an extent. But Alan thinks Jeremy Jenner might say things to him he wouldn't say to other investigating officers.'

'I won't press you for details, naturally. I dare say the reason for her death will come to light eventually. Things have a way of working themselves to the surface. On a general note, ever since I came to Bamford, it's struck me that people hereabouts are adept at keeping secrets. On the surface, all looks calm, workaday, normal. But the stories I hear, you'd hardly credit.'

'Alan spends his time finding out about people's secrets, too.'

'Indeed. The astonishing thing,' James added in sudden earnestness, 'is how long memories are. Something happens today and the root of it goes back years. It's a sad fact that many people are what Robert Louis Stevenson described as "wonderful patient haters".'

Markby wasn't sorry to find, when he got to Overvale House, that Alison Jenner was out walking the dog. Jeremy, wearing old corduroy trousers and a disreputable sweater, received him with a kind of resigned civility. It told the visitor Jenner had had more than enough of police officers of all ranks and both sexes enquiring into his private affairs, but accepted it as an unpleasant necessity. Jenner, in his professional life, had learned leadership, self-command and how to keep a clear head in an emergency. It stood him in good stead now. Markby thought the man was like a once-great singer who can no longer quite make the difficult notes but who can rely on training and experience to carry him through a role.

'I'm still sure you should be looking for the blighter who wrote the letters,' he said.

'We are looking for him.'

'Don't play silly buggers,' Jeremy said irritably. 'You know I mean you should be looking at him for the murder of my daughter.'

'We have him in mind. But we'd be making a mistake if we closed our minds to the possibility of someone else being responsible.'

'Whoever killed her, first stabbed her. He knew she was dead!' Jeremy's eyes blazed with sudden fury. 'He didn't need to do anything else. Logically he ought to have left her where she was and got out of there before someone came along and spotted him. But he didn't do that. He took time to strike her on the head and dump her body in the lake. That was deliberately done to let us know he'd done it. How many people know about Freda Kemp's death? It has to be him.'

'I'm beginning to wonder,' Markby said. 'Just how many people *do* know about the death of Miss Kemp and Alison's trial.'

Jenner leaned back in the chintz-covered armchair. They were in the comfortable drawing room where Jess had spoken to the Jenners. The fire smouldered in the hearth despite the sunny day. Markby thought Jenner's complexion looked unhealthily grey.

'I know this is stressful,' he said carefully. 'I'd like to suggest that both you and Alison call your doctor if it gets too much.'

'I've got pills,' Jenner said testily. 'I'm not going to keel over, if that's what you think.' He made a gesture of waving aside some inconvenient object. 'I want this fellow found, Alan.'

'We're doing our very best. Inspector Campbell is in London visiting your daughter's flat today. I understand you weren't happy at the idea of your daughter's possessions being searched, but it might well turn up a clue.'

To his surprise, Jenner looked positively shifty. 'Harrumph!' he said. 'Quite so.' He got up and went to the fire. Seizing the poker from the companion set in the hearth, he rattled it energetically in the ashes before taking another log from a basket and adding it to the flames. When he stood up and turned back to Markby, the effort and the heat of the fire had reddened his pale complexion.

'Look here,' he said. 'If she's been poking round the flat today, there's something I ought to tell you.'

'Yes?' Markby raised his eyebrows. Mentally he had heaved a sigh of exasperation. It was not an unfamiliar situation. People in possession of information didn't yield it up until they had to. Even when keeping something back would hinder an investigation they wanted carried out as quickly as possible, they hugged their secret facts to their chests and watched the police struggle on without them. What had Jenner hoped would remain hidden but was now to be revealed?

'I asked Toby to pop up to London today and go there, to Fiona's flat.'

'May I ask why?' Markby's tone had hardened. He had sympathy for the Jenner family but not towards anyone who sought to confuse a police inquiry, even with the most innocent of motives.

'I want to tell you something in the strictest confidence, Alan.' Jenner paused, obviously awaiting confirmation that his information wouldn't be passed on. He didn't get it.

'I'm a police officer,' Markby said wearily. 'This is an investigation into murder.'

Jenner appeared all at once deflated. He sank back into the armchair. 'Stupid of me. You'll report everything, you have to. The thing is, I don't have facts. All I have is what may turn out to be a mere suspicion. My daughter was a very beautiful girl and a wealthy one. I had expected that, by now, young men would be queuing up wanting to marry her, or even, in the modern way, she'd have set up house with some chap. She never told me if anyone was hanging round. Of course, she's – she *was* quite entitled to keep such matters private. We have never been close, Fiona and I. I'm sorry about that but it couldn't be helped. She was brought up by her mother, largely in France.' Jenner rubbed his hands together nervously. 'I want you to understand, Alan. My intention was simply to protect my daughter's reputation. That's why I asked Toby to go to London today. I didn't actually tell him exactly why, which was probably unfair, but I thought, if it should all turn out to be my fevered imagination, it was better I didn't start a rumour.'

'A rumour of what?' Markby asked patiently.

'Some weeks ago, I was in London and I had the idea of calling on Fiona, just to see how she was getting on in the flat. I rang the number to let her know I'd be coming over and a young woman answered. I didn't say who I was. I just asked, was Miss Jenner there? She replied, "Fi's out. This is Tara. Do you want to leave a message?" I said I didn't and I made an excuse for the call. I said I was her bank, just routine. You know how banks ring up these days, wanting to sell you everything from home insurance to health plans. I didn't say anything to Fiona about it. But I began to think things over. She used to ring someone up on her mobile phone when she was here, and receive calls. She was always very secretive about them. There was the total absence of close men friends. I have to say, I was pleased that she seemed to get on so well with young Toby. But I'm afraid the idea had lodged itself in my brain that she preferred women. There, I've said it.'

'And you wanted to know for sure, so you sent Toby to the flat today, ahead of the police, as you hoped.' Markby shook his head. 'That was foolish. It's put Smythe in a difficult position.'

'It's my fault entirely,' Jenner said vehemently. 'Toby's a decent chap. He didn't want to let me down.'

'Well, then,' said Markby. 'Let's hope Inspector Campbell got there before he did.'

Markby left Overvale House and hesitated by his car for a moment. He was angry with Jeremy Jenner for withholding information and letting Jess Campbell go up to the London flat unprepared. He was even angrier that Jenner had sent Toby there and that Toby had agreed to go. If Toby got a bit of a shock when he got there, serve him right! Markby felt he wanted fresh air. He began to walk across the lawns in the direction of the lake.

146

It was deserted when he reached it. Signs of the police presence remained, strips of blue and white tape which lay trampled in the mud or still encircled the trees. He wondered that Stebbings hadn't removed it but perhaps Stebbings was avoiding the spot. Markby had found that there were two main reactions to a murder scene. Either people were drawn there by a dreadful fascination or they walked a mile out of their way to get round it. The corpse had long been removed but remained as an unseen presence, an unquiet spirit. Even now Markby felt as though he were being watched. He shrugged away the notion as fanciful.

The mini-tent which had been erected over the impression of the tyre tread had been taken away. It didn't look as if the tyre tread impression would be of any use to them. The divers had turned up nothing in the lake. They were looking in the wrong place. The girl's body had been dumped here. No, not dumped, he thought. Artistically arranged in the lake, according to Stebbings. They had only the gardener's word for it. No one else had seen her there. By the time the family arrived at the scene, the body was lying on the ground by the water's edge, dragged from the lake by Stebbings, and by the time the police had got there the body had been manhandled even more.

Markby sighed. This had not been how he'd planned to spend the Easter holiday with Meredith. Nor had Meredith planned all this disruption. It had just happened, as these things did. Only this time, of course, they had both been drawn into it by Toby Smythe's request. There had been a time, Markby recalled, when he'd occasionally felt a twinge of jealousy with regard to Toby Smythe. It had been groundless because, as he now knew, that wasn't the way Meredith felt about her FCO colleague. She liked the chap to a degree Markby couldn't understand. But that's as far as it went. She also appeared to be prepared to forgive Smythe any amount of difficulty he caused. Sometimes, Markby had wondered if some sort of latent maternal instinct prompted this. It was not something he'd ever had dared to suggest to her. But she did always seem to think she had to damn well look after him.

There was a further dimension to Markby's discontent. Now he'd reached senior enough rank, the inconveniences of his chosen calling ought not to intrude quite so often into what was supposed to be his private life. But they still did and still would. He was unhappily aware it had been one of the reasons behind the collapse of his first marriage. There had been other reasons why he and Rachel hadn't lasted but the constant interruption of official matters, disrupting their social life and leading to endless upsets on the home front, had been one of the first to make itself felt. Only too well, he remembered Rachel, her face puckering in disappointment, wailing, 'But I've *arranged . . .*' Disappointment had eventually turned to anger and then to resentment. 'Honestly, Alan, I think you do it *on purpose . . .*' That won't happen this time, he told himself. I'm not called out so often now they've stuck me behind a desk and, in any case, Meredith isn't like that.

He thrust aside these thoughts and instead studied the lakeside area. Even with the memory of death hanging over it, it was still beautiful. He cast his gaze across the surface, wondering where the murder weapon might have entered the water, if it had. The police divers hadn't found it, but it hadn't been an easy place to search. He could see where the rushes had been beaten down and the shrubs had clearly been disturbed. And they were being disturbed now. Out of the corner of his eye, he saw a distinct movement in the leaves. A bird, he thought, nesting in there. But then the leaves moved again and he caught a glimpse of some solid object. Not a bird but a person. While he had been looking at the lake, he himself had been watched. It hadn't been his imagination.

Markby began to stroll idly along the water's edge until he reached the bushes. Then he stopped and called out loudly and firmly, 'I'm a police officer. Come out at once.'

The bushes remained in place. It wasn't possible to hear another person holding his breath but Markby was distinctly aware that, in among the foliage, someone was doing just that.

'Don't be stupid,' he said wearily. 'I'm not going away. Either you come out or I come in and get you, it's your choice.'

At this there was an upheaval in the greenery, which parted; a slim dishevelled figure pushed his way out and stood before Markby, looking defiant and frightened in equal part.

'Darren Stebbings,' said Markby, 'if I remember rightly. What were you doing in there?'

'I didn't know who you were,' mumbled Darren. 'So I hid.' He was an unprepossessing youth, puny of build and fighting a losing battle with teenage acne. His features were small, his nose snub and lips thin. His ears, on the other hand, appeared a little too large. Odd fragments of leaf and twig drifted from about his person as he spoke and added to his elf-like appearance. He didn't strike Markby as particularly intelligent, either, and he was a rotten liar.

'You know who I am,' he said. 'You've seen me before, down here by the lake, the morning Fiona Jenner's body was found. You were holding a sack with that goose in it, the one that used to patrol down here.'

'I forgot what you looked like,' muttered Darren, scuffing his trainer shoe in the already disturbed earth. 'I forgot you were a copper. You might've been the murderer. I didn't know. I was scared.'

'Come off it, Darren. You knew perfectly well who I was and you were hiding for some other reason. What is it?'

Darren didn't reply. He fixed his gaze on the ground and stood before Markby in a hangdog attitude. Markby had met the type before. The boy didn't have the courage to own up but, perversely, his very fear gave him the strength to remain silent in the face of repeated questioning. He could ask Darren what he'd been up to over there until he was blue in the face. Darren wouldn't tell him. He'd have to find out.

Markby walked over to the bushes and pushed his way in. The spot where Darren had been secreted was easily identifiable by broken twigs. Markby parted the foliage and peered into it. Ah, there it was! He reached out and gently removed the little digital camera which Darren had thrust into the bush before emerging in response to Markby's demand.

He came back to Darren, the camera held up in his hand. 'What were you doing, come on, Darren. You were taking photographs? What of? The lake? Of me?'

'Of you,' Darren muttered sulkily.

'Why?'

'Practice,' said Darren.

Markby thought this over. What was it Fiona had said? Darren wanted to become a snapper of the stars? 'You were practising creeping up unobserved on your target and taking a photograph?'

'That's it,' said Darren. 'I'm going to make it my career. Photograph famous people when they're not looking and sell the pictures to the papers.'

Oh, yes, thought Markby grimly. I've definitely met your type! A little older than you are now and a great deal grubbier, hanging round like a vulture outside a courthouse, pushing your camera in front of the faces of the grief-stricken, not even the dying escaping the lens.

'Right,' he said. 'Now then, you tell me about other occasions you've done this, crept up on people.'

Darren looked even more sullen. 'I haven't done it often. I haven't had much chance. I took some pictures of Mrs Jenner when she was out walking the dog.'

'And what about Fiona Jenner, a young, beautiful girl? Don't tell me you didn't take any snaps of her.'

'I took some,' Darren admitted. 'But my dad tore them up. He took the memory card out of the camera as well. He doesn't understand.'

'But I do, Darren, believe you me. Tell me about the pictures of Fiona Jenner.'

'They weren't mucky!' said Darren suddenly with unexpected vigour. He looked up, his pinched features flushed. 'I didn't go creeping round looking in windows or anything like that. The ones Dad destroyed, they were taken down by the paddock when she was with the horses. She liked the horses. They're Mrs Jenner's horses but Fiona always rode them when she was here. I took some last summer, too, when she was in the swimming pool round the back of the house. They weren't bad but the ones with the horses were better and my dad just tore them up!' Resentment burned in Darren's voice.

'Hm, I think I'll have a word with your father. Where is he now?'

Darren looked nervous. 'You're going to tell him I was taking a picture of you?'

'I might. It depends. Where could I find him?'

'He's down at the copse,' said Darren reluctantly. He turned and pointed towards some trees about a quarter of a mile away. Markby could just make out a thin curl of smoke rising into the clear air. 'He's clearing it out. Here, you don't want me to go down there with you?'

'No,' said Markby to the boy's obvious relief. The relief was short-lived. Markby's next action was to slip the camera into his pocket.

'Oy!' yelped Darren. 'What are you doing? That's my property! You can't do that.'

'I can. I'm confiscating it. I have reason to believe you have been taking unauthorized pictures of a police investigation. Now clear off home.'

For a moment he thought Darren was going to throw himself at him and attempt to wrest the camera from him by force. Then his face crumpled and he looked more as if he was going to cry. 'I paid a lot of money for that,' he snivelled.

'I dare say you did. Don't worry, you'll get it back when all this is over.'

Markby walked away leaving Darren glowering after him. About halfway to the trees he stopped and took out the camera to check on the youth's photographic progress. There was quite a good picture of Markby gazing across the water like one of Arthur's knights waiting for a lily-white arm to appear from the depths. There were also two good ones of police activity around the lake's edge. Here was Jess Campbell, looking straight into the lens but completely unaware of it.

Markby let out a hiss of annoyance, thrust the camera back into his pocket and strode on towards the trees.

As he got nearer the copse he could smell the burning wood and hear the crackle of the flames. Showers of golden sparks flew up into the air. Mixed with the odour of dry debris being consumed by the flames was the more unpleasant one of damp or decaying matter. He could see the gaunt figure of Stebbings nearby. The man had taken off his jacket and rolled up his sleeves above his sinewy forearms. In his hand he held a sickle and was stooping to slash at undergrowth.He presented a strange, medieval figure such as might have been found in the margins of some illustrated Book of Hours. There was a dirt track running along the edge of the copse back towards the main drive up to the house. A ramshackle and ancient Land Rover was parked on it. It had clearly been kept out of doors in all weathers because moss was growing round the window frames.

The wood was a tangle of native trees. Beneath them, stretching into the shadows, Markby could see patches of bluebells and a carpet of white wood anemone. Peeping out here and there were the yellow faces of a few late primroses and celandine.

The woodland edge where Stebbings was busy was a tangle of dead and live brambles, seedling trees, woody nightshade, nettles, dock and grasses. The man worked methodically, the sickle swinging back and forth, reducing rampant nature to uneven stubble. As he worked the fire behind him consumed a pile of branches and dead wood as if in a mock auto-da-fé.

'Good morning!' called out Markby, as soon as he got near enough. He checked his wristwatch. 'I see it's not quite noon. Your son told me you were down here.'

Stebbings moved away from the edge of the wood and studied Markby from beneath his bushy eyebrows. The sickle dangled at the end of one long arm by his side. He didn't look friendly. 'What do you want me for, then? Your sergeant came and looked at my old Land Rover.'

'Nothing to do with that. Your son's interested in photography.'

Stebbings scowled and rubbed the grimy fingers of his free hand across his beard. 'He is. Waste of time, I keep telling him. What's it to you if he is?'

'I understand he took some photographs of Fiona Jenner which you destroyed.'

Stebbings looked surprised and then angry. His fingers tightened on the handle of the sickle. 'The stupid kid's not told you that?'

'Very wisely he owned up. Unwisely, you destroyed them. He says you tore them up. What did you do with the memory card?'

'I burned the lot,' Stebbings told him. 'I burned the bits of the photos and I burned the little card thing. It wasn't anything much, just pictures of the young lady petting the horses. But things having turned out the way they have, I thought it best you lot didn't know about them. So I got rid of them. I told Darren to say nothing.'

'I understand you wanted to protect your son,' Markby told him. 'But in the absence of the photographs I have only your word and his as to what they showed. I have confiscated his camera, by the way, as a matter of prudence, until this is over.'

'I should have taken it away from him,' growled Darren's father. 'I should have taken it away from him the day he brought the damn thing home. Pleased as punch he was with it. I told him it was a powerful lot of money for a dinky little gadget like a kid's toy. He reckons he can make a living at it one day. You reckon he can?' Stebbings posed this question unexpectedly.

Markby raised his eyebrows at being thrust into the position of careers adviser. 'I am afraid that your son has a definite talent. I don't doubt he will successfully misuse it one day.'

'Ah,' said Stebbings. 'Very likely the little bugger will, then, if you say so.'

The bonfire crackled and spat a few sparks.

'It's a lot of work for one man,' said Markby, nodding towards it.

'It is. All that stuff burning there is what I cleared in January when the winter storms brought down a couple of trees. But I didn't have the time to burn it before now. Too wet, anyway. Then Mr Jenner, he came down here and saw that the grass and brambles had spilled on to the path. He told me to cut it back. I told him, better to leave it until later. Birds might be nesting in some of it. Not that I've found any nests. Mr Jenner said he didn't give a damn about birds' nests, get it cleared. So I looked for Darren this morning to come down and give me a hand but he's skived off somewhere.' Stebbings gazed discontentedly at his work.

Markby nodded and then suddenly uttered an exclamation. He grabbed a long branch from the heap Stebbings had piled up ready to add to the flames, and thrust it into the bonfire. Watched by the astonished gardener, he pulled if out and held it towards the man. 'And what's this?'

'I dunno,' said Stebbings, peering at the end of the branch. 'What is it?'

'I'll tell you what I think it is,' Markby told him. 'I think it's Fiona Jenner's red hair band which she was seen wearing when she left the house on the day she died, but wasn't wearing when next seen by her family, dead by the lake. Perhaps you'd like to tell me why you're burning it?'

When Markby got to Regional HQ, with the red scrunchy in a plastic bag, he was waylaid by Ginny Holding with the news that Inspector Campbell was on the phone.

'I'll speak to her,' he said. 'Put her through to my desk.'

'Hello, sir,' came Jess's voice down the line. 'I'm calling in to say I'm making my way home. I had a couple of surprises at the flat. Mr Smythe was there when I arrived.'

'I've just come back from Overvale House. Jenner told me he'd sent Toby there. Had he done any damage?'

'He'd only just got there, I think. He apologized. Then we were both interrupted by the arrival of someone called Tara Seale who lives there with Fiona Jenner. Her partner, if you see what I mean, sir.'

'Ah, yes. Jenner told me about that, too. That is to say, he wasn't a hundred per cent certain of the situation but he had guessed Fiona hadn't told him something. Unfortunately, he hadn't forewarned Smythe, let alone you.'

'No, sir,' said Jess tetchily. Jeremy Jenner clearly wasn't her favourite person at the moment. She was also doubtless annoyed that both her pieces of information had failed to surprise the superintendent. 'I felt a bit of a fool but not as much as Mr Smythe did.' There was some satisfaction in Campbell's voice as she said this. 'I waved my ID at Tara Seale and got him out of there sharpish. Seale didn't know Fiona was dead. I'm sure about that. She wasn't acting.'

'Where's Smythe now?' Markby asked her.

'I don't know for sure, sir. He said he was going for a walk along by the Festival Hall. I think he's probably gone somewhere to drown his sorrows.'

'Well,' Markby said, 'things are certainly happening on all fronts. Fiona's red hair scrunchy has turned up.'

'Where?' He had to smile at her startled tone.

'Near a copse on Jenner's land. I was just in time to stop Stebbings burning it on his bonfire. We'll have to get a team down searching the wood. Oh, and his son had been snapping the police at work by the lake. He took a good picture of you.'

'*What?*'

Markby chuckled and put down the phone.

Chapter Nine

'What did Stebbings say?' asked Meredith, moving her head on Markby's shoulder so that she could look up at him.

'He said he hadn't noticed it. He'd been clearing out the undergrowth by the edge of the wood. It might have been in that, or it might have been on the ground where he built his fire. Or perhaps somewhere between the edge of the copse and the place where the bonfire was. It could have been caught up in branches as he dragged across the stuff to burn. After a long and, I might say, quite lively discussion about this, he decided it had probably been lying on the track which runs by the wood and got caught up in the rubbish as he dragged it across.'

They were reclining on the old sofa in Meredith's living room before a blank television screen. When Meredith and I move into our house together, Markby thought, the television is going into some sort of cabinet with doors, so it can be shut away. Why should the thing dominate the room even when no one is watching anything? It's like being always under the eye of a petulant elderly relative, demanding attention, emanating waves of reproach at being ignored.

Having arranged for the scrunchy to be sent for forensic examination and for a team to start combing the woods, Markby had informed everyone that he was now going out for a very late lunch. But as soon as he'd got in the car, he'd made up his mind to skip lunch and drop by Meredith's place instead. Jeremy Jenner, Toby Smythe, Jess Campbell, Harry Stebbings and young Darren, they all besieged his mind. He needed to distance himself from them for an hour or so. He wanted to get what they'd had to say into some kind of perspective. Perhaps talking to Meredith would help.

'You believe him, then? That he wasn't burning it on purpose?' Her voice, by his ear, sounded incredulous.

Well she might find the whole thing hard to believe. Markby shrugged, which was injudicious because it jolted her head. 'Sorry,' he said and bent his head to kiss the top of hers. 'I have no reason to disbelieve him.'

He sensed scepticism emanating from her and sighed. 'Look, if he'd wanted to destroy it, he'd have made a point of doing so before now and not kept it only to chuck it on a fire with a lot of other stuff. That's what he did with the photographs. He destroyed them at once. It's still a very important discovery. We've now seriously to consider that Fiona died there on that track. There were already indications she hadn't died at the lakeside. We've got people searching the woods now. They're looking for Fiona's mobile phone, among other things. If they find that we'd be pretty sure that is where she was attacked. So far, no luck. Stebbings swears he's found no mobile down there. He showed me his own battered old model, as if to prove he hadn't nicked Fiona's. He's a strange man. I fancy he chooses to work and live out in the country like that, on his own, because basically he doesn't like being with people. Being a loner doesn't make you a crook and I don't think Stebbings is of a criminal mind.'

But what is a criminal mind? he asked himself. When does being uncooperative, or thoughtless, or just plain stupid, turn into wilful obstruction? Stebbings didn't want the police at Overvale any more than his employer wanted them there. Jenner reluctantly accepted them because he wanted something from them: the identity of his daughter's killer and that of the writer of abusive letters to his wife. Stebbings, on the other hand, saw Fiona's death as no reason to welcome the police. They remained strangers on his patch, snoopers into private matters. Did most people see them like that?

Meredith's voice recalled him to his surroundings.

'So she died in or near the woods? It makes sense. Her killer wouldn't attack her out in the open where someone might see.'

'Yet look at the risk he took taking the body to the lake and spending time arranging it in the water.' It wasn't right. The actions contradicted one another. What kind of killer behaved so erratically? Or had he changed his mind? What had caused the change? Was there, after all, some macabre purpose in arranging the body as it had been found? Or was it found exactly so? Who found it? Stebbings. And Stebbings, by his own admission, had moved it, pulling Fiona from the water and attempting resuscitation.

Aloud he said carefully, 'There are alternative scenarios. Was she waylaid at the woods by someone who had driven down the track to that point and waited for her, knowing perhaps that she ran in the morning? Or was it a pre-arranged rendezvous? She knew her attacker and had agreed to meet him or her at a spot familiar to both of them. Does that mean they'd met there before? This time there was some kind of quarrel. Whoever it was stabbed her, put her body in his vehicle, drove back along to the track to where it joined the main drive, up the main drive a short way and then across the grass to the lake. Unfortunately for us, only when he got to the lake was the ground soft enough to take an impression of his tyres. There's been so little rain lately that everywhere else is rock hard. Even more unfortunately, Stebbings and his son pretty well obliterated the impression in chasing after Spike. The search team isn't only looking for the mobile in the woods; they're looking for a possible murder weapon.' Markby ended with some emotion, 'I just hope Stebbings hasn't found and zealously removed that!'

'Stebbings might not be a criminal, as you say,' Meredith observed. 'But he seems to have been a thorough nuisance and got rid of quite a bit of evidence, accidentally or on purpose, including his son's photos of Fiona.'

'There are people like Stebbings in every walk of life,' Markby returned gloomily. 'As if things aren't complicated enough, they seem to go out of their way to make them worse. Incidentally, your chum Toby is perilously near being in that category, too!'

Meredith sighed. 'He didn't mean any harm. All right, all right! He shouldn't have gone to Fiona's flat. It was so stupid of Jeremy Jenner not to have told Inspector Campbell that he suspected his daughter had a partner living at the flat. It was inexcusable not to tell Toby and to persuade poor Toby to go up there. I don't know what Toby was meant to do. Just look around and come back and confirm Jeremy's suspicions, or not, as the case might be. If Toby didn't find anything, Jeremy would have kept quiet about his guess that Fiona had a partner. What a mess. It's a good job your Inspector Campbell found him pretty quick before he turned everything upside down and was caught red-handed by Tara Seale! At least Campbell could wave her ID at Ms Seale and give Toby a chance to get out of there.'

'It was a good job he was caught by Campbell for his own sake and ours, never mind Tara Seale. It's only because Jess turned up before he started turning out cupboards and drawers that he's not facing a charge of obstructing our inquiries! Campbell wants to talk to you tomorrow morning by the way,' Markby added, as if by an afterthought. 'She'd like your impression of Fiona. She's interested that you think Fiona might have written the poison pen letters. You're still taking the rest of the week off?'

'Yes.' She sighed. 'Obviously Toby's not safe left unsupervised. Perhaps I can keep an eye on him.'

'Hey, you are not his keeper! He's a grown man. A grown man with very little common sense, but still old enough not to have to keep hold of nurse!' Markby couldn't help sounding annoyed.

'I'm not nursemaiding him,' she retorted defensively, just a little too defensively, he thought. 'I just want to be around so he can come and talk things over with me. He's been knocked sideways by all this. He'd never have agreed to oblige Jeremy by going up to the flat in London, if he'd been thinking straight. Poor Toby, he must be feeling really low.'

After a moment, Markby said, 'You feel you need to watch out for Toby. I'm watching out for Jeremy Jenner who, like Smythe, seems to have left common sense behind somewhere. What a family. It must be genetic.'

'I suppose,' Meredith defended the Jenners, 'that at a time like this, they can't be expected to think reasonably.' She reached up and touched his face. 'Like you, I had hoped we'd get some time together over the Easter break and the way things have turned out we've hardly had any. That's partly my fault. I agreed to talk you to about Toby's cousin's wife and her problem and let us in for going to lunch there.'

'It's just sod's law,' said Markby, catching her fingers and kissing them. 'What did you do this morning?'

'I went to the vicarage and found poor James Holland up to his eyes in packing cases and newspaper. He's decided to start clearing out ahead of his removal. The new vicarage is ready and he can move in. That means we can start early on renovating the present vicarage. I long to get my hands on that kitchen. It will all have to be torn out and everything done new. There's loads of space. There's also a Victorian kitchen range. At least Mrs Harmer didn't use that, but she did use the gas cooker which is a sixties model and I doubt that it's now safe. Honestly, Alan, you never saw so much junk. He's got to get rid of it all. I advised him to just put it all in a special jumble sale.'

'Be careful. Sometimes quite valuable items get thrown away in the rush to clear out!'

'Not this time,' said Meredith firmly. 'I know junk when I see it. James will never be able to put it all in the new vicarage. I stayed for an hour and helped him wrap up some of it and put it in boxes. I went outside and walked round the garden. It's a bit of jungle but it could be made really nice. I've been thinking again about that garden furniture those two guys make. I thought, while

I'm home, I'll go down and ask them to make some for us, like Alison's only a little simpler.'

At this point Markby's stomach gave an aggressive rumble announcing it felt it had been empty long enough. Meredith sat up with a start.

'Oh, poor Alan! Haven't you eaten? Why didn't you say? I could at least have made you a sandwich! Let me make you one now.'

'No, no,' he said. 'Don't bother. My fault entirely. I should have picked up something on my way over here.'

'Don't be noble, please,' she pleaded. 'This doesn't say much for my domestic skills, does it?' Her expression of dismay was quite comical.

Markby grinned at her. 'Funnily enough, I'm not marrying you for your domestic skills. If I wanted a cook-housekeeper, I'd find someone like Mrs Harman.'

'You wouldn't want a Mrs Harman. I don't know how poor James survived all that time under her regime. She boiled all the green vegetables for fifteen minutes by the clock and made him a milk pudding every day.'

'I survived for seven years at boarding school on a diet like that,' he reminisced. 'Look, I know what we'll do. We'll walk up to the Crown. They do an all-day breakfast. I'll have that and you can have a cup of tea or whatever you fancy.'

'The Crown?' Meredith asked. 'It's grim.'

'Isn't it under new management? I don't care if it's grim. It can fry up bacon and eggs. I know it's not the sort of place I'd normally invite you to join me at, but we're midway between lunch and dinner now and everywhere decent isn't serving.'

The Crown was an old hotel in the town's centre. The occasional tourist strayed into it but mostly it catered for travelling reps and people who found themselves unexpectedly stranded in the town overnight. They didn't ask questions at the Crown. They signed in whoever turned up and then pretty well left guests to their own devices. The bar was usually busy in the evenings with trade which came in off the street. The restaurant had always been a dark, half-deserted room presided over by an elderly waitress. Diners settled the bill at reception on the way out, if they weren't staying there, or on leaving, if they were.

Markby had more than a passing acquaintance with the Crown because it was here that the police had from time to time lodged witnesses or temporary staff. He was therefore greeted as an old friend by the receptionist, a chirpy young woman in a tight black sweater.

'Hello,' she said. 'You again, then, Superintendent?' She treated Meredith to a rapid up-and-down assessment. 'You want us to put this lady up?'

'Er, no,' he said. 'We just dropped in for something to eat. The restaurant's open?'

'It's always open,' she said cheerfully. 'But it depends what you want. Three-course meal is from six o'clock. Chef's got some haddock.'

'Nothing like that. Just a snack.'

'That's all right, then,' she said, waving them through to the dining room with a flash of her gold-painted nails.

'Hey,' said Meredith, as they took their seats in an otherwise untenanted restaurant. 'How many women do you lodge in here?'

'You'd be surprised! Hello, Florrie.'

'Nice to see you, Mr Markby,' said Florrie, who had come plodding across the room to their table, notebook in hand. 'You want the all-day breakfast again?'

'I don't,' said Meredith hastily. 'I'll just have a cup of tea.'

Florrie dismissed her with a glance and concentrated on Markby. 'Bacon, two eggs, black pudding and fried bread?'

'Alan,' said Meredith when Florrie had taken her bunions off to the kitchen with the order. 'You come in here regularly!'

'Quite often,' he admitted.

'And you always eat that fry-up? It's a heart attack on a plate, you do realize that?'

'I don't care,' he said mutinously. 'I like it. Anyway, I only eat it here.' And in the police canteen, but there was no need to tell Meredith that.

'By the way,' Meredith said. 'Being in here reminds me of the Feathers and that reminds me of something I meant to mention to you. Dolores Forbes, you remember her?'

'How could I forget her? Once seen, never forgotten, our Dolores!'

'She told Toby and me that Fiona had been in the pub one evening.'

He looked startled. 'Fiona? In the Feathers? What was she doing, slumming?'

'Both Toby and I were taken aback. It couldn't have been her sort of place. Dolores thought she must have been with someone but didn't notice any one person who seemed to be her companion. But the place was full.'

'How often is the Feathers full?' Markby asked drily. 'When was this? Recently?'

'I didn't ask. But it was the night of a darts match so it ought to be possible to find out the exact date from Dolores.'

The tea arrived in a large brown earthenware pot accompanied by milk in a chipped jug and two cups with mismatched saucers.

'If they want any more crockery like this, James has got stacks of it,' Meredith observed waspishly. Also on the tray was another object which Florrie set down on the table before departing.

Meredith picked it up and gazed at it in wonder. 'Do you realise this must be the last place in the country to serve ketchup in a red plastic tomato? I never thought I'd say it but the Crown makes the Feathers look almost normal. I thought you said this place was under new management?'

'So I was told. I hope they don't do away with the all-day breakfast.'

The meal in question arrived at that point and was set before Markby with a flourish. He picked up the plastic tomato.

'Alan,' said Meredith in a strangled voice, 'if you're going to squeeze that all over your plate, I'm going to the ladies.'

'Don't forget your tea,' he said cheerfully.

The ladies' room at the Crown was clean but the hand-dryer was broken and, of the two cubicles, only one could be locked. When Meredith re-emerged into the reception area, she found it was occupied by a new arrival. She was engaged in a spirited exchange with the receptionist.

At first glance, a casual passer-by would have thought a young girl was checking in. The female figure was out-proportioned by her large suitcase. But then, perhaps aware of Meredith's scrutiny, she turned her head and revealed herself to be a woman in her forties.

She was the sort of person one couldn't ignore. Despite possessing the dimensions of a thirteen-year-old, she had an air of a woman of the world, a disconcerting combination. She wore baggy pants and a figure-hugging top but her most striking feature was her hair, or rather her lack of it. It was clipped short in a crew-cut, almost shaven, the resultant fair bristles covering her well-shaped skull. She was, however, carefully made up and wore large hooped earrings. The overall effect was a blend of artistic and chic and was carried off with formidable poise.

The woman assessed Meredith briefly and dismissed her as of no interest. She turned away to address the receptionist in a slightly irritated tone. 'I am Madame Plassy. Madame Chantal Plassy. I telephoned you to reserve a room.' Her accent was faint but unmistakable, even so.

'That's right, Mrs Plassy!' said the receptionist, unhooking a large key. 'Number seven, top of the stairs. It's got an en suite shower.'

'I asked for a bath,' Chantal protested.

In vain. 'We don't do baths en suite,' said the receptionist. 'There's a bathroom on the landing, though.'

'There is at least someone who can take my case upstairs?'

'I'll get Mickey out of the bar. You just leave it there,' she was told.

Chantal turned aside and Meredith stepped in front of her. 'Excuse me,' she said. 'I'm sorry to accost you like this, but you're not Fiona Jenner's mother, by any chance?'

This gained her a sharp look and another, this time much closer, assessment. 'Yes, and so? Who are you?'

'My name is Meredith Mitchell. I'm just having a cup of tea here with my fiancé, Alan Markby. He's the superintendent in charge of investigating your daughter's – um – unfortunate death.'

Finely plucked eyebrows twitched. 'I was not aware my daughter had had an unfortunate death. I understand she was murdered. I think that's rather worse than just bad luck, don't you?' Without giving Meredith a chance to recover, she went on, 'Where is this Markby? Take me to him!'

Markby had fortunately just about finished his all-day breakfast when Meredith reappeared with Chantal. Introductions and explanations were made and Chantal joined them at their table. Meredith was already wondering whether she'd acted wisely in intercepting Fiona's mother. Closer observation showed the lines of stress beneath the make-up and, together with some expensive perfume, there emanated from Chantal an aggressive electricity fuelled by suppressed rage. She was bereaved, she was shocked, and, above all, vengeful. She wanted someone's scalp. It was like being in the company of an unexploded bomb.

Florrie made her majestic way to them and removed Markby's plate. 'Can I get you something, madam?'

Chantal pointed a beautifully manicured index finger at her. 'The coffee, is it from a jar?'

'We can do it from a jar if you want it from a jar,' said Florrie helpfully.

'Of course I do not want it from a jar! You don't have real, proper coffee?'

'We've got a machine does it, if that's what you mean,' said Florrie.

'Then I would like black coffee.'

'I'm very sorry about the death of your daughter,' Markby said to her when Florrie had gone. 'Meredith and I did meet her, just the once, at lunch.'

Chantal assessed him coolly, taking her time. 'You have established the cause of death?'

'Yes. She was stabbed.'

Chantal's neat fingernails rapped a tattoo on the table as if the pent-up energy in her must find some outlet. 'Jeremy didn't tell me this. He phoned me to tell me she had been killed, murdered in the grounds of the house while jogging. He said her head was injured and she had been thrown into a lake. That is typical of Jeremy. Instead of giving bad news all in one piece, he chops it up and delivers it bit by bit, as if that could make it any better!' Bitterness filled her voice and perhaps the memories of past occasions and old disputes. She leaned back in her chair to think over the new information. Her eyes glowed as if it had fed new power to her inner rage.

Impulsively, Meredith asked, 'Does Jeremy know you're here?'

'I saw him this morning,' Markby added. 'He didn't mention he expected you in Bamford.' But then, Jeremy being Jeremy, he probably wouldn't.

'He knew I was coming, of course!' she retorted sharply. 'I told him at once I would come. He invited me to stay at Overvale House, but I refused. It's not, I think, *bon ton*, to stay under the same roof with your successor, one husband and two wives, like a harem. Besides, Fiona told me his present wife is very dull.'

'You've resumed your maiden name?' Markby asked her.

The fine eyebrows twitched again. 'No, I am remarried. My husband couldn't come with me to England. He has business matters in Switzerland where we live. Besides,' (an elegant shrug) 'he didn't know Fiona.'

Florrie brought the coffee. Chantal eyed it dubiously.

'When were you last in touch with your daughter?' Meredith fancied she heard a certain sharpness in Markby's voice.

'I saw her in London in January. I came over for the sales. I didn't buy anything. The London sales are not what they were. I spoke with her on the phone two or three times after that.' Her tone and manner indicated that her relationship with her daughter was not Markby's business.

'Then you perhaps met Tara Seale?' Markby asked.

Chantal gave a dismissive nod. 'Yes, I met her. I liked her. She was intelligent and chic. You obviously know about their relationship and you are going to ask me how I felt about it. It didn't worry me, if that is what you want to know. *Au contraire*, I was pleased Fiona had found someone. At that time she hadn't told her father about Tara. I advised her to do so. It wouldn't be easy because Jeremy is so stuffy. But he had to be told. She said she would. I don't know if she did.'

'But you haven't mentioned the existence of Ms Seale to Jeremy at any time since then?'

Chantal's eyes widened. 'Why should I? It was not my job to tell him. It was Fiona's. Anyway, I am not normally in touch with my ex-husband. When he phoned me to tell me Fiona had died it was the first time we'd spoken in two years.'

There was a momentary pause and for the first time an expression of sadness touched her face. For the loss of her daughter? For the break-up of her marriage? For both? They were not to know. The emotion was wiped away. She became brisk again.

'Now, let me ask you a question. What are you doing about this?' Her tone brooked no nonsense.

'Pursuing investigations. We don't yet know why your daughter died but we think we know where. Not by the lake where she was found, some distance off near some woods.'

'What about the weapon? Have you found it?'

'Not yet,' he admitted.

'So, why aren't you out there looking for it? Why are you sitting here drinking tea and–' Chantal sniffed the air delicately – 'eating fried food? The smell of the English breakfast is unmistakable.

Why are you eating it at four o'clock in the afternoon? I never understand the English.'

She picked up her cup and sipped, grimaced and put the cup down again. 'Or their terrible coffee.' She studied her surroundings. 'I think I will phone Jeremy and accept his kind offer to stay at Overvale, after all.'

'I would like,' said Meredith as they left the Crown, 'to be a fly on the wall when Chantal arrives at Overvale with her luggage and tells them she's changed her mind about staying there.'

'I, on the other hand, wouldn't,' Markby returned with feeling. 'That woman is a loose cannon. The less I see of her the better! Campbell can deal with her.' He frowned. 'You know, Chantal made a shrewd remark about her former husband. She said he parcelled up bad news and let it out bit by bit. He does that with all information.'

'Boardroom skills,' said Meredith. 'Keep something up your sleeve. Fox the opposition.'

'The trouble is, the police are not the opposition. We are supposed to be on his side . . . and he's supposed to be on ours! But it makes me think that if Jenner really has something he doesn't want us to know, it'll be the very devil prising it out of him.' Markby heaved a sigh. 'Where are we going now?'

'It's getting a bit late. Why don't we walk on down to the Watersmeet estate and take another look at Rusticity?'

They began to walk through the centre of the town towards the outskirts. 'What about the poison pen letters?' Meredith asked. 'Has any progress been made with those?'

'No. That's getting more complicated by the hour,' he grumbled. 'For someone who has no enemies – according to Toby – Alison Jenner appears to be unpopular with quite a few people.'

The trading estate was jammed with cars and visitors. Families struggled through the throng with wailing infants in buggies. Customers from the garden centre staggered back to their vehicles laden with greenery. One optimist was balancing a stepladder over his shoulder and carried a giant tin of paint in his other hand.

'It's still the Easter break,' Meredith said, 'and the great British public does what it likes best – shopping for DIY or home improvements.'

'This is horrible,' he replied in awe. 'Thank goodness we didn't bring the car. We'd never have got in – or out again.'

Rusticity, like the other outlets, was packed. Nevertheless they were spotted and hailed by Ted who appeared from behind a gaggle of elderly ladies. His snub-nosed face bore a broad grin. He looked as if he was having the time of his life.

'Hello, there, Miss Mitchell! Got Mr Markby with you today, I see?' There was something incredibly suggestive in the way he said this.

'Yes, we've come to take another look at the table and chairs.'

'Help yourself,' said Ted. 'Let me know if you want any information. I'm back there in the office.' He pointed towards the building behind them. 'See you later.' With this, he vanished into the throng but not before directing a final grotesque wink of complicity at Meredith from what Ted supposed to be behind Markby's back.

'What's the matter with him?' asked the bemused Markby, who had turned round just in time to catch the tail end of the wink. 'Why is he grimacing like that?'

'He saw me at the Feathers with Toby. He thinks I'm two-timing you. So does Dolores.'

'Hussy!' he declared dramatically.

'Will you ever forgive me?' Meredith placed a hand on her bosom. 'I hope Ted isn't going to behave like that every time I see him. I shall buy my garden chairs elsewhere!'

One of the elderly ladies cannoned into Markby with her walking stick.

'Let's go home,' Markby pleaded. 'We can come and look at his chairs another time.'

They went home.

⋆　⋆　⋆

Cherry Basset had been told by her mother that she'd been named after Mrs Basset's grandmother. Cherry didn't think that a good enough reason. She was sixteen and, at that age, anything one's parents think is nice is automatically the pits. Cherry's father had played no part in deciding on his daughter's name. Six weeks before she was born, he had announced one evening that he was going down to the corner shop for a packet of smokes, left the house and never returned.

Mrs Basset had taken his departure philosophically. 'He never could take responsibility, your dad,' as she'd later explained to his abandoned daughter.

In due course, Mr Basset's place in the household was taken by someone called Uncle Gary, although as far as Cherry had ever been able to ascertain he wasn't any kind of relative. She described him to anyone who asked as 'Mum's friend'. Uncle Gary had been there so long now that everyone took it for granted he was part of the ménage. From time to time Mrs Basset would confide to a neighbour, 'If I knew where my husband was, I could get a divorce, and Gary and me could make it legal.'

But Mr Basset had not divulged his whereabouts. Mrs Basset hadn't looked for him, perhaps disinclined to find him. As for Uncle Gary, he hadn't shown any interest in 'making it legal', so things just went on as they were.

None of this worried Cherry much. True, there had been that incident about a year earlier when Uncle Gary, ever one for the inappropriate squeeze in a dark corner or a doorway, had made a suggestion, immediately rejected with contempt by Cherry.

'No, I won't, you dirty old man! What do you think I am? And if I was going to do it, I wouldn't do it with a bald-headed old geezer like you!'

After this Uncle Gary wisely kept his hands and his suggestions to himself. Mrs Basset knew nothing of this episode and Cherry had almost forgotten it. Her one concern was the burden she laboured under – her name. But recently she'd made a decision. She had learned from perusing the front pages of the tabloid press that the name of the wife of the current prime minister was Cherie. It should be said that Cherry wasn't a great reader of the newspapers or, indeed, of anything else. But she worked in a local newsagent's and so saw the press, or at least the front pages, in the line of business. She had been struck by the similarity of spelling to her own name and remarked upon it to her employer. He had reliably informed her that '*chérie*' meant 'darling' in French. Cherry found that really cool and decided to modify her own name forthwith. It had to be better to have the same name as a prime minister's wife than that of a flavour of yoghurt.

'Why not call me "apple" or "pear"?' she demanded of Darren Stebbings.

Darren was Cherry's boyfriend. They had been drawn together by a shared sense of injustice, Cherry at her name and Darren at his father's lack of understanding for his son's ambitions.

'Me mum's not so bad,' said Darren, ignoring Cherry's question which was, after all, unanswerable. 'She doesn't understand but she doesn't grumble. It's Dad. It's like talking to a blooming brick wall.'

'My mum don't understand. I told her, I said, I want to spell it C-H-E-R-I-E. She said, why can't you spell it like you've always done?'

'He took it off me,' said Darren passionately. 'Just like that. He had no right!'

The burning resentment and heartfelt injustice permeated through Cherry-Cherie's self-absorption. 'He took what?'

'My camera! I've been telling you. Haven't you been listening?'

'Yeah . . .' said Cherry-Cherie doubtfully. 'Your dad took it?'

'No! That bloody copper! He had no right. It took me a year to earn the money for that camera, working Saturdays down at the Watersmeet estate, carrying stuff out to people's cars.'

'Well, you can do that again, earn some more,' said Cherry-Cherie with simple logic.

'He said he'd give it back, but you can't trust coppers. I'm not carrying stuff out to cars for another year. I don't have to, I reckon.' A look of cunning crossed Darren's face.

Cherry-Cherie was intrigued. 'Go on.'

'They're not as clever as they reckon. They're like all old people. They don't know nothing about modern technology.'

'What do you mean?' Cherry-Cherie frowned and chewed the end of one lock of dishevelled blond hair.

'I reckon,' said Darren, 'I've got a way of making some money real quick. Just you wait and see.'

His companion, her interest already waning, said, 'All right, then. I will.'

Chapter Ten

Now that she had her end-of-terrace cottage in Station Road on the market, Meredith's housekeeping skills were being sorely tested. She had taken to watching those TV programmes which advised would-be house-sellers of the things possible buyers looked out for and the things they particularly didn't like. Tidiness was very much liked. Fresh flowers in the house were strongly recommended, along with bowls of fruit in the kitchen. Tidiness, she had realized, was very much a question of habit. Keeping the fruit bowl filled was more of a problem. As soon as she'd got a display worthy of a still life, she ate it. The flowers Alan had given her on Easter Sunday still stood resplendent on a table by the window, the early sunlight falling on yellow and pink roses, red-tipped apricot-coloured carnations and purple iris. She checked they still had sufficient water this morning and that it hadn't gone green, and looked round the room with the mild surprise of one who couldn't quite believe she had managed this unusually high standard of Home Management.

The first person through the door this morning, however, was Jess Campbell who turned up promptly at ten. Meredith made them both coffee and they retired to the shining and neat sitting room and settled down.

'This is a nice place,' said Jess, looking round her.

'I think so. It's got two bedrooms. Originally it had three but one had to be converted into a bathroom. When the house was built, bathrooms didn't exist. I suppose they sat in a tub of water in front of the fire downstairs. There's not much garden but that's suited me. I don't have time to garden. I had a new kitchen put in and a new bathroom when I bought it, and I also had that porch built on the front. I think it ought to suit a young couple without children or a single person, like me. I know that years ago people raised large families in houses like this, but times have changed, I recognize that. You won't know the old Bamford vicarage in the middle of town, the one Alan and I are buying?'

Jess shook her head.

'It must be three times the size of this, and it does worry me a little, I admit, that we might have gone over the top. It's in a run-down state; everything needs doing up and will take us ages. But Alan and I both liked the place. Alan particularly likes the garden. That's in a state, too, but he's keen to get going at recreating it. Where are you living?'

Jess told her. 'I'm only renting, of course. I'd like to buy. The rented flat is pretty grotty.' She sighed. 'Oh, well, I suppose I ought to get on with what I came here for. The superintendent suggested I talk to you. He said you were observant.'

'Did he?' Meredith sounded surprised 'I'm interested in people. Perhaps that makes me look at them and listen to them.'

Jess had taken a small tape recorder from her capacious beige leather bag and put it on the coffee table among the cups. 'You don't mind if I record our talk? Or I can take handwritten notes, if you prefer. I'd prefer the tape because it saves me time in the long run.'

'I don't mind the tape.' Meredith watched as Jess set it running and spoke the date and time into it. Against the background of its soft whirr Meredith went on, 'Alan did say you wanted to ask about Fiona Jenner. But I only met her once and in the rather artificial circumstances of a lunch party. It was rather an odd gathering, not a proper social one. More like a working lunch. We were there to hear about the poison pen letters Alison Jenner had been receiving. Fiona said little, but as we were leaving she was waiting for us by the gates and flagged down our car. She seemed keen to ask what Alan was going to do about it. I got the impression there was some resentment towards Alison and possibly also towards her father. I might have got a better impression of Fiona if I'd talked to her just one-to-one on general subjects, got to learn her views, her likes and dislikes. But she wanted to talk to Alan, not to me, and the conversation centred round Alison and Jeremy Jenner. Earlier at the house, as I said, she took little part in things. I took a good look at her when I met her, because we hadn't been told she'd be there, but I was really concentrating on Alison.'

'And what was your impression of Mrs Jenner?'

'She was very nervous. That's understandable. She seemed a nice person and deeply grateful to her husband because he'd never referred to the trial during their marriage. I thought, well, he wouldn't, would he? He was the last person who'd want it made public knowledge. He had been a public figure himself in the business world. He's retired now but I dare say his name is still widely known and respected. I can't say I really took a shine to him. I thought him pompous and a snob. But he was worried about his wife, so . . .' Meredith shrugged. 'Perhaps he was just being protective.'

'Did Fiona have nothing to say at all?'

'Hasn't Alan told you? She asked him about identifying the typeface the letters were printed in.' Meredith hesitated. 'I did suggest to him afterwards that Fiona might have written the letters, or at least knew who did.'

Jess smiled. 'Yes, he did say that. What made you think so? Just because you sensed something you called resentment on Fiona's part towards her father and stepmother?'

'To tell you the truth,' Meredith confessed. 'I was casting about for a suspect. The weak point of my theory is that Alison didn't tell Fiona about the trial until after she'd received several letters. The person who wrote the letters knew about the trial and that seems to rule Fiona out. When I said I sensed some resentment, I must stress there wasn't any overt antagonism between Fiona and her stepmother, not in front of strangers, anyway. That's what I mean about a lunch party being an artificial sort of stage for people to play out roles on. Good host, good hostess, polite daughter . . . well, she wasn't *that* polite. She suggested that, back in the days of the investigation into Freda's death, the Cornish police had been keen to stitch Alison up, to use Fiona's phrase for it. She was a bit spiky, perhaps even a little arrogant in her manner. I did wonder about the circumstances in which Jeremy and Fiona's mother had parted company. By the way, have you met Chantal Plassy?'

'Fiona's mother? Not yet. I hope to interview her later today. I believe she's planning to stay at Overvale House.'

'She was going to stay at the Crown.' Meredith grimaced. 'But when she saw it, she changed her mind.' She contemplated the little black tape recorder whirring away among the coffee cups, soaking up her words and recording them for posterity. 'I feel as though I'm gossiping about people whose hospitality I enjoyed, whatever the circumstances. It's embarrassing.'

Jess Campbell was a police officer and she had learned to control any embarrassment she might feel. But she said sympathetically, 'I understand. It's not nice. But I wasn't at that party and you were. I know the superintendent was there, but women notice different things to men. Was resentment of Alison for ousting her own mother the only reason you thought Fiona might have had for writing the letters?'

'Well, no, I wondered if there might be a money angle. But since then I've learned that Fiona was wealthy in her own right. Money probably wouldn't have been a motive. In fact, my suspicion of Fiona was unfair. I didn't have any reason to suspect her. I've no reason to suppose she could have known about the trial earlier. I was . . .' She wriggled awkwardly in her chair. 'Alan would say I was playing detective. But it wasn't a game and I was out of order.'

There was a pause. The tape recorder whirred on. Without warning, Jess changed the subject. 'You know Toby Smythe well, I understand.'

Meredith blinked and bridled. 'Yes, I've known him a long time. If you think Toby had a hand in writing the letters, you're barking up the wrong tree! He's got no reason to do anything like that. He likes Alison. He's a nice guy.' She glimpsed the barely perceptible twitch of Jess's mouth. 'I know he went up to London to Fiona's flat. He shouldn't have done that. He did it to oblige Jeremy. He's sorry.'

'Oh?' Jess's finely drawn dark eyebrows were raised again. 'He's spoken to you about it?'

'He rang me last night.' A long and agonized phone call it had been, and somewhat rambling. Meredith had suspected Toby had had a couple of drinks. She had advised him to make an early night of it.

Jess Campbell, Meredith decided, was an attractive woman despite a tense professional manner, not exactly inquisitorial, but dauntingly on the ball. She was of athletic build and her dark red hair was cropped short, though not as severely as Chantal's. She wore no jewellery. Her grey trousers and jacket were smart, if unexceptional, but teamed with a very nice turquoise silk shirt. Her feet were shod in medium-high-heeled black ankle boots. Her fingernails were carefully manicured. She's struck a good balance in her appearance, thought Meredith with respect, knowing how hard this was to do in the workplace. No woman wants to look dowdy. But no woman wants to look like a bimbo, either. This is a big case for her, she thought in sympathy. I know what it's like. If a woman slips up in doing the job, there's always someone to suggest a man might have done it better. Even now, even after all these years of change in the workplace. It's human nature that doesn't change. She's new here, too. Everyone will be watching her, listening to every word, noting every gesture, forming an opinion of her.

She realized that her visitor was aware Meredith was studying her. In return, Jess was watching her hostess and waiting patiently for Meredith to make up her mind. Meredith said, 'Sorry. But I did tell you I look at people. They interest me.'

'No sweat,' Jess said casually. 'Did Mr Smythe tell you he'd been thinking of proposing marriage to Fiona Jenner?'

'Yes, he did tell me that.'

'You weren't surprised?'

'Why should I be surprised?' She had been surprised, but she wasn't going to admit it to Jess. It wouldn't do to suggest that Toby had started acting out of character. Meredith eyed her visitor. 'He didn't know then she had a partner in London. He told me that last night on the phone, too.'

'She was a cousin. People do marry cousins, I know,' Jess observed. 'But I think it's fairly rare these days.'

'But not illegal!' Meredith said tartly, pushing away her own reservations which she had expressed to Alan. 'In any case, she wasn't a first cousin. Her father and Toby's father were cousins. Would that make her a second cousin, or a cousin once removed?'

This gained a faint smile from Campbell. 'Not such a close relative, as you say. Did he strike you as very upset over her death?'

'Yes, he was – is!' Meredith said firmly. 'But Toby's not the sort of person who mopes around. He has a very positive attitude.'

Jess didn't look altogether persuaded, Meredith thought, so she added, 'People react to shock or tragedy in individual ways. What you see is Toby's way. It doesn't mean it hasn't hit him hard. He'd known her all her life, remember.'

Jess leaned forward and switched off the little tape recorder. 'Thank you,' she said.

'I've not been very helpful.' Meredith grimaced.

'Everything helps.' Jess hesitated. 'Do you mind if I ask you a question which is nothing to do with this investigation?'

'Go ahead.'

'What kind of price are you hoping to get for this place?'

A little taken aback, Meredith told her. Jess thought about it for a moment. 'I know this is a frightful cheek.' She sounded almost shy. 'It's extremely rude to ask to view a property without making an appointment . . .'

'You want to look round?' Meredith grinned. 'Sure, why not? Oh, I've eaten the fruit.'

'Fruit?' Jess looked puzzled and gazed round her as if expected to see a pile of apple cores and orange peel.

'The decorative display of fruit in the kitchen, as recommended to impress prospective buyers. But I have washed up.'

They both laughed.

While Jess Campbell was talking to Meredith, Markby was holding an interesting conversation of his own with ex-Chief Inspector Alec Barnes-Wakefield. At the end of it he put down the phone, his expression thoughtful. About an hour later, a long e-mail arrived, also from Barnes-Wakefield. At the end of that, Markby was not merely looking thoughtful; he'd begun to look worried.

He found his way to the operations room and asked if Campbell was back yet. She wasn't. He asked for a message to be given to her to come along and see him as soon as she arrived. Shortly before twelve, she did.

'You want to see me, sir? I've been out to interview Miss Mitchell.' She'd have been back earlier if she hadn't lingered to be shown the house but, unless he asked, she saw no point in telling him that now.

He wasn't interested, in any case. 'I've been talking to Barnes-Wakefield,' he said.

Jess trawled rapidly through her memory. 'Oh, the investigating officer in the Freda Kemp case.'

'Yes, sit down.' While she was doing this, Markby ran briefly through his prepared speech. It wasn't going to be an easy one. The conversation with and ensuing e-mail received from Barnes-Wakefield had both been illuminating, though perhaps not surprising.

Though his acquaintance with the man was of the briefest, and he had never actually set eyes on him, he had quickly recognized the type. Barnes-Wakefield had certainly been a hard-working and reliable officer, tenacious and determined to get his man, or woman. So far, so good. The flaw came with an inability to be deflected from his own interpretation of events. This had become evident in the opening sentence of what had sounded like a lengthy and at times aggressive self-justification. Barnes-Wakefield had not only been willing to talk about the Kemp case. He was thirsting to put his view of it, a view which hadn't changed an iota in twenty-five years.

The first thing he had insisted upon was the correctness of his initial interpretation of the scene. It was, Barnes-Wakefield had decided and still believed, the scene of a murder. Once he had decided that, he had to find a killer. Alison had fitted the bill.

In fairness, thought Markby, she was the most likely suspect. Alison had borrowed money from her aunt and Alison was named as her aunt's heiress. Motive a-plenty in the book of someone like Barnes-Wakefield, who had worked hard all his life for every penny and never borrowed a cent, apart from his mortgage. Thereafter, Markby suspected, the chief inspector's approach had been that of a man finding facts to fit his theory. Inconvenient objections were ruthlessly pushed aside. Alison's alibi had not been checked as it should have been. Not surprisingly, when the case came to court, the whole thing blew up in his face.

It was typical of such a man that he still clung to his belief in Alison's guilt and saw the failure to get a conviction as a deeply personal affront. Markby explained this as tactfully as he could to Jess Campbell. She sat listening in silence, her pale face tense beneath its cap of dark red hair. She understood. What was worse, more awkward, was that she had grasped what he hadn't said.

'We have here an officer with an unblemished career who probably retired respected by everyone,' Markby said, placing emphasis on the last words. 'OK, he made the occasional mistake but we all do that. Unfortunately for his own peace of mind, Barnes-Wakefield appears still to be raging over the fact that things didn't work out as he wanted them to in the matter of the Kemp case.' He fell silent.

Jess asked quietly, 'Do you want me to add him to the list of possible poison pen writers? He's waited twenty-five years, if he did write them.'

'What's twenty-five years when you have a bee in your bonnet?' Markby muttered. 'With every passing year it gets stronger. The sense of injustice grows. He was severely criticized by the press after the trial. That obviously hit him hard and he hasn't forgotten it.' He walked to the window; his hands clasped behind his back, and stared out.

'So, if he was going to kill anyone, he'd kill Alison,' Jess said unwisely.

It gained her a quick put-down. Markby spun on his heel to face her. 'Is that a joke, Campbell? It's in poor taste if it is. Barnes-Wakefield isn't a killer. He spent his working life chasing and catching killers and other violent types. He wouldn't join them.'

'But he might write the letters?' Jess persisted, despite the cold anger in the blue eyes boring into hers.

She saw the look in his eyes falter and he turned his gaze away. 'I was thinking aloud just now,' he said stiffly. 'I didn't intend you to draw any conclusion from it.'

She didn't press the matter any further. He hated the idea of a policeman going wrong, whether it was a serving officer or a retired one. They all did. But his own dogged honesty meant he had to mention the possibility. His anger wasn't directed at her. It was directed against himself. He felt disloyal because he even thought this of a one-time fellow officer.

'Is that all, then, sir?' she asked.

'Yes, that's all,' was the curt reply.

The postman drove his van down the bumpy lane past the Stebbings' cottage (he seldom delivered any mail there) and turned through the gates of Overvale House. The sun was pale this morning but the air dry. The horses had been moved from their usual pasture and it had been occupied by a number of large birds which looked to him like seagulls. If they were, he didn't know what they were doing there. They ought to be by the sea, following fishing boats, at least so he understood. These were patrolling the centre of the paddock, round and round one small area, occasionally pecking at the ground.

When he reached the house, the postman saw that another vehicle had got there before him. It was a taxi and from it had climbed a small, neat female with the shortest hair he'd ever seen on a woman. He wondered whether it was the result of chemotherapy, a first tentative regrowth after losing the lot, but it appeared more a fashion statement. Women did weird things with their hair, he told himself, but he hoped his girlfriend never decided to trim hers down to stubble. Despite that, the taxi passenger looked really sexy, even though she wasn't that young. A large suitcase stood on the drive by her feet and she had just finished paying off the driver.

The postman pulled over to one side to give the taxi turning space and got out with the assorted mail in his hand.

'Morning!' he said cheerfully to the small woman, trying hard not to stare at her strange haircut.

'Good morning,' she returned. 'Will you ring the bell or shall I?' She had a foreign accent. She was French, he guessed.

In the event, neither of them had to. The door was opened suddenly by Jeremy Jenner.

'There you are, Chantal,' he said, not sounding very enthusiastic. 'I thought I heard the taxi. Oh, post, thank you.' He held out his hand.

The postman gave him the letters; then, although he would dearly have liked to linger and find out what all this was about, he had no option but to get back in his van and follow the taxi down the drive.

Jeremy carried his first wife's case into the hall and set it down. As he did, the dining room door opened and Alison came out. She moved forward to greet her guest with an outstretched hand.

'Chantal? How nice to meet you. Have you had breakfast?'

Chantal gripped the outstretched hand briefly and cast a rapid glance over her hostess. 'No, they make terrible coffee at that hotel and the bed was lumpy. *Affreux.*'

'Oh dear,' Alison sympathized. 'Do come and sit down. Jerry will take your case upstairs and I'll get Mrs Whittle to bring you some fresh coffee and some toast.'

She ushered the visitor into the comfortable sitting room which Jess had seen and returned to the hall on her way to the kitchen. She was just in time to see her husband, who had obviously been riffling through the morning's post, stuffing a small white envelope into his pocket. He looked up guiltily.

Alison's heart seemed to stop beating and then give a great lurch. 'What is it?'

'Nothing, darling, just circulars and business stuff.'

'No, I mean, what was that one you put in your pocket?'

'From the bank,' he said easily, moving away towards the study.

'It's not the right size or shape for a letter from the bank,' Alison said. 'It's another one of those letters, isn't it?'

He turned back and saw that she had held out her hand towards him. 'Look, Ally . . .' he began.

'It'll be addressed to me,' she said calmly. 'May I have it?'

'Best to let me deal with it,' he urged.

'I have to see it, Jeremy,' she said. 'You know I have to see it and then we'll take it to the police.'

He pulled the now-crumpled envelope from his pocket but still held it fast. 'It might not be what you think.'

'Then it won't matter.' With a slight edge to her formerly calm tone, she added, 'I'm not a child, Jerry.'

Reluctantly he handed her the envelope. 'Perhaps,' he said. 'We ought not to open it, just give it straight to the police as it is.'

'As you said, it might not be what I think it is. Then we'd look silly. I have to open it.' She tore it open as she spoke, took out the single folded sheet and spread it flat.

Her husband saw the colour drain from her face. He moved to

185

her side so that he could read the letter. Her hand shook but the printing was clearly decipherable.

NOW THERE IS ANOTHER ONE. JUST LIKE AUNT FREDA, FOUND IN WATER. DEATH FOLLOWS YOU AROUND, DOESN'T IT, ALISON?

Jeremy took it gently from her hand. 'Leave it to me. I'll go and phone the police from the study. You just sit down quietly.'

She shook her head. 'No – no, I've got to see about Chantal's coffee . . .'

'Then you do that. I'll see about this.' His voice was gentle but firm.

She looked up at him desperately. 'Jeremy?'

'Go on, now.' He touched her arm.

Alison turned away, walked in an awkward, disjointed robotic fashion down the hall and disappeared through a door at the far end.

Jeremy Jenner folded the letter and was slipping it back in the envelope when a faint sound caught his ear, that of someone breathing.

He looked up sharply. Chantal had come out of the sitting room and was leaning in the open doorway, her arms folded across her chest and her polished nails pressed against her forearms.

'Trouble, Jerry?' The voice was all innocence but her eyes gleamed with spite.

'Family business!' he said angrily. 'Nothing to do with you, Chantal!'

'Oh, I'm not family any longer, is that it? I'm not still your only child's mother?'

'Don't start,' he said wearily. 'It was Alison's idea to invite you to stay, not mine. At least don't make trouble while you're here.'

'I thought,' she said in a voice which quivered with suppressed rage, 'there was trouble here already. My child, your child, has been murdered! That isn't trouble? It isn't a problem? We're going to sit around here and make conversation about the weather as the English love to do and we are not going to mention Fiona? Don't be foolish, Jeremy. I'm here precisely because of the trouble. This is what we're all thinking about, isn't it? And what we're all going to be talking about. But it seems there is something else. Why must you give that letter to the police?'

'I told you!' he shouted and then, as his voice rang round the hall, he made an effort to speak quietly. 'I told you, it's private to me and to Alison.'

Chantal shook her head and the hoop earrings swung. 'No,' she said, cool now, her own moment of unveiled anger conquered and the rage put back in its box. 'No, my dear Jeremy, it isn't just private to you and to her. It is of interest to the police. That suggests to me it has a bearing on the death of my daughter. That means it is of interest to me. May I see it?'

'No,' he retorted, breathing heavily. 'You certainly may not.'

'Then let me guess at it.' Her voice was unrelenting. 'It is an anonymous letter. Am I right?' When he didn't reply, she went on, 'Let's see, it's addressed to Alison, yes?'

'Why should it be addressed to her?' Jeremy's voice appeared to have been forced from his throat through a constricted opening. The sounds were distorted and barely audible. 'You're wrong, it's addressed to me.'

She shook her close cropped head again. 'You are being silly, Jeremy. No, it isn't. It's for Alison. She is the one with the past.'

He moved towards her threateningly. 'Past? What do you mean?' His voice rose. 'Stop all this nonsense, Chantal, at once!'

'You can't bully me, Jeremy. I'm not your wife any longer. I'm not some underling in your office. And you are the one who is being silly. I know about the murder trial and I know about the other letters, too.'

He gaped at her and croaked, 'How?'

'Because Fiona rang me and told me about it, naturally, as soon as you told her.'

He looked stunned. 'She had no right—'

187

His ex-wife interrupted him briskly. 'You always have to be the person in control, don't you, Jeremy? You give the orders and no one does anything without asking you first. No one else has the right to act independently no matter how important it is to them. Of course Fiona told me. It wasn't only right, it was necessary. You had presented this woman to her as her stepmother. Then she learned you'd replaced me with a woman who had been charged with a murder. She was shocked. I'm her mother, so she picked up the phone and talked to me. It was the most natural thing to do. What's the matter? Did you tell her to keep it a secret?'

He shook his head in a dazed way. 'No, no . . . I thought she would do that, anyway. It was a family matter.'

'And I'm not family now. We're back to that. But I am, and I was then, Fiona's closest relative, her mother. Do you think I shouldn't have been told? You yourself should have told me! But you kept your sordid little secret, you and Alison; because you knew I would insist Fiona cut all her links with you.'

'Why the hell should she do that?' he shouted at her. 'You talk about people making up their own minds. In the next breath, you say you would have insisted Fiona cut herself off from me.'

'For her own safety!' she threw back at him.

'Alison was innocent of that charge! She was cleared by the court! Fiona *was safe*!' Jenner broke off and gave what sounded a strangled sob.

'No!' Chantal snapped viciously. 'She wasn't, was she, Jeremy? She wasn't safe and now she's dead!'

'Get out of this house!' he ordered, panting, his face suffused with blood.

'Oh, I'm not suggesting Alison killed her, Jeremy. Naturally not. But neither am I convinced her actions had nothing to do with it. First poison pen letters come to this house. Then my daughter is murdered here. Do you think the police have made no connection? Do you think the police aren't wondering about Alison? After all, one doesn't meet people who have stood trial for murder every day. You can't just, what's the English expression? You can't just sweep it under the carpet.'

'Damn you!' he snarled at her. His hands were opening and closing involuntarily as if they would have liked to fasten themselves round her slender neck. 'How many people have *you* told about it?'

She shrugged elegantly. 'Actually, none. It's not the sort of information one mentions at the dinner table. But once people do know about something like that, they don't forget. People have long memories for murder, Jeremy.'

'You can't imagine what it's like,' said Toby that evening.

The three of them were seated round a corner table in the Saddler's Arms, one of Meredith and Alan's favourite pubs. It was a tiny place with low beams, which had made no concessions to modern desires for slot machines, wide-screen television or piped music. But the atmosphere was relaxed and the welcome genuine.

Toby, however, was not relaxed. 'Do you know the Noel Coward play, *Blithe Spirit*?' he asked.

'I've seen it on television. They showed a wonderful old film of it, only recently. Rex Harrison played the lead and Margaret Rutherford played Madame Arcati, the medium,' Meredith told him.

'Isn't that the one where the dead wife comes back to haunt the husband and his new wife?' Markby said, raising his pint to his lips. 'I saw it, too. We watched it together at your place.'

'Then you'll remember,' Toby went on, 'that at the very end of it all three of them are dead, the husband and both wives. Rex Harrison's ghost is sitting on a wall with a ghost wife on either side of him, and he's stuck with them both bickering over him for eternity. Well, that's what it's like at Overvale now. That's why I had to come out tonight. I had to get away or risk losing my sanity. Jeremy sits there between Alison and Chantal. Chantal hardly speaks to Alison. Jeremy hardly speaks to Chantal. Alison hardly speaks. All three, including Alison when she does speak,

speak to me. I have this three-handed conversation going all the time, punctuated by the most awful silences which I feel I'm expected to break. It's like trying to do a particularly difficult juggling trick. I can't stand it.'

'Poor Toby,' said Meredith, trying to hide a smile.

She wasn't successful. 'It isn't funny!' he said bitterly.

'I'm not unsympathetic, believe me,' she assured him. 'But it has got a funny side.'

Alan, with the heartfelt tones of a man who had been through divorce, added, 'You've got my sympathy!'

'And on top of it all, Alison got another letter this morning. But you know that,' Toby said to him.

'Yes, it's being looked at by forensics. It's an interesting development.'

'Jeremy thinks it's from the killer, he's always thought the writer murdered poor Fiona. Chantal thinks so, too. Do you think that?' Toby stared hard at Markby.

Markby, regretting the conversation he'd had with Jess Campbell that afternoon, was tempted to reply sharply but managed to keep his cool.

'Oh, I'm a cautious copper. I keep my thoughts to myself. One thing this new letter does tell us is that the writer hasn't been put off by the murder. Now, that is interesting. Whether or not he was involved in Fiona's death, one might have thought that with all the attention being paid to it he would have taken fright and not written again. After all, this is hardly the moment to draw the spotlight on to himself. I am interested in our letter writer. He's turning out to be a rather curious fellow.'

Toby was looking at him with doubt written on his face. 'But you don't think he killed Fi?'

'I don't know who killed Fiona Jenner.' Alan smiled and shook his head. 'But here we have a man – we're still assuming it to be a man – who couldn't resist the opportunity of Fiona's death to write to Alison again. I will say this to you, because it's obvious anyway, that putting the body in the water does appear to link the letters and the death. But what is he going to do now, that's the question.'

There was a silence while all three of them sipped their drinks and thought over the problem.

'Perhaps,' Meredith suggested, 'the fact that he can't seem to resist the temptation to write again makes him vulnerable. With every letter he writes, he takes a risk.'

'Oh, yes, he'll slip up eventually,' Markby agreed.

Toby set his empty glass down with a thump on the table. 'So what are the police going to do? Sit around until he makes a mistake which leads you to him? Caution is all very well, but he's laughing at us, all of us! Well, I won't sit about. I intend to do something about it.'

Markby looked startled and opened his mouth. Toby held up his hand to forestall him. 'Don't panic. I'm not planning to interfere in your murder investigations. I'm just going to do a little research, if you like to call it that.'

'Toby!' Meredith broke in and kicked his ankle beneath the table.

'Ouch!' said Toby. 'Yes, I know, Meredith. The police don't like independent action by the public. But I'm not proposing to turn myself into a vigilante, am I?'

'I hope not,' said Markby. 'I'd have to warn you off formally.'

'Stuff your formal warnings. Sorry, Alan, but I'm thoroughly sick of all of it and having Chantal here has brought things to a head. I'd forgotten what a spectacularly dreadful woman she is. I hadn't seen her since their divorce, years ago.'

'Did she always have that haircut?' asked Markby unexpectedly, gaining himself a quizzical look from Meredith.

'Yes, she did,' Toby told him. 'She's an artist, or so she claims. She paints squiggles on large canvases. They're all called "Untitled". That's because she doesn't know what they are. Look here, Alison is a walking nervous breakdown. It just can't be left until something turns up. Or what will turn up will be yet another wretched letter and, if that happens, Alison will crack. Believe me, she's clinging on by her fingernails. She doesn't need Chantal roaming round the house like a vengeful harpy. She needs the whole business to be sorted so that Chantal can go back to Switzerland and get out of our hair. I particularly need her out of *my* hair. Jeremy is arguably a cause for my concern, but Chantal definitely is not.'

'She lives in Switzerland now, does she?' Markby asked.

He nodded. 'I gather she lives in a splendid villa on the banks of Lake Geneva with a banker husband and some pedigree dogs of a small and hairy variety. She showed me pictures of them. They looked like those electrically operated shoe brushes you find in hotel corridors. I ought not to be unkind about her. I know she's lost her only child. But she makes it very difficult for anyone to sympathize with her. I have to say Jeremy doesn't make it easy. I've stood by him and given him all the support I've been able to do. I even agreed, stupidly, I admit, to go up to London to Fiona's flat for him. I made myself look a complete fool in front of that woman inspector of yours. But I did it because Jeremy's a relative and an old friend. Well, everything has its limits. I'm not getting involved in Jeremy's marital arrangements, present or past, and certainly not when faced with the present and the past at the same time. Jeremy's going to have to sweat it out on his own.'

'I can understand that,' Markby said. 'But what are you proposing to do? Because I do need to know, if for no other reason than so that I can be ready to rescue you if you get into trouble. Not, by the way, that I might always be able to do that. It depends on what kind of trouble you get into!'

'What are you planning, Toby?' asked Meredith in a practical tone. 'Are you going back to London to your flat?'

'What would I do there but mooch around, thinking about it all, and remain just as frustrated because I can't do anything? No, I'm going down to Cornwall.'

'*Cornwall?*' exclaimed Meredith and Alan together.

Toby looked gratified at having elicited this joint response and at the dismay on both his listeners' faces. 'Thought you'd like to know,' he said smugly. 'Anyone care for another drink?'

'What will you do in Cornwall?' Alan asked him bluntly.

'I don't know yet. I'll go to this place where Aunt Freda had her cottage – Alison's given me the address – and ask around. Someone will remember the crime. After all, people don't move house in rural areas, they stay stuck in the same spot all their lives.'

'Honestly, Toby,' said Meredith, 'you have very preconceived ideas about country life. Cornwall is a tourist destination and lots of its old cottages have been bought as holiday homes. People retire down there, just like Aunt Freda did. You'll probably find that nearly everyone you speak to has only lived there for about ten years and won't remember a thing about a twenty-five-year-old crime.'

'Hold on, now,' said Alan. 'I understand that in her will Freda Kemp left everything including the cottage to Alison. Does Alison still own it?'

Toby nodded. 'Yes, she does. She doesn't use it herself because of the sad associations it has for her now. You can understand that. It would be a bit creepy trying to sunbathe in the garden where old Freda was found head down in the pond. Alison rents it out as a holiday let, just as you were describing, Meredith. But . . .' Toby didn't rub his hands in satisfaction at this point, but looked as though he might. 'But the people she had let it to for Easter cancelled. It's empty. I can stay there. I've got the key.'

'You seem,' Alan said sourly, 'to have the keys to a lot of properties, one way and another.'

'People trust me,' said Toby serenely. 'You might not, but others do.'

'We do trust you, Toby,' Meredith told him. 'Even Alan, don't you, Alan?'

'No,' said Markby. 'Since I might as well be honest, I don't know what the heck you're going to do once you get down to Cornwall, Toby. With respect, Meredith, neither do you!'

'Then I'll go with him!' she said promptly.

This temporarily silenced both men.

Toby spoke first. 'Don't you have to go back to work?'

She shook her head. 'No, I took the rest of the week off. I was only going to take one day, because Jess Campbell was coming to see me. But then I thought, well, I'll take the rest of the week, even if it doesn't make me very popular at the office. I feel I should be around to – to keep an eye on things,' Meredith concluded somewhat obscurely.

Toby wasn't fooled. 'You mean, to keep an eye on me!'

'To support you, Toby,' she amended. 'I felt I should be here for you.' She looked at Markby. 'You don't mind my going down to Cornwall with Toby, do you?'

'Yes.' There was an obstinate set to Alan's jaw and a glint in his eye.

'Oh, come on, Alan,' Meredith reasoned. 'You want to know what he does down there. I'll be there and I can tell you.'

'Thank you very much,' said Toby stiffly. 'Much as I'd normally appreciate your company, Meredith, I don't want a police spy following me round.'

'I'm not a police spy, don't be silly. Two heads are better than one. Sometimes people will talk to a woman rather than to a man, it's less threatening.'

'Oh, well, in that case, come along.' He brightened. 'In fact, it's a good idea because you can drive us in your car. Otherwise, I've got to borrow Alison's car again. I sold my car when I left Beijing and now I haven't got one. I'm waiting to see where they send me next. Look, Alan, Meredith's absolutely right. She'll keep me in order.' Toby looked hopefully at Markby.

'How long for?' demanded Markby.

'Three days. We can't go wrong in three days.' Toby seemed to feel his optimism might be misplaced. 'Not very wrong, anyway.'

'Go with him, if you want to,' Markby said with a sigh. 'Chauffeur him around while he bothers everyone.'

'Great! I really appreciate this, Alan. I'll look after her. I'll get another round of drinks? Same again?' Toby jumped up and made for the bar.

Meredith leaned across the table. 'Alan, please, don't be difficult. Of course I don't really want to go with him to Cornwall. But if I don't, I'll be worried sick about what he's doing, and so will you be. At least I'll be there and I can stop him getting into some silly fix or other. It's particularly useful that I'll be his driver because, without me, he can't go anywhere! I'll know his every move.'

'I'm less worried about any trouble he may get himself into than I am about his dragging you into danger with him!' Markby retorted.

She blinked. 'You think there might be danger down there in Cornwall?'

'Listen,' he hissed, as Toby was making his precarious way back towards them with three brimming glasses balanced on a very small tin tray. 'He is proposing to go down to a quiet neck of the woods and stir up waters which have been lying undisturbed for twenty-five years. Who knows what he might turn up on his fishing expedition? And I know you. Don't tell me you don't want to go with him and snoop around.'

'Here we are!' said Toby cheerfully, putting the tray on the table. 'That chap Ted is over there at the bar, by the way.'

'Ted Pritchard from Rusticity?' Startled, Meredith peered across the smoky room and sighed. 'So he is. What's he doing here? I thought he drank at the Feathers. Did he recognize you?'

'Oh yes. He was tickled pink. He'd seen all three of us sitting here drinking together.'

At that moment, Ted, at the bar, caught Meredith's eye, winked and raised his glass to her in salute.

'Oh, wonderful,' she said. 'Now he thinks we all live in a *ménage à trois*.'

'I'm beginning to think it myself,' said Markby gloomily. 'I really do understand how Jeremy Jenner feels.'

'Let's hope Ted doesn't find out about Merry and me going down to Cornwall, then!' said Toby. 'Cheers!'

Chapter Eleven

When Alan Markby had referred to Cornwall as a quiet part of the world, he hadn't been thinking of the effect of the Easter holidays on a renowned tourist destination. The roads were clogged and they made slow progress. The interior of the car was stifling. Meredith had drunk her bottle of water and they had eaten all the boiled sweets.

'There's another caravan up ahead,' said Toby obligingly when they found themselves stuck in yet another tailback. The road here was little more than a lane between high banks bright with pink flowers.

'Thanks. How much further is it to this cottage of Alison's?'

Toby consulted the map. 'Not far. Fifteen miles.'

Meredith groaned. Fifteen miles might just as well be fifty in present circumstances. She looked at her wristwatch. This was all going to prove a ghastly mistake.

Toby, on the other hand, had cheered up since they had entered the county and no amount of traffic problems could quench his enthusiasm.

'I love this area. I used to come down here with my parents during school holidays. I remember sunbathing on the beach at Daymer Beach and, later, learning to ride the surf at Polzeath. That was when I was much older, of course. In our earlier years, my brother and I used to scramble over the rocks seeing what we could find in the pools, and several times we nearly got cut off by the tide. It comes in very fast along this stretch of coast.'

'Where is your brother now?' enquired Meredith.

'He's a marine biologist. He puts that down entirely to those seaside holidays in Cornwall. But he's working in Australia now.'

'What about your parents?'

'Retired to Portugal,' said Toby. 'Well out of it. They were sorry to hear about Fiona, of course. But I doubt they'll be coming back here for the funeral.'

It was the first mention Meredith had heard of funeral arrangements for Fiona Jenner. 'Has the coroner released the body?'

'Not yet, but Jeremy's putting pressure on. The thing is, Chantal will stay until Fiona's decently sent on her way and the rest of us have to put up with it. I think Jeremy was all for throwing her out of the house before she'd been in it five minutes, but Alison wouldn't hear of it. The funeral is going to be an awkward affair. There's that girl in London, Tara. She'll want to be at the service. I pointed that out to Jeremy but he mumbled that he meant it to be family only. I said that in the circumstances Fiona had looked on Tara as family. But that didn't go down well, and I didn't get a proper reply. I think she's been on the phone to him.'

'Tara Seale has?'

'Yes. At least, I'm fairly sure. It's difficult to be absolutely certain because, as I said, Jeremy won't talk to me about it. I think he's annoyed now that I went up to the flat and found Tara there. But it was all his idea! I overheard him talking to Alison. Tara was mentioned followed by something about her having no rights. My guess is that Jeremy is trying to freeze her out and I think that's unfair. She was Fi's partner, after all. I think Jeremy wants to get her out of the flat. It appears Fiona didn't make a will. The whole thing is basically rather petty. I had thought Jeremy had a more generous nature, at least a modern attitude. He seems to be turning into an aggrieved Victorian paterfamilias. I think that he and I are heading for a vigorous disagreement about it, but I don't want to row with him just yet, not while he's got so much else to worry about. Even so, I'm not going to let him freeze Tara out. It's not right. It's not what Fiona would have wished. It's downright cruel, if you ask me. He's not going to get away with it. I won't let him.' Toby gave a determined nod.

'He's grieving,' Meredith reminded him. 'Grief doesn't listen to reasonable argument. Give him a week or two.'

'No one's listening to anyone just now, that's the trouble.' Toby folded the map carefully into a neat rectangle. 'I don't have time to wait for Jeremy to change his attitude, anyway. He's got to be made to see Tara has to be included right now. Alison would be kind to Tara, I'm sure, just as she's tried to be kind to Chantal. But I can't ask for her help with this. Since that last letter came, Alison's been as jumpy as a cat on a hot tin roof. She's given up on Chantal and it's not just the moment to talk to her about Tara, I'm afraid. Turn right here!'

Meredith turned right and found to her great relief that they had left the traffic behind them. They now followed a narrow twisting lane which led them up hill and down dale until they reached a pub, two or three cottages and a ramshackle garage.

'This is the village,' said Toby confidently.

'Are you sure?' Meredith peered doubtfully at the two petrol pumps sited in isolated splendour before a large dilapidated building bearing a board reading: G. Melhuish. Repairs. Tyres and Exhausts. MOT.

'Must be, it's on the map. We go on for a quarter of a mile towards the sea.'

The sun was starting to go down when they finally reached their destination. The cottage stood in an exposed position atop the cliffs with a magnificent view of the River Camel estuary below. As Meredith got out of the car, the wind caught her hair and sent it flying wildly around her head. She could smell the salt spray of the sea rushing up the beach below. There was no one to be seen and the red glow of the setting sun bathed them in a strange, other-worldly light. The cottage, a curious affair, half stone and half timbered, looked as if it might have started life as some kind of barn. She mentioned this to Toby.

'I think it did.' Toby's expression, flushed with the dying sun's rays, was almost exalted. 'Alison said there was a story that smugglers kept their illicit cargoes in it during the eighteenth century. But every old building along this part of the coast will tell you a similar tale. Mind you, they did land contraband along here in the bad old days, in the smaller bays like Trebarwith and Tintagel or Boscastle and, of course, at Polperro. Sometimes the excise cutter would intercept and arrest the smugglers but they had their work cut out. Informers didn't last long and local people kept their mouths shut. No one saw anything wrong in it. The most respectable ladies bought their tea at the back door late at night. The West Country has always been at odds with authority.'

' "Brandy for the parson, 'baccy for the clerk",' Meredith quoted Kipling, but Toby was pulling their suitcases from the car and didn't hear her. She turned back to the odd little building which was to be their base.

It had the abandoned air of a habitation which wasn't lived in except for occasional weeks here and there. There was life, however, in the form of a dozen small rabbits hopping about the front garden. At the human approach they scattered, bouncing away across the dry turf in a dozen directions.

'There must be a warren nearby,' Meredith commented.

Apart from the rabbits, the only other sign of life was an occasional seabird wheeling overhead. As a holiday cottage, a place to get away from the hurly-burly, it would be ideal. As a place to retire to and live out your final days, much less so. Freda Kemp, thought Meredith, must have been very lonely in her last years. She must have looked forward eagerly to her niece Alison's visits. Even the daily visit from her cleaner, Mrs Travis, must have assumed a huge importance.

'Mrs Travis,' said Meredith as they opened the front door. 'We ought to try and find Mrs Travis.'

'Will she still be alive?' Toby asked.

'Why not? She had a ten-year-old son way back then, twenty-five years ago. She probably wasn't much more than my age now, in her mid-thirties. She can't be more than in her sixties at the most, and we ought to be able to find her.'

'She didn't like Alison,' warned Toby.

'So, we won't mention Alison.'

They carried their provisions in from the car and stashed them in the cupboards and fridge. The cottage was comfortable and attractive, furnished inside with modern pine pieces. Quick inspection of the neat kitchen showed that it was equipped, as such lettings usually were, with the standard six of everything in the way of crockery and cutlery. Alison must have cleared out everything reminding her of her aunt. Only in the living room did two old but nice rugs suggest they might have survived from earlier days. There was a splendid wide-screen television set. In a cupboard, in case the weather turned against the holidaymakers, they found a supply of board games and much-thumbed paperback novels.

Meredith went to sleep that night listening to the roar of the incoming tide as it surged up the estuary until it reached the rocks below the cottage. Once there, the waves growled angrily against the base of the cliff. The creak of the house timbers mingled with the sea noises. It made her more than ever conscious of the loneliness Freda Kemp must have endured. Endured, she thought, was the word. Why hadn't she sold up and moved somewhere livelier? Perhaps her decision to stay had been due to a wrong-headed obstinacy. She had made her choice and she would stick with it. But people differ in their idea of lonely. Perhaps Freda hadn't felt her isolation. There were people who were happy enough on their own. Freda might have been one of them.

The following morning was bright and clear. Their attempt to find Mrs Travis was held up, however, by Toby's insistence that they climb down to the beach.

'Because the tide is nearly out now,' he said simply.

Meredith didn't know what time the tide had turned but Toby was right. It was racing back towards the open sea, slowly exposing the yellow sands. Luckily, they hadn't to scramble down the rocky incline using hand- and toeholds. There was a concrete stairway from the cliffside path to the beach below. The sand, now that they'd reached it, could be seen to be dotted with wormcasts, shells, the occasional dead crab and odd strands of seaweed. In places the smooth surface was broken by groups of large boulders. The rocks here were pale grey with tinges of pink and blue. Meredith discovered that, if viewed through sunglasses, the pinks and blues became quite startling. In the far distance someone was walking a pair of large dogs which gambolled happily along the water's edge, splashing in and out of the shallows. Otherwise they were alone. Toby seemed to have regressed to his childhood, clambering over the boulders and exclaiming in delight over tiny finds of crabs or shrimps in the rock pools. Eventually Meredith dragged him sternly away.

'Look, we came down here to try and find some clue or other to what's happened back at Overvale. We won't do it like this.'

Regretfully Toby followed her back to the steps and they climbed up to the road at the top.

'Where first?' he asked.

'It's too early to try the pub. Let's go back to that garage. I could buy some petrol and ask a question or two, just casually.'

But when they drew up at the garage, that also seemed to be deserted. They got out of the car and looked about them.

'There must be someone about,' Toby fretted. 'The doors are open.'

At that moment there was a clang from inside the large rickety building and the sound of a robust oath. They made their way towards it.

Meredith stepped out of the bright sunlight into the interior and a shutter seemed to come down before her eyes, isolating her in a world of darkness which smelled strongly of oil and grease. Then her eyes accustomed themselves to the dim light and she saw she was surrounded by all the contents of a garage workshop. Something moved at the far end and a bear-like figure materialized, coming towards them, wiping his hands on a grimy rag.

'Hello,' he greeted them. 'What can I do for you, then?' He looked even bigger close at hand, clad in extremely dirty overalls and strong boots. He had a mop of curly hair and very bright blue eyes which made her think of Alan. Meredith guessed him to be G. Melhuish, owner and chief, if not sole, mechanic.

Meredith put in her request for fuel. As she sorted out the money to pay for it, she wondered how to begin a general conversation. But she needn't have worried. They were strangers, the first visitors of the day, and the garage owner was keen to talk to them.

'Down here on holiday, then?' he asked affably, leaning one blackened hand against the nearest pump.

'No—' began Toby but was overridden by Meredith.

'Yes, but not a proper holiday. Just a couple of days.'

'Where are you staying, then?' The man looked from one to the other of them as if fixing them in his memory.

'At the cottage along there, on top of the cliff.'

'Ah, the old Kemp place,' he said, and scratched his chin leaving a smear of grease.

'I understand it belongs to a Mrs Jenner,' Meredith said carefully. 'Who are the Kemps?'

He gave her a canny sideways look. 'Only one of them, an old lady. She used to live there. It'll be a while back now.'

'But everyone still calls the cottage after her? Why is that?' Meredith affected wide-eyed innocence but had the feeling he wasn't fooled by it.

'She died,' he said. 'Can't say I knew her. Before my time.' He pushed himself away from the pump. 'Well, got to get some work done! I hope you enjoy your stay.'

His desire to chat seemed to have evaporated. He began to amble back to the garage.

'Can you tell us whether there is there a shop around here?' Meredith asked loudly.

He stopped and looked back at them. 'If it's groceries you want, you can find shops at Polzeath. We've a post office down the road here. That sells a few things. If it's a supermarket you're after, you'd do best to drive to Wadebridge.' He nodded and carried on his way.

'He knows about Freda Kemp!' Toby said fiercely as they got back in the car. 'He just wasn't going to tell us.'

'It's understandable,' Meredith pointed out. 'We're staying in the cottage. It might spoil our holiday to know an unexplained death had taken place there.'

'Well,' Toby mused. 'At least it shows we didn't come down here on a complete fool's errand. People do remember Freda Kemp living there.'

'One person,' she corrected him. 'That's all we've found so far. He's probably telling the truth, too. It was almost before his time. He'd have been a young boy twenty-five years ago. He wouldn't have known much about it.'

'A possible murder?' Toby exclaimed, turning to her. 'In a place like this? You bet they talked about nothing else, young and old! When I was ten years old I'd have been there, hanging round the police at the scene of crime, snapping them with my camera, keeping a scrapbook. Little boys are ghouls.'

'That's why I was hoping there would be a local shop,' Meredith sighed. 'We could have asked there and found someone with a long memory. Let's try this post office.'

But the woman in the post office, though affable, couldn't help. She had only been there a couple of years.

They went back to the cottage, drank coffee and wrangled over what to do next. As it was after midday by then, they decided to walk to the pub and see if they could get some lunch.

'And some information,' said Toby hopefully. 'Good places for that, pubs. You know, all the old inhabitants gather there. They like to gossip and if we buy them a pint or two . . .'

Sadly it didn't work out like that. The pub didn't do lunches, only sandwiches. Like the postmistress, the people who ran it had only been there for two years. They had come from Basingstoke to live in Cornwall. No oldest inhabitant obligingly showed his face, only a pair of tourists and a tough-looking young man with an earring and tattoos.

'No use talking to him,' whispered Toby. 'Once he realizes we want information, he'll tell us anything we want to hear in return for fifty quid, and all of it straight from his imagination.'

'We'll try again this evening,' Meredith suggested, as they left. 'Perhaps more people will be there. After all, you can't expect the locals to turn up at lunchtime. They're probably all working somewhere.'

They ended up walking along the clifftop path above the beaches below. The tide had receded so far that there seemed to be only a strip of water left between them and the far side of the estuary where they could make out the roofs of Padstow. They had run out of conversation and ideas and mostly walked in silence, buffeted by a stiff breeze from the sea. Meredith was aware how much she missed Alan. Perhaps, when all this was over, and after they were married, she and Alan could come here and spend some time just relaxing and walking. But that wasn't what she and Toby were here to do now. There had to be some other way of getting back to what happened twenty-five years earlier.

'Alan hasn't dropped any hints, I suppose,' Toby asked wistfully. 'You know, to give us a lead.'

'No, not a thing. He hasn't said a word about the investigation since you and I decided to come to Cornwall. He didn't say a lot before, except to tell me they'd found Fiona's hairband.'

Meredith stopped walking. 'But I have just had an idea!'

'What?' asked Toby, taking off his shoe to shake out the grit and small stones.

'There is one person we may well be able to find and who would know all about Freda Kemp. The police officer in charge of the case at the time.'

'He'll be retired, he must be,' said Toby.

'He may be retired but he could still be around. If you worked in Cornwall, would you retire somewhere else? What's more, I know his name, Barnes-Wakefield. How many people will there be in the telephone directory for the area with that name? What we need is a public library.'

The idea appealed to Toby, who cheered up considerably. They drove to Wadebridge and sought out the library where, as Meredith had hoped, there was set of telephone directories. There was only one Barnes-Wakefield.

'That has to be him,' said Meredith firmly. 'See, he still lives in Cornwall. I'll phone him now.'

'What do we tell him? We'll need an excuse to go asking him about Alison.' Toby eyed her hopefully, trusting she'd have the answer.

'We tell him near enough the truth,' she said simply. 'You're Alison's cousin, or more or less her cousin. After all these years, she's still anxious to clear her name. She feels the court verdict didn't entirely do that. She was very fond of her aunt and she wants to know the truth about how she died. Barnes-Wakefield will buy that, believe me. You're appealing to him for help, for his special knowledge. That flatters him. He might not want to help Alison, but he'll still meet you and chat about it. It gives him a chance to show off. Look, it's human nature. He won't refuse to see us.'

The retired Chief Inspector Barnes-Wakefield lived in an immaculately presented bungalow on the outskirts of Newquay. The front garden was largely taken up with a rockery and a minute fish pond. Two small brightly painted figures hunched by the pool with tiny fishing rods.

'Gnomes!' exclaimed Toby. 'I don't believe it. People really still put those things in their gardens!'

'Toby,' said Meredith. 'You have got to look upon DCI Barnes-Wakefield as you would a senior member of the diplomatic staff of a not very friendly nation. Watch every word you say, right?

You love his garden. You particularly like the gnomes. Tell him about your happy childhood holidays in the area. Get him on our side.'

'You don't have to tell me!' replied Toby huffily.

Barnes-Wakefield had warned Meredith on the phone that he might not answer the doorbell and, if he didn't, to try the back of the property. They walked down the path beside the bungalow and found themselves in a neatly tended garden. At the far end was a greenhouse and they could see a figure moving about inside it.

Toby strode forwards, leaving Meredith in his wake, and put his head through the open greenhouse door. 'Chief Inspector? My name is Toby Smythe. I understand you're expecting us? I'm really very grateful to you for agreeing to see us.' He stuck out his hand.

Barnes-Wakefield was a wiry, grey-haired man with the tanned skin of someone who spent most of his time out of doors. His eyes had probably been quite dark once, but age had faded the irises to a milky brown. His gaze, beneath his bushy eyebrows, was nonetheless sharp. He was treating Toby to a very comprehensive assessment.

'And this is Meredith,' Toby surged on, 'a friend and Foreign Office colleague of mine.'

'You have a lovely garden here,' she told him promptly.

The old man smiled and his expression became marginally less wary. 'Yes, it's very nice, isn't it? The air carries a lot of salt here and one has to be careful to choose plants which tolerate it. The garden was always my hobby and has pretty well been my life since my wife died last year.'

Meredith and Toby both expressed their regrets.

Barnes-Wakefield heard them out, staring into the distance. When they had finished speaking, he said. 'Would you like to go indoors and talk or stay out here?'

Toby glanced briefly at Meredith. 'I think it would be nice to sit out here. It's quite warm. I spent a lot of time in Cornwall as a kid and it's really nice to be able to just sit and breathe Cornish air.'

'Then make yourself comfortable on the garden seat over there. I'll just go and wash my hands.'

They watched him amble across the lawn and disappear into the house.

'He seems quite willing to chat,' said Toby. 'I don't suppose he gets many visitors.'

'It's sort of sad,' Meredith said. 'He's lost his wife and his hobby is all he's got. I hope Alan doesn't end up like that.'

'Look on the bright side,' Toby urged. 'You're not married to the guy yet. Don't make him a widower.'

Barnes-Wakefield was coming back, carrying a tray with three mugs on it. He set it down on a small wooden table.

'I made us coffee. You do drink it? I brought sugar separate. I take three spoonfuls myself.'

When they were all three settled with coffee Barnes-Wakefield sat back and fixed his deceptively milky gaze on his visitors. 'Now then, you want to ask me about the Kemp case.' It wasn't a question but a statement.

'It's as I tried to explain on the phone—' Meredith began.

'Alison Harris, as she was, is now Alison Jenner and married to a cousin of mine,' Toby interrupted. 'She's been getting some poison pen letters.'

Barnes-Wakefield sipped his coffee. 'You won't want to hear me say this of a member of your family, but I thought then, and I think now, we had enough evidence to support the case. The jury thought otherwise. I was disappointed we lost it.'

'Look, sir,' Toby said frankly. 'I don't want to get into a discussion about that. We obviously differ in our opinions as to whether my cousin's wife was responsible for Miss Kemp's death. By the way, she thinks it may have been an accident.'

Barnes-Wakefield shook his head slowly. 'No, it wasn't an accident. A murder set up to look like an accident, that's how it looked to me then – and now. We live in a country where we accept a jury's verdict. But I've not changed my mind and I've spent quite a long time during my retirement mulling over the Kemp case. No investigating officer likes to lose one.'

There was something frighteningly implacable about this nice old gentleman, thought Meredith. He had made up his mind early in the case that Alison was guilty. He still believed it. His investigation had probably been overshadowed by his determination to charge her. He wouldn't have wanted to hear any counter-arguments. He didn't want to hear them now. Thank goodness Alan isn't like that, she told herself. Whatever the circumstances of the case, Alan always tries to keep an open mind.

'The person who has been writing to Alison knows about the case,' said Toby. 'But it was twenty-five years ago. Do you know if there were ever any books written on it?'

Barnes-Wakefield shook his head. 'None that I ever heard of. There was a lot in the newspapers at the time.'

'Especially around here?' Meredith prompted.

The pale sharp gaze moved to take her in. 'Oh yes, the local press had a field day.'

'I understand,' Toby said, 'that the housekeeper had rather a lot to say at the time.'

'You'll mean the cleaning woman, Mrs Travis?'

For the first time Meredith sensed a slight loss of confidence in Barnes-Wakefield's voice and demeanour. Her own antennae tingled.

'Yes,' she said. 'That was the name. Alison felt that she had never liked her.'

'Travis . . .' said Barnes-Wakefield slowly, giving himself time to think, thought Meredith. 'Yes, I remember her. She had a lot to say and I agree, she didn't like Alison Harris.'

'Have you any idea why?' she asked.

Barnes-Wakefield was definitely avoiding her gaze now. 'Well, she was fond of the old lady, I think, protective, you'd call it. Miss Harris was a city girl, a bit brash in her ways. Whenever she turned up, it unsettled Miss Kemp. Mrs Travis, she was the old-fashioned type, a local woman.'

Meredith was thinking rapidly. Mrs Travis would have been unlikely to have had any transport other than a pushbike. She must have lived very locally in order to work for Freda Kemp. Aloud, she asked, 'Did she live in one of those cottages just before you get to the Kemp cottage?'

Now the milky gaze swung round to her. 'I fancy she did. But we didn't rely on her testimony, if that's what you're thinking.' He turned back to Toby. 'I wish I could help you. I'm afraid I can't. I had a long chat on the phone with a chap in your part of the world, a Superintendent Markby, about the case. I answered his questions to the best of my ability and followed it up with an e-mail setting out my reasoning at the time. Briefly, I pretty well told him what I've told you. I don't think you'll find the answer to Miss Harris's – Mrs Jenner's – present troubles down here.' The milky gaze assessed Toby again. 'Some people court trouble. When you've had as much experience as I've had, you'll find that out. I'm not surprised your cousin's got herself into another spot of bother.'

'E-mail?' Toby sounded surprised.

Barnes-Wakefield looked a little smug. 'Oh yes, got to keep up with the modern ways of doing things. The computer has been very useful to me. I browse the Internet.' He put down his mug and stirred in his chair. 'As far as these letters are concerned, I don't think there's anything I can say that'd be of any use to you.'

The implication was clearly that they had reached the end of the interview.

Meredith plunged in. 'We would like to speak to Mrs Travis.'

'Would you now? I wonder where you think that would get you. You'll have a job finding her. I doubt she'll live in the same place. You'll have to knock on doors, like the police do. Old-fashioned investigating.' He smiled at them but the faded brownish eyes weren't amused.

★   ★   ★

'Whew!' said Toby when they had left. 'What did you make of that? Alison never had a chance.'

'No, and the worst of it is, he never had anything but the best of intentions. He wanted to find the killer of Miss Kemp. He thought he had found her.'

'He didn't like losing the case, that's for sure!' Toby drummed his fingers on the car dashboard. 'Do you think he might have written the letters, Merry?'

'Barnes-Wakefield?' she exclaimed, startled.

'Why not? Nice old fellow, pottering in his greenhouse, a widower and all the rest of it but, underneath it, a vindictive old guy, I bet you! Losing his wife might have made him bitter, too. He's got nothing to think about, by his own admission, but his garden. Also by his own admission, he's spent a lot of his retirement mulling over the Kemp case. Let's say he feels that justice wasn't done. He's got a computer. He knows not to make the kind of mistakes which will set the police on his trail. He feels safe. So he starts writing to Alison to let her know the whole thing's not forgotten and not everyone was prepared to accept the Not Guilty verdict!'

'The letters were postmarked Oxford,' she objected.

'He gives them to someone to post for him. The person doing it may be quite innocent. Barnes-Wakefield has made some excuse. It could be some former police subordinate of his. The chief inspector says do it, and the guy still does it. No questions asked.'

'How would Barnes-Wakefield have found Alison? And you're forgetting Fiona. You're not suggesting he would have killed Fiona as part of his vendetta?'

Toby's enthusiasm subsided. 'No. But perhaps we're being misled by this business of Fiona being found in the lake. Perhaps the letters and Fiona's death aren't connected.'

'He's right in one thing,' Meredith observed. 'We've got to knock on a few doors. I have this gut feeling that Mrs Travis has the answers. Barnes-Wakefield was definitely uneasy when we started to talk about her. I believe he was influenced by her testimony and now he's aware that it may have been flawed. He's been pushing the thought away but it niggles at him.'

That afternoon, having decided on a new approach, they knocked on the doors of the other cottages in the vicinity of the Kemp cottage.

'Sorry to bother you,' Toby began. 'I used to come down to this part of the world for holidays when I was young and I'm trying to find a family named Travis who lived here then . . .'

The first cottage belonged to a couple originally from Bristol who had retired there. They had been there four years.

Sorry to bother you, I used to come down . . .

The second cottage belonged to people who only used it at holiday time and were down for Easter.

Sorry to bother you, I used to come down . . .

The third cottage belonged to a retired clergyman, a small white-haired sparrow of a man who listened carefully to Toby's request.

'I'm afraid I can't help you,' said the Reverend Simmons, when Toby fell silent. 'Normally I'd suggest you went and asked the local vicar. He might know of people who *would* know, if you understand me. But I know the local man has only been in the parish six months.'

'That's a pity,' Toby said despondently. 'It was a good idea.'

Mr Simmons brightened. 'I'll ask my wife. When I'm stuck, I always ask her. She generally thinks of something. Come in.'

In the Simmonses' comfortable chintz-furnished sitting room they found Mrs Simmons.

'I won't get up,' she said as they were introduced. 'My arthritis won't allow it. But do sit down and Piers will make tea.'

Toby and Meredith exchanged slightly guilty glances.

'Can I tell you the whole story?' asked Toby suddenly. 'It's quite true that I used to come down here for my holidays and it's true I want to find a Mrs Travis. But there's a bit more to it than that.'

The Simmonses, husband and wife, had probably dealt with this kind of request time without number. Mrs Simmons beamed kindly at them. Mr Simmons invited, 'Fire away!'

Between them, and over tea and fruit cake, Toby and Meredith explained about Alison, Freda Kemp, the letters and eventually Fiona's death. At the end of it all, their hosts looked serious.

'What do you think, Phyllis?' enquired Mr Simmons of his wife.

'Well,' she said slowly. 'I was thinking of Eileen Hammond. You did say this Mrs Travis had a child?'

Mr Simmons turned proudly to his visitors. 'There! I said we should ask my wife. She always comes up with something. Eileen Hammond, the very person.'

'Who . . .?' ventured Toby.

Mr Simmons raised a blue-veined hand. 'Ah! Yes. Miss Hammond was for many years the headmistress of the local primary school. The school, sadly, no longer exists. But we've become acquainted with Eileen through attendance at the same church. If Mrs Travis had a son, then he may well have been Eileen's pupil and, if he was, she'll remember him!'

'Eileen never married,' explained Mrs Simmons. 'Her pupils were her family.'

'I'll phone her,' said her husband. 'Right away.'

Eileen Hammond lived in a neat bungalow very like that belonging to ex-Chief Inspector Barnes-Wakefield, except that it didn't have a pond or any gnomes.

'Thank goodness!' said Toby.

Miss Hammond was a spare, angular woman with white hair tucked into an untidy bun. She was also apparently a tapestry fanatic. An unfinished piece of work lay on a chair and around the walls of her sitting room were several framed examples, chiefly floral in subject. They accepted more tea and more fruit cake and, when these formalities were over, they were allowed to explain what had brought them. Miss Hammond listened attentively with her head tilted to one side, her eyes fixed on the speaker's face. This might simply have been a habit gained as a schoolteacher but Meredith suspected it might be because their hostess was slightly deaf.

'Edmund Travis,' Eileen Hammond said when they had finished. She hadn't spoken at once but sat, sifting through her memories as she might a card index. When she found what she wanted, she gave a little nod of satisfaction. The filing system had worked. 'The little boy's name was Edmund and I remember the family very well. They weren't a problem family in the sense of being in any trouble. There was never anything like that. But the father had left home and the mother had to work very hard to support herself and her son. This is a country area and was even more so, back then. Attitudes change slowly. The fact that Mr Travis had done a bunk—'

Meredith started, slightly surprised to hear this slang expression coming from precise Miss Hammond.

Miss Hammond noticed and smiled. 'That's what the local people called it. It was a sort of scandal in those days, believe it or not. A Victorian attitude still persisted that a deserted woman wasn't quite respectable. People were embarrassed to be around her. They felt they ought to do something but they didn't know what, and they didn't want 'wrong ways' rubbing off on their own families. They didn't want the problem transferred, like an illness that was catching. Yet Mrs Travis was the epitome of respectability. She had to be, because of her deserted status. It was a struggle for her although, because they were a low-income family, Edmund got free school lunches. He used to ride to school on a terrible rusty bike I believe he found in a skip.'

'Alison remembers him as being sullen,' Toby remarked.

Miss Hammond disapproved of this word and said firmly, 'He was always polite. He never misbehaved in class. He paid attention. He wasn't clever but he worked hard and achieved average results. His best subject was art. His mother was devoted to him so, although his father had abandoned them both, there wasn't any lack of love at home.'

'What about his mother?' asked Meredith. 'What else do you remember about her?'

Miss Hammond shook her head. 'Not a great deal. I knew her less well than the child. The child, you see, was my province.' Eileen smiled at them. 'As I told you, the mother was a hard-working, very respectable woman, a little old-fashioned in her ways. She was a countrywoman and older than some of the other mothers of children at the school. I think Edmund had come along late in life. She had no time for fads and fancies.'

'And what happened to the boy and his mother, do you know?' Meredith held her breath and was aware that Toby, beside her, was leaning forwards intently.

Eileen shook her head. 'I'm sorry. I don't know. The mother remarried. She moved away with her new husband – I don't recall his name – and took the child with her. I lost touch at that point.'

'Remarried?' Toby exclaimed tactlessly. 'She sounded a bit of a gorgon from all Alison said!'

'A little dour,' Miss Hammond corrected him. 'But not a gorgon. I believe she married an older man. I can't even say that for certain. It's an impression I got. Anyhow, they left.'

There was a silence. Meredith asked, 'Do you remember the Kemp case?'

Eileen raised her eyebrows. 'Indeed I do. I knew Miss Kemp slightly. A very nice woman and, I think, a lonely one. She was devoted to her niece.'

'And do you think her niece killed her?' Toby asked bluntly.

Miss Hammond shook her head again. 'I really have no idea. I hope not, because Freda loved the girl. Anything could have happened. It was a very strange affair.'

'Mrs Travis was Miss Kemp's charwoman.'

This observation by Meredith gained her a severe look from Miss Hammond. 'So I believe. She was, I know, very distressed at Miss Kemp's death. She made some rather wild statements about it all, accusing the niece. The police listened to her perhaps a little too attentively. My personal opinion, and I say this to you in confidence, was that Mrs Travis wasn't altogether sane on the subject. She'd had so many misfortunes and with Miss Kemp's death she lost a job she needed. It was one more blow, one too many.'

'Was Edmund happy at the idea of his mother being remarried?' Meredith asked.

'Oh, yes, I'm sure he was. The family's financial position improved. He got a new bicycle.' Miss Hammond glanced at a carriage clock on the mantel shelf. It was time for them to go.

'That's it, then,' said Toby when they left Eileen Hammond's home. 'I don't think we can get any further.'

'We can try the pub again tonight.'

But the pub proved no more a source of information that evening than it had done the previous lunchtime. The retired couple from Bristol called by for a modest tipple, greeted Meredith and Toby with polite smiles, and left early. The garage man, Melhuish, leaned on the bar all evening and was still there when Toby and Meredith left. He nodded to them but did not appear to want to get into any conversation with anyone. Everyone else there was a visitor, down for Easter.

The following morning, Meredith drove Toby back to Bamford.

'We've not achieved much,' sighed Toby. 'Unless you count digging out Barnes-Wakefield, and it turns out Alan had already been in touch with him. Just following behind Alan isn't what I came to Cornwall to do. I wanted to find out something new!'

'I think we've achieved quite a lot,' Meredith argued. 'At least you know now how Alison came to be suspected and accused. Between Mrs Travis and Barnes-Wakefield she had no chance!'

'But did he write the letters?' Toby wasn't giving up his theory.

'I don't know,' Meredith mused. 'I think he'd be capable of it, but that doesn't mean he did do it. And he had no motive to kill Fiona.'

'Poor Fi,' said Toby. 'Her death put the whole business in a different league, didn't it?'

The previous evening, about the time Toby and Meredith left Eileen Hammond, Alan Markby was walking through Bamford. He was thinking about Meredith and, coincidentally, thinking about Barnes-Wakefield. In fact, the two subjects were not unconnected in his mind at the time. He missed Meredith. She'd only gone down to Cornwall for a couple of days, but heck, he still missed her. He understood something of the loneliness Barnes-Wakefield must feel since his wife's death. Markby's own first marriage had finished in divorce. At the time it had seemed a relief to get the arguments and acrimony behind him. But later, in a strange way, he'd missed Rachel. Rather, he'd missed going home at the end of the day and finding someone there. Even if it had been someone complaining he was late again and the dinner ruined. He'd missed going to bed with someone else and disliked waking to an empty room. He disliked sitting alone before a television set with no one to complain to about the direness of the programmes. At social functions he became again the single man he had been at twenty. When you're twenty, that's fine. Life is full of opportunity for the unattached male. In one's thirties a slight unease sets in as all about you pair off. At forty comes the need to explain one's unattached status. Old age alone begins to appear frightening. It was something Toby was envisaging and it had led him to the crazy plan of proposing marriage to Fiona. Fortunately, he hadn't done it.

'Or,' murmured Markby, 'he says he didn't. But did he? And was it so crazy? She was a rich young woman.'

Don't talk to yourself, he admonished himself. Not a good sign and, in a copper, positively dangerous.

Markby's own isolation had ended when Meredith entered his life. He still felt a kind of surprised gratitude that life should have been generous enough to give him a second chance. And he missed her. He wanted her here, not roaming around Cornwall with Toby Smythe.

At that moment he realized he was being hailed from the far side of the street.

'Mr Markby!'

It was Stebbings. He stood by the kerb in his grubby waxed jacket, waving his long arms in a wild semaphore. His hair and beard were even more unkempt. Passers-by gave him a wide berth. Seeing he had attracted the superintendent's attention, Stebbings lurched across the road with his long arms still flailing as though he had lost all control of them. 'I want a word!'

Markby wondered if the man was drunk. It was early in the evening, but that didn't mean anything. He couldn't smell any drink but he eyed Stebbings cautiously.

'I want a word!' said Stebbings again when he reached him.

'Go ahead,' invited Markby.

'Where's my boy?' Stebbings demanded.

'I don't know,' said Markby immediately. 'Where should he be?'

'At home, that's where!' Stebbings yelled in his face. People turned their heads.

'Come along,' Markby said soothingly, 'we'll walk on and you tell me about it.'

Having to walk alongside Markby put an effective brake on Stebbings' belligerence. His manner remained truculent, however. 'I've been looking all over town for him.'

'It's not yet seven,' Markby pointed out.

'He's been gone since yesterday evening, dammit!' roared Stebbings.

'I see. Has he spent the night away from home before, without telling you?'

'No!' Stebbings stopped and forced Markby to stop also. They were outside a betting shop, which was a little unfortunate. 'He doesn't do that,' said Stebbings in a quieter voice. 'My wife, she's going crazy. She's reckons he's had an accident.'

Markby's brain was racing, throwing up a variety of scenarios. 'It might be a girl,' he said. 'He's that age.'

'I've been to her house,' said Stebbings. 'Cherry Basset. She's got no more sense than her mother. But she hasn't seen him. She was at home last night, mother swears to it. So does the bloke who lives there with them.'

'We'll check the hospitals,' said Markby. 'Have you told the police?'

'I told them, told the local chaps. Do you think they showed any interest? Not a bit. Like you, they said he'd be with a girl or a bunch of his mates.' Stebbings snorted. 'He doesn't hang around with a crowd of others, Darren. He's a loner, like me.'

'Oh, I'm interested,' said Markby. Anyone, even Darren Stebbings, who was connected with Overvale House was of interest. Darren's absence might be easily explained, but the fact remained he had chosen a bad moment to go missing. Markby was getting that feeling of all not being well.

'You go home,' he said, 'and reassure Mrs Stebbings. We'll do everything we can to find him.'

Stebbings gave him a wild look and stabbed a grimy forefinger against Markby's chest. 'You find him soon.' He lurched away, his long hair flying.

Markby stood in silent thought on the spot where Stebbings had left him. He was roused by a hiss at his elbow and looked down to find a small wrinkled face looking up at him.

'Hello, Ferdy,' he said resignedly.

Ferdy Lee, one of the small-time crooks (or, as the man himself described it, entrepreneurs of the neighbourhood), smiled delightedly at being recognized. He had broken nicotine-stained teeth. 'I've got a good tip if you want a flutter,' he said.

'Tip? Flutter?' Markby suddenly remembered that he was standing in front of the betting shop. 'No, thanks all the same, Ferdy.'

'I expect you don't want to be seen going in, you being well known in the town,' said Ferdy with kindly understanding. 'I could put the bet on for you.'

Markby thanked him again and hurried away. Anxious to leave Ferdy behind, he had not consciously chosen a direction, but found himself walking down the road in which, if he remembered correctly, Jess Campbell had rented a flat. He dredged the number from his memory and rang her doorbell.

She was so surprised to see him that he was embarrassed and found himself apologizing profusely. 'I just dropped by to tell you a piece of news which may or may not have a bearing on the Jenner case.'

She invited him in with a clear reluctance. He thought at first she might have company, or she might just object to being called on without warning when she was off duty. But as soon as he saw the interior of the flat, he understood her unwillingness. A television set flickered in one corner and, by a cruel irony, was showing one of those make-over programmes in which a run-down property was being transformed.

'It's not much,' she said, seeing the expression on his face. 'But it's temporary.' She followed his gaze to the television set and added wryly, 'Yes, right . . .' She went to switch it off.

'I won't stay long.' His own embarrassment was growing and he felt she realized it. This was an awful place. Was it the best she'd been able to find? There was a glass of white wine on the stained coffee table.

'Can I offer you a drink?' She indicated the wine glass. 'That's all I've got, I'm afraid.'

'That's fine. Thanks.'

She retreated to the kitchen and returned with a second glass and the bottle. Markby seated himself in the rickety armchair and accepted the filled glass she held out.

'We can surely find you somewhere better than this,' he said.

She shook her head. 'Don't worry. It's given me the necessary encouragement to buy. Meredith showed me over her house. I liked it very much. I've been wondering, if she hasn't accepted any other offer, if I could make one.'

'Oh?' He tried not to look startled. 'As far as I know, she hasn't accepted any other offer. She's rung to let me know she and Smythe come back from Cornwall tomorrow.'

'Cornwall?' Jess looked puzzled.

Markby's embarrassment, which had been lessening with the arrival of the wine, returned. 'Er, yes. She and Smythe went down there for a brief visit. You can ask her about the house tomorrow evening.' He buried his nose in his glass and tried not to wince as the liquid struck his palate. It was the sort usually sold by supermarkets in large bottles. 'I called by because I've just had a meeting with Harry Stebbings in town. Darren has gone missing.'

He explained the details, such as he knew them, and Jess looked serious.

'It's a dodgy time for him to go missing,' she said.

'It is. I took his digital camera off him the other day.' Markby gave a rueful grin. 'I confess I felt a little mean doing it, he was so distressed. But the little blighter was too good at snapping people unawares. And I've been thinking about that. Perhaps, in the present circumstances, Darren's hobby was a dangerous one.'

'We can get a search warrant,' Jess said promptly. 'Turn over that cottage where he lives with his parents. They won't like it. But it might turn up some reason for his going missing. At the very least, we can take away all his photographic material and his computer.'

'Computer?' Markby set down his wine and blinked at her.

'He might have stored some of the digital images he took on the computer,' Jess explained. 'He's bound to have one.'

Chapter Twelve

It turned out to be a busy day. It began during the night when someone threw a brick through the glass door of a hairdresser's salon in the centre of Bamford. Robbery didn't appear to be a motive. A notice in the window informed passers-by that no money was kept on the premises overnight. The cash till was left open so that anyone still doubtful and peering through the window could see how empty it was. The owner, called to investigate, confirmed no one had helped himself to the hairdryers or cleared the shelves of bottles of spray and gel. It was probably, the local police decided, just some home-going merrymaker who was even now sleeping it off somewhere. When he woke up, his own actions would be lost in a fog and even if he were found and accused of breaking the door, he'd vehemently deny it with the confidence of one who simply couldn't remember.

Constable Wallace was sitting in the police car outside the salon at seven thirty that morning. He was waiting for his colleague, still inside the premises with the owner, to join him. The salon was next door to a newsagent's which was already open for business. The delivery boys had arrived to collect their satchel of papers and cycled away laden. A steady trickle of customers had been going in and out of the shop either to buy the morning news or to stock up with cigarettes for the day ahead. At the moment things were quiet; a girl came out of the shop and walked up to Wallace in the police car. She stooped down by the window indicating she wanted to speak. Wallace let down the window cautiously. He recognized her as the girl who worked in the shop. She had long, unkempt hair and small, truculent features like a terrier. Her name, he seemed to recall, was Cherry.

'Oi!' said Cherry Basset by way of greeting.

'Yes?' returned Wallace. 'Something I can help you with?'

She stared at him as if he'd said something particularly silly. 'No,' she said. 'I got some information for you.'

Wallace brightened. 'About the breakage?' He nodded towards the door.

Cherry turned her gaze to the salon's damaged door and contemplated it for a moment as if assessing whether it was worth her attention. Apparently it wasn't. She shrugged. 'No.'

'What then?' asked Wallace tersely.

'My boyfriend, Darren Stebbings. He's missing. You lot are supposed to be looking for him.' She didn't appear to have much faith in their ability to do this.

'Yeah,' said Wallace. 'We know about him. You seen him?'

'No, of course I haven't seen him,' she snapped. 'If I had, he wouldn't be missing, would he? I'd know where he was! But I've been thinking.'

'Oh yes?' Now it was Wallace's turn to sound doubtful about her abilities.

'The last time I did see him, he said something to me about he knew where to get some money. He didn't explain. It might have something to do with it.'

'You didn't ask where he was going to get this money?' Wallace sounded sceptical.

'No,' said Cherry. 'I didn't know he was going to go missing, then, did I?'

'All right,' said Wallace wearily. 'I'll tell 'em back at the station.' His colleague was emerging from the salon accompanied by the owner. 'We've got to take care of this first,' he added.

'All right,' said Cherry, tossing back her dishevelled locks. 'Just don't say I didn't tell you.'

★　★　★

'Caro?' Michael Fossett called out his wife's name from the yard behind the back door. If he wanted to go in the house, he'd have to take his boots off. Easier to stand outside and shout.

She appeared in the doorway. 'What is it?' She'd been at the computer working out the farm accounts and was annoyed at being called away. She held her glasses in one hand and a sheet of paper in the other. The sunlight fell on her face and made her blink at him.

The sight of her made him smile, not because he was amused, but because he felt happy whenever he saw her. She had been a very pretty girl and he thought she was still pretty. She'd put on some weight, of course, and her hair was just starting to grey, but she was the same in his mind. Over the last few years, when so much had gone wrong, as the farm turned slowly but inexorably into a loss-making concern and their future looked ever bleaker, this had been the one thing which had kept him going: his marriage and his family life. The thought that something might threaten it frightened him. That fear had been growing slowly in him since Fiona Jenner's death.

Aloud he said, 'I've been thinking about those sheep over on Jerry Jenner's land. I'll think I'll move them down here. It'll take me the best part of the morning.' He and Caroline ran the farm between them with the sporadic help of an elderly farm worker, not here today. His back had 'slipped out again', something it tended to do after a late night drinking at the Feathers. 'Do you want me for anything before I start?'

She shook her head. 'No, but if you should see either Jeremy or Alison . . .'

'I'll be doing my best not to see them.' That sounded cruel and he hadn't intended to sound cruel or uncaring. But he had enough troubles of his own. He couldn't take on board all the bad luck of others. It was terrible for Jenner to lose his daughter. The Fossetts had sent flowers and a note of condolence, Caroline had organized that, and Michael supposed they'd turn out for the funeral, when it was held. They couldn't do any more. It was a private thing, a death in the family. Even a violent death at criminal hands as Fiona's had been. The police had been to the Fossetts' farmhouse asking if they'd noticed anything unusual during the days leading up to the death. Any strangers? Any strange vehicles parked suspiciously? No, he'd told them. If he'd seen a car parked on his land, he'd have investigated. A year ago they'd had a spot of trouble with some local youths using a remote area of his land for dog-fighting. Since then he'd kept an eye open, in case they came back. So he was sure he hadn't seen anyone.

He shrugged now. 'I'm really sorry for them, but what can I say? I'm hoping I don't bump into either of them.'

She hesitated. 'Take care.'

That was new. She would not have said that to him before the tragedy at Overvale. Farming was a lonely life and it didn't do to be nervous or worried if you found yourself far from human habitation or company. But there was a new element out there these days in the familiar landscape. It was more of a threat than the dog-fighting or the occasional discovery of signs of badger-baiting. Both these activities were illegal and nasty but they went on all the time, all over the countryside. This new intrusion was different, more insidious, more personal. It had, as yet, no face. No one, to their knowledge, had seen it. But all of them felt its presence.

He whistled to his dog and set off. His wife watched him go and went back to her computer. But before she did, she locked the back door. That, too, was something new.

Fiona's death had brought other concerns than their personal safety. Dorcas Stebbings was not the only one who was worried what the tragedy might mean in changed circumstances for all of them. Leasing the extra grazing land from Jenner, at what was frankly a trifling rent, was very useful to the Fossetts and Michael had plenty to think about as he strode across the fields. He'd been making use of Jenner's land since the man had bought Overvale. Jenner had no use for it. He was happy for Michael to take care of it and over the years Michael had begun to look on it as an extension of his own land. But the Jenners might not want to stay, now that young Fiona was dead. A new owner of Overvale might not be willing to lease out the land – or might be willing, but at a vastly increased rent. Michael scowled to himself. A new financial problem wasn't something they could easily deal with just now.

The dog was running ahead of him. She was a six-year-old black and white border collie and her name was Marge. She had been named after a television cartoon series character and the name had been chosen by the Fossetts' own daughter, Bridget. Bridget was staying with her grandparents for the Easter school holiday. Holidays were unknown to Michael and his wife. They were too busy on the farm and there was no one to look after the stock even if they had had time. Bridget knew it and was happy to hang round the farm when she came home for the school holidays but on this occasion, with a murderer on the loose in the district, they had decided she'd be better off visiting Caroline's parents in their North Wales retirement bungalow. Bridget was a good kid but her school fees ate a large hole in the farm's revenues. Slowly but surely, the Fossetts were going broke. Caroline could jiggle the figures any way she liked on that computer, the facts remained the same.

Marge had suddenly scuttled off to the left. Michael called to her but, usually so obedient, she didn't come. She was running round in a circle, head low to the ground, tail tucked in, her whole attitude one of distress.

Her unease was being caused by something lying on the ground. A dead sheep? Michael began to stride across the springy turf towards the spot. The dog looked up, barked once and then stood waiting, guarding whatever it was there.

Michael was near enough now to see what it was, and it wasn't a sheep. He called again to the dog, more sharply. This time she came.

'Wait here, Marge!' he ordered and she dropped to the ground.

He walked on until he reached the thing on the ground. His first thought had been that it was just a bundle of old clothes.

People had no compunction about dumping their rubbish in the countryside. Burnt-out cars, old bedsteads and fridges, plastic sacks of domestic refuse or garden clippings, he'd found the lot over the years. What did the fly-tippers think the farmer did with all that? He had to pay to get it cleared up, that's what he did. It wasn't as if there wasn't a council dump not five miles down the road where people could take stuff. They just couldn't be bothered to drive so far. In the case of the burnt-out car, it had been stolen and used, the police guessed, in the commission of some crime.

Much as he detested all of this, he would have preferred any of it to what he found now. This was a body. He would have expected it to be some old tramp who had died out here from hypothermia or heart failure or some other natural cause. Death was common in the countryside, usually dead stock, but once before, some years ago, they'd found an old chap huddled in a crude shelter made from branches and rags. The tramp himself had been so emaciated and his skin so tanned and leathery with weather and a layer of ingrained grime that he'd looked like a mummified figure. But this wasn't a tramp; and since Fiona's Jenner's murder, another, grimmer, possibility lurked and had now raised its unwelcome head.

Michael dropped on to his heels and balanced by the side of the body which was sprawled face uppermost, its arms flung out to either side. He recognized who it was, of course. It was that kid of Harry Stebbings. What was his name? David? No, Darren, that was it. He was dead, no two ways about that! And it wasn't natural causes. There was blood on his T-shirt just below the breastbone.

'Bloody hell!' Michael said softly.

He took the dead boy's wrist, forcing himself to touch the clammy skin. He could lift it, but there was definite resistance. He released it, then stood up and gazed around him. How the devil had the poor little tyke got here? There was no reason why Darren Stebbings should be walking across country. But there was a track over there, skirting the edge of the pasture. It ran across the landscape and joined the other track which ran down the edge of the woods. Darren might or might not have come that way. More to the point, someone else probably had. Michael had a spontaneous, father's, thought. Thank God Bridget wasn't staying at home this Easter. They'd been right to send her to Wales. Bridget could have been wandering about out here . . . This could have been his daughter.

Once that thought had left his mind, another entered it. Michael hesitated. This would put the finishing touch to it. A second death meant that the Jenners would almost certainly leave. For a mad moment, Michael toyed with the idea of moving the body, hiding it somewhere. A stupid idea, he told himself. It would turn up. Besides, this was pure selfishness. This was more important than the farm's troubles.

He dug his mobile phone from the pocket of his quilted body-warmer and called the police. Then he rang Caroline and told her what had happened. She didn't say much, only that he should watch out. The killer was long gone, he assured her. The boy was stone cold and stiffening. 'You keep that door locked!' he ordered.

'It's locked,' came her quiet voice, its calm ruffled by worry and growing shock.

The news came as a sombre and unwelcome development to Markby and to Jess Campbell. Inevitably, the first thought of both of them was that they should have treated Darren's disappearance with more urgency. It had rung alarm bells and they had tried to find him.

'But not tried hard enough!' said Markby grimly.

Now Jess was being driven to the scene by Steve Prescott. They drove in silence, Jess thinking furiously what this new death might mean.

Prescott spoke once to say, 'If he died out here in the middle of nowhere, it's no wonder we didn't find the poor little bugger.'

Jess supposed that was Prescott's attempt at consolation. He knew what she must be thinking. In a sense, he was right.

To search miles of open land was a marathon task. In the case of any missing person, one began first with tracing his regular contacts and places he visited. No one had suggested that Darren, despite or perhaps because he lived in the country, spent his free time hiking up hill and down dale. At every opportunity he headed for Bamford and that was where they'd looked first.

They passed by the Stebbings' cottage. As they reached the gates to Overvale House, a few metres further on, a figure lurched from behind the gate post and brought them to a halt by the simple process of standing in the middle of the drive in front of them. It was Stebbings himself, wild and hirsute as ever, waving his long arms up and down as usual, giving the impression that the arms were operated not by him, but by some unseen puppeteer.

'Damn!' said Jess.

They hadn't contacted Stebbings yet. Their intention was to remove the body, once it had been photographed and the pathologist had seen it, and request Stebbings to come and make formal identification at the morgue. But that wasn't to be so, it seemed.

Stebbings stumbled to the car and crouched by Jess's window. She let it down.

'What's going on?' he demanded hoarsely. 'I saw the police cars going up there.' He pointed in the general direction of Overvale House. 'Has it got anything to do with my boy? Have you found him?'

Jess took a difficult decision. 'We've had a report of a body, Mr Stebbings. We don't know for sure whose it might be.' The identification by the farmer, Fossett, was probably right but they would still need that of a family member to be quite sure. 'Why don't you go home,' Jess went on, 'while we investigate it? I'll get in touch with you as soon as I've anything to tell you. This might not be anything to do with Darren.'

She felt the foolishness of saying this, even as she spoke.

Stebbings, rightly, had no truck with it. 'My boy's missing. Now you've found a body. Who the hell should it be? I'm coming with you.'

He grasped the handle of the rear door. Prescott was out of the car in an instant and on his way to intercept him. Jess called out to stop him. Stebbings would certainly resist and there would be a regrettable scene. Things were already regrettable enough.

'All right, Mr Stebbings, you can come with us. But please, do as we tell you. We'll look at the body first and if we think it's necessary—'

'I'm coming with you!' said Stebbings obstinately.

Prescott opened the rear door to allow Stebbings to get in. Unfortunately, while they had been concentrating on the man, they had failed to see his wife. She must have seen them drive past the cottage and had run out and followed, catching up with them at the gates. She presented an incongruous figure in her apron, her lank greying hair fixed in a row of pin curls across her brow. She said nothing, simply opened the other rear door and got in beside her husband.

'No, Mrs Stebbings, I'm sorry,' Jess exclaimed. 'Your husband will come with us and he'll—'

'I'll not be getting out,' she said in a sullen, obstinate voice. 'You'll not get me out.'

Prescott, who had known it take three strapping constables to get one drunken female teenager into a police car, murmured, 'It won't be easy, ma'am, not unless her husband . . .'

'Do you go on back home, Dorcas,' ordered Stebbings.

'No, Harry,' she replied in the same obstinate tone.

Stebbings apparently recognized it. 'She won't go,' he said flatly.

Jess heaved a sigh. 'All right, Mrs Stebbings, but when we get there I must insist you remain in the car, is that understood?'

Michael Fossett had waited by the body, sitting on the ground with his arms resting on his bent knees. The dog lay on her stomach beside him. Watching the dead, thought Michael. It was an ancient custom, he'd heard, that the dead were not to be left alone. Overhead birds wheeled in the sky. Crows. They knew there was carrion below. It was as well he and Marge were here and had discovered the body so early in the day. Otherwise the crows would have found it first and he'd seen what crows could do to the carcass of a dead sheep. It was a wonder foxes hadn't scented the body during the night. A fox has sharp teeth and isn't fussy what he eats.

The first police officers to arrive came by way of the track which ran by the woods. They parked their car at the edge of the field and walked over it towards the waiting Michael, who rose to his feet. Madge stood up too.

'His name is Darren Stebbings,' Michael said by way of greeting as they reached him. Both of them were very young. They probably weren't that much older than the dead youth. One of them looked queasy. 'He's stiffening up,' Michael added. 'He must have been lying there all night.'

The constables consulted together and he heard the words 'missing person'. They phoned for back-up and soon all manner of people began to arrive. One of the constables took Michael aside and started to take a statement from him. He asked if he could leave but was asked to just stay a few minutes, because the inspector would be there shortly and might want to speak to him.

About ten minutes after that the inspector arrived and turned out to be a young woman with short red hair. She wasn't alone. She had a burly sergeant with her and, worse, she had Harry Stebbings lurching along beside her. Both she and the sergeant looked put out and Michael guessed there had been some argument with Stebbings about this. Stebbings had won.

Michael felt a strange mixture of emotions, pity certainly, but also deep embarrassment and shame. Death ought to be a private matter. Here they all were standing around gawping at Stebbings' boy as he lay there, looking young, vulnerable, unattractive and lifeless. Now they were staring at a father as the man first set sight on the body of his son. All this ought to be done behind closed doors, decorously, the body neatly laid out, flowers and candles nearby. But that was sentimentality and this was raw life.

Stebbings stared down at his son in silence for a long moment then muttered, 'Yes,' and turned aside.

That was when the door of one of the police vehicles parked over by the woods opened and a woman got out. She began to run towards them, stumbling over the rough ground and uttering weird cries like seagulls make as they wheel in the air. To his horror, Michael recognized Dorcas Stebbings. Who on earth had brought her here? But probably, he realized, she had refused to be left behind.

She was near enough now to be seen clearly. She still wore her old-fashioned pinafore. Her hands, which she waved in the air, were oddly whitened and Michael guessed that this was caused by flour. She'd been baking when the news had come.

Two officers had moved to intercept her but she swept them aside. Both Harry and the woman inspector tried to catch at her but she eluded them, too. Her wild progress was inexorable, beyond any human interference. She had seen the body now and her voice rose even higher in a kind of squeal such as pigs make when being loaded up for the slaughterhouse. She flung herself at the body and they all rushed forwards to drag her away, but she had wrapped her arms round the stiff corpse and was trying to hold her child to her bosom as she must have done so many times when he was a toddler and had fallen and cried for comfort. But the body was cold and rigid in her arms.

'Leave it be, Dorcas!' Harry shouted at her and took her arm to drag her away.

'Please, Mrs Stebbings,' the woman inspector was pleading. 'Please, you mustn't touch . . .'

'Not touch!' Dorcas shrieked at her. 'Not touch my own child!'

They pulled her away and, as they did, she caught sight of Michael.

'They've taken our children!' she screeched at him. 'They've taken Mr Jenner's girl and they've taken my boy! Where's your girl?'

'She's staying with her grandparents,' Michael heard himself say.

She uttered a long moan. 'You've still got your child. But they've taken mine! I've got nothing now!'

'For Christ's sake,' Michael muttered to the woman inspector. 'Can't I go now? I've made a statement. My wife's alone at the house. I must get back. You know where to find me.'

The inspector said he could go. He set off as quickly as he could, turning his back to the grisly scene, Marge scurrying at his heels. But he was still able to hear those crazy cries from the distraught mother. He wanted to put his hands over his ears, blot them out, but it would be in vain.

Her mind has gone, he thought in frozen horror.

By the body, one of the constables who had first arrived on the scene approached Jess Campbell.

'Wallace, ma'am, from Bamford station,' he introduced himself. 'We had a call out to a break-in this morning and while we were there, his –' Wallace indicated Darren – 'his girlfriend turned up. She wanted to tell me something.'

'I'm sorry,' Jess said later. 'It should not have happened that way and I didn't mean it to.'

She had been describing the scene by Darren's dead body to Markby. He had listened quietly and without interrupting, but she could see the reproach in his face.

'I know the body should have been removed to the morgue and then the father called there to make a positive ID. But they'd both seen the police car pass by their cottage earlier. They knew something was up. Stebbings was waiting by the gates to Overvale House and jumped out in front of my car. I had to admit there was a possibility we'd found his son and then he insisted on coming along. He seemed calm enough. I agreed. I hadn't counted on the woman. She must have seen my car and come running out of her cottage. She came up while I was talking to her husband. She still had her apron on and her hands covered in flour. She just got in the car. I couldn't order Prescott to drag her out.' Jess's voice was miserable.

'No, it shouldn't have happened that way,' Markby agreed. 'But sometimes events take over. Has a doctor seen Mrs Stebbings?'

'Yes. He's given her something. She – she just lost it completely. I suppose I should too, in her situation. To see her cradling that body, it was awful.'

'Come on!' Markby said briskly. 'We see awful sights all the time in our job. I feel badly, too, because I've got the poor little blighter's camera and he was so upset when I took it off him.'

'What do you think he was planning?' Jess asked. 'We've spoken to Cherry Basset again. She insists that she only knows he was sure he knew a way of getting some money.'

'Which we can bet was blackmail. I'd taken his camera and he wanted to buy a new one. He'd taken a photograph he knew was worth money. He went to someone and told whoever it was about it. That someone was the killer. The boy wasn't the brightest. He wouldn't think about that, only about the money.'

Jess had handled the discovery of Darren's body badly. Dorcas Stebbings shouldn't have been allowed anywhere near the grim scene. But would Darren have been lying dead there if Markby hadn't taken his camera? It was something Markby would have to live with.

Aloud, he said, 'Let's concentrate on this computer of the boy's.'

Darren's computer and other photographic paraphernalia had been brought from his attic workroom to HQ to be looked at by an expert. The expert in question, a young Asian man, looked up as Markby and Jess came into the room.

'Pretty straightforward,' he said. 'He stored several of the photographs he took with the digital camera on the computer's hard drive and the rest on disk.'

'Can we see them?' Markby asked.

'Sure, no problem.'

The images appeared one by one on the screen. Fiona Jenner in her bikini lounging by the pool. Fiona Jenner walking with her hands in her pockets and her long hair flying in the wind. Fiona riding one of the horses.

'His father didn't understand that the images could be stored like this,' Jess mused. 'Or he'd have ordered Darren to destroy them. He was keen on Fiona, wasn't he?'

'She was the nearest he could get to a celebrity,' Markby said sadly.

The images flicked on. But now they were different. These hadn't been taken at Overvale. They'd been taken, it seemed, in a pub car park. The pub itself could be seen in the background and was familiar.

'That's the Feathers!' Markby said, excitement touching his voice. 'Fiona went there at least once, we know that.'

There were several people in the frame. Most were young men and wore identical white T-shirts with some slogan on the breast.

'A team,' Markby said. 'The darts team, arriving for the match. There was a darts match the evening Fiona was seen at the Feathers.'

Here was another frame showing the darts players but, this time, the home team with the pub's name on their shirts. With them were a few women.

'There's Fiona!' Jess said. She pointed at the screen. 'Look, her body's obscured by that other woman, but her face is clear. It's Fiona Jenner! She must have gone there with someone on the home darts team.'

'And that,' said Markby, pointing at another figure, 'is Ted Pritchard, from Rusticity. It could be coincidence. He drinks at the Feathers. It makes sense he belongs to their darts team. Or, he could have met Fiona at Overvale House,' he added, 'when he was delivering the garden furniture there.'

'Got chatting to her and asked her out for a drink,' Jess said. 'Suggested she come along for the darts match?'

'But why would she agree?' Markby said thoughtfully. 'Not for his company, we can be sure of that. Fiona wasn't interested in male company other than Toby's and he was a relative. I don't suppose she was a darts fan, either. But there might have been something else linking them . . .'

As he spoke another picture appeared on the monitor screen. Markby recognized it as the track beside the woodland where he'd spoken to Harry Stebbings. A white van was parked on it and standing by the van, deep in conversation, were Ted Pritchard and Fiona Jenner.

'That's it!' Markby snapped. 'We need to talk to Ted Pritchard at once! Come on, we'll drive down to Rusticity now!'

It was lunchtime and Markby called by the Feathers first. It was situated on the way from Regional HQ to the Watersmeet trading estate and they knew Ted sometimes drank there at lunchtime. But he wasn't there today and Dolores Forbes hadn't seen him. Her whole person quivering with curiosity she offered them a drink, on the house. They declined it. She looked half disappointed and half relieved. She wanted to know why they sought Ted Pritchard, but she didn't believe in handing out free drinks as a matter of principle.

They drove on to the trading estate. At Rusticity they found Ted's business partner, Steve Poole.

'Ted's lunch hour,' said Steve, his pale gaze inquisitive. 'What do you want him for?'

'Just to check something,' Markby said vaguely. 'Where might he be?'

'You could try the Feathers. He goes over there for a pint and a sandwich some days.'

'We've already called in. He's not there.'

Steve scratched his thinning hair. 'Then he's probably out on his bike.'

'*His bike?*'

'Oh, keen cyclist, is Ted.' Steve nodded wisely. 'Keeps himself fit that way. He'll have gone home to collect his bike and cycle miles before he comes back here to work.' Steve pointed down the road towards the open countryside beyond the trading estate. 'He'll be out there somewhere.'

Chapter Thirteen

Meredith and Toby had made better time on the return journey from Cornwall, leaving very early in the morning and arriving on the outskirts of Bamford at lunchtime. They were now heading for Overvale House so that Meredith could drop Toby there. As they travelled they had spent the time in urgent discussion as to what Jeremy Jenner was to be told.

'There isn't much, is there?' Toby said morosely. 'Poor old Jerry will be waiting, hoping we've turned up something interesting. But we didn't even manage to find Mrs Travis. Luckily we did find Barnes-Wakefield and I've definitely got my eye on him!'

'But we don't tell Jeremy that!' Meredith said firmly. 'Not until we've spoken to Alan. We don't know what Jeremy might do. Alison's been afraid he'll do something irrational. I'm sorry, but you're just going to have to tell Jeremy we drew a blank.'

There was normally little traffic on this lonely road but now, suddenly, a police car swept past them, driving in the opposite direction, towards Bamford.

'Did you see that?' Toby asked incredulously. 'Harry Stebbings was in that car.'

But Meredith was overtaking a cyclist who, head bent, helmeted and goggled, was pumping his legs up and down again the increasing incline. She hadn't seen the passenger in the police car. 'Are you sure?' she asked, when she had negotiated the obstacle.

'Of course I'm sure. You can't mistake Stebbings. What's going on? Could they have arrested old Harry?'

'If they have, Jeremy will know,' Meredith told him, still not really believing it.

They reached the gates of Overvale House and turned in. As they drew up before the front porch in a swirl of gravel chips, Jeremy Jenner came hurrying out to greet them. There was an expression almost of panic on his face and when he saw who had arrived he looked momentarily bewildered and then relieved.

'What's going on?' Toby asked, scrambling from the passenger seat. 'We've just seen Stebbings in a police car, heading for Bamford. Or I saw him, Meredith didn't. It was definitely Harry.'

Jenner put a hand to his forehead. 'Yes, it was Harry. You won't know it, but there's been another death.'

They stared at him in horror.

Toby whispered, 'Who? Not – not Alison?'

'Alison's safe. No, not her, thank God.' Jenner shook his head as if to clear it of a haze. 'One oughtn't to be grateful for being spared if it means someone else has suffered. But of course I am. The death is of Harry's boy, Darren. He'd gone missing and this morning he turned up dead.' Jenner waved a hand in the general direction of the countryside. 'Mike Fossett found him. It's a hell of a business. It just keeps getting worse. Come in, come in . . .' He gestured towards the door.

'I won't, if you don't mind,' Meredith said hastily 'I need to go home and unpack. I'll call back later, if I may.'

The news had shocked her deeply. Stebbings wasn't a likeable man and his actions had been consistently obstructive, but how had this happened? How did Darren, of all people, fit into the scheme of things? She had a mental image of the youth as he'd arrived at the lakeside where they'd surrounded Fiona's lifeless corpse. Pale, scrawny, acne-plagued, wearing well-worn jeans and a much-washed T-shirt, he'd been scared out of his wits at the sight of the body. Above all, he hadn't appeared to be any threat or even likely ever to become one. He was just a youngster going through that awkward age between boyhood and adulthood when your hormones are treacherous and the world generally seems to be against you. It's an age of self-obsession. That Darren could play any part in any of this just seemed so unlikely as to be unbelievable.

She wanted to get back home and hear what Alan had to say, although she might not be able to contact him until the evening. With this new death to add to present inquiries, he'd be busy all day.

Toby was giving her a reproachful look which said she was abandoning him in his hour of need. She steeled her heart against it. Toby could tell Jeremy about the Cornish visit without her help. To be frank, their journey west now took on the appearance of supreme self-indulgence. What had they hoped to achieve, she and Toby, on their amateur fishing trip? Here, at Overvale, was where the mystery lay and the answer to it. Toby was looking glum. But he was going to have to cope on his own. Echoing Alan's opinion on the subject, she found herself thinking: Toby doesn't need me. He's perfectly capable.

The same could hardly be said of Jeremy Jenner. The man looked ill, his face gaunt and grey. He was already a shadow of the confident man she'd met for the first time only recently. Had the general strain done this, or was it Darren's death coming so soon after Fiona's? Two bodies found on his land. That wasn't something Jenner's long years in the business world had equipped him to cope with.

Meredith's eye caught a movement at an upstairs window and glimpsed a face before the person up there stepped back out of sight. Chantal was still present. That couldn't be helpful. *But it's not my problem*, Meredith told herself. *I'm not a member of this family. If Jeremy is breaking down, it's for Toby and Alison to take care of him.*

She drove out of the gates and turned on to the rough road which led to the main road. It took her past Stebbings' cottage and she slowed to look at it. It appeared deserted, despite the fact that washing flapped on the clothes line. She remembered the woman they had seen pinning it up on their first visit to Overvale.

Mrs Stebbings, the bereaved mother, where was she? What awful effect must this have had on her?

The person who has done these things, Meredith thought, is very wicked. Yet this stretch of countryside was so beautiful and appeared so peaceful it seemed that evil deeds must be an anachronism, some sort of historical mistake. That, though, failed to take account of human nature which can also appear serene and at peace but, at the same time, harbour violent emotions.

She had reached the main road and pressed her foot on the accelerator. Almost at once, however, she was forced to brake. There was an obstruction in the road ahead. A bicycle lay on its side, wheels spinning. There was no sign of the rider. Meredith drew up and got out.

As she neared the spot she could hear muffled groans coming from the roadside ditch. She hurried towards the sound and peered down into the tangle of hedgerow plants. The cyclist was sprawled in the bottom among the dank nettle roots and rotting debris. With his helmet and goggles he looked like some sort of spaceman who'd made an unscheduled earth landing. Seeing a concerned face looking down at him, he gasped, 'Give us a hand!' and reached up as he spoke.

His voice was familiar. Meredith scrambled into the ditch and began to assist him to rise. He scrambled out and got unsteadily to his feet. As she watched he unbuckled the helmet and took off the goggles. It was Ted Pritchard.

'Ted?' exclaimed Meredith in astonishment. 'What are you doing out here? What happened?'

'Bloody bird!' muttered Ted. 'I was riding along, enjoying a bit of fresh air, and it came swooping down right in front of me. Sparrow-hawk, I reckon. It saw something in that ditch and just dived for it like they do. It skimmed my nose, I felt its wings.'

He was dusting himself down as he spoke. His solid muscular frame was clad in cycling shorts and figure-hugging Lycra jersey but didn't appear to have suffered any grazes or cuts despite lack of any protection. Landing in the ditch had at least been a soft landing. He picked up his bicycle and began to examine it anxiously for damage.

'What are you doing out here at this time of day?' Meredith asked him again. 'Shouldn't you be at work?'

'It's my lunch hour, isn't it?' Ted defended himself. 'I don't go cycling every lunch hour, mind. But sometimes, when it's a nice day like today, I go home, get the bike out and just ride round for a bit. Otherwise I don't get fresh air at all, you know. Steve and me, we work round the clock at the business. You've got to, when you're working for yourself. There's no one else to do it. I spend the best part of my day breathing in sawdust, stuck inside the workshop.' He gave the bicycle an experimental push back and forth. 'Something's buggered,' he observed gloomily.

'Look, where do you live?' Meredith asked. 'We can put the bike in the boot of my car, tie it in somehow, and I'll give you a lift home with it.'

He brightened. 'Thanks, that's nice of you. I appreciate that.'

To get the bicycle in the boot they had first to take out Meredith's suitcase and put it on the back seat. They then struggled to wedge the bicycle in the boot and secure it with the tow-rope Meredith kept in there.

'Expensive bike, this!' gasped Ted as they finished the job. 'I'll have to strip it down completely.'

'Where do you live?' she asked, when they were both in the front of the car.

She expected him to give an address in Bamford, but instead he said, 'I'll show you. Easier that way. I've got this place out in the country here. I bought it cheap, pretty well a ruin, and I'm fixing it up. Go on down here about a mile and turn left.'

Turning left took them on to a dark, tree-shadowed track worse than that which led to Overvale. Nobody but himself lived down here, said Ted, which Meredith could well believe as they made bumpy progress along it. The cottage, when they reached it, was a single-storey stone building, one end of which had crumbled into a heap of blocks. Trees and undergrowth had encroached on the premises until leafy fingers scraped at the walls. It would have been easy to assume no one lived here if one end hadn't been restored after a fashion, curtains at the window and the door freshly painted. Rusticity's white van was parked at the cottage's side.

She helped Ted unload his bicycle from the boot. He pushed it to the side of the road and propped it against an untrimmed hedge. With his back to her, rummaging in the saddlebag, he called cheerily, 'Come on in and a have a cup of tea or something!'

'Thanks, but I've only just got home after a couple of days away. I need to unpack. I won't, if you don't mind.' She moved back to the car.

But Ted had turned towards her and advanced a few steps, his round, imp's face still wearing a cheery smile. Automatically Meredith paused and waited.

'No, no,' he said. 'You've got to come in. I insist.'

That was when she saw the sharpened screwdriver in his hand.

The inside of the cottage was uninspiring. Ted's work of restoration hadn't got beyond the exterior walls and roof. The room they were in served both as living room and kitchen. There was a rusting wood-burning iron range in the hearth, long disused. A simple gas cooker fed by a butane gas bottle provided Ted's needs. Nor did he appear to have electricity. There was a paraffin lamp on the rickety pine table. The impression was not so much that he lived here as that he camped out. He had, however, made a partial effort to brighten the place up with pictures. They were a mix of sketches and watercolours, carefully framed in pine, and dotted haphazardly about the walls.

'I haven't got round to doing anything much in here,' said Ted, still affable and smiling. 'I want to get the outside of the place fixed up first. So if it's not quite *Homes and Gardens*, you'll have to excuse it.'

'Yes,' said Meredith, not knowing quite what else to say. He was still holding the screwdriver pointing towards her. She didn't want to look at it but her eye was drawn to its dull gleam and wickedly sharpened tip. She asked carefully, 'What's all this about, Ted?'

'Oh, you know what it's all about, I think,' he returned. 'Because you're the bright sort and you hang around with a top-notch copper. A working man like me is good with his hands. Not that I haven't got quite a good brainbox of my own. But I've always said, if you want really smart, look for a woman. Women can't knock a nail in straight or fix a bit of electrical wiring, but give them a problem to chew on and they've got it solved in no time at all. Sit down, why don't you? That chair there is the best.' The screwdriver wavered as it was used to point at the piece of furniture.

Meredith obediently sank down into a worn armchair. It wasn't very comfortable. She could feel the springs beneath her. But that was the least of her worries. Ted pulled up a wooden chair and sat down before her. The sharpened screwdriver was steady again in his hand.

'I saw it was you when you overtook me in your car. You had that fellow with you, the one who's been staying at Overvale, and I reckoned you must be headed there. So, when I heard a car coming towards me, I thought I might be in luck, you'd just dropped him off and you were coming back. There's never much traffic on that stretch. I put the bike on the road and jumped in the ditch. You've been on a little trip with your gentleman friend, have you?' he went on in his friendly way. 'Been down to Cornwall, I hear.'

'Hear from whom?' snapped Meredith. 'I've only just got back.'

'George Melhuish, he gave me a call. He said you and the other chap were down there poking around. Staying in the old Kemp cottage and asking about Miss Kemp. George hadn't told you anything but he knew you were still asking other people. I wasn't worried about the other chap but I was worried about you. You're the bright one and you've got that copper boyfriend. You and he might go talking over what you'd heard in Cornwall. That's why I threw the bike in the road to stop you. I just don't want you and that copper putting your heads together.'

Meredith said nothing. She was thinking furiously. Ted was watching her in an amused way, as if waiting for her to come up with the answer. Seeking inspiration, Meredith stared at the collection of pictures on the walls. It struck her that there was something familiar about them and she began to take a closer look, all the while aware of Ted's amused yet chilling gaze. Yes, that was surely the wide sweep of the beach at Polzeath and that was Stepper Point across the estuary. Those were the ruins of Arthur's castle at Tintagel. That was the tiny habour at Padstow crammed with boats of all kinds. It all began to click into place.

'Ted,' she said at last, slowly. 'That's the abbreviation for Edward. But some people might use it as an abbreviation for Edmund, a less popular name. Was Pritchard your stepfather's name?'

He nodded delightedly. 'That's it! I knew you'd work it out. My mother married old Dougie Pritchard and we left Cornwall, went off to live in Dorset first of all, then Kent, and eventually we finished up living in Lewisham, outskirts of London.'

'You lost your Cornish accent along the way,' Meredith observed. 'But you kept in touch with George Melhuish?'

'Oh, he was my best mate at school, was George, pretty well the only friend I had. Yes, we've kept in touch all these years, just the odd letter, you know, Christmas card, that sort of thing. George has always said, I ought to go back home, as he calls it, and go into business with him in the garage line. But my stepfather, he was a carpenter, and I followed him into that trade.'

'Where did you meet Steve Poole?' Meredith had no idea what she was going to do about this situation but it made sense to keep him talking. At the moment he was prepared to chat. He wanted to find out what she knew. After that he'd kill her. He'd killed Fiona and Darren and after a while, she supposed, it became almost an automatic reaction to a problem. There was no doubt she wasn't to be allowed to walk out of here alive.

246

'Prison,' said Ted casually. 'Well, not proper prison, it was a young offenders' institution. They were very keen on teaching you a trade there and I was already by way of being a carpenter, seeing as I'd been working with my stepdad. So I enrolled on the course to get a certificate to my name. Steve, he was on the same course. Like me, he was in the institution because of a spot of burglary. We decided, when we got out, we'd go into business.'

'But Ted!' Meredith couldn't help exclaiming. 'What you're telling me is a success story. Both you and Steve got into some sort of trouble as boys, but you got out of it, started a proper legitimate business. Why would you do anything to endanger that?'

'Ah,' said Ted, pointing the glittering tip of the screwdriver at her. 'I'm not going to let *you* endanger it, that's for sure.'

For one awful moment she believed he was going to lunge at her with it, there and then, and to distract him she blurted, 'You always had a bike, didn't you? Eileen Hammond said you had a bike.'

Ted looked surprised and then gave her a nod of approval. 'So you found Miss Hammond, did you? I'm surprised she's still around. She must be over eighty. Yes, I had a bike, rusty old thing. The other kids laughed themselves sick at me over it. But when Dougie married my mum, he bought me a proper new bike. He wanted to get me on his side, see? He didn't want me making any trouble because he could see me and my mum, we were close. He was an oldish chap already, Dougie, and he'd married my mum because he wanted someone to cook and clean for him. She knew that. She reckoned it was a fair enough deal.'

'Is your mother still alive?'

This was an unwise question. Ted's cheery expression faded and was replaced by a scowl. Now Meredith could see the sullen child described by Alison Jenner. 'She's alive. We'll leave her out of this.'

'You wrote those letters to Alison,' Meredith said.

Ted looked aggrieved. 'I printed them out on our computer in the office back at Rusticity. But I didn't make up the words. She told me what to say.'

Meredith's spine tingled. 'Fiona Jenner?'

He nodded. 'See, I recognized Miss Harris straight away when she came to the workshop about the garden table and chairs. She was Mrs Jenner now, living in that big house, lots of money. But I knew she was old Miss Kemp's niece, Alison. She hadn't changed, looked much the same. She'd always known how to find someone with money to look after her. She used to come down and visit her auntie and more often than not, every time she did, the old lady would give her some money or agree to pay for something for her. My mum told me so. My mum reckoned it was shocking, the way Alison used Miss Kemp.'

'So where did Fiona come into it?'

'I went up to the house, delivering that garden furniture they'd ordered from us. Nice set of furniture, that.'

'Yes, it is,' Meredith agreed. 'That's why I want to order some like it.'

Ted's eyes glowed with suppressed mirth. He didn't intend Meredith to be ordering anything. Meredith was to be, what? Buried under the floor of the ruined part of this cottage and a new concrete floor laid over her? That, thought Meredith, is what I'd do, if I were Ted.

'She was there, was Fiona. I chatted to her, friendly like. But she was a real stuck-up piece. Thought I was nothing, just a workman. So, to take her down a peg or two, I said I knew something about her stepmother that none of the Jenners would want revealed. I was fairly sure Fiona wouldn't have heard about it already. For all I knew, old Jenner himself hadn't. It was something Alison would want kept quiet. Her husband was a rich man. They'd got posh friends and Alison was enjoying swanking around playing lady of the manor. "What?" says Fiona, all hoity-toity, but dead curious. So I told her. "Your stepmum got away with murder." You know what?' Ted sounded bemused. 'She didn't react at all the way I thought she would. She didn't turn a hair. I

248

had to admire her for it. She just asked how I knew and how could I be sure? So I told her and she was tickled pink.'

Ted paused and reflected. 'She didn't like Alison, see? So she, Fiona, she says to me that, for a joke, we'd send the letters. She'd tell me what to say and I'd print them out. She liked a joke, Fiona. That's why I put in her the lake, smashed her head first, just like old Miss Kemp. I thought, if Fiona could see me do it, she'd appreciate the joke.' Ted smiled but it wasn't his normal cheerful grin. His eyes were cold.

'But,' whispered Meredith. 'Alison has always believed Miss Kemp's death was an accident. The police were wrong.'

'It was meant to look like an accident!' snapped Ted. 'That bloody interfering copper with the double-barrelled name . . .'

'Barnes-Wakefield?'

'That's him.' Ted nodded. 'Mum said he'd think it was an accident.'

'Your mother killed Miss Kemp?' Meredith forgot that mentioning Mrs Travis wasn't wise.

'Of course she didn't!' Ted shouted furiously at her. He leaned forwards and jabbed the screwdriver at her face.

It grazed her cheek as she threw herself to one side. 'There wasn't anyone else!' she gasped.

Ted chuckled. It was an unexpected sound and it chilled Meredith's blood. 'Wasn't there, eh?'

There was a moment's frozen silence as the words hung in the stuffy air.

'You . . .?' she gasped. 'But you were a ten-year-old boy . . .'

'I was a ten-year-old boy who had to go to school all winter in wellington boots because my mum hadn't the money to buy me leather shoes. Miss Kemp, she never gave my mum a bit of extra money so that she could buy me proper clothes, did she? She had money, too, more than an old woman like her needed. Do you know how she made it, her money? She ran an agency in London that found domestic staff for people. That's how she always treated my mother. A servant, that's what she was. Do this, do that!

That's all Mum heard from Miss Kemp. Never a "thank you" or a "would you mind?"

'And that old bike I had to ride! I found that bike in a skip. Someone had thrown it out, it was that rubbishy. But I got it out and cleaned it up. The other kids laughed at me because of it, and because of the wellington boots and all the rest of it! You know what being poor is?' Ted's eyes glowed. 'No, of course you don't. I'll tell you. It means everyone despises you, even snotty-nosed school kids.'

There was blood trickling down Meredith's cheek. She could feel it but she dared not put up her hand to wipe it away.

'What happened?' She had only minutes now to get out of here now. How?

Ted shrugged. 'I didn't mean it. You could say it *was* a sort of accident. It was Sunday. I was fed up with hanging round the house and went out just walking. I was by Miss Kemp's cottage and I saw Alison drive off in her nice car, going back to London. Then the old lady came out and began pottering around her garden. She liked her garden. She'd left the door open. I thought, no one's there. Mum didn't work there on a Sunday, see? I could slip in and see if Miss Kemp had any money lying about anywhere. It was because of the bike. I wanted to buy a proper bike and I was saving up. I thought, I bet Miss Kemp has agreed to give Alison some more money to buy things in London. It's only right I should have some, too. If she wouldn't give it to me, mean old biddy, I'd take it. I slipped in and started looking round. Some people had stopped outside the cottage and were talking to her, a pair of cyclists, it was. I saw them from the window, so I reckoned I was safe. I was looking in a desk drawer when she came back in and caught me at it. I was terrified. I was only ten years old and I didn't think. I just grabbed a paperweight on the desk and jumped at her, striking out. She was very old, frail. She went down like a ninepin and lay there, not moving. I ran home and told Mum. She came running to Miss Kemp's cottage. She said Miss Kemp was dead. We'd make it look like an accident. We'd put her in the pond and they'd think she'd drowned. So we did that. It was awkward carrying her. She was only little and thin but she weighed more than you'd have expected. That's what they mean when they talk about dead weight. It was the same when I moved Fiona but I had the car that time. Mum cleaned off the paperweight and put it back on the desk because she said it might be missed. Then we went home.

'But that old Barnes-Wakefield, he wouldn't have it was an accident. He said there was no water in Miss Kemp's lungs. He couldn't see anything by the pond she'd hit her head on so he couldn't explain the wound. He reckoned it was murder and Mum and me, we were scared stiff. So, we had to give him a murderer, didn't we? Mum told him it must be Alison. He listened to Mum.'

'Yes,' Meredith said. 'He did. He still believes Alison killed Miss Kemp.'

'Yes, we made a good job of it.' Ted stood up. 'I always make a good job of things.'

Now . . . thought Meredith. He's going to kill me now.

'I can't go driving all over the countryside on the off chance I'll see him!' Markby said crossly.

Steve Poole stared at him. 'You want him that urgent, do you?' He squinted suspiciously at Markby and Jess. 'What's he done?'

'Should he have done anything?' Jess asked.

'No, we got a good business here.' Steve looked round him and his expression grew anxious. 'We've got a good business,' he went on, sounding worried. 'He'd better not have bloody screwed it up!'

'Has he been in trouble before?' Markby asked.

Steve's gaze swivelled back to him. 'Well,' he said reluctantly. 'Not for years. He and I, we both got into a bit of trouble when we were kids. Pinching things, you know, just casual, from unlocked cars mostly. Or we'd watch for people leaving a door open and nip in and just grab what was to hand. We both got sent to one of those young offender places. That's where we met. But we set up the business when we got out and we've gone straight since. Never even fiddled the books.' He sounded aggrieved.

'You can't give me any better information about where he might be?' Markby snapped. 'Come on, think, man!'

'Well,' Steve stared miserably at him and then at Jess before returning his gaze to his chief tormentor. 'To get the bike, he'd have to go home first. He took the van. He'll take the bike back to his house when he's finished, pick up the van and come back to work. So you could go to his place. If the van's still there, that means he's not come back yet and all you'd have to do is wait for him.'

'Right!' Markby said. 'You listen to me. You are not to contact him the moment we leave, understand? I don't want him to know we're on our way.'

'He's got no telephone at his place,' Steve said defensively. 'Right dump, it is. Part of it's falling down. He hasn't even got electricity.'

'I expect he's got a mobile phone. I don't want you using that.'

Poole was shaking his head again. 'He lost his. Although, the other day, I saw he had a new one. Not that I've ever seen him using it. He leaves it in the office.' He grinned briefly.

'What's funny?' Jess asked him.

Poole shrugged. 'Nothing. Just that it's a fancy thing, not like you'd expect him to have at all. It's got flowers on it. I joked about it when I asked him for the number. He wouldn't give me the number. He said it was one of those phones where you prepay for calls and all the credit was used.'

'Show me!' Jess was already moving towards the boarded-off area which marked Rusticity's office.

Inside the cramped area papers were lying around in untidy stacks, box files formed unsteady towers, elastic bands and pens were housed in washed margarine tubs and, among this sea of office equipment, Jess spotted a computer and monitor. Neither

Poole nor Pritchard, it seemed, was good at office management.

But Steve Poole seemed to know where to look for anything. He pulled open a drawer and produced a small mobile phone with a decorative cover, blue, patterned with daisies.

'We'll take that!' Jess said.

'More like a woman's thing isn't it?' said Poole.

'I wish we'd known about that pair having a criminal record!' Markby said angrily as they drove out of Bamford.

'If this mobile turns out to be Fiona's, he's got to be number one suspect,' Jess said. 'But I don't understand what motive he could have to kill her.'

'The poison pen letters,' Markby said tersely. 'Fiona must have met Ted when he and Poole delivered the garden furniture to Overvale. Meredith suspected Fiona from the first of being the letter-writer. But I think we'll find Fiona used Pritchard to write the letters at her dictation and to post them. When I appeared on the scene, Fiona got cold feet. She wanted the letter-writting to stop. She forgot that, while money wasn't a motive for her, it might be one for Ted. He'd no intention of giving up something which he hoped, eventually, could turn out highly profitable. They quarrelled and he killed her. When Darren approached him with his photos showing Ted and Fiona together, Darren became the next victim.'

Jess had been consulting the rough road map sketched for them by Poole and now said sharply, 'Here's the turning!'

They drove slowly down the track until the cottage came into view.

'There's the white van, sir,' Jess pointed ahead.

'And there's Meredith's car!' he replied. 'Damn! Pritchard's ahead of us. He's been ahead of us all along. We'll stop here and continue on foot, but call in for back-up first. I've a bad feeling about this!'

When Jess joined him a few minutes later he was observing the cottage from behind an overgrown hedge.

'No sign of life,' he whispered. 'We can wait until back-up gets here. But time might not be on our side.'

'The others are on their way. But if you think we can't wait, I could go round to the back,' Jess returned in the same low voice. 'You kick in the front door, I kick in the back door or smash my way in by the window.'

'Easier said than done! We need to know that Meredith is in there—'

There was a crash of breaking glass and something flew through the window by the front door and landed in the garden.

Meredith's panicking gaze had flickered round the squalid room and found the paraffin lamp on the table. Fear sent the adrenalin pumping through her. She leapt up and lunged towards it, her fingers closing on the base.

Perhaps her previous quiet manner had deceived Ted into thinking she wasn't going to move or perhaps he had been caught up in his own narrative. Now he swore and dived towards her. She threw the lamp at him with full force. He dodged aside. The lamp carried on and smashed through the front window, flying out into the garden. Ted, off balance, stumbled back and staggered as he came up against the side of the armchair. The screwdriver flew out of his hand, described an arc through the air and clattered to the stone-flagged floor.

Meredith ran for the front door. Ted was behind her. She could feel the heat of his body. As his hand gripped her shoulder, her fingers wrestled with the door handle. The door opened, the material of her shirt ripped, loosening his grip. She threw herself through the narrow gap out into the overgrown garden. As she did, she heard a shout, but not from Ted. Here, outside. Her fleeing body cannoned into another and, with the breath knocked out of her, she fell to the ground entangled with the other person.

'Come on!' Markby shouted.

He and Jess rushed towards the cottage as the paraffin lamp

shattered on the ground. It had been some years since Markby had been required to kick open a door. It occurred to him as he ran that he might not be able to do it. Fortunately he wasn't called upon to try.

Before Markby could act, the door was jerked open by an unseen hand. Meredith hurtled from the darkness inside, crashed into him and sent him flying. Ted leapt over their prostrate bodies and sprinted towards the white van. Struggling to disentangle himself, Markby yelled at Jess. Ted had almost reached the van when Jess caught up with him, flung her arms round his legs and brought him crashing to the ground.

By the door, Alan and Meredith had both managed to achieve sitting positions.

'All right?' he demanded.

'Yes!' she gasped.

'I've got to help Jess!' He scrambled to his feet and headed for the white van.

But Ted was lying face down beside it with Jess Campbell kneeling on his back. 'Got him, sir!' she said, turning a flushed triumphant face towards the superintendent.

When the overpowered Ted Pritchard was safely in the hands of the back-up team which had just arrived, Markby observed, 'That was a splendid flying tackle, Campbell.'

'Thank you, sir. I used to play women's rugby!'

'Women's rugby?'

She grinned at his appalled expression. 'I think Meredith's waiting for you, sir.'

'Lord!' exclaimed Markby. He hadn't forgotten her, he'd just been busy. He hurried to where Meredith was waiting, sitting on a rustic bench by the front door. She looked pale and shaky.

'Sorry to dash off. I saw you were OK,' he said, still breathless and attempting to smooth his hair. 'I had to lend Jess a hand. I'm getting too damn old for this.'

'She seemed to be doing rather well by herself.' Meredith managed a wry smile.

'She plays women's rugby.' He returned the smile and then said soberly, 'This isn't funny. He's killed twice already. I thought we might be too late.' He pointed at the shattered remains of a paraffin lamp lying by his feet. 'Is that what you threw through the window?'

'It wasn't my intention to throw it through the window. I didn't know you and Jess Campbell were out here. Back in there, I thought my last moment had come. Ted was all set to finish me off the same way he killed Fiona Jenner. I lunged for the paraffin lamp on the table, grabbed it and hurled it at him. I wanted to make him drop the screwdriver!'

'What screwdriver?' he demanded. 'What's that blood on your face?'

'The sharpened one . . . He did drop it but the lamp went straight on through the window.' She wiped away the blood. 'It's nothing, a scratch.'

'Murderous little monster,' said Markby bitterly. 'They were writting the letters between them, I suppose.'

'Oh, yes, I was right about Fiona. It was all her idea, he says. He wrote them but she thought the idea up.'

'I wonder,' Markby mused, 'how she found out about Alison's trial and why she decided to use Ted to do the letter-writing.'

'Because he's Edmund Travis,' Meredith told him.

Chapter Fourteen

'She's expecting you.'

The warden of the Lewisham retirement home smiled in welcome at Jess and Sergeant Ginny Holding, but her eyes were watchful. She was a middle-aged woman, stout in build, bearing a name shield on her breast, and wearing her spectacles slung on a cord round her neck.

The retirement home was a pleasant, if nondescript, modern building with large windows letting in plenty of light and a view of a scrap of dusty lawn between it and the busy road outside. There were flowers in vases and, on the walls, pictures of distant landscapes which probably meant little or nothing to the residents. A large notice pinned to a cork board in the entrance reminded them that the travelling library would visit them today and please to have ready any books they wanted to exchange. The whole was permeated with a smell compounded of floor wax, disinfectant, memories of yesterday's boiled vegetables and that indefinable odour of sickly old age.

'It's not the proper travelling library,' the warden explained to Ginny, who had been looking at the notice on the cork board. 'One of the local librarians brings a selection of suitable books, large print, you know, and sets up shop for an hour in the residents' lounge.' She turned back to Jess. 'If I could just have a quick word with you in the office before you see Dorothy?'

The office was like offices everywhere: cluttered desk, fax machine, computer terminal, filing cabinet. The warden pulled out a couple of uncomfortable-looking chairs and offered them to the two police officers.

'Dr Freeman and I have discussed your visit.' She paused as if expecting some comment on this. When none came, she appeared a little disconcerted. 'Dr Freeman is in charge of the medical care of our residents.' The words were emphasized and accompanied with a minatory look.

'We've cleared our visit with your local police station.' Jess was not to be outdone in the matter of references. They had also cleared it with the Devon and Cornwall constabulary, whose case the murder of Freda Kemp had been and on whose files it still remained open. She saw no reason to tell the warden that.

'Oh?' The warden appeared not to know what to make of Jess's answer. After a brief consideration she dismissed this counter-claim of authority. 'Indeed?' Outside these walls the police might have some jurisdiction but inside them Dr Freeman ruled the roost.

'I gather,' she began again briskly, 'you want to talk to Dorothy about her son. Is he in some kind of trouble?'

'He's involved in our inquiries,' Jess said carefully.

'She's devoted to him,' the warden told her. 'She'll be upset if he's in trouble.' Her tone was reproachful as if, somehow, the trouble was Jess's fault.

'Does he come and visit her?' This question came from Ginny.

'Oh, yes, quite regularly, once a month. He doesn't live in the London area now. Dorothy looks forward to his visits. They keep her going, really. He's all she has. I must say, he does seem devoted to her.'

'Mrs Pritchard is fit enough to see us?' Jess asked her. Her heart was sinking. Surely they hadn't come all this way to be told Mrs Pritchard was too frail to be questioned?

The warden pursed her lips. 'Physically, yes, she's certainly fit enough, although she suffers badly from arthritis. That's why she lives here. Otherwise, she could certainly manage on her own. She isn't yet seventy, you know, and most of our residents are a lot older than that. I feel quite sorry for Dorothy, because she's had to come into a place like this at such a relatively young age. I think she resents it. One can understand her frustration. She's got all her marbles and, frankly, some of our residents . . .' The warden let the words trail away.

'So she will remember something that happened twenty-five years ago?' Jess asked cautiously.

'Oh, good heavens, yes! Mind you, they nearly all remember things that happened years ago. It's the things that happened last week they can't remember! But Dorothy isn't in that category. Dorothy's as sharp as a button. It's really only because she can't manage for herself on account of the arthritis that she's here. I should warn you, she can be very outspoken.'

'I'm hoping she will be,' Jess told her.

'Mm,' said the warden doubtfully. 'Well, as I say, Dr Freeman and I see no reason on medical grounds why she can't be interviewed but, at the same time, we are responsible for her general well-being here. We wouldn't wish her to become distressed in any way. If she does show signs of that, the interview will have to stop immediately. Is that quite understood?'

'Of course!' said Jess, trying not to show her impatience.

The warden sensed that further delay wouldn't be welcome and got to her feet. 'Come along, then.'

She led them along the corridor to a lift. They went up to the first floor and along another corridor until they reached the last door. The warden knocked and opened it.

'Dorothy, the two police officers are here to see you.'

Jess couldn't hear a reply. Presumably there had been one because the warden went on, 'I'll leave them with you. But I'll come back in a minute, just to see you're all right.'

Jess and Ginny exchanged glances. To be fair to the warden, she hadn't been told the exact nature of the inquiries the police were following up. But however the warden and the absent Dr Freeman thought of it, to Jess and Ginny this was a murder inquiry and Mrs Dorothy Pritchard (formerly Travis) was part of it.

The room into which they had been shown was a good size and pleasantly furnished with a traditional look: chintz fabrics and wallpaper smothered with pink rosebuds and sprays of forget-me-nots. But it was unbearably stuffy and overheated. Jess felt herself wilt. She felt trapped and looked automatically towards the window. It was tightly sealed. This room was at the front of the building and the view admitted was that of the busy main road outside the residential home. At least Mrs Pritchard, incarcerated here by her affliction, had a lively scene to watch. On the other hand, the noise of passing traffic must be a nuisance and perhaps that was why the window was kept shut. There were a few personal knick-knacks around, in pride of place among them a framed portrait of a round-faced, unsmiling boy of about twelve in school uniform. His hair had been brushed ruthlessly flat and he stared at the photographer with a level gaze that held just a touch of insolence.

Mrs Pritchard sat in an easy chair facing the door. She did not bear any particular resemblance to her son, being thin with short-cropped iron-grey hair and deep-set dark eyes which were fixed on her visitors with the kind of hungry intensity one sees in birds of prey which have spotted their next victim. She was dressed in navy-blue trousers, beneath the hems of which protruded swollen ankles and feet thrust into maroon velvet slippers. Despite the uncomfortable heat of the room, she wore a woollen green jumper. It was unadorned with any jewellery. Nevertheless, she had made an effort to dress up for her visitors by the application of make-up. The attempt had not been a success. Her hands, knotted with the disease which had brought her to live here, rested on the arms of her chair. The application of powder and lipstick had been understandably clumsy. The red gash of her mouth was crooked. The loose powder she had used lay in pale patches on her skin and caked up the wrinkles. Her whole facial appearance, the eyes apart, was uncomfortably close to that of a corpse laid out for a formal wake. Jess noticed that Dorothy Pritchard no longer wore her wedding ring. Perhaps now she couldn't slip it on and off her finger past the swollen joints. Perhaps, Mr Pritchard having died some years earlier (they had learned this before coming here), she just didn't bother with the outward symbol of matrimony any more.

Mrs Pritchard subjected them both to an unsmiling appraisal and then said curtly, 'Girls!'

Behind her, Jess heard Ginny murmur, 'Oh-oh . . .'

'Good morning, Mrs Pritchard,' Jess said politely. 'I'm Inspector Campbell and this is Sergeant Holding. Here's my warrant card.'

She held it out. Mrs Pritchard glanced at it dismissively. 'I was expecting men. They told me police officers. Naturally I expected men, not girls.'

Was it the expectation of male visitors which had led the woman to experiment so disastrously with make-up? Jess didn't know whether to find this tragic or farcical.

'Well, we're here now,' she said calmly. 'May we sit down?'

'Suit yourselves.' They were not men and they were to be allowed neither the authority Mrs Pritchard would have recognized in male officers, nor accorded the civility she might have extended to them.

Mrs Pritchard, Jess thought with sudden insight, didn't like sister women. She had not liked Alison Harris. Alison thought that had been due to the difference in their personal circumstances and the fact that Mrs Pritchard (at that time Travis) had resented Alison's easy lifestyle. It went deeper than that. The unease which Jess had felt on entering this room, and which she had attributed to the stuffiness and heat, deepened.

They seated themselves, Jess directly before the painted resentful figure in the armchair, and Ginny slightly to one side of her.

'You're here about Edmund,' Mrs Pritchard said abruptly before either of them had time to open the conversation. 'He's a good boy. It's no use you telling me he's done something wrong. He hasn't.'

'He's been arrested in connection with the murder of a young woman called Fiona Jenner, Mrs Pritchard. Did you know that?'

She sniffed. 'Yes. He told his lawyer to phone me and explain why he couldn't come and see me. It's his regular time, tomorrow. He ought to be here then. He won't be, because you've got him locked up. You have no right.' The hooded eyelids drooped briefly over the fierce raptor's eyes. 'Who is this young woman Fiona?'

'Fiona Jenner? She was the daughter of a retired businessman, Jeremy Jenner, and the stepdaughter of his present wife, Alison, who was formerly Alison Harris.'

It was hard to tell whether Mrs Pritchard was disconcerted by this news. She ran the tip of her tongue over her desiccated lips, smearing the cheap lipstick even more disastrously. Jess found herself thinking it made it look as if Mrs Pritchard had been eating raw meat. She pushed aside the fanciful notion of a vampire. Yet there was something frightening, inhuman, about this grotesque woman.

'She was always trouble, Alison.' Mrs Pritchard's dark eyes sparkled with hate. 'Has she got Edmund into this fix? It's the sort of thing she'd do. She was always a bad lot, Alison Harris. I *know*!' The last word was spat out viciously.

'We have evidence connecting your son with the death of Fiona Jenner.' Ginny Holding took up the interview. 'And he has confessed.'

A look of scorn greeted this. 'You've tricked him, you mean. I know the police and their artful ways, their so-called confessions. Edmund's an innocent. Anyone could get him to sign anything. It won't count, you know. You can't get a conviction on the basis of a confession alone. I asked the lawyer. He said you've still got to prove it.'

'Not exactly an innocent, though, is he?' Ginny pointed out. 'As a young man he was sentenced to a term in youth custody for several offences of house burglary and theft from cars.'

The woman's thin cheeks flushed and she darted a vicious look at Ginny. 'He got into bad company. He didn't realize what he was doing. I told you, my Edmund is a good boy and an innocent, easily led astray.'

This conversation was going nowhere rapidly and time was ticking by. The warden would be back soon, checking Dorothy wasn't distressed. Distressed! thought Jess. The old harridan is on the offensive. If we let her, she'd make mincemeat of us. Meat. Blood. There is was again. That vampire image was lurking at the back of Jess's mind and wouldn't go away.

'Mrs Pritchard,' she said briskly. 'We haven't come to talk about Fiona Jenner. We've come to talk to you about an event which happened twenty-five years ago. Do you remember the death of Freda Kemp?'

There was a silence. The dark eyes blinked once. 'Of course I remember it. I worked for Miss Kemp. She was a nice old lady. Alison was her niece. She twisted Miss Kemp round her little finger. She was always so sweet and loving when she arrived for a visit.' Mrs Pritchard adopted a high-pitched babyish voice. "Oh, Auntie Freda, how lovely to see you!" ' Mrs Pritchard's voice dropped again to its normal level. 'Then, within an hour of being there, she'd have wheedled money out of her aunt. Shocking, it was, to see it.'

'Your name was Travis then?' Ginny asked her.

Mrs Pritchard again transferred her gaze briefly to Ginny, this time treating her to and up-and-down appraisal. She pursed her lips and nodded. 'It was. I married young. I didn't know better. Ron Travis was no good. He wouldn't work. Spent any money he got in his pocket down at the pub. In the end, he left. He told me there was no work to be had in Cornwall and he was going out of the county to find some. He was going to Taunton. So he went and I never saw him again. Never expected to. Good riddance to bad rubbish, I say. But he left me with a child to care for and no means of doing it. Typical.' She leaned forwards and her dark eyes glowed. 'I've had a hard life. You modern women, you've no idea.'

Unwisely Ginny began, 'There are still single mothers—'

She was interrupted. 'Half of them are single by choice! I had no choice. I had to go out cleaning floors and looking after people. You girls with your good jobs and your cars, money in your pockets, foreign holidays, going out dancing at night . . . What do you know? I never enjoyed any of that!'

'Do you remember the day Miss Kemp died?' Jess asked loudly, putting an end to this tirade.

'I do.' Mrs Pritchard blinked again and for the first time a note of caution sounded in her voice. 'That is to say, I knew nothing of it at the time. It was a Sunday and I didn't go to the cottage on a Sunday. It was my one day off. Day off? I spent it working in my own place, doing all the laundry and scrubbing and polishing I didn't have time for during the week because I was out doing it for other people. That's why my hands are the way they are now, useless. Hard work did that. Anyway, I went to the cottage on the Monday morning, same as usual. The doors were all unlocked but Miss Kemp wasn't in the cottage. I thought, perhaps she's in the garden. So I went out to see, and there she was, lying face down in the pond. I thought first of all that she'd drowned. But the police said later that couldn't be because there was no water in her lungs. They said it was murder. So I told them, I knew who'd done it. It was Alison. She'd been there that Sunday. She'd arrived on the Saturday and I saw her. She was the same as usual, buttering up Miss Kemp. She couldn't wait to get her hands on Miss Kemp's money. I told that police officer . . .'

'Mr Barnes-Wakefield?' Ginny asked.

'That's the one. I told him, he had to look no further than Miss Harris.' Mrs Pritchard gave a satisfied nod and sat back in her chair.

'But,' Jess said quietly, 'that's not how it happened really, is it? Not according to Edmund.'

The dark eyes blazed at her. 'Edmund was a ten-year-old child at the time! What did he know about it? What have you made him say? You've been tricking my son! Making him say things, say nonsense!'

'Edmund tells us Miss Kemp found him in the cottage, after Alison left. He was looking for money.'

'It's a lie!' Mrs Pritchard's voice filled with room. Her face contorted with rage. 'It's a wicked lie!'

'He was frightened and struck out with a paperweight. Then he fetched you and it was your idea to put Miss Kemp in the pond, to make it look like an accident.'

Mrs Pritchard leaned forwards again. Her arthritic hands made clawing motions and the green jumper heaved with emotion. The red gash of a mouth worked soundlessly for a few seconds and then the words burst out as if released from a dam. 'Lies – lies – all of it! It's *wicked* to say such a thing. Alison killed her auntie. Alison did it!'

'Judge and jury cleared Alison.'

'Pah!' She actually spat. The woman spat, not much and to one side, but a thin arc of saliva crossed the air and landed on the carpet. Both Jess and Ginny Holding had been spat at before, by drunks and yobs, but in this floral-decorated room it was doubly shocking.

If Mrs Pritchard was aware of how she had dismayed her audience, she didn't show it. She continued with her tirade. 'She hoodwinked that jury. She put on her usual act: all sweetness and light, butter wouldn't melt in her mouth. She was just a nice young girl and everyone was being so nasty to her . . . They all fell for it. Just as Miss Kemp fell for it. But I never did, never!'

Disgusted by the spitting and unable to disguise her repugnance, Jess said sharply, 'Your son is also to be charged in relation to offences against another woman. She was forced by your son into his cottage. He threatened her with a sharpened screwdriver . . .'

'It's a lie! My Edmund wouldn't do that! Do you think I don't know my own son?'

Now the woman's voice was shrill. Her whole body writhed with anger. The red mouth jerked into extraordinary shapes. The dark eyes were venomous in their intensity. 'I know all about you girls . . . You never knew any hardship! Men like my Edmund aren't safe from you girls! Not from Alison, the scheming little bitch, nor from this Fiona person you told me of. Whoever she was, my Edmund had nothing to do with what happened to her. If someone killed her, so what? She was probably just another rich spoilt brat who got what was coming to her! It's all lies, filth, wickedness . . . You call yourselves police officers and you're supposed to know about right and wrong but you twist it all to trap the innocent, you do the devil's work . . . I know your type . . .'

By now she was becoming incoherent. The words bubbled out of her mouth accompanied by a stream of spittle. She swayed back and forth. The words, screeched at them, echoed off the walls of the chintzy little room. Jess and Ginny gazed at her in horror, appalled by the sight and powerless to interrupt. In the middle of it all, the door opened and the warden walked in.

'Dorothy? Dorothy?' She ran to Mrs Pritchard and then turned on the two police officers. 'I heard her shouting. I told you, I made it quite clear, you weren't to upset her! Whatever will Dr Freeman say?'

'Can we charge her with anything?' Ginny asked as they left. She sounded shaken.

'I doubt it,' Jess returned. 'Ted Pritchard has told us what happened at the Kemp cottage, but there's no corroborating evidence. We can't even charge his mother with obstructing police inquiries. He says they put the body in the pond. She says they didn't. It's her word against his. She had nothing to do with the Fiona Jenner murder. She had nothing to do with the poison pen letters. Mind you, hate mail would be just her style. But with her arthritic hands, she couldn't write it. Couldn't even use a keyboard, probably, if she tried, and I don't see her trying to. She's vicious, twisted woman and if you want to look at it that way, she's at the bottom of it all. But charge her? No. There's nothing we can bring against her. It's not a crime to be unpleasant.'

'Chantal wanted Fiona interred,' Alison said, grasping Meredith's hand. 'So Jeremy agreed. Perhaps having a grave to visit is helpful, better than – than the other way. That's so final. Thank you for coming today.'

They were gathered in a quiet country churchyard. The church was only partly in use and no burials had taken place here for some time. It had been a matter of getting permission from the bishop but that had not been a problem.

The churchyard lay in a slight hollow so that all around them the lichen-encrusted tombstones formed a circle, suggesting unseen spectators. The spirits of those whose mortal remains crumbled away here now watched with interest as a new arrival prepared to join their number. Father Holland had come from Bamford, as usual on his motorbike, to conduct the service. The bike was discreetly hidden away in the shadow of massive old yew trees which must have stood here as long as the church had, perhaps even longer. Father Holland, surplice fluttering in the wind, had led them from the interior to a grassy spot in the lee of a crumbling stone wall. There they had remained, in silence, heads bowed, as Fiona was finally committed to the earth.

'How is Jeremy?' Meredith murmured.

Both she and Alison glanced towards Jenner. He was still standing by the open grave, aloof from the other mourners, hands folded, staring down at his child's coffin. They saw Father Holland approach and speak to him. Jeremy nodded but appeared to be paying little attention.

'He feels the unfairness of it so,' Alison whispered back. 'She was young, beautiful and, well, rich. The world ought to have been at her feet. Chantal's managing rather better because she's been able to weep and her husband's come from Switzerland to support her.'

Chantal Plassy was being consoled elegantly some distance away by a distinguished-looking grey-haired man in an expensive suit.

'I ought to go and speak to Tara,' Alison said. 'So please excuse me. You will come back to the house? Just a buffet lunch.'

She pressed Meredith's hand and moved away towards a slim young woman whose pale features were set in an expression of deepest misery. Meredith wondered whether Alison or Toby had persuaded Jeremy to relent and allow Tara to attend. As Meredith watched, Alison put an arm round the girl's shoulders.

'I'll be glad when this is over,' Alan Markby said by Meredith's ear. 'Jeremy looks as if he needs a good stiff drink.'

James Holland was still talking earnestly to Jeremy and still getting as little response. As they watched, Toby joined in and his presence seemed to rouse Jeremy from his trance-like state. He nodded and mouthed a few words. James Holland, perhaps satisfied now that Jeremy was in good hands, left them and came over to Alison. There was a brief conversation and they all began to move off in a straggling procession towards the gate and the cars parked beyond. In the background, partly concealed by the shadow of the church building, Meredith glimpsed two men with spades, leaning on their tools and waiting for the area to be cleared so that they could complete their task. She shivered.

Jeremy had joined his wife and they had moved up to the head of the group. They reached the gate first and, as they passed through it, the others saw Jeremy sway and then crumple to the ground. To the onlookers it all seemed to happen, as shocking things often do, in slow motion. To Meredith, Jeremy's figure in the dark overcoat seemed to deflate slowly and fold in on itself. Alison put out her hands as if in some way she could catch him and keep him upright and as he was. Toby leapt forward but he, also, was too late. His fingers caught Jeremy's sleeve but the dark figure continued its inexorable collapse until it sprawled on the ground and stayed there, unmoving.

The spell was broken. They all ran to the spot. Jeremy was now supported on Toby's arm and his face was contorted, his breath coming in spasms. Alison knelt by his side, holding his hand and calling his name desperately. Behind them, Chantal Plassy clung to her husband's arm, her face frozen in horror. Markby summoned the ambulance, but before it could reach them Jeremy's gaze clouded and the painful breathing stopped altogether.

At Overvale House Mrs Whittle took the telephone call, then went into the dining room. She gazed briefly at the untouched buffet, so neatly laid out, before she began methodically to take it all back to the kitchen.

Chapter Fifteen

Alan Markby, Meredith and Toby were sitting in Alan and Meredith's favourite pub, the Saddlers' Arms. It was early in the evening and the place was only a quarter full. From the bar came a murmur of voices as two regulars settled in. The barman was taking time to chalk a careful message on a blackboard above their heads. 'Special today,' it read. 'Sausages and mash with leeks. Vegetarian broccoli and pasta bake.' They were the same specials as last week and, very likely, they'd be the specials next week, but nobody cared. If there had been any change to the familiar menu, there might even have been some murmurings of discontent. The customers of the Saddlers' Arms liked things to remain just the way they were.

Although it had rained sporadically throughout the day, a ray of evening sunshine was now falling through the window and across Meredith. It picked up golden highlights in her brown hair matched by the gleam of the horse brasses tacked to the ancient blackened beam above her head. Alan Markby smiled at her and she smiled back.

Toby, intercepting the smiles, looked sad for a moment. Aloud, he said, 'So you matched up the tyre treads, after all?'

Markby turned his attention to him. 'The van treads, yes. We found the Rusticity van's tracks by the woods, too. The ground was softer there, hadn't dried out, and we got better prints. Forensics went over the interior of the van and found traces of Fiona's blood. It was just the evidence we needed. The photograph of Ted and Fiona together made it hard for him to deny his involvement but we had to link him to the body itself. He should have resisted the temptation to be clever and left her lying on the track by the woods. On top of that, the mobile phone he'd left in the office at the firm turned out to be Fiona's. But he hasn't been denying it. Ted's main problem is that he can't resist showing off. He was showing off when he put Fiona's body in the lake. He's showing off now, telling us about it. Oddly enough, it's a common enough criminal trait. A planned crime like murder must of necessity take place in secret. But secrecy is galling to the murderer. He wants to show the police and anyone else interested how clever he is, how he can hoodwink anyone. Murderers are especially sure of their own cleverness and it's particularly satisfying to them to tease the police. It's like dangling a piece of string, with a twist of paper tied to it, above a kitten. The kitten can see it but he can't catch it. "Catch me!" the murderer wants to say. "Look, here I am. Are you quick enough or am I quicker?" Ted says putting Fiona in the lake was a joke. I think it was intended to bait us and yes, it was a joke, Ted's private joke, laughing at all the rest of us.'

'I bet he's not laughing now,' Toby observed grimly.

Markby sipped his pint. 'In a way he still is. Being caught, even being convicted, doesn't alter the murderer's mindset. He still thinks he's cleverer than the rest of us. He has no morality as we understand it. He has no compassion. He sees no reason why he can't act just as he wants to. He began his criminal career with a murder. As you know he's been telling us how, as a ten-year-old, he slipped into Miss Kemp's cottage to see if she had any spare cash lying around on that fatal Sunday. She disturbed him and he struck out. If you ask me, it wasn't the first time he'd stolen from her. The old lady was getting confused and probably hadn't missed the odd pound or two. Later on, he practised the same kind of opportunist theft from unlocked cars and by taking advantage of open doors or windows. It landed him in a young offender's institution.'

'Where he met up with Steve Poole and they set up a business. He could have gone straight,' Meredith said. 'It seems such a pity.' She pushed back her thick brown hair with both hands and the gold highlights rippled.

'Going straight was proving hard work physically. He and Steve were working all hours for modest return. Ted suddenly saw himself presented with the opportunity to make some easy money. From the moment he recognized Alison, he knew he could turn it to his advantage. At first he wasn't sure how, but then he was tempted to tell Fiona the story and Fiona had an axe to grind of her own. She resented Alison, a resentment fuelled at a distance by her own mother in Switzerland. Chantal seems happily married now but after her divorce from Jeremy she went through several unsatisfactory relationships and she envied the security she'd lost and which she saw Alison enjoying. She'd persuaded her teenage daughter that she had to be sent to the hated boarding school in England, not because that suited Chantal but because of the divorce which meant Chantal couldn't offer Fiona a settled home.

'Fiona came up with the idea of the letters and Ted was happy to go along with it. He had to handle it carefully and not frighten Fiona off. His long-term objective, when she was so involved she would find it hard to get out of it, was to start asking for money. That was what Fiona misunderstood. She was a rich young woman and she didn't understand how the prospect of a golden goose would appeal to someone like Ted. She thought at first she was using Ted to write letters and give Alison a fright. But she wasn't stupid and she soon began to be suspicious of his intentions and to realize that, just possibly, Ted was using her. When Meredith and I turned up that day for lunch, and the whole thing was discussed in detail, she began to get seriously alarmed. She phoned Ted on her mobile and arranged to meet him in their usual spot down by the woods early the next morning. She told him the letter-writing had to stop. Ted however had no intention of stopping. Nor did he trust her not to own up to what they'd done. She had a loving family. They'd be shocked and disappointed if she told them but, after an almighty row and some recriminations, they might well forgive her. She was Jeremy's only child, after all.

'But he had a criminal record and he had actually printed off and posted the letters. No one was going to be magnanimous towards him. Jeremy Jenner would want someone's head on a plate, and it would be Ted's. Jeremy couldn't pretend the letters hadn't happened and he'd want to exonerate his daughter. Ted would be the fall guy. He'd go to gaol. It would be the end of the business he and Steve Poole had so laboriously built up. Poole wouldn't forgive him. So he killed her. Later, when the wretched Darren tried his hand at blackmail, he killed him. Killing gets easier.'

Toby said quietly, 'Those are not the only deaths he's responsible for. We've mentioned Freda Kemp's, but we oughtn't to forget his part in Jeremy's.'

After a silence, Meredith said, 'Yes, there's Jeremy's.'

'So,' Toby said to Alan, 'what is murder? You'll have a legal definition of it. I have a moral one. Ted Pritchard killed Jeremy. Oh, I know it was his heart which gave out,' he went on, before either of the others could comment. 'We knew his heart wasn't in good shape. It might have helped if he'd been a more expressive sort of guy. You know, broken down and sobbed on Alison's shoulder, got it all out. But that wasn't Jeremy's style. He stayed buttoned up and kept it all contained, smouldering away inside him. In the end, the built-up stress was just too much. But you can still put his death at Ted's door.'

'It's not so simple, is it?' Meredith objected. 'Why not say Dorothy Pritchard, formerly Travis, was behind all their deaths? She brought up her adored son Edmund, known to us as Ted, with an obsessive devotion and filled him with her own particular kind of poison.'

'Old hag,' growled Toby. 'It all started with her. She accused

Alison and persuaded that dinosaur, Barnes-Wakefield, that he needn't look any further for his murderer.'

Markby sipped his pint thoughtfully. 'Yes, Jess Campbell feels much the same way as you, I fancy, and was disappointed she couldn't find anything with which to charge Mrs Pritchard, or Travis, whatever you want to call her. The odd thing about it is that looking at it without personal emotion getting in the way, if you can, Dorothy Pritchard has had a hard life. One might even feel sorry for her in other circumstances. Her husband, Travis, had been a poor provider and finally deserted her. She lived in a poor area of the country where there was little work for an unskilled woman so she had to go out cleaning for a living. Can you imagine how she felt when her son, the only good thing in her life, came running home to tell her he'd attacked her employer, Freda Kemp? Then finding he'd actually killed Miss Kemp? Of course, she tried to cover it up. It wasn't the right thing to do but it was the human thing, the thing a mother would do. Now, because Ted is almost certainly going to gaol for a long time, she'll be deprived of even his visits in that home she's in. She'll sit there with her useless hands, unable to do anything and with nothing to look forward to. She's not a woman who ever had time for hobbies, even reading, and I doubt she's developed any now. The company in that home mostly consists of people much older than herself and even if they're willing to chat to her, she's not the sort of woman to indulge in long chats. I think that's punishment enough, don't you?'

'Perhaps I could feel more sympathy for her if she'd accept some responsibility for what happened to Alison . . .' Toby began and then fell silent.

Markby shook his head. 'People can rewrite history in their heads with remarkable success. That's what Dorothy Pritchard has done. She's still saying that, if anyone killed Miss Kemp, it was Alison. Even though one part of her brain knows that the accusation came from her alone and that Alison had nothing to do with Miss Kemp's death, another part of her brain has adopted the fiction that she and Edmund really did nothing on that fateful Sunday afternoon. You won't persuade Dorothy to change her tune. She sees herself as a martyr and Edmund a victim of others' misdoing. He was led astray as a teenager and so ended up in a young offenders' centre. He was led astray by Fiona Jenner and conned into writing the letters on her behalf. When she was told about Fiona, she burst out into a tirade against another young woman 'who only got what she deserved'. Some people envy the rich, but Mrs Travis nurses a terrifying hatred for anyone more fortunate than herself. Her hatred of Alison is as strong today as it ever was.

'Her influence on the child Edmund must have been considerable. That and the humiliations he suffered at school, which even his old teacher remembered, led the youngster to see the world as owing him some recompense. He had a right to pilfer spare cash from Miss Kemp. He had a right, later on, to steal it from careless members of the public. He had a right to plan that Alison should be made to pay him, literally, for all the trouble she'd caused him. The road leading to murder is sometimes a long one. Edmund Travis was an unhappy little boy whose sensitivities were warped and blunted. Much of that can certainly be laid at his mother's door. That way murder lies.'

'The trouble Alison caused *him*!' Toby exploded. 'That's more than warped, that's lunacy! Poor Alison did nothing!'

'But it's how he sees it,' Markby repeated patiently. 'Alison belongs to the fortunate of this world. Such people see others, like Ted and his mother, struggle and do nothing to help. I'm not saying it excuses any of the things he did. I'm just saying that's how Ted sees it.'

'He's nuts!' insisted Toby.

'No,' Alan said, 'he's as sane as you or I.'

'How is Alison?' Meredith asked Toby. Toby's jaw had set and he was settling in for an argument. It seemed the moment to drop the matter of Ted's state of mind.

He turned his attention to her. 'Coping fairly well. Chantal cleared off after the funeral and that helped. Alison's had experience of dealing with traumatic situations, as we know. She's quite tough, really, when she needs to be.'

'That's what Fiona said,' Meredith murmured.

'She could have coped with the letters better if she'd been alone,' Toby went on. 'If it had concerned no one but herself she'd have taken some action, perhaps even gone to the police. It was because she was worried Jeremy would find out, and what the effect would be when he did, that she found it impossible to do anything. Now, of course, that's not an issue.'

A small group of people came into the pub, chattering and laughing. Its tiny bar was filling up and the evening was underway. Someone was even ordering the vegetable bake. Toby looked towards the newcomers and grimaced.

'Life goes on.'

'Yes,' Markby said. 'It does.'

'Do you remember,' Toby asked him, 'the occasion we saw Ted Pritchard here? He didn't normally drink in this pub. He was a customer of the Feathers. Do you think it was coincidence he was here that evening or was he checking on us?'

'I think he was checking on us,' Markby said promptly.

'Do you think he heard us talking about Cornwall?' Toby went on. 'And tipped off George Melhuish to look out for us, for me and Meredith?'

'He hasn't said so,' Markby told him. 'It's just possible.'

'And what,' Toby asked with a grim smile, 'do you think he planned to do with me, after he'd dealt with Meredith?'

'He hasn't told us that, either – yet.' Markby gazed blandly into the distance. 'Perhaps he wasn't so worried about you.'

Meredith gave him a reproving look but he affected not to see it.

'Point taken,' said Toby equably. 'I wouldn't have worked out he was Edmund Travis. Still, I suppose he might have had it in mind to tidy things up completely, and tricked me into meeting him by the woods where he used to meet Fiona.'

'He might, indeed,' Markby agreed.

'What will Alison do now, Toby?' Meredith asked him, changing the subject again.

He brightened. 'Well, I've got this new posting, as you know. Warsaw. I go out there at the end of the month. Once I've settled in a flat, Alison's planning to come out for a holiday. It will get her right away from this place and give her a chance to think what she'll do about Overvale House. She'll sell, I think. As she says, it's too big and it has too many gruesome memories. After that, I don't know. But she's resourceful. I think she'll be OK, given enough time.' He checked his wristwatch. 'Speaking of time, I have to get back. I told her I'd only be a short while.'

'I hope we see you again before you leave, Toby,' Meredith said.

He grinned at her. 'Sure you will. And Warsaw's not too far away to prevent me coming back here to dance at your wedding, as I said I would.'

He shook Markby's hand and made for the door. When he reached it, he turned and gestured in farewell. Markby had moved his arm to put it along the back of Meredith's chair. The ray of evening sunlight now fell across them both and the rest of the bar room was a dusty, shady place inhabited by shadowy figures. Toby looked at the pair of them for a moment, a rueful smile crossed his face, and he was gone.

'What do you think?' Meredith asked Alan. 'Alison's only forty-eight. She's a nice-looking woman. Perhaps Toby needs someone older to look after him. Given his inclination to think about marrying within the family . . .'

'Don't!' Alan begged. He put out his hand and gently laid it over her mouth. 'Don't matchmake for him! It doesn't bear thinking about. Forget about him. Think about *us*.'

Jess Campbell closed the door and gazed round the rented flat. She loathed this place. But, with luck, it wouldn't be home for much longer. She'd gone into the financial aspect of it and she was well able to take on a mortgage. She'd make an offer for

Meredith's house. She meant to get in touch with Meredith and tell her tomorrow.

The notion of buying a house was quite exciting. She'd have to buy some furniture. Perhaps her mother could lend her a few pieces to start her off. The family home was crammed with stuff her parents didn't use. At the thought of her family her excitement was replaced with a touch of sadness. Her brother had returned to his medical work. She missed Simon. Perhaps it was being a twin that made her feel the absence more. Perhaps it was the knowledge that all she really had was her job. She liked her job and thought, on the whole, she did it well. True, she made the occasional slip-up. Allowing the Stebbingses to see the corpse of their son at the scene had been one of them. But the superintendent had expressed his satisfaction at her handling of the case, now it was closed.

'Well,' said Jess aloud, 'it's as closed as it can be before a trial. Who knows what a jury may decide?'

She put her Marks and Spencer's chilled moussaka in the microwave and took the bottle of white wine from the fridge. She poured a glass and raised it in a toast. 'Cheers! Here's to crime!'

The sun was setting over the lake at Overvale. Against the darkening sky a shape appeared, nearing the spot. With a rush of wings it swooped down and landed close to the jetty. Spike settled his feathers, squawked once triumphantly, and slowly and with dignity began to patrol his domain.